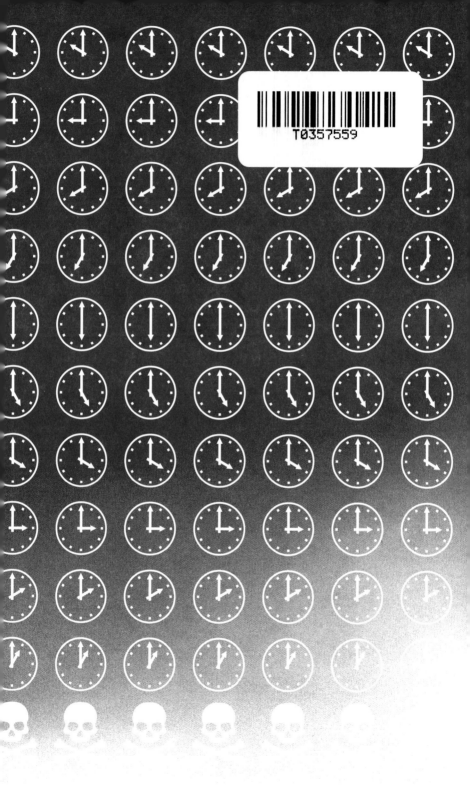

THE SURVIVOR WANTS TO DIE AT THE END

ALSO BY
ADAM SILVERA

THEY BOTH DIE AT THE END SERIES

They Both Die at the End

The First to Die at the End

THE INFINITY CYCLE

Infinity Son

Infinity Reaper

Infinity Kings

STAND-ALONE NOVELS

More Happy Than Not

History Is All You Left Me

WHAT IF IT'S US DUOLOGY (WITH BECKY ALBERTALLI)

What If It's Us

Here's to Us

THE SURVIVOR WANTS TO DIE AT THE END

ADAM SILVERA

Quill Tree Books
An Imprint of HarperCollinsPublishers

*For those who feel like liars when they talk
about the future. Take one day at a time.*

*Shout-outs to my dog, Tazzito, and my therapist, Rachel,
for saving my life time and time again.*

*And to Luis Rivera. I would have not survived
at the end without you. LYTM, Kidd.*

Quill Tree Books is an imprint of HarperCollins Publishers.

The Survivor Wants to Die at the End
Copyright © 2025 by Adam Silvera

ISBN 978-0-06-324085-8 (trade bdg.)
ISBN 978-0-06-345861-1 (international ed.)

Typography by Erin Fitzsimmons & David Curtis
25 26 27 28 29 LBC 5 4 3 2 1

FIRST EDITION

AUTHOR'S NOTE

This book touches on suicidal ideation, contains graphic descriptions of self-harm, and mentions suicides. If you choose to move forward with this story, I offer a spoiler in the next line about whether you can expect to witness a suicide in this novel, but if you don't want to be spoiled, just skip ahead to the next paragraph: (SPOILER) While characters will die in this book, as is the nature of this series, neither of the main characters will die from suicide. (END SPOILER)

If you're suffering and need help, reach out to the Suicide and Crisis Lifeline at 988. If you still don't feel good after the first call, then hang up and call again. And again and again and again until you're safe from harmful thoughts. I have made those calls myself in the past, and I'm here to tell you that today.

Let's go to tomorrow together.

PART ONE
The Not-End Days

Death-Cast has changed not only how we

all live before dying but also the lives of those

contemplating their own deaths. If Death-Cast

has not called the hurting, then it is not their End

Day. Simple as that. It has been heartbreaking

to watch people try to prove Death-Cast wrong.

My greatest wish is that by living, each and every

soul will heal so they no longer await our call.

—Joaquin Rosa, creator of Death-Cast

LOS ANGELES

July 22, 2020

PAZ DARIO

7:44 a.m. (Pacific Daylight Time)

Death-Cast never calls to tell me I'm gonna die. I wish they would.

Every night between midnight and 3:00 a.m. when the heralds are alerting people about their End Days, I stay up and stare at my phone, willing it to ring with those haunting bells that will signal my early death. Or my late death if we're being real about how little I've wanted to be alive. I dream of the night when I can interrupt my herald's condolences over how I'm about to die and just say, "Thank you for the best news of my life."

And then, somehow, I will finally die.

My phone didn't ring last night, so I'm forced to live through another Not-End Day.

I'm always performing a will to live for all the people working hard to keep me alive: my mom, obviously; my stepdad, who used to be a guidance counselor and still acts like one; my therapist,

3

who I lie to every Friday afternoon; and my psychiatrist, who prescribes the antidepressants I overdosed on in March. I almost feel guilty wasting everyone's time since I'm a lost cause. But if I can't convince everyone that I only tried killing myself because of that documentary about my childhood incident, then I'll be sent to a suicide treatment facility where I'll not only have even more people working to keep me alive, I won't stand any chance at trying to kill myself again.

If this Not-End Day goes as well as I hope, I might be happy to stick around.

For the first time in almost ten years, I have a callback. And not just any callback but a chemistry test to be the love interest in the movie. And not just any movie but the adaptation of my favorite fantasy novel, *Golden Heart*. All it took was one killer self-tape and lying about who I am.

Now I gotta go book my dream role.

I'm pacing my bedroom, going over the audition sides, even though I've got these lines down. Everything in here is black and white except for the novels, plays, and video games that entertain me on my Not-End Days. Mom got me this big Zebra plant, which, despite the name, doesn't match my room's vibe. It was a nice thought to get a natural pop of green in here, but I've had a hard enough time nourishing myself, so the plant has browned from neglect; I gotta throw it out because I can't watch a plant die before me.

Okay, it's time to get ready. I tuck my audition sides into my hardcover of *Golden Heart* as a 912-page good-luck charm and then stuff it into the backpack I usually use for hiking. I grab the black T-shirt and jeans requested by casting, and I'm about to hit the shower when I notice my 365-day journal on the floor. I'm quick to throw it back in my nightstand, since I forgot to do so around 3:00 a.m.; I can't have anyone looking in there.

I crack open my door, hearing a Spanish song playing from the old radio I moved to the top of the fridge after we got rid of all the alcohol. Mom and Rolando are laughing as they cook breakfast before she goes to work at this local women's shelter. It's the little moments like this when Mom isn't bringing me plants or supervising my antidepressant dosage that give me hope that she will actually be okay if I die. Even if she said otherwise after my suicide attempt—I'm only talking about the one in March, since no one knows about the second.

Before I put on a show as Happy Paz for Mom and Rolando, I have to get ready, just like any actor who goes through hair and makeup. I've only ever been on one movie set, back when I was six, but I remember thinking how cool it was to have artists help me get into character before a director calls, "Action." Now I do all of this by myself before performing happiness.

I rush down the hall and into the bathroom that's still warm and misty from Rolando's morning shower. I wipe the steamy mirror, trying to see the villain everyone else sees, but I only see a boy who has dyed his dark hair blond to book this job and who is growing out his curls to hide the face everyone knows more from the docuseries about the first End Day instead of his small but once promising role in the last Scorpius Hawthorne film.

The cold water of the shower shocks me awake before I twist the knob so far that the hot water turns my tanned skin red. I force myself to stand there even though my body wants to take control of my legs and back away. The body eventually wins, and I get out.

The sink is cluttered with all of Mom's and Rolando's things, like her brush with a forest of black and white hairs, his comb and gel, the cactus soap they picked up from the Melrose Market, and the porcelain plate where she leaves her engagement ring when she's going through her moisturizing routine. No real sign of my existence except for the toothbrush inside the orange plastic cup with theirs. That's on purpose. When I'm dead, I want Mom to forget about me for as long as possible. That means not seeing my things around our shared spaces. If Mom's haunted by my death, she'll be forced to move again to escape my ghost like we did after Dad's death, but this tiny house that Mom and Rolando bought together is her favorite part about living in Los Angeles. It represents our fresh start.

What was supposed to be our fresh start, at least.

In addition to a suicide note for Mom, I should leave another for Rolando to set up a Graveyard Sale because I know Mom won't have the heart to sell my things herself. She's the bread-winner of the house, but barely; we're talking stale, week-old bread breadwinner. They can probably make a few thousand by selling my copy of the last Scorpius Hawthorne book that was signed by the author as well as the Polaroids she took of me with the cast.

That trip to Brazil with Mom to film my scene was mind-blowing, I still can't believe I got to visit the iconic set of the Milagro Castle and—

Nope, no going down memory lane for my time as young Larkin Cano when I have a different role to play now. Not the one for the audition. The role I play every Not-End Day.

Fully dressed and clean, I grab the doorknob and whisper, "Action."

I become Happy Paz.

"Good morning," I say with an Oscar-winning smile as I enter the living room.

Mom and Rolando are eating breakfast tacos in our dining nook and playing Othello, the board game I used to love as a kid. They look up with genuine smiles because Happy Mom and Happy Rolando aren't roles they're playing.

"Morning, Pazito," Mom says.

Being called Pazito is something else I used to love as a kid.

"You ready for your audition?" she asks.

"Yup."

Rolando fixes me a plate. "Eat up, Paz-Man. You'll need your strength."

I force-feed myself because they'll get suspicious if I don't eat. The truth is that while I don't usually have an appetite for food, I'm always starving for life. Sometimes I feel so empty that my stomach aches, like it's growling for happiness, but there's never anything to eat or nothing looks good or when I'm finally in the mood for something it feels like no one wants to take my order.

"Would you like help running lines?" Rolando asks.

I pass because when I originally filmed my self-tape, Rolando was my reader, and he was way too dramatic, like he was auditioning for some telenovela from behind the camera. I had to kick him out and prerecord the other character's lines in a deeper voice, filling in the silent spaces I reserved for my character. That performance got me this callback. I don't want Rolando getting in my head again.

"How about a ride to the audition?" Rolando asks, always desperate to show that he's different than my dad, which yeah, I know.

"I'm gonna walk. I want the fresh air."

He holds his hands up in surrender. "I'm taking the day off if you change your mind."

"Don't you need a job to take the day off?" I fake a laugh so it sounds like a joke, but Mom scolds me anyway while Rolando laughs too. His laugh is also fake.

"I am taking the day off from hunting for a job," Rolando says while brewing tea and talking about the work he's gonna do around the house.

I zone out.

Last month Rolando got laid off at this local college because of funding. It sucks because he loved having an office job again, especially after homeschooling me for most of high school, but the mounting mortgage and medical bills suck even more. He's being precious about the next job he takes. "Nothing that gets me emotionally involved," he keeps saying.

The career adviser gig was perfect because it was just a job talking about other jobs while also scratching his itch to help people. Unlike his draining years as an elementary school guidance counselor. "Who knew children could have such troubles?"

he has said more than once, even around me, someone who faced a lot of troubles as a child. And then of course there was his most short-lived but taxing job as one of the world's first Death-Cast heralds. It's been almost ten years since he quit on the first End Day. The same day that changed my life so quickly that I became that child with a lot of troubles.

It's gonna be wild if I book this movie before he gets a job.

Rolando brings Mom tea and a kiss. "Enjoy, Glorious Gloria."

"Thank you, mi amor."

I'm so happy Mom is in love—true love this time—but sometimes it's hard to watch, knowing that I'm gonna die without being loved. Every night when I'm in bed alone, hoping that Death-Cast calls, I wonder if I would start to fear for my life if I had someone next to me. Someone holding me. Someone kissing me. Someone loving me.

But who would ever fall in love with a killer?

No one, that's who.

I go clean my dish, letting hot water burn me again. I switch off the faucet before anyone can notice my hands are cleaner than the plate.

"Pazito?"

"Yeah, Mom?"

"I asked if you're okay."

To be a great actor, you have to be a great listener, but I was so in my head just now that I didn't hear my scene partner. Now I'm staring like I've forgotten my lines. I'm falling out of character, like my Happy Paz mask and wardrobe's threads are being pulled off of me, exposing me as a nonworking actor who doesn't even deserve to work. No, I'm a great actor, and yeah, great actors have to be great listeners, but they also have to act truthfully. So I'm gonna tell the truth—well, *a* truth.

"Sorry, Mom, I'm just on edge over this audition," I say while staring at the floor, like I'm embarrassed. That part might be an act, but I'm selling the truth that, yeah, my mood is off, but check me out, I'm talking instead of hiding everything like last time. Then I top it off with a lie: "I'm okay."

The legs of Mom's chair begin screeching and then halt. She's desperate to comfort me, but I've told her that I need some space whenever I express myself because all the hovering makes every little thing feel much bigger than it is. I used all the right words from my therapist to get that across, and it's working, but I know how hard it is for Mom to not be able to mother me.

It's hard for me too. If only a hug could save me.

"The best thing you can do at this audition is be yourself," Mom says.

"Doesn't he have to be a character?" Rolando asks.

"He has to bring the character to life, like only he can," Mom says. She's been this encouraging of my dreams ever since I was a kid. "Go make this callback your comeback, Pazito."

"I will," I say.

The stakes have never been higher. If I don't book this role, I won't have anything to live for.

I start heading out when Mom calls after me.

"Let me grab your . . ." Her voice fades as she goes into her bedroom.

I already know she's getting my daily antidepressant. The bottle with my Prozac is hidden somewhere in her room because I can't be trusted to respect my dosage after the first time I tried killing myself.

I had my reasons.

In early January, Piction+ started streaming their limited docuseries *Grim Missed Calls* about the Death's Dozen, the twelve Deckers who died on the first End Day without warning due to some mysterious error with Death-Cast's equally mysterious predictive system. The episodes aired weekly, each revolving around a different Decker. The finale was about my dad, who didn't believe in Death-Cast. The filmmakers wanted to include us, but Mom declined and begged them not to move forward with this project because it would reopen a terrible wound (as if it ever really closed). Her pleas were ignored because "history needs to be remembered." It wasn't surprising when we found out the filmmakers were pro-naturalists, people who wish to preserve the natural ways we have always lived and died before Death-Cast. That docuseries was never about remembering history. It was a hit-piece against Death-Cast. And I got caught in the cross fire.

As if my anxiety wasn't sky-high enough as we counted down to the finale's premiere, the episode aired during the same week the government issued that stay-at-home order to prevent the spread of the coronavirus, guaranteeing that everyone would have nothing to do but freak out and watch TV. It was suffocating watching that press conference with the CDC and Death-Cast where they projected that over three million people could die worldwide if we didn't do our part immediately by staying indoors, and the docuseries only made that worse for everyone by casting doubt in Death-Cast because of their forgotten fatal error almost ten years ago.

No matter what happened—pandemic or no pandemic—my world was always gonna become more unlivable after the finale aired. I never watched, but the filmmakers apparently sensationalized my traumatic childhood incident and the trial that followed, portraying me as nothing but a psychotic hit man groomed by Mom so she could continue her affair with Rolando. And millions believed this.

So, on the fourth day of sheltering in place, an hour after the Death-Cast calls ended, I tried proving Death-Cast wrong by swallowing my entire bottle of antidepressants and washing it down with my stepdad's bourbon.

Then I waited to die, which is becoming the story of my life.

My vision got hazy, I started burning with a fever, and I began passing out, shocked that I was finally dying. I was too weak and drugged and drunk and near death to cry over how much it sucked that I'd reached this dark place, but also happy I was getting out for good. I would've died if Mom hadn't woken up from her usual nightmare about Dad, only to find something worse: me unconscious in a puddle of my vomit.

To this day I don't remember falling out of my bed or the ambulance ride or my stomach getting pumped, but I'm still haunted by waking up in the emergency room, handcuffed to the bed's rails like I was the dangerous criminal the docuseries made me out to be, and my mom removing her surgical mask as she begged me to never do anything like that ever again.

"I'm a planner," Mom had said through tears, gripping my hand. "But I will not plan to live in a world without you, Pazito. If you take your life, then I will plan to take mine too."

I spent three days in the psych ward thinking about what Mom said. I love her so much, but I hate that threat about killing herself too if I die by suicide. She has so much to live for, even if she'll no longer be a mom because her only child will be dead.

I can't handle this pressure to keep living when I have nothing to live for.

I need to live my life—and my death—how I see fit.

I've been biding my time because I learned my lessons about trying to prove Death-Cast wrong. There was that suicide attempt in March, but the one from my birthday last month has to stay a secret or I won't get the chance to try again in ten days on the ten-year anniversary of my dad's death.

Mom comes down the hall and gives me one pill.

I swallow my Prozac and smile like it's already anti'd all my depression.

Then Mom keeps staring, almost like she's a casting director who isn't buying my performance as Happy Paz and is only seeing an actor overacting, which is the last thing any respectable actor wants. But that's not it. She sees me as her baby, her only child, the kid she once accompanied to auditions, the kid who she tickled during Halloween costume fittings, the kid who used to believe in prophecies because he used to believe in the future.

The kid who thought he was being a hero when he saved her life.

The kid who grew up and now wants to die.

"I hope you feel better, Pazito."

"Me too, Mom." I'm telling the truth, but I know better.

Then I leave the house.

"And scene," I whisper.

I'm no longer Happy Paz. And I haven't been since the first End Day when I killed my dad.

NEW YORK

ALANO ROSA
11:00 a.m. (Eastern Daylight Time)

Death-Cast didn't call because I'm not dying today, but others have with death threats simply because I'm the heir to the Death-Cast empire. At least they're giving me a warning. That's the Death-Cast way, after all.

Over the years I've had people tell me I shouldn't be bothered by death threats because I've grown up knowing my End Day. That's not true. There are many privileges I receive from my father creating Death-Cast, but knowing when I will die isn't one of them. In fact, my father has been accelerating my training to inherit the company on his own End Day. When that will be is as much a mystery to him as mine is to me, but with the rise of the Death Guard radically pushing their pro-natural agenda on behalf of their favored presidential candidate, my father knows he's a target as those cultists call for the end of Death-Cast. The irony of my father not having his affairs in order before dying isn't lost on us.

We need to be cautious, even here in New York, where it

was rare to find pro-natural propaganda around the city before this year. That all changed on Sunday, March 29, when the two-week lockdown period ended and people returned outside to find *DEATH-CAST IS UNNATURAL* posters on the subway and bridges and in churches and grocery stores and every public place imaginable. If the Death Guard had their way, millions of people around the world would've died from the coronavirus without warning for no other reason than that's what they believe was part of the natural order.

The natural order of life and death changed on Thursday, July 1, 2010, when President Reynolds told the country all about Death-Cast. What I didn't know at nine years old was how things would eventually get so divided between those who believed in Death-Cast's mission and those who opposed it. President Reynolds wasn't prepared for this either. Two months into his second term, President Reynolds received his Death-Cast alert and spent his End Day hiding in an underground bunker, only to be assassinated by his most trusted Secret Service agent, who decided to fight for pro-naturalism instead of his president.

This morning, I was finishing President Reynolds's biography instead of an early copy of my father's upcoming memoir when I received a call from an unknown number.

"I'm going to kill you, Alano Angel Rosa," a young man threatened.

"Thanks for the courtesy call, friend," I said before hanging up.

That was my forty-seventh death threat. It was followed by

another six calls from other harassers within the hour before I deactivated the line and set up my new phone. It's always annoying to have to log in to my Death-Cast account and update my number every time mine gets leaked, but that will soon be resolved by my father's latest creation. Not much else I can do unless I abandon having a phone completely. My parents ask that I block unknown numbers and report threatening texts without answering, but I can't help myself. If someone wants me dead, I have to know how much they know. If they have only my name and phone number, then that can be anyone, anywhere. Historically it's been an empty threat. But if someone says they're watching me walk home through Central Park when it's dangerously close to midnight, I take that threat seriously and run for my life.

The most unnerving part about the original caller was that his voice sounded familiar, but I can't fully place it. He sounded young, but not too young. It could be anyone who wants revenge on Death-Cast, but I'm inclined to believe it might be a relative of one of the Death's Dozen.

There's Travis Carpenter, whose older sister, Abilene, was hit by a truck in Dallas, Texas. On Friday, August 27, 2010, my father personally apologized to the family, only to be threatened with a shotgun by Travis Sr. I wondered if both Travises are working together to make my father feel the loss of a child, but according to my research, Travis Jr. seems to be busy pursuing his political science degree. Travis Carpenter is also still registered for our services, unlike Mac Maag, whose uncle, Michael Maag, was robbed and stabbed to death on the first End Day. I have no idea if Mac

Maag supports the Death Guard since his social media profiles have been inactive for the last three years, but I like to believe he's just living a peaceful pro-natural life. And then there's Paz Dario, who I knew about before the first End Day since he was the cute boy in *Scorpius Hawthorne and the Immortal Deathlings*, but he's more famous now for being the boy who killed his father, Frankie Dario. I used to check in on him a lot before he deactivated his social media from the unjust backlash that spawned because of *Grim Missed Calls*. I hope he's doing okay.

As for me, I'm not concerned about this morning's death threats, especially not while I'm here at our primary Death-Cast headquarters, where we have the best security money can buy. I'm able to focus on the work at hand, which right now involves shadowing a meeting in the boardroom between my parents and Dalma Young, the creator of the Last Friend app.

"Death-Cast has rewritten death, but it has always been about changing lives," Pa says.

"That you have," Dalma says, sitting across from my parents while I stand in the corner with my tablet.

"As have you, young lady," Ma says.

Dalma is twenty-eight years old, but she can honestly pass for twenty-one, maybe even nineteen like me. She looks like a goddess with her black halo braid, glowing brown skin, and the white caftan dress. "You're sweet, but my aching back doesn't make me feel young at all."

My father laughs. "Hard work hurts. We would like to honor you for yours."

Dalma's brown eyes look between my parents. "Honor me how? You've already done so much for me. The grants, your advertisements promoting Last Friend. Not to mention your inspiring commencement speech at my graduation, Mr. Rosa."

My father has an ego, something my mother has spent years trying to tame, but he's too unique a beast, like a dragon flying in a sky of pigeons. There is no grounding him as long as he's the only soul alive to create a company as special as Death-Cast. "The connections forged through the Last Friend app have inspired me, time and time again. That is why at next week's Decade Gala we will be naming you our inaugural recipient for the Death-Cast Life-Changer Award."

Tears slide down Dalma's cheek. "For real? Isn't there someone more deserving? What about the Make-A-Moment founders?"

"The Holland sisters are among the incredible innovators who have helped shape the age of Death-Cast, but you changed the lives of all Deckers who needed company in their final hours."

Dalma tries controlling her sobs as she shakes her head. "Lives have been lost because of me too."

As the Last Friend app approaches its five-year anniversary on August 8, there have been some really thorough profiles recognizing all the good it's done as well as the crimes committed through the platform's history. Deckers inviting Last Friends into their homes only to be robbed of their possessions. Solicitation for nudes and sexual favors as if it was the Necro app. Relentless harassment from Death Guarders who scare Deckers away. Abuse where Deckers have been treated like punching bags for people needing to blow off some steam. The darkest stain on the company's history has to be the summer of 2016, when the Last Friend serial killer murdered eleven Deckers. Everyone believed the killer had gone and died himself since the killings stopped for several months, only for him to claim his final victims on Friday, January 13, 2017, and Thursday, May 25, 2017, before being caught.

I know a lot about the Last Friend serial killer. My best friend's brother was the first victim.

There's a familiar, haunted look in Dalma's eyes as if it's impossible for her to not see the blood on her hands even though she didn't kill those thirteen Deckers herself.

My father's brown eyes are distant too as he stares at the empty corner of the room. "It is admirable to take accountability for any shadows cast over your company, as we have, but you must understand that the despicable serial killer who preyed on innocent Deckers is no more your fault than Deckers dying after receiving Death-Cast alerts is mine."

Dalma nods, but she doesn't seem to believe it. "Mr. and Mrs. Rosa, I'm deeply honored that you think so highly of me, but I don't feel comfortable accepting this award. Sometimes I think Deckers are better off if I terminate the app so nothing horrific like that ever happens again."

My parents look between each other, lost for words.

"You've done so much good, Ms. Young," I say, surprising everyone. Shadows aren't supposed to speak. "I was so touched by *Time* magazine's profile on people who choose to be Living Last Friends for Deckers seeking companionship. I haven't had the honor of serving as one myself, but I really hope to, even just once to make someone's End Day brighter."

I pull out a chair and sit next to Dalma. "You can't bring back those thirteen Deckers any more than we can resurrect the Death's Dozen, but both companies deserve to survive because we've done far more good than harm. Your app's record holder, Teo Torrez, has served as a Last Friend over one hundred and thirty times since January 2018 to honor his son, Mateo, who lived his best End Day thanks to his Last Friend, Rufus Emeterio—the very same Rufus whose trio of friends known as the Plutos started an annual trend on September 5, 2018, where they each serve as Last Friends to commemorate him. This constellation of connections exists because of you, Ms. Young. Terminating the app won't terminate death, but it will terminate those life-changing End Days."

Dalma rubs her teary eyes, and I grab her a box of tissues. "You sound like my therapist," she says, blowing her nose.

"I've read a few self-help books."

"Time well spent."

"Does this mean you will accept the award?" Pa asks.

Dalma nods. "I'll prepare a speech."

"Fabulous," Ma says, coming around the table to give Dalma a tight hug. "We're looking forward to celebrating you. Please feel free to invite the whole family."

"My mother and stepfather are spending the summer in San Juan, but my sister and her girlfriend—sorry, fiancée—are in town. I'll invite them. Dahlia loves a cocktail party."

Pa gets up from the table. "Congratulations to your sister

and her partner. Pass along their contact information when you get a chance so we can send over formal invitations." What he really means is we need their names so our private security force, Shield-Cast, can do extensive background checks before allowing them in the building. "I believe your friend Orion Pagan has already RSVP'd yes. That right, Alano?"

Earlier today I went over the guest list with Pa's chief of staff. "Mr. Pagan is confirmed."

Dalma's lips purse before she smiles. "That's wonderful." It doesn't sound like it.

I was under the impression that Dalma Young and Orion Pagan were best friends. It was Orion's connection with a Decker—Valentino Prince, who my father personally called on the first End Day—that inspired the Last Friend app, after all. Now it would appear there might be some drama at the Decade Gala. I make a mental note to have security surveying them throughout the night.

After an attendant arrives to escort Dalma back to the ground level, I walk with my parents down the hall toward my father's office, followed by all our personal bodyguards, Ariel Andrade, Nova Chen, and Dane Madden. This building is the safest place to be, but it doesn't hurt to be extra careful.

"Nicely handled," Pa tells me.

"I didn't overstep?"

"Not at all. Was that *Time* profile about Living Last Friends in your brief?"

It's my job to know everything about everyone. If we're

meeting with someone, I spend hours researching who they are and writing comprehensive reports. Everything from where they were born to what they do now to their favorite hobbies and even what topics to avoid in our meetings. I prepared one for Dalma Young that made me feel qualified to be her personal biographer.

"It was," I answer. I even provided a TL;DR that went unread.

"I will be more on top of it next time," he says, patting my back. "Nonetheless, your being up-to-date saved the day. I was especially impressed with how compassionate you were about Dalma's ghosts and your ability to motivate her to continue her necessary work so Deckers never have to die alone. You will make a great leader one day, mi hijo."

I've grown up knowing I will one day inherit Death-Cast when my parents retire, but my father has always been adamant that I climb the company ladder instead of stepping into the role. He can tell me everything there is to know about being CEO, but it's the experiences that will make me successful. That's why I spent last summer as an assistant and have been fully with the company since Monday, January 6, after spending New Year's Day/my birthday in Egypt. I'm not in love with the administrative duties like inputting information into spreadsheets or ordering supplies, but that's not why my father hired me. It's because I'm a naturally gifted learner who loves research; I believe I was a historian in a past life. I take great pride in this work and would do it for free.

That's hardly saying anything since my family is so wealthy that we will die before we can spend all our money, but that doesn't stop my father from trying. We mostly live in our penthouse condo that overlooks Central Park, but he also purchased a house in the Chicago suburbs, a bigger house in Orlando, and the biggest out in the Hollywood Hills with a mind-blowing view of Downtown Los Angeles. Oh, we also have the house in San Juan. We haven't been there in a couple years unfortunately, but at least my mother's family is making it their home, unlike our other residences, which remain empty ever since we discovered old family friends bugged our condo to try to discover Death-Cast's secret method for predicting deaths.

We're fortunate enough to put the money back into the community too. My family has donated and invested so many millions that my father was famously downgraded from billionaire to millionaire. Everyone celebrated him even though it was my mother who started the charity Give-Cast, but she doesn't have my father's ego. She works hard to ground me in this lavish life so I'll one day inherit the company but not the ego.

That's why we live by a very important rule: never accept anything for free that we can pay for ourselves. No comped dinners, no matter how gracious the chef is that Death-Cast allowed her to have a beautiful End Day with her husband, who would've died unexpectedly otherwise. No Super Bowl suites compliments of the coach who last year put his tight-end superstar in the game despite a doctor's warning of a potential fatal injury, only for that player to score four times, including the winning touchdown that broke the tie. And no free tickets to this past

Met Gala, even though the legends at Saint Laurent wanted to dress us for the carpet, so I begged my parents to go because I've loved fashion forever and this was the honor of a lifetime. I don't ask for much, so they said yes and bought my ticket. I got to stun on the carpet in a dark sequin blazer suit with a white silk necktie blouse and forge a relationship with their creative director, who is dressing me again for the Decade Gala.

The pay-for-everything rule has applied to college too. I was offered a scholarship to Harvard because of my 4.0 GPA, but everyone believed my family bribed the admissions committee since I was homeschooled (as if homeschooled students can't qualify for scholarships) and that my parents bribed my private tutors to manipulate my grades (as if I'm not naturally brilliant). It didn't help when I rejected the scholarship as a goodwill courtesy. The only way I could get everyone to stop accusing me of being an unworthy cheat was showing up to the first week of classes last fall knowing everything the professors were teaching after I spent the entire summer studying the textbooks front to back, all while vacationing in Ibiza, where the vegetarian paella at La Brasa is to die for. (Not literally. No food is worth dying for, but I would have that paella flown in on my End Day.)

I had to quit college after that first semester. I couldn't focus on my studies as people tried cozying up to me, if not outright badgering me, for company secrets despite telling everyone who asked how Death-Cast can predict the deaths that my father isn't sharing that information with me until I'm older. No one believed me. But I mainly left for safety reasons. On Monday, December 2, 2019, we all returned from Thanksgiving break and I was immediately attacked by a student, Duncan Hogan, whose mother died at 12:19 a.m. on Thanksgiving before the heralds could alert her at 12:35 a.m. Duncan understandably hated being caught off guard and felt robbed of a goodbye and grieved by beating me bloody in Burden Park. He then started a pro-natural club on campus that harassed me all month. My bodyguard attending classes didn't make things better, so I didn't come back after the holiday break. It's a shame because I loved my professors and a taste of a normal student's life, but it's not as if university would ever truly prepare me to become CEO of Death-Cast anyway.

I've been so committed to this role that I was promoted to executive assistant on Wednesday, July 1, and I now attend every meeting and I'm on every call, whether it's with the board of directors, business owners, security, grant recipients, politicians, or even the president of the United States.

"Your job is to know everything possible," my father said upon giving me the promotion. "Until it is time for you to know the once impossible."

The Death-Cast secret.

I'll know my training has been completed when he sits me down for that talk.

For now, we all return to my father's corner office, where there are monstera trees in front of the windows that overlook Times Square, a grand seating area for the rare guests invited inside, a bookcase wall full of nonfiction where I regularly borrow books—most recently biographies about President Reynolds, Ada Lovelace, and Vincent van Gogh—a desk modeled after the

Resolute desk in the White House except it has the company's hourglass logo carved into the face instead of the presidential coat of arms, and a bronze globe where my father's bar cart used to be before he went sober on Tuesday, February 11, for his fiftieth birthday after suffering blackouts.

"Your eleven thirty with Mr. Carver got pushed back to one o'clock, so you'll be meeting with Aster instead," I remind Pa. His chief of staff has a long list of items to go through before next week's gala and before Pa will meet with his manufacturer to receive production updates for his exciting new creation. Code name: Project Meucci.

"I think it's time, Alano."

I double-check my watch. "You have another twelve minutes."

"Not that."

Ma looks confused too. "Then what is it time for, Joaquin?"

"Time for Alano to get proper fieldwork at Death-Cast," Pa says. He stares at me, preparing to ask me to do something I've been avoiding for years, and I would be happy to continue doing just that for the rest of my life. Something my father has only ever done once himself. "Tonight, you will call your first Decker."

LOS ANGELES

PAZ

8:38 a.m. (Pacific Daylight Time)

It's been one year since we moved from New York to a neighborhood in Los Angeles called Miracle Mile, and I gotta say, it hasn't lived up to its name.

An angry, late-night Google search taught me that this part of LA is known as Miracle Mile because of its once "improbable rise to prominence" from a dirt road to million-dollar properties. I don't know the first thing about building buildings except that it's gotta be hard. But can it be harder than rebuilding my reputation after killing Dad? Isn't it harder for me to rise to prominence than all these museums and restaurants and parks? And would it be so hard for someone to give me a miracle so I can get my life back on track?

Mom calls our home a miracle. She leased the place off Zillow before we even moved out here, and it was love at first sight: a single-story, white-bricked Spanish colonial house with the clay-barrel-tiled roof that all our neighbors have; two bedrooms, which we desperately needed after squeezing into

Rolando's apartment for years; a tiny but big enough backyard that Mom loved when it was greener and not looking like its own dirt road; and it's walking distance to all those miraculous museums and restaurants and parks, which was great since we didn't have our car yet. Mom believes the biggest miracle of all was when the original owners decided to sell to her in December, but I think the true miracle was that they didn't have her and Rolando evicted for housing a killer.

To get to the casting office sooner, I cut through the La Brea Tar Pits even though I hate the smell of sulfur. The first time I heard about the tar pits I thought it was gonna be so much cooler since it's the only Ice Age fossil site in an urban city, but it's basically just a park with models of prehistoric animals getting stuck in the very real bubbling tar. On the suicide survivor forum, Edge-of-the-Deck, I read about a man who tried killing himself in the tar pit, but it took so long for him to sink that he changed his mind and fought his way out. I've looked into a lot of ways to die, but that's not something I would do after my first failed attempt. It needs to be faster with no time to second-guess myself.

This whole thing makes me want a cigarette.

Most people quit smoking in January, but that's when I started. The holiday season is always depressing, but this last one was the worst in years. I couldn't go on my secret Instagram without seeing happy families dressed in their holiday sweaters or go on TikTok since the feed was flooded with gift unboxings. Meanwhile we had another quiet Christmas with a simple tree that I hated decorating because I can never get through that holiday without remembering the times I sat on Dad's shoulders to put the star on our tree. Then on New Year's, after Mom and Rolando shared their midnight kiss while I stood alone as usual, Mom got down on one knee and asked Rolando to be her life partner. I didn't know she was going to propose or that Rolando could cry from happiness. Knowing that Mom felt safe enough to marry Rolando after being so scarred by her relationship with Dad was beautiful, but it also made me feel even lonelier.

That's when I started smoking to help take the edge off. Sometimes when I'm smoking, I picture my pink lungs blackening with every inhale, just to remind myself why I'm still doing this even though I hate the taste and smell. This isn't me being rebellious, Mom and Rolando still have no idea because I cover my tracks with the mints and the extra shirt I usually carry on me. I smoke because I'm chasing death. Smoking isn't the fastest way to die, but if dying is gonna be a long game, then I need to play as much as possible to win.

But I'm not gonna smoke right now. I gotta be fresh and need healthy lungs for this role I'm gonna book.

Once I exit the park, I take a left on Sixth Street and go up Fairfax, where the Academy Museum of Motion Pictures is under construction. Before this callback, I swore that I would never be given a chance to achieve something worthy enough to be featured in this Death Star–looking building, but we'll see.

A couple blocks down, across the street from the Writers Guild, I arrive at the Hruska Casting office, where I'm hoping to make a name for myself.

A better, different name for myself.

"Checking in?" the clerk asks.

"Howie Medina," I lie.

I'm sent to the waiting area upstairs.

Look, I love my name, but that docuseries was watched by hundreds of millions of people, and there aren't exactly hundreds of millions of Paz Darios running around the world. I needed a new identity if I was gonna have any shot of booking my dream role. So I'm honoring my roots with Mom's maiden name as well as the actor Howie Maldonado, who died in a car crash three years ago. Howie played Scorpius Hawthorne's evil rival, but when I was on set playing his character's younger version for the flashback scene, he couldn't have been chiller. He even testified as a character witness in my trial (not that anyone would know, since the docuseries apparently excluded anything that would make me look good). I legit believe Howie would like that I'm representing him through my stage name.

I exit the elevator, and there's another guy in the waiting area. He's dressed in all black like me, but he's gorgeous, with natural blond hair, the brightest green eyes, a sharp chin, and lean muscles. He must usually get booked off his headshot alone. The guy—my competition—politely smiles, and he has a goddamn dimple.

"How's it going?" he asks in a voice deeper than I thought, like he might look young but he's older than you'd think, which is perfect for the character. I hope to everything that he can't act, not that it matters in Hollywood when you're this hot, but I'm screwed if he's legit.

"I'm good," I lie as I take a seat on the opposite couch. "You?"

"Excited. I'm Bodie."

"Pa— Howie," I say, clearing my throat. "Howie."

"I've been wanting to do a big fantasy movie. I can't wait."

It's almost like he thinks he's booked it already. Maybe that smile wasn't polite. Maybe it was victorious because he doesn't see me as real competition.

"It'll be epic," I say, like the role is mine.

He squints, sizing me up—or trying to recognize me. "Have you acted before?"

Yeah, in the biggest fantasy franchise of all time, motherfucker is what I wanna say.

"Just a small role" is what I actually say.

That seems to give Bodie some relief.

"You?"

"A few things," Bodie says, like he must have some booming IMDb page. "But I've never been the star of anything. This project seems like it's going to be huge."

"Yeah, it's based on a bestselling book. You should check it out."

"It's like a thousand pages." He shrugs. "I'm going to put my own spin on the character."

As a fan, I already know I would hate watching his interpretation. "Good luck with that."

The door opens, and an assistant lets Bodie know the casting director is ready to see him.

"Thanks," Bodie tells us both, stepping inside with his shoulders held high, like he's about to claim his destiny.

This adaptation deserves actors who give a shit about the source material. Someone like me.

Golden Heart is an epic love story between the Immortal and Death. It's about this once-nineteen-year-old, Vale Príncipe, who falls into an unmarked grave while staring at a total eclipse, and when he climbs out, he's been graced with a golden heart that grants him immortality. He spends his long and lonely life caring for others, particularly the sick and the dying. Throughout the first century of his immortality, Vale is visited by Orson Segador, the latest incarnation of Death, who doesn't understand why Vale won't die. They get to know each other whenever Orson appears to claim the souls of Vale's companions. Then Orson starts mysteriously dying, and he needs Vale's golden heart to survive and reap souls as the natural order demands. That's when it gets wild because the Immortal has to choose between letting Death die so all the sick and dying he tends to can be graced with immortality too or surrender his golden heart to save the only soul he's ever loved, even if that means the Immortal has to die so Death can live.

The novel is so damn epic and gonna make an amazing movie and break millions of hearts. The scene where Vale discovers he's immortal is gonna be the first scene that does people in; it definitely got me. Basically, Vale returns home from his first date with a boy who once tended to his family's garden, and when he shares the news with his parents, Vale's father beats him to death. Except not really. Vale awakens during a terrible storm as his parents are dragging him through the woods and toward the ocean. They're shocked to discover he's alive, and his mother questions where all his bloody cuts have gone, but the father shakes it off as nothing but the rain washing everything away. The father ties Vale's hands behind his back with fishing wire, stuffs his pockets with stones, and casts him off a cliff. Vale plummets through a crashing wave and tumbles around in the ocean before sinking. Minutes pass, and Vale knows he should be out of breath, but somehow he's surviving . . . then he sees Death for the first time. Death is nothing but a dark, skeletal-shaped blur at first, and he swims around Vale, waiting for him to die, but Vale keeps living against all odds. He breaks free from the fishing wire, ditches the stones, and swims back to the surface, where the storm has cleared and the sun is bright and Death is gone.

The actor playing Vale needs range, which I think I got, but not only has Vale already been cast by a young movie star, it's also not my dream role.

I'm auditioning for Death.

The first time I read the book, I felt so connected to Death because he was feared and viewed as nothing but a soulless soul-taker and an enemy to living beings. But then that connection deepened when Death's backstory gets revealed. He was once a boy who chose to die by suicide, and since he chose death, that's what—who—he became when he killed himself while staring at the same eclipse that made Vale immortal.

A suicidal soul that's treated like a killer? Yeah, I was born to play Death.

I also have another deep connection to this book. I sorta know the author, but it's very complicated.

The author, Orion Pagan, is alive today because he fell in love with a guy, Valentino Prince, who literally gave him his heart on the first End Day. He wrote this novel to keep his memory alive.

I also met Valentino on Death-Cast Eve, when he moved into the old building my dad used to manage. I only got to talk to him for a couple minutes, but he was a really nice guy. Brave too.

I'm getting anxious, like I'm about to mess up or I won't be good enough. I try focusing on the audition sides, but my nerves are too damn strong, the words are blurs. There's so much riding on this audition, it's literally life or death for me. It should feel like a win-win scenario because if I don't get this, I get to go die. But I've read enough stories on Edge-of-the-Deck to know that it isn't that simple, especially since no one has ever proven Death-Cast wrong and I'm gonna have to be the luckiest person in the world to be the first one—and my life has been anything but lucky.

The door opens, and Bodie steps out with a smile. "Have fun," he tells me before heading to the elevator.

Is he telling me to have fun playing Death while I can because he just locked down the role? I can't let this get to my head, but when the casting assistant calls me in, I'm one hundred percent letting this get to my head, even though I shouldn't because I knew I wasn't the only one auditioning; I just didn't think I was auditioning against a more experienced actor who looks more like Orson fan art brought to life than I do.

I should just leave now.

No, I gotta do this. I can't write in my suicide note that I gave it my all if I don't even try. Honestly, what's the worst that can happen? It's not like I can get sadder than I already am.

I show my anxiety what's what and go inside. I hand the casting director, Wren Hruska, my headshot and résumé, which lies about my name, work experience, and representation. I'm super confused, though. The studio is very familiar to past auditions—table for the casting team, tape on the floor for my mark, camera set up on tripod, soft box lights—but this isn't a regular audition, it's a chemistry test with the other actor, but I'm the only actor in the room. Did something change? Is the casting director or her assistant reading the scene with me? Was I supposed to bring in a monologue? Did someone email an update to the fake account I made up for my fake agent?

Or maybe Bodie really got cast on the spot.

"Are we still doing the chemistry test?" I ask, looking around.

"Yes, Zen is changing. His other shirt was washing him out," Wren says. "You'll be on the green mark this morning."

I go stand on my mark, relieved that I'm still in the running.

A door opens, and the young movie star, Zen Abarca, steps out of the changing closet in a black turtleneck that's perfectly tight against his pecs and arms. His muscular build comes from years playing Agent Early in the Young Smiths movie franchise about teenage spies. Yeah, he's gorgeous, but he can genuinely act, and I've watched tons of interviews where you can tell he loves the craft. I also believe Zen was born to play Vale. He's openly gay, has sun-kissed skin, messy hair as black as the oily tar in the park, and even the bags under his blue eyes suggest he's lived a long life while still being youthful.

Then someone else comes out of the changing closet wearing a baggy white cashmere sweater, blue jeans, and dark books, his brown curls sneaking out from under his faded Yankees fitted cap. I'm both starstruck and panicking at the sight of Orion Pagan.

There's a lot of reasons I'm perfect for the casting of Death, but there's one huge reason why I might not be welcomed anywhere near this project.

My dad wasn't just Valentino's landlord. He was also his murderer.

NEW YORK

ALANO
12:16 p.m. (Eastern Daylight Time)

When I was nine I wanted to be a herald, but I've long outgrown that childhood dream and I'm now dreading making my first Death-Cast calls tonight.

I believe heralds have the most important job in the world. Before the age of Death-Cast, doctors were the closest profession society had to heralds since they could gauge how long a sick patient had to live. Hours, days, weeks, months, sometimes years. They weren't always right. Heralds always are when alerting Deckers. The older I got, the more I realized how sad that was. A patient told by their doctor they're dying could still hold on to hope that they might survive, but Deckers don't have that privilege. Their fate is ironclad.

I couldn't spend years telling people they would die without being haunted. I'm not even sure that I'm ready to do it for three hours, but my father thinks I am because of how I conducted myself with Dalma Young.

"You were sympathetic but swift, the true talents necessary for a herald," he had said.

I may not want to be a herald in the long run, but my father believes it's necessary for my succession to be able to relate to the increasing weight of grief that heralds carry night after night. I didn't bother arguing that he must be as light as a balloon, since he only ever made one call, ten years ago, because I know what he would say: "I have enough ghosts."

So do I. Tonight I'll gain some more.

For now, I'm distracting myself with other Death-Cast business. I'm in my father's office with my parents and our chief of staff, Aster Gomez, who was first hired as a customer success engineer during the company's inception because of her people skills—people skills that could've been utilized for herald work, but she didn't want to do that either. Now thirty-five years old, she oversees all department heads, a role my father anticipates I will one day take over once Aster receives another promotion.

Aster has spent the past forty-five minutes leading us through updates and requests for the Decade Gala: Scarlett Prince's final counter for more money before she will agree to have her studio photograph the event; reviewing the guest list, which now includes Dalma Young's half sister, Dahlia Young, and Dahlia's fiancée, Deirdre Clayton; the rush order placed for Dalma's award engraving; the final menu from the chefs at our local World Travel Arena and their head count for catering staff; the hiring of undercover security; goody bags that include all-inclusive getaways to the Rosa Paradise, our resort in Culebra, Puerto Rico; the silent auction for a week on our yacht, *The Sunshine Decker*; the recasting of a new actor for our Project Meucci commercial since the first refused to sign the NDA;

approving promotional trailers from our sponsors, the scripts and routes for the tour guides, and the headshots and instrumentals for our in memoriam ceremony; and making all final decisions for the run-of-show.

"Would you like the Life-Changer Award presented before or after the Project Meucci reveal?" Aster asks.

Pa considers this. "When do you think would be the best time, Alano?"

I'm confused why he's asking when I remember there's a surprise I've been coordinating for our three employees who have remained at the company since the start: the head herald, Andrea Donahue; the onboarding director, Roah Wetherholt; and Aster Gomez.

"Do the award before," I suggest. I budgeted five minutes per person for Ma to share some quick words and present their plaques, paid sabbaticals, and a check worth enough to fulfill some bucket list dreams.

"Very well. It will be good to honor Dalma's innovation before introducing the company's next phase," Pa says.

Aster notes the decision on her tablet before looking up again. "Moving on from the gala, I spoke with publicity, and the campaign for the Lifetime Lottery begins tomorrow morning."

We will be running a lottery on our anniversary where ten households will win lifetime subscriptions to the service, and we'll also be announcing our intention to repeat this every year for the foreseeable future. It might not be free for all, but my father is always working on reducing pricing. Ten years ago

Death-Cast cost $20 for a single day, $275 for a month, $1,650 for six months, and $3,000 for a whole year. As more and more people registered, the price kept dropping; supply and demand. This earned my father a lot of goodwill because most founders would've kept hiking their charges for a company that's not only successful but one of a kind like Death-Cast. Today, subscriptions cost $12 a day, $90 for a month, $500 for six months, and $900 for the year. Hopefully by the time I'm running the company it will be even more accessible if not completely free.

My phone buzzes. I have Do Not Disturb turned on while at work where no one can reach me except company contacts; this is mainly so my best friends don't distract me with memes. Our publicity director, Cynthia Levite, has messaged me and Aster with a media hit from NBC. *How would Mr. Rosa like to respond?* she wrote.

The article is about a twenty-one-year-old Death Guarder who was arrested after posing as a Last Friend to kill a nineteen-year-old Decker. The Decker was stabbed three times as the Death Guarder issued a warning—or threat: "Your time is almost up, Death-Cast!"

Here we are planning for the company's future, and someone is threatening it.

"Excuse me," I say, interrupting Aster as she shares the pre-order sales for my father's memoir. "There's been another Death Guard attack. A Decker was murdered." I share the article's highlights: the who, the what, the where, the when—and the threat.

"Our time is almost up?" Pa asks, his fist sitting tight on the table.

"How would you like to respond?" Aster asks, her stylus pen at the ready.

My father closes his eyes, composing himself. "Release a statement on our newsfeed. Say that we continue to oppose the violent attacks from the Death Guard and we will be investigating the assailant's threat." He opens his eyes, his gaze drifting as if he's distracted by someone behind me, but there's no one there. "Extend the company's condolences for the Decker. He was robbed of a long End Day and even longer life."

Aster notes everything. "Would you like to review the copy before it goes live?"

"No," Pa says. He trusts her.

"I'll submit this after our meeting—"

"Submit it now."

"Yes, sir." Aster leaves the office.

Ma sighs. "Dead at nineteen. That young man's life was just getting started . . ."

"As was his End Day," Pa says. "I hope he made the most of it."

"I'm going to check in on Dalma and have security look into the assailant's background," Ma says, leaving too.

Did I make a mistake convincing Dalma Young to keep Last Friend alive?

Pa stares at the brass globe where his bar cart used to be.

"Can I get you anything?" I ask, wanting to take his mind off drinking. "Maybe a punching bag with Carson Dunst's face? I could have one here within the hour."

"I would much prefer punching Carson Dunst's actual face for egging on those cultists, but thank you for the offer." My father comes around his desk and rests a hand on my shoulder. "Have Agent Madden escort you home and get some rest, mi hijo. You will need to be alert for your shift tonight. Deaths depend on it."

The pressure is mounting. I need some fun to take my mind off this task ahead. I turn off Do Not Disturb mode. The group chat with my best friends is alive and well as they're both sending listings for the apartment we're secretly wanting to get together.

"I'm going to go hang out with Ariana and Rio."

"Where?"

"Maybe grab a bite at Cannon Café." That's Rio's favorite diner, a block from his house, where the waitstaff don't mind that we stay there for hours talking and playing cards; probably something to do with the big tips I leave. But I realize this is not the answer my father was looking for, especially today.

"A boy your age was just murdered, and your own life was threatened this morning."

"But I'm not dying today," I say. We know that because of his creation.

"That does not mean you can tease Death."

There's a fire growing inside me, but I snuff it out, just as my father has been known to do when I try lighting my own matches. It's a shame that I'm being primed to oversee a company that encourages everyone to live their best lives without being able to do so myself.

I envy the Deckers who live more on their End Days than I get to with my entire life.

LOS ANGELES

PAZ

9:17 a.m. (Pacific Daylight Time)

I have no idea if Orion Pagan hates me or not, but I'm about to find out.

In the almost ten years since Dad killed Valentino, I've been in the same room with Orion only twice. The first time was during my trial, when Orion took the stand and called my dad a monster. The second time was when Orion came to LA on his book tour last November and I was next in line to meet him when I got nervous and left. Orion has never reached out to me, not even when the docuseries had everyone on the internet dragging me. I get Orion hating Dad, but why would he hate me? If anything, shouldn't he thank me?

I'm the reason Valentino's murderer is dead.

I can't believe Orion flew out from New York for this audition. No, I can't believe I'm stupid enough to be surprised by Orion flying out here for the audition. This story means everything to him. He even wrote the screenplay himself because he didn't want Hollywood bastardizing the material like we've

44

seen happen to too many great books. Of course Orion is gonna make sure that the actor playing his magical self-insert is the right person.

"What's up," Orion says, greeting me with a hand on his heart, the heart that he received from a transplant after Valentino was declared brain-dead because my dad kicked him down a flight of stairs for trying to save my mom.

If only I had been a little bit faster with getting the gun—

"Howie?" Orion asks.

At first I think Orion is questioning my identity, but he's actually just getting my attention.

"Sorry, I'm just nervous. I didn't know you were gonna be here. I love your book."

The lie is kind of true, but I'm genuinely more nervous about Orion recognizing me for who I really am than I am about the audition.

"That means a lot," Orion says, hand on his heart again. "We've seen thousands of people for this role, and your self-tape legit blew us away. I seriously got chills watching you become Orson. Your performance was so grounded and haunting."

The casting director nods. "You have a raw power of emotion that's hard to find in young talent these days," Wren says.

"Don't be nervous," Orion says. "You got this."

"Don't be nervous about this either," Zen says as he takes his mark with a knife in his hand. "It's just a prop."

Okay, so no one here knows who I really am, which is great, but I really gotta act my ass off before, during, and after this audition if I'm gonna get cast as Death. I'll come clean to Orion once I book the job . . . or maybe after I sign the contract . . . or when we're on set . . . or done shooting . . . or during the premiere's red carpet . . . or I'll take it to my grave and be buried as Howie Medina.

"When you're ready," Wren says.

The scene for our chemistry test is one of my favorites from the book.

I get into the right headspace by using the "moment before" technique, where I break down everything I—Death—was doing before this scene begins: I appeared in this forest to claim the soul of an orphan girl Vale had been taking care of after her parents were killed in a war, and when Vale's pleas for me to not take the girl failed, it leads to this moment where my scene with Zen opens. Zen transforms into Vale—his posture slouching like he's carrying the weight of the world, his breath building as his blue eyes become oceans, and his hands shaking as he plunges the knife straight into his heart. The fake blade retracts into the handle, but I'm not an actor seeing a prop or a suicidal guy who wishes his reflexes would shut down so he could kill himself the same way. I'm Death watching the Immortal attempt suicide, my head cocked as I imagine the golden lights emanating from his heart.

Vale throws the knife across the forest and falls to his knees, crying.

"Stop taunting me, Immortal," I sneer.

"I am not taunting you. I am begging you to take me."

There are hundreds of other souls waiting to be claimed by me as I hover over the Immortal, all threatening to turn into violent ghosts the longer they remain in this plane, but I cannot understand how this boy continues to defy my grasp. I kneel before him and hold his face, shivering even though he is warm. I cannot carry him into the afterlife. He is hyperventilating because he does not know why this is happening to him, but if it is not my responsibility to comfort the dead, I certainly do not have to tend to an immortal who cannot breathe when he will survive this just as he has drownings in oceans and plummets from tall towers and now knives to the heart. I am ready to depart when he asks if this is happening because of the eclipse. The same eclipse that made me Death. It is strange that our journeys as extraordinary beings began on the same day, but it is also less lonely. The universe may have gifted Vale with immortality because his life was threatened by unloving parents, but it does not feel that way to me.

"To kill oneself only to be anchored to eternal life is punishment," I say.

"Living is painful, but it does not have to be a curse."

"I am not living. I am Death," I say, turning away to go vanish into the shadows.

The Immortal grabs my hand, his touch now burning. "Becoming Death does not mean you do not deserve this second chance at life. I am terrified of walking this world alone. If we are to cross each other's paths forever, perhaps we can get to know one another."

I stare down at our hands. It feels nice to be touched, to be wanted, but there is no way this will end well. If I have not always been Death and he has not always been the Immortal, that must mean that something will go terribly wrong here. I will not make the same mistakes of having my heart broken.

"I am not alive, and I will not fall into the trappings of life," I say, snatching my hand out of his. I look the Immortal up and down before turning my back on him, knowing that I will not be able to stay away from this soul, whose company I will miss if I ever carried him into the afterlife.

Then applause rings through the air. The forest turns back into a studio. Vale changes back into Zen. And I become myself again.

"Holy shit!" Orion shouts over his own clapping. "Guys, that was fucking amazing—excuse my language—no, fuck that, I said what I said!"

"You were locked in," Zen says, patting my back like he's impressed.

I honestly feel like I disassociated and became the character. I'm still sinking back into myself. I'm Paz, I'm nineteen, and I'm an actor who just crushed this audition.

"Off-the-charts chemistry, guys," Orion says, and the casting director agrees.

"I mean, we're kind of a destined match. Our names mean peace," I say.

Zen looks puzzled. "Howie means peace?"

I tense up. I just said something really stupid and career-costing. Orion is no longer looking at me like I'm the perfect casting for Death and instead like I'm a plot point he's working out in his book. Does Orion know Spanish? Would he know that my name, my real name, actually means peace? I gotta distract from this.

"I mean, no, your name means peace and calm and all that," I tell Zen, flustered. "But my name has a lot of meanings. My favorite is 'heart brave.' That feels so perfect for this story, right?" I only know that because Howie Maldonado told me.

"Totally perfect," Zen says. He's looking at me like I'm just an awkward actor again.

Orion isn't as sold on that performance, but the casting director is, so she excuses me, letting me know that she'll be in touch one way or the other.

"Thank you for your time," I say, rushing out before Orion can solve the mystery.

I'm waiting for the elevator, pressing the button a thousand times to make it go faster, when Orion steps out into the hall and shouts, "Hold up!"

I can't run away, not even when the elevator doors finally open. "Hey, Orion."

"Dude, your performance was seriously phenomenal. It's kind of an author's dream come true to watch a character so personal brought to life so beautifully."

Wait. Am I about to get an offer?

My heart is pounding. "I'm so honored, I would kill for the chance to play this role."

"You sort of have," Orion says. "Didn't you, Paz?"

NEW YORK

ALANO
12:40 p.m. (Eastern Daylight Time)

My bodyguard is teaching me how to fight for my life inside the Death-Cast gym.

Agent Dane Madden has been tasked with protecting me since June 1, 2019, because my father wanted me to have a younger personal bodyguard who could better blend in with me at college. Agent Dane (as I call him since he won't stop addressing me as Mr. Alano) is twenty-one years old and was hired because he worked security at Death-Cast affiliates such as Clint's Graveyard, a club for Deckers, and Make-A-Moment, a virtual reality station where Deckers can experience risk-free thrills. He's devoted to the cause, unlike President Reynolds's bodyguard, who assassinated him.

Since Monday, March 16, Agent Dane started teaching me Muay Thai during the lockdown.

I'm laying into this ninety-pound heavy bag after Agent Dane coaches me through different moves, but my jump switch roundhouse kick keeps suffering from the switch itself. I finally mastered the timing for swinging my rear arm down to generate power into my kick, but I can't seem to find my balance to fully rotate my hip and lead foot for execution. An opponent would easily knock me over in the ring, not that I'm doing this to compete. This started off as a mental exercise to expel the negative energy clouding my judgment, but lately it's been physical training in the event I might have to actually fight for my life.

Agent Dane folds his tattooed arms against his big chest. "You're not focusing."

"I am absolutely focusing," I say, panting.

"Then you're focusing on the wrong thing."

I'm used to learning things naturally—history, business, languages, other crafts, even people's lives—that not being anywhere near close to mastering this one move is bothering me. "What should I be focusing on, then?"

"Surviving," Agent Dane says.

"My survival is your job."

"Only because Mr. Rosa knows that danger still exists even though it's not your End Day."

I think back to how my father just told me to not tease Death. "There's such a thing as being too careful, though."

"Not in my profession," Agent Dane says. Back when he was guarding Clint's Graveyard and Make-A-Moment, he had to retrain his brain to remember that not receiving his Death-Cast alert didn't mean he was safe, especially since he was working with Deckers whose deaths were daily threats to his well-being.

Even his life. "I operate as if you are a Decker who can be saved. I need you to start doing the same."

"What does this have to do with not getting my kick right?"

"Everything. If you don't believe you have to fight for your life, you will not give it your all." Agent Dane nudges me back away from the heavy bag, sweat dripping from his blond buzz cut as he demonstrates the kick step-by-step again. "Now, instead of focusing on how hard or fast you would hit your target, focus on everything you stand to lose if you die." He becomes a blur as he executes the jump switch roundhouse kick, his tattooed foot hitting the heavy bag so hard that I can't imagine a human skull surviving that impact.

There's a lot I know about Agent Dane, but he holds some cards close to his chest. What he stands to lose if he dies is one of them.

I square up to the heavy bag, trying again and again to nail this kick, but I'm so angry at my father for forcing me into a life that is so equally disrupted by his creation and for preparing me for a destiny that I never asked for, a destiny that I only feel obligated to fulfill for atonement and atonement alone. I collapse onto my knees, panting as I rest my head against the heavy bag. My lungs and abs are on fire, but my heart is broken that fighting for a life as restrictive as mine is so pointless.

"It's okay," Agent Dane says, helping me up. "This is what I'm here for."

My survival is his job.

If only the people whose lives I've ruined had bodyguards too.

LOS ANGELES

PAZ
9:41 a.m. (Pacific Daylight Time)

Orion Pagan is frozen as if Valentino Prince's lifesaving heart has stopped beating.

We're down the block from the casting office, sitting on the curb. He wanted to speak privately, but he's not speaking. He keeps staring at me like I'm a ghost.

I feel nine years old again with good intentions but bad judgment. "I'm just gonna go."

Orion shakes his head. "No, I want to talk to you," he says, but that haunted look hasn't left his hazel eyes. "I'm just a little thrown off, especially because you're rocking blond hair now."

That bleaching burned my scalp, just like my steaming hot showers, and it only got worse when the stylist wrapped my hair in foil and sat me under a heat lamp. There was no escaping that feeling of my head being on fire. I couldn't switch off the faucet or jump out of the bath like my body always forced me to. That pain was worth putting myself through to show Orion that I'm the perfect actor to cast as Death, and to set me down a path where I wouldn't seek out pain again.

"I dyed my hair to do Orson justice," I say. There were so many lines I highlighted in the book, but I quote back my favorite about Orson's blond curly hair. "'Death's hair was as golden as the Immortal's heart and as twisted as their love for each other.' Something like that."

"Exactly like that," Orion says. "And for the record, you didn't need to dye your hair to do Orson justice. You got the heart of his character down."

"That means everything coming from you."

Then Orion looks down. "I'm sorry I never hit you up to see how you were doing, but I promise I've thought about you a lot over the years, Paz. Before and after that trial, the documentary, anytime someone brought up your father. I've even stupidly wondered if you read the book. I figured we'd cross paths outside that courtroom eventually."

"Thanks for that, by the way."

"You were just saving your mother from a man who would've killed her like he did Valentino. I couldn't have you rotting in jail like your father deserved to be, but sometimes I hope hell is real and he's burning—" Orion's rapid-fast response comes to a halt. He takes a deep breath, his stubbly cheeks still flushed. "Sorry, dude, it's one thing for me to carry that anger and another to throw that your way. I hate that man, but you probably feel differently."

There are days where I hate Dad because of how much he tortured and terrified Mom. Other days where I hate Dad because of how much killing him ruined my life. And then there are days where I feel the guiltiest because I don't hate him at all.

Seeing how Orion hates Dad over a single tragic moment only makes me think about how everyone treats me like I'm a monster because of my one incident.

"So, how old are you now?" Orion asks, like he's remembering he's the adult in this conversation.

"I turned nineteen last month."

"Nineteen. That's how old Valentino was when . . ."

When Dad made sure Valentino would never age another day.

Now it's my turn to rescue us from an awkward silence. "I almost met you at your book signing, but I backed out at the last minute. I was happy to hear how healing this book has been for you. It's gotten me through some hard times too."

I ramble about some of my favorite moments: Vale comforting a depressed Orson after he escorted his parents to the Eternal Realm; when Vale drunkenly sang a cherished childhood song to a dying man with Alzheimer's and how Orson joined in even though he always avoided interacting with the living until it was time to cross them over; and when Orson took Vale to a cave for a picnic and opened up about the struggles that led to his suicide.

"I, um, I've been really suicidal," I say. This is the first time I'm talking about my struggles with someone who Mom isn't paying to help me. "Ever since I killed Dad I get treated like I'm dangerous. I got bullied hard as a kid. I've watched my dreams die. It was hard reading about Vale becoming immortal because living forever felt so suffocating. I honestly saw Death as the true hero since he saved people from having to live in this terrible world."

Orion is nodding, even when I'm done talking, like he's deep in thought. "I don't talk about it a lot, but I really struggled with living after Valentino died. It didn't always make sense to outsiders, not even my best friend, because Valentino and I only knew each other for a day, but his loss is still so damn heavy. I wrote about Orson becoming Death because my depression and grief were so powerful, like I would never escape them, not even in my next life. It made living hard, but Valentino wanted me to live, so I'm going to bust my ass to keep living." He reaches out and pats my shoulder. "You got to do the same, Paz."

Orion was able to write his way out of his depression. I'm gonna act my way out of mine.

"I finally found a will to live when I saw your book was becoming a film. I'm sorry I lied about my name, but I had to get an audition to be Death. I knew I'd kill it—crush it." I really gotta watch what I'm saying, especially around Orion, who might be my only lifeline. "Look, that docuseries has made me out to be some psycho killer, but I'm a good person trying to live my life without being treated like I'm a villain. Your movie could be my comeback." I might as well be down on my knees begging. "Please back me up."

The way Orion is staring makes me feel like I've just blown it. I should've played it cool and let this audition process unfold without putting pressure on him or asking for special treatment.

"I will back you up, but I got to tell the team who you really are. You cool with that?"

"I totally get it."

"Then I'm happy to put in a good word for you."

It sucks that I can still get rejected after my performance because of how the incident and docuseries damaged my reputation, but Orion fighting that fight for me means the world.

I wonder if this hope is what Orion felt when Valentino first offered his heart.

"Thank you, thank you, thank you!"

Orion stands and helps me up from the curb. "I'm down to do what I can; you don't deserve all the shit you get."

I'm so damn happy that I feel like I've died.

I reach into my backpack and pull out my copy of *Golden Heart* and the pen I once used to write hateful things on myself. "Can I get your signature?"

Orion flips through my hardcover, finding so many passages highlighted and notes scribbled in the margins. Then he signs my copy, but before he gives it back, he stops and admires the book's cover as if he hasn't already seen it a billion times. The cover has two anatomical hearts laid over each other—one in dull black, the other in a gold foil that's shining under the sunlight—against a white background with the title on top and his name on the bottom. During Orion's cover reveal on the *Today* show he mentioned that the illustrations were inspired by the actual scans of Orion's and Valentino's hearts taken on the first End Day.

"Here you go," Orion says, handing the book back.

It feels magically blessed, like it's been enchanted with a spell for happiness, I don't know, but I'm feeling amazing.

"Thank you so damn much for this story. And for everything."

He smiles. "Okay, I should run back up. You got to promise something, though. If this movie doesn't work out, you got to take care of yourself."

"I promise," I lie.

"Boom," Orion says, giving me a fist bump. "I'll catch you later."

He walks back toward the casting office, and I go the other way.

Who would have thought that Orion and I would bond over the tragedy that changed our lives forever?

I remember meeting Valentino on Death-Cast Eve when he moved in down the hall. I asked if he was gonna be our new neighbor, and we introduced ourselves and he said I had a cool name. I don't remember telling him he had a cool name too, and I wish I had. Dad got mad at me for not being in bed, even though I couldn't sleep because I was trying to find him, since I was scared about all the Death-Cast stuff, which he just told me wasn't real, like it was some monster in the closet. Then I didn't see Valentino again until the next night, when Dad was beating up Mom and Rolando at home and Valentino appeared at the top of the stairs. I didn't know Valentino was a Decker when I screamed at him to help, but he rushed inside anyway like a hero, even though he must've known it was gonna lead to his death. I just wanted to stop all the fighting, so that's when I ran into the closet to grab the gun, and by the time I came back out, Valentino was gone.

Those memories have me turning around and running down the block.

"Orion!"

He stops right outside the casting office. "Hey, everything okay?"

I'm shaking as I spit out, "I'm sorry I couldn't save Valentino too."

Orion sucks in a breath, speechless.

"I'm really sorry," I say, tearing up and turning away, crying on the streets after what has really been one of the most promising days of my life.

I'm heartbroken that nine-year-old Paz was seconds too late to kill Dad before he could kill Valentino. I wish things had gone differently, even if that means that Orion would've never written *Golden Heart* because Valentino would've never died, and maybe Orion would've been dead instead due to heart failure. But I can't play the what-if games. I can't undo anything I did or didn't do, but I can own up to my past, especially with Orion, who is looking out for my future.

At a stoplight, I open my copy of *Golden Heart* and I'm touched by the simple message Orion has written in my book: *Paz, keep living.*

Here's hoping Hollywood calls instead of Death-Cast.

NEW YORK

ALANO
5:35 p.m. (Eastern Daylight Time)

Even with sixteen years of memories without my best friends, I don't like remembering life without Ariana Donahue and Rio Morales. They're lifers, for sure.

It's been hard making friends these past ten years without wondering if someone wanted to get to know me for me or for the company's secrets. I've spoken about this a lot with President Page's son, Andrew Jr., who has grown up in the White House's shadow for the past twelve years thanks to his father being sworn into office as President Reynolds's vice president before being voted into office himself. Our talks across various ceremonies and rallies made me feel less alone, but he was a few years older and lived in DC.

Then I met Ariana on Sunday, December 25, 2016, when she accompanied her mother, Andrea Donahue, who came in to Death-Cast to work both Christmas Eve and Christmas Night for the holiday premium pay. I was also there that night because the head herald, Henry Tumpowsky, was depressed from both the holiday season and the job itself so he quit hours before his shift. My father abandoned our plans to take over the duties, and my mother and I helped out where we could. I eventually wandered into the cafeteria, where Ariana was sitting alone since she wasn't allowed in the call center.

"You're Mrs. Donahue's daughter, right?" I had asked, recognizing her from the holiday party.

"Ms. Donahue," Ariana corrected. "My dad's not in the picture."

"Sorry to hear that."

"Don't be. It's his loss," she said with a shrug. "I'm awesome."

Even back then I admired how confident she was. I wasn't surprised to discover that she was attending LaGuardia to train for Broadway. She graduated last month and will be starting at her dream college, Juilliard, in the fall.

Right now, since I'm forbidden from existing in the outside world, Ariana and I are at my penthouse, sunbathing on the rooftop garden as my German shepherd, Bucky, sits at the foot of my chaise.

"Babe, I'm destined to win a Tony, but even I can't act like I think you calling Deckers tonight is a good idea," Ariana says after letting me vent about my father's assignment. "Working that shift is going to be unforgettable. Like, bad unforgettable, Alano. I don't even think my mom can train you how to detach."

It's no secret that Andrea Donahue has a reputation for being emotionally detached at work, openly admitting that her one rule for surviving the job this past decade has been her refusal to see Deckers as people. My family doesn't endorse that mentality, but Andrea shamelessly sees it as a necessary compartmentalization skill to prevent turnover, something she told my mother when applying to become the new head herald. Grief won't overwhelm her as it did the previous head.

But Ariana is right: there is no training that will make me heartless to Deckers. Their grief does threaten to overwhelm me.

I pet Bucky between his big brown ears, as I always do when stressed, but looking at him doesn't take my mind off death this time.

On Leap Day, I found out my dog was dying.

Before that, my parents were busy coordinating efforts with the CDC to help prevent the spread of the coronavirus, but on Thursday, February 20, I'd noticed that Bucky was sick too, so that became my number one priority. After nine and a half years I'd grown used to Bucky getting sick and needing to sleep it off for a couple days, but this was different. He didn't come running at the jingling sound of his leash. He wasn't eating his food or mine and even refused broccoli and strawberries, his favorite snacks. After two days of this I scheduled an emergency vet appointment. Dr. Tracy drew Bucky's blood, performed a sonogram, and extracted fluids. One week later, Dr. Tracy called and diagnosed Bucky with hemangiosarcoma, a highly invasive cancer that's most prominent in large dog breeds, including German shepherds. Like Bucky.

That call was the closest thing to a Death-Cast alert an animal can receive.

Bucky was given five to seven months to live.

That was five months ago.

Unlike Death-Cast alerts, there is still hope for survival. I was willing to do anything to extend Bucky's life, even if it was only for another month or week. A day, even. Bucky underwent surgery on Saturday, March 14, right before lockdown. We were fortunate enough to be sheltering in place here, where Bucky could enjoy fresh air in the garden while recovering. Once the lockdown was lifted, we returned to the hospital for chemotherapy. He's now cancer-free.

Still, no one truly knows how much more time I have with Bucky, so I'm making the most of it. I spoil him with new toys even though he always gravitates back to the giant carrot squeaky toy I bought at Target. I'm still feeding him the healthiest food while sprinkling in more treats. And wherever I go, he goes. I'm never leaving the city or country without him again. There's all the exercise too, of course, and while the walks have been taking longer this year, I don't mind. I block out that time for Bucky so that when he does die, I'll trust that I gave him his best life.

If only my father showed me the same care I show my dog.

"Hey," Rio says, entering through the balcony's double doors. "Can you get Dane to ease up on pat-downs? I'm starting to feel like he should take me out to dinner."

My parents only started allowing me to have guests over after the lockdown, wanting to make sure that my friends and I would have a safe space to hang out in the event we had to shelter in place again. But no matter how close we are to someone, they must be inspected every time to make sure no one is planting bugs in here ever again. This will change when my friends and I get our own place.

"Why are you so late?" Ariana asks, braiding her long brown hair.

"He was playing *A Dark Vanishing*," I say.

Rio's eyes widen. "How'd you know that? Did you bug my place? Maybe I should be patting you down too."

The thought of Rio patting me down makes me warm in the face but also weird in the head because over the past three years of being friends we've regularly been mistaken by strangers as brothers, cousins, even fraternal twins. I used to think it was just people being racist, since we're both tall, light-skinned Latinos with dark hair, but honestly, I see the resemblance too. I'm both honored by the comparison because Rio is very handsome, but I'm also disgusted that people think we're related because we don't have a history of behaving like brothers.

"I didn't bug your place." I point at Rio's shirt that says *I PAUSED MY GAME TO BE HERE*.

Rio laughs. "Three reasons why you're wrong. Number one: I was actually playing the sequel, *A Dark Vanishing: New Dawn*. Number two: saying that I was playing the game is really reductive when I was protecting the realm from a resurrected demon queen. On hard mode, by the way. Number three: I didn't put on this shirt to make a statement. I've been wearing it since yesterday."

"Ill." Ariana points at the chaise closer to me. "Sit there."

"I only came for the dog anyway," Rio says, patting his thighs. "Come here, Buckboy."

I'd rather Rio use any of the other nicknames I've given Bucky over the years—Buck, Buck-Buck, Buckaroo, Million-Dollar Buck, Buckingham—but I'm moving on at this point. Bucky usually ignores him anyway, and I'm honestly just relieved Rio is no longer calling him Buck-Fuck.

"Good boy, don't listen to Tío Rio," I say, scratching Bucky's head.

When I got Bucky's diagnosis, Rio was pissed that Ariana's demonic cat Lucyfur—actually just named Lucy—would outlive Bucky even though she's twice as old and half as sweet. Ariana took offense, even though she knows no one will miss leaving her house with fresh scratches. Ariana and Rio kept me company during Bucky's surgery, distracting me with their hot takes, like how Ariana believes the Scorpius Hawthorne movies are better than the books, and Rio thinks that TV shows should stop using Death-Cast as plot devices, and they both squeezed my hands when the doctor exited the operating room to let me know Bucky's fate.

I can always count on them.

Except when it comes to Rio being on time or responding to things in a timely fashion.

"Did you get my text?" I ask.

"I got it," Rio says. We stare at him. It's not until Ariana laughs that he notices we're waiting on him to say more. "What?"

"Any thoughts?"

"You said you don't want to do it, so don't do it."

"My father thinks it's good for the company."

"Then do it."

"But I don't want to."

"Then don't."

Rio is very opinionated but usually holds back from speaking his mind. I think it's because he grew up a middle child who didn't like causing any trouble. But I've been encouraging him to be honest now so nothing gets left unsaid, like when his older brother, Lucio, died. He leans in with his palms pressed together, a sign he's about to share his unfiltered thoughts.

"It's absolutely insane that heralds still exist in the first place. That would be like the town criers from medieval England still walking around today telling people the news. Death-Cast should collectively send Deckers an automated message at midnight instead of calling them individually. It would not only save the company a lot of money, it's better for the Deckers who get screwed over for valuable time when they're called so late into the night."

"Logically, all that makes sense," Ariana says. "Selfishly, that would put my mom out of a job, which would suck for me because then she can't pay for Juilliard, so I'm Team Heralds, even if that means Alano having to take one for the team tonight. Sorry, babe."

This isn't the first time Death-Cast has been criticized for the decision to not have automated messages.

"No one should find out they're dying from a computer," I say.

Over the years, my father has been approached by numerous AI companies who wanted to program automatic alerts, and he always tells the founders to get their heartless asses out of his building.

"Are you at least getting time and a half for working so much in one day?" Rio asks.

"He's inheriting a Fortune 500 company," Ariana says.

"Then all the more reason to fire the heralds and pocket the change."

Ariana flips off Rio, and he blows her a kiss.

I love them, even if I sometimes feel like the middle child between them. They rarely hang out without me; meanwhile I have my own relationships with them. Ariana and I go to plays and musicals, visit museums, sign up for random classes at the 92nd Street Y, and go thrifting every chance we get. Rio and I mostly go for long walks and talk about everything and nothing while trying not to kiss. We're usually successful, but we're humans who crave connection, and our past makes that easy.

Rio snatches my sunglasses off my face and puts them on. "I forgot mine at home."

"That's not my fault."

"It's your fault that we have to be locked away up here, Rapunzel."

"I didn't threaten my own life."

Ariana shudders. "The death threats are so creepy. Any leads?"

"No. Security usually traces the calls back to dummy phones. Probably a pro-naturalist."

"Death Guarder," Rio corrects.

"Death Guarder," I echo.

It's a necessary correction. The Pro-Natural Order is a movement largely made up by those who prefer living life without knowing their fates. This can be dictated by their age, faith, or simply personal preference. Pro-naturalists generally don't harbor ill will toward pro-casters. The Death Guard, on the other hand, are extremists who want Death-Cast to collapse. They spread conspiracies about Death-Cast presenting itself as a public service company and accusing us of playing God and deciding who dies. They stage and record fake Death-Cast calls, and the videos later go viral when the Decker never died; this trend is known as "crying Death-Cast." They even troll real Deckers who are posting about their End Days on social media, which makes them abandon sharing their stories, diminishing the circulation of genuine narratives that encourage people to sign up for our service. Now the Death Guarders are going so far as to kill Deckers and threaten my life.

"Whoever wants to kill you is just a hater," Ariana says.

"A dangerous hater," Rio says. "You should fire Dane."

"Why are you trying to fire everyone?" Ariana asks.

"Especially someone good at his job," I say. "Look at me: I'm alive."

Rio keeps staring out in the city. "If Shield-Cast won't investigate who's out to kill you, then I will."

"Is Detective Rio making a comeback?" Ariana asks.

Rio used to dream about becoming a detective, back when he was waiting for the professionals to solve the mystery of the Last Friend serial killer. "If that's what it takes to keep Alano alive. Alano, give me the call log and tell me everything you remember. Did the original caller have an accent? Any background noise? Was he trying to extort you?"

I hold out my hands, gesturing for Rio to breathe. "I appreciate you, but I'm okay. Shield-Cast is taking this seriously. I promise."

Rio nods. "Okay," he says, resigned. I wouldn't be surprised if the next time I go to his house, I find a bulletin board with strings connecting photographs of suspects with other clues.

"On a brighter note," Ariana singsongs while braiding her hair. "I thrifted the shiniest suit for the gala."

I should be up-front about this morning's update. "About the gala . . ."

"You better not be uninviting us," Ariana says. "It was a thrift, but not my thriftiest thrift!"

Rio shrugs. "I can return my RainBrand suit."

I settle Ariana down. "You're both still going. At least, I hope you are," I say, shifting to Rio. "My father has decided to honor Dalma Young with our inaugural Life-Changer Award at the gala."

I wish Rio wasn't wearing my sunglasses so I could see his reaction, but it's already clear that he's never going to celebrate Dalma Young's creation. Not when Last Friend is the reason his brother is dead.

On Sunday, June 19, 2016, Lucio Morales received his

Death-Cast alert at 2:51 a.m. He shared a bedroom with Rio and their younger brother, Antonio, so they all jumped out of bed to the blaring alert, not knowing who Death-Cast was calling. Rio and Lucio both thought the other was playing some cruel prank. No one was laughing when Lucio signed on to Death-Cast and verified his fate. The Moraleses hosted a funeral in the middle of the night, and once everyone finished their eulogies and began mapping out the best routes to Lucio's favorite places to give him the best End Day possible, Rio found Lucio sneaking out to be with a Last Friend instead of his family.

"Lucio didn't want his death to scar us," Rio had explained.

But it was impossible not to be scarred by Lucio's death when his corpse was discovered, bruised and bloated and branded and dismembered. All because of a murderer who posed as a friend—as a Last Friend.

Rio removes the sunglasses, his near black eyes staring at me. "How can you honor Dalma Young when her app got another person killed today?" he asks.

"That was the Death Guard threatening Death-Cast."

"A life was still lost," Rio says.

Defending the Last Friend app to a victim's brother is never going to go well.

"That was an absolute tragedy," I say about today's killing. I should have checked in on him sooner. "I understand if attending the gala is too uncomfortable for you."

"No, I'm not going to let Dalma get in my way again. I just won't clap for her."

"That's fair," Ariana says.

"I also wouldn't be mad if Dalma Young appeared on your call list," Rio tells me.

"That's dark," Ariana says.

"I'm kidding," he says.

I know he's not.

There are a lot of opinions Rio has that I don't agree with, including how during the angrier stage of his grief, he would regularly voice that Dalma Young is as guilty as the Last Friend serial killer, H. H. Bankson, or how he believed the death penalty should be used on all murderers.

"Serving life sentences means they're still living," Rio had said. "If someone takes a life, they should lose theirs. An eye for an eye, a life for a life."

That's not justice. That's revenge, and revenge is what Rio wants against his brother's killer, who is alive in prison instead of six feet under. I'm not surprised he wants Dalma Young dead too.

"The Last Friend app should definitely shut down," Rio says.

I keep quiet.

Rio and I got close after his brother's death, but if he ever found out I convinced Dalma Young to keep Last Friend alive, it would kill our friendship forever.

LOS ANGELES

PAZ
8:12 p.m. (Pacific Daylight Time)

I keep daydreaming about what life will look like when I'm cast as Death.

I might resurrect my old Instagram account to share my casting announcement as a massive middle finger to everyone who bullied me off social media. I'll get to fly down to Puerto Rico to shoot the movie, and during my downtime I can connect more with my roots, finally meet my aunts, and learn some Spanish. I'll get tight with Zen Abarca during our long hours on set, and who knows, we might become best friends. Maybe more. More than anything I can't wait to become my dream character. It'll be nice to become famous for something good.

Even though I haven't booked the role yet, Mom and Rolando cooked a celebratory dinner and baked flan for dessert. Normally I'd hide out in my room this time of night, but I'm still on such a high (and now post-dessert sugar high) that I'm hanging out with Mom and Rolando in the living room.

We're trying to find something to watch. HGTV is airing one

of their Graveyard Sale specials of *Flea Market Flip*, where the vendors have strong emotional connections to the things they're selling because they once belonged to beloved Deckers. I'm so relieved I won't be putting Mom through this pain. We skip that since she's already seen that episode and keep skipping and skipping and skipping until we end up all the way back to the local stations. There's that cringey drama *Beth vs. Death*, which is about a Death-Cast herald, Beth, who uses her psychic powers to save the lives of the Deckers she calls. I'm desperate enough to be working again that you could pay me to be on that shit show but not to watch it. We land on NBC, where a news anchor is reporting on the murder of a nineteen-year-old Decker who got tricked by a Death Guarder on the Last Friend app.

"Holy shit," Mom says.

"Poor boy," Rolando says.

I know what it's like to be tricked on the Last Friend app, but my abuse was more psychological than physical, though definitely physical too. Not that anyone knows about one of the saddest nights of my life.

It's been hard to make lifelong friends, so after my suicide attempt, I started befriending Deckers on the Last Friend app. They were so desperate for company on their End Day that they were down to hang out with killers like me.

I've been a Living Last Friend for six Deckers.

My first Last Friend was Amos, who was very nice, very nervous (understandably), and very sick from cancer. We had a long talk at his synagogue about the afterlife—the next world, as he called it—and his wishes to be buried alongside his brother as soon as possible for his soul to find peace. I never found out how he died, but I envied him and his soul, whatever happened. My second Last Friend was Carter, this guy a year older than me who was as attractive as he was horrible to me: very. I don't like talking about him. My third Last Friend was Darwin, one of my favorites. No deep talks, but we had fun at this arcade where we talked about his favorite video games, anime, and fantasy movies. He wasn't a fan of the Scorpius Hawthorne movies, and I found his rants funny. Not only did he die at sixteen, he ended up on the Dumb Deaths website for suffocating on a spoonful of cinnamon for some influencer's channel. My fourth Last Friend was Robin, this girl who drowned at the World Travel Arena. My fifth Last Friend was Marina, who ended up ditching me thirty minutes into our breakfast because her best friend finally woke up to see all of Marina's missed calls and texts, which I respected but which made me sad because I've never had a best friend of my own. And my sixth Last Friend, Kit, was the worst of them all. He was a liar, rude, and the two hours spent with him had me racing home to self-harm because he made me feel absolutely worthless.

I swore to myself I would never be someone's Last Friend again, but maybe if things get bad again, I'll sign up so some Death Guarder can do my dirty work for me.

My phone buzzes, and all that tension and sadness gets swallowed up. "Orion just texted."

Mom sits up. "He has your number?"

My phone number was one of the only true things on my

résumé. "He wants me to call," I say, my heart pounding. "Do you think it's bad news? Good news? Maybe it's no news?"

"Only one way to find out, Pazito," Mom says, trying to contain her excitement too, but I see that glimmer in her eyes.

I stare at the ten digits that make up Orion's phone number. It's gotta be good news. Why else would the author of my favorite book and the screenwriter of this movie text me so late after I crushed my audition today?

"Record my reaction," I say. I love videos where actors find out they booked roles. I can use mine during my comeback post.

I call Orion on speaker and pace as the phone rings, crossing my fingers as I pass Mom's camera.

"Hey, Paz," Orion says against a noisy airport background. "How's it going?"

"I'm good, I'm just— Yeah, I'm good."

"Listen, I'm catching a flight back to New York, but I wanted you to hear all this from me. We shared your tapes with our studio partners at See-All, and every single producer loved you. You were so dialed in as Death, and your chemistry with Zen was undeniable. I got chills every damn time I rewatched the video today."

I'm tearing up. Every horrible thing I've had to push through has led me to using my pain for my dream. All's well that ends well, right? Mom's hand is shaky as she and Rolando keep smiling at each other. I can't even get mad at how this might be messing up the video, I'm legit so damn happy too. Happy Paz isn't a performance for once—

"But they're nervous," Orion says.

I freeze. "Nervous about what?"

"The reality is everyone's trying to cover their own asses, protect their jobs. I got a lot of shit for adapting my book when studios kept throwing out names for Oscar winners to do the script instead. This is how they work out in Hollywood, and I hate it, but they're not sure how casting you will play out in the long run."

My thigh is already tingling, like it knows what's about to happen to it.

"But they liked my performance," I say.

"They loved your performance, Paz. If this was just about acting, you would have the part. But Hollywood hates risks, so they want to go with a safer choice. They're concerned that this movie they're investing tens of millions of dollars in might get boycotted because—"

"Because I saved my mom from getting killed?! Because I was declared innocent during trial?!" I snap, which can't be helping my case, but fuck it, all anyone is ever gonna see me as is a loaded gun anyway.

Mom turns off the camera and tries calming me down, but I keep pacing, taking Orion off speaker.

"Come on, there's nothing else you can say? Maybe set up a meeting so they can see I'm a good guy. Tell them I'll do the movie for free. Please!"

Orion is quiet. All I can hear is an airport attendant announcing boarding for a flight to New York. "I'm sorry, Paz, but I've done everything I can."

Now I'm not saying anything, just breathing and breathing

even though I don't wanna. I'm about to throw my phone against the wall when Orion calls my name. "What?"

"I get that you're pissed, but remember your promise," Orion says, but I don't believe he actually cares about me. He's trying to cover his ass too, just like those ass-covering assholes at the studio. "I'll hit you up soon to see how you're doing."

Soon? How long is soon? A day or two? A week? Right now a week sounds as long as an immortal life.

"Okay. Thanks, Orion," I say, hanging up as he's saying bye.

I stare lifelessly at Mom's phone on the couch. I want that reaction video deleted.

"I'm sorry, Pazito," Mom says, blocking my path from pacing more.

"It's not your fault."

"This isn't your fault either."

"It is, you heard him."

Mom grabs my hands. "No. Orion and those Hollywood people do not know what they are talking about. Everything that happened was all Frankie's fault."

"Yeah, well, Dad's dead."

"You are not, Pazito, because you and I, we are survivors," Mom says, pulling me in for a hug. "We have been through so much, and you will get through this too."

I hate being called a survivor like it's a good thing, but Mom is right, I will get through this.

I just have to wait until I'm alone so I don't end up on suicide watch again.

NEW YORK

ALANO
11:25 p.m. (Eastern Daylight Time)

I'm in the training room of Herald Hall along with our three new hires and onboarding director.

We're sitting at a long glossy white table, one of the four originals from the first End Day; my mother thought it would be nice to repurpose this piece from the past for the same space where the next generation of heralds receive their training. The new heralds—Fausto Flores, Honey Doyle, Rylee Ray— have been taking notes the entire session. Even though I know everything being taught from reading every handbook we've internally published since inception, I take down notes too so they don't feel even more self-conscious than they already do while sitting next to the creator's son.

Roah Wetherholt regularly travels the country for onboarding heralds, but my father has them stationed in New York until the end of the month for next week's gala and to oversee the training of our new hires. If Roah wasn't in town, this responsibility would fall on the head herald in charge, and Andrea Donahue doesn't have the right touch. There's a reason why Roah was promoted from herald to head herald to training manager within our first year of operation and director by year five. They've even contributed to recent printings of the herald handbook.

Before anyone gets hired as a herald, we perform extensive background checks and have them interviewed by a human resources manager or chief of staff. If approved, the applicant goes on to the last stage, where they perform a series of practice calls, recorded and supervised by the head herald on duty. Those videos make their way to my parents, who have the final say, not leaving the world's most important job up to chance.

I was given everyone's profiles tonight before meeting them.

"Make sure we were right," my father said. He'd like to see me involved in the hiring process within the year.

The training tonight has been both a refresher on everyone's preboarding lessons—telecom etiquette, active listening, de-escalation techniques—and other important matters such as the desired window of time for each call, how to speak with a Decker's proxy (like a child's guardian, for example), what to do when the Decker doesn't answer, dispatching police if foul play is suspected, time zone logistics when Deckers are traveling, and more.

Roah moves on to a new lesson. "A Decker will ask you how Death-Cast works. Who can tell me the best response?"

I can, but I don't count.

Honey Doyle sheepishly raises her hand. I get her hesitation; I doubt she had to manage matters of actual life or death in her previous customer service role at AT&T. She says, "I'll tell the Decker I don't know how Death-Cast works."

"That's close, but I advise you to be more specific and conclusive to prevent follow-ups. It can be as simple as 'I'm afraid that information isn't available to heralds' or 'I'm not aware how Death-Cast works, only that our predictions have never been wrong.' Then return focus on their End Day for both their sake and the Deckers in waiting."

Everyone takes note; I scribble some lines.

"I have a question," says Rylee Ray, a former sales rep who moved to New York from Georgia with her husband, Brian Ray, who's unemployed but currently being screened for a security escort position here due to his extensive background in the field. "What happens if we see a Decker who we know on our contact list?"

"Do you mean someone you personally know or someone famous?" Roah asks.

"Personally."

If she had answered celebrity, it would have been a red flag that I would've reported to my parents. HR is usually skilled at identifying who wants to be a herald for the right reasons and who's trying to get intel on public figures dying to sell that information to news outlets or abuse their power by pranking people from our lines (a felony, as of 2013) or simply get a foot in the building so they can discover the Death-Cast secret. If we suspect they could be guilty of one crime, we consider them risks for all.

"Seeing someone you personally know can be hard," Roah says. "We recommend passing that call on to another herald. History shows that when a Decker has ties to an active herald, it can lead to suspicion that maybe they aren't dying, prolonging their stage of denial and even risking them not believing in their End Day. Once the Decker has been alerted, the head herald on duty can give you space to personally reach out and offer your condolences."

There's quiet in the room, like everyone is imagining what names they dread seeing on their contact sheets. I would lose it if I saw my parents or best friends on that list.

Roah asks if anyone has any final questions, as they'd like to get us in the wellness room so we can collect ourselves before midnight.

Fausto Flores speaks up. "What happens if we're working and it's our End Day?"

I'd be surprised if everyone hasn't gone from imagining a loved one's name on their contact list to their own.

"The moment we discover it's your End Day, we will pull you from the floor to deliver the news personally," Roah says.

This has happened six times in Death-Cast history.

"Will you know before our shift starts?" Fausto asks.

Roah shakes their head. "The contact lists are active as of midnight in each respective time zone, not a second before. Every night, your head herald is tasked with scanning the new roster as soon as possible for any heralds to relieve you of your duties so you may capitalize on your End Day."

"Good to know."

Fausto Flores is eighteen, the youngest full-time herald in Death-Cast history. Death-Cast doesn't have any major reservations about hiring young apart from the heaviness of the job, but between being up-front about the realities heralds face and the support we offer with our on-site therapists, we ultimately trust everyone to know their capabilities. The reason we haven't hired any eighteen-year-olds before has been because no eighteen-year-olds genuinely want to work here. Except Fausto Flores, who has never had a job before this, but Aster Gomez vouched for him.

There's a last call for questions, and no one answers, so Roah escorts everyone a few doors down for our active resting.

I breathe in the lavender and eucalyptus oils permeating throughout the wellness room as serene harp songs cycle through the speakers in the corner. The public is always surprised to learn that this is a mandatory part of the job because companies don't typically pay their employees to relax for thirty minutes before their shifts. Death-Cast wants our heralds at their very best and that means getting them in the right headspaces before their daunting tasks. To help release endorphins and alleviate anxiety, we have a steam room, tubs for cold plunges, studios for yoga and dancing, a craft room to create bright art, a waiting room with healthy snacks, and a quiet zone where you can relax with an eye mask and go on a guided meditation journey.

Every herald chooses how they will best prepare for these

three hours of their night, these three hours of their life to prepare others for the end of theirs.

Roah Wetherholt heads for the craft room; Honey Doyle walks into the waiting area; Rylee Ray bravely goes to the dancing studio, which no one ever does on their first night; and Fausto Flores strips down to his underwear and takes a cold plunge. You can learn a lot about someone from how they spend this time.

I grab an eye mask and headphones and go into the quiet zone. No one else is here, so I have my choice of where I want to relax. I feel like Goldilocks bouncing between the beanbag to the velvet rocking chair to the bouclé swivel chair to the leather massage chair, but it's the faux fur bed that looks like a dog bed made for humans that strangely feels just right. I go through the audio options, most tempted by recordings of rain pouring in a jungle, birdsong by a river, and small waves hitting a beach while children laugh in the background, but I opt for the guided meditation in the hopes of taming my mind from focusing on the weeds in my life instead of the flowers.

In the darkness of my eye mask, I begin my meditation, guided by a soothing voice. I settle into my comfortable position, trying to find peace, and as if my guide can read my mind, they tell me that my stress is normal. I inhale for five seconds, exhale for eight, anchoring myself to my breath, but I can't help but think about this exercise not being enough for people who are about to find out they're Deckers. How can anyone breathe after getting this information? How aren't more people dropping dead from heart attacks the moment they hear that blaring alert? I try catching up with the meditation as the guide tells me to show compassion toward myself, but I've always been better about extending that to others. I work hard to be compassionate toward myself for getting distracted after hearing how our brains are skilled to take us out of the present moment; my brain doesn't just take me out, it always transports me, whisking me away. Right now I'm going back to this afternoon, when Agent Dane's training made me feel as if I don't have a life worth fighting for. I have to stop imagining myself as a defeated Decker and refocus as a herald who must push through all trials to make sure no Deckers die unwarned. I repeat this intention to myself over and over as I begin fading. The meditation comes to an end with a final message about allowing gravity to keep me grounded so I can take on the unfolding night ahead.

It's ten minutes to midnight as all the heralds gather by the wellness room's front door.

I blend in with the heralds in my uniform: a white button-down shirt with our insignia—an hourglass with radio waves in place of sand—and a gray tie with matching slacks. This has been the dress code since launch. I've sketched concepts for new uniforms that could make our heralds more comfortable during a harrowing job, but my father said he wanted to create a separation between work and home.

"It may be difficult, but it is not impossible," he said. "If firefighters and police officers and doctors can keep their gear—and thoughts of their work—at their stations, so can our heralds."

Right as we're all about to file out to the call center, Andrea Donahue walks in, a slight limp from an old injury that used to require her elegant wooden cane that was adorned with chamomile flowers. Her gold hoop earrings distract from her black disheveled hair, and she looks less like a spy when she removes her shades and tan trench coat. Ariana looks so much like her mother that staring at Andrea feels like getting a glimpse of Ariana at fifty-five. Hopefully not in personality, though. Andrea simply nods at the new heralds, not bothering with any small talk or welcomes. She doesn't typically invest her energy into any coworkers unless they survive one month on the job. Even then, she doesn't seem to have a social life outside her daughter. She's about to lead the line to the call center when she sees me and does a double take.

"Alano?"

"Good evening, Ms. Donahue."

"Are you working with us tonight?" she asks, observing my uniform.

"Yes, ma'am. My father wants me to have the experience." I'm sure Roah Wetherholt would've notified Andrea beforehand, but I'm more surprised she doesn't already know this from her daughter. "Didn't Ariana tell you over dinner?"

Andrea shakes her head. "No, I haven't seen her tonight. I wasn't home."

I'm expecting her to expand, but in all my attempts of getting to know her personally, Andrea doesn't divulge too much about her life.

"Have you had a chance to say hello to the new heralds?" I ask.

Andrea seems offended at first, then seems to remember I'm the Death-Cast heir. "Not yet. I'll be sure to check in on them during the shift," she says, and then checks her watch. "We should be going so we're not late."

This coming from the woman who was an hour and a half late without notifying anyone. This isn't the first time, but Andrea has expressed to my mother and HR that the active resting period of her shift doesn't put her in the right headspace. She's always forgiven because of her productive outreach. But being late to call Deckers would be a bigger offense.

All twenty-one of us file out of Herald Hall and ride the escalator from the ninth floor to the tenth.

The call centers have evolved since the start of Death-Cast, all the layouts designed by my mother. First there were open-floor plans with the glossy white tables and fountains stationed around the workspace so that the sounds of flowing water could soothe the heralds between their calls. Then the glossiness became sterile and made the heralds feel like test subjects in a cruel experiment to see how long it takes for the job to break a person. So every Death-Cast facility swapped in colorful furniture and cheerful paintings with buckets of blue used throughout because psychologists said it's a productive and calming color. The call centers were updated again in January with healthy and happy plants in every corner, elegant wallpaper that looks like an aerial shot of an ocean in motion, beaming light bulbs that mimic sunlight so the graveyard shifts feel brighter, and cubicles with black oak veneer desks and glass partition panels so that even though heralds have more privacy and less noise interference during their calls, they can still see their colleagues nearby and know they are never alone.

I'm stationed between Andrea Donahue and Fausto Flores. Unlike the other established heralds, my desk doesn't have any personal items on display, something the handbook encourages for heralds to be rooted to their own lives between the calls. My desk has only the headset, phone, sleek computer monitor, mechanical telecom keyboard, and a binder with prompts for Deckers, all of which I've long memorized.

A hand squeezes my shoulder, familiar.

I wasn't expecting my father to check in beforehand. "Hey, Pa."

"You ready, mi hijo?" he quietly asks, as if his presence hasn't already been noted by the heralds, particularly Andrea, who straightens up.

"I'm as ready as I can be," I say.

"You will do well."

I will because I have to. Messing up means messing with someone's life and death.

Andrea spins in her chair to face my father. "Good evening, Mr. Rosa."

"Evening, Andrea. All well with our newcomers?"

"Absolutely. I'll be supervising them."

"Excellent. I'll quickly introduce myself and get out of your way."

My father greets Fausto Flores, Honey Doyle, and Rylee Ray, unaware that Andrea had no role in preparing them for the evening. Even if we had time to discuss this I wouldn't want to. She's our head herald, but most important, she's my best friend's mother. I let my father exit the call center and choose to focus on my job.

I'm here to do a job—and that begins in one minute.

I put on my headset, switch on the monitor, and ready my phone so I can call people and tell them their lives are over.

LOS ANGELES

PAZ
9:00 p.m. (Pacific Daylight Time)

The one and only time I was on suicide watch made me even more suicidal.

Mom and Rolando would stay up with me every night, waiting until Death-Cast was done with their calls so that they knew I wouldn't be successful in killing myself. Not that that stopped me from trying last time. That very threat is why Mom slept in bed with me as Rolando camped outside my door in a sleeping bag in case I tried running away, which wasn't my plan but definitely became an urge the longer I didn't have privacy. Rolando removed the doorknobs from every room in the house so I couldn't lock myself in anywhere, even though it wasn't possible to try overdosing again, since all his alcohol had been dumped out and my antidepressants were hidden somewhere. It didn't stop there. One time I had a headache and went to the medicine cabinet for Excedrin and found the shelves cleared of everything except toothpaste and cotton balls. It took weeks before household meds were reintroduced into the bathroom, and it's a great thing no one ever caught on that I had started burning myself with the shower's steaming hot water or Mom would've probably bathed me in the backyard with the garden hose.

I only got off the intense suicide watch thanks to crafting Happy Paz.

Sometimes it's sad being so good at acting that loved ones believe I'm okay.

Across the country, the Death-Cast calls are beginning, but no one can know I'm counting down these next three hours before lucky souls start receiving theirs in LA, or that I'm hoping I'll be one of them.

NEW YORK

July 23, 2020

ALANO

12:00 a.m. (Eastern Daylight Time)

Death-Cast hasn't called to tell me if I'm dying today, but I'm about to call people who will be.

In this three-hour outreach window, I'm charged with calling thirty Deckers. Every call should be done within five minutes. There's some cushion to go over, but not a lot. During quarterly meetings there's always complaints from heralds, especially the new ones, that five minutes isn't enough, but the truth is if we allotted more time per Decker then Death-Cast would have to expand the outreach window by another hour (as we already had to do in year two to support the demand), and that increases the chances that someone could die before receiving their alert. Making sure Deckers don't die unwarned is a herald's one job.

My contact list appears with all thirty names randomly ordered to ensure no one receives special treatment. Over the years, millionaires and billionaires have wined and dined my father, encouraging him to offer a premium service where subscribers pay extra to have their names automatically bumped to the top of the list.

"You'll make a fortune off people buying time," one billionaire said.

But my father refused anyway, telling him what he tells everyone else: "We are all equals in life, but we are never treated that way. I can at least ensure the proper balance by making us all equals in death." Then he always picks up the tab to prove he doesn't need to exploit anyone for more fortunes.

The first Decker on my list is Harry Hope. His last name is so beautiful, but so sad. The only hope he can hold on to after my call is a long End Day. Our studies have shown that the average Decker is dead before 5:00 p.m., but Harry will have a leg up on the others. I tense, stunned that I'm about to deliver this life-changing news, and I wish I had undergone training with test calls like the others. That experience could've better prepared me than knowing every word in the handbook. As I see Andrea Donahue already extending her sympathies on behalf of Death-Cast to her first Decker of the night and Fausto Flores dialing his, I accept that I'm going to be the bearer of bad news and can only hope that he takes it as well as can be.

I click his name to get his phone number from his profile. As it's ringing, I wish there was more information about Harry Hope apart from him being a twenty-nine-year-old in Brooklyn and his emergency contact being his mother. I'd love to know his interests, his dislikes, even a photo so he's more than a faceless voice on the other line.

Then I hear his voice. "Hello?" He sounds surprised, which I'm not.

"Hello, this is Alano from Death-Cast calling to speak with Harry Hope."

He responds only with some sniffling. I'm about to continue through the rest of the standard formalities before remembering I need to confirm his identity.

"Is this Harry I'm speaking with?"

"It is," he says as he begins sobbing for his life.

I want to validate his feelings, but the handbook recommends taking advantage of the silence while you have it. "Harry, I regret to inform you that sometime in the next twenty-four hours you'll be meeting an untimely death. While there isn't anything we can do to suspend that, you still have a chance to live."

I click open another window that has information about today including the forecast, special activities, promo codes for different Decker-friendly businesses, instructions for funeral arrangements, and more.

"Do you have any End Day plans in place? If not, I'm ready to present some ideas for you."

"I can't believe it," Harry says, hyperventilating. "I can't— I c-c-c-an't believe it."

He's not in a place yet for activities. I have to de-escalate. "I know this is difficult news to receive, Harry, but it's all done in service to set you up for success while you still have time. How about we take a deep breath together—"

"It's going to work," Harry mutters. "I can't believe it's going to work."

Hair raises on the back of my neck. "What's going to work?"

There's a lightness to Harry's cries. Almost like he's happy-crying.

I try asking again. "What's going to—"

There's a gunshot. I drop to the floor, hiding under my desk. I'm scared that we're under attack before realizing the gun was shot on the other end of the line.

Did someone kill Harry or did Harry kill himself?

I can't believe it's going to work, Harry Hope had said.

Was he talking about suicide? Is that why he was happy-crying?

Did I deliver good news?

The gunshot keeps ringing in my head. Did Harry already have the gun in hand when I called, or did he pick it up after knowing he would die? I don't know what he looks like, but that doesn't stop me from picturing real brains being blown out of a skull.

I look up to find Andrea staring at me from her chair while still speaking with a Decker. Fausto is kneeling before me, offering a helping hand. I stay under the desk, trying not to throw up or cry. Maybe I've gotten all of this wrong. Harry could still be alive. The obvious alternative for why he would've fired a gun isn't any better, but maybe no one was shot, he could've fired a gun into the air, like a starting pistol for a race, but maybe it's to celebrate his End Day.

"Harry, are you there? Harry? Harry, are you there? Please, Harry . . ."

I'm supposed to alert the authorities and his emergency

contact, but it's one thing to call people to tell them they're dying. It's another to call a mother to tell her that her son has shot himself to death.

I can't speak.

I can't *breathe.*

I'm having an asthma attack. I pat myself down, but I forgot my inhaler in my other pants. Am I going to die? Andrea was supposed to inform me at the start of the shift if I'm going to die, but I don't know if she even reviewed that list before jumping straight to work. Fausto calls for help, and Roah rushes over, but they're pushed to the side by my father, who is panting hard. He grabs an emergency inhaler from inside his jacket, something he always carries on him after my tenth birthday, when I didn't have my inhaler and was fighting for my life during an asthma attack that we suspected might lead to death even though I didn't receive my alert.

I pump the medicine in between sobs.

My heartbeat is pounding in my head, but that single gunshot playing on a loop is louder. I had no illusions that Harry Hope would die today, but did I have to hear it?

By the time I can breathe again, I wish I couldn't after that unforgettable, haunting call.

12:25 a.m.

"You did all you could do," my father says, resting his hand on my back as I sob into my mother's shoulder.

We're alone in the wellness room. No nature sounds or cold plunges or dance parties will make me forget that traumatic

Death-Cast call. If I hadn't read all six editions of the herald handbook I would be turning to it now for insights on how to recover from this, but there are no entries for the rare case of a Decker happily crying as they take their own life while still on the call.

"I didn't do anything except give him clearance to die," I say.

"This is not your fault," Ma says.

"If he did indeed kill himself, it is because he was unwell," Pa says.

We don't know for a fact yet that Harry Hope died by suicide, but his final words support that theory.

In the past decade, Death-Cast revolutionized how everyone lives before they die and that includes suicidal people, some who try proving our predictions—or lack thereof—wrong. But as we've continued gaining trust with the public, there have been fewer suicide attempts as people fear what will happen to them when—not if—they fail. We can only hope this continues so suicide isn't a leading cause of death in this country like it still is today, doubling the amount of homicides. The downside is that there's been an increase in self-harming as a coping mechanism during the so-called Not-End Days, a term coined by suicidal people who are struggling after not receiving a Death-Cast alert.

When announcing his presidential candidacy on June 18, 2019, Carson Dunst pinned the rise of self-harm on Death-Cast.

"Outrageous," my father said while watching President Page's former vice president build his campaign by attacking our company. "This nation, the very nation Dunst hopes to lead, has always failed to recognize suicide for the epidemic it is."

Later that night, after composing himself, maybe even reckoning with some truth to the fact that Death-Cast might be responsible for the rise in self-harming, he told me, "My greatest wish is that by living, each and every soul will heal so they no longer await our call."

That wasn't the case for Harry Hope, who was told that he would die sometime in the next twenty-four hours and killed himself three minutes after midnight.

"How about we get you to Tamara?" Ma says.

I shake my head. I don't want to see the on-site therapist.

"How about Roah? They have more experience with this than we do."

Before working at Death-Cast, Roah Wetherholt was an operator for a suicide-prevention hotline. If they have stories about people killing themselves over the phone, I don't want to hear them.

"Then talk to me," Pa says. "I understand what you are going through."

I rack my brain for a memory of my father speaking with a suicidal Decker who killed himself, but there's nothing. "Your one and only call went to a Decker who lived a historic End Day."

"A call where a man was shot."

That man was William Wilde, the first Decker in the Death's Dozen, who was shot to death by a masked assailant in Times Square while my father was on the phone with Valentino Prince. It's upsetting, but it's not the same thing.

"You don't know that man's voice," I say. I knew Harry's for only three minutes, but I'll never forget it.

My father is about to argue, but he pulls back. "Let's get you home if you do not want to talk with anyone."

It would be nice to cuddle with Bucky until I fall asleep, or call my friends, but I have work to do. "I'm going to finish my calls," I say, quickly exiting the wellness center as my parents chase me down Herald Hall.

"Alano, stop," Ma says.

"You are not working in this state," Pa says.

I stop at the bottom of the escalator, enraged. "You told me to do this," I say, pointing at my father. "What did you think would happen? That I would only speak with one-hundred-year-olds who have lived long and happy lives? I was always going to be scarred, you know that I can't—" I stop speaking because there are cameras, and we have to watch what we say as a family with many secrets. My father doesn't need me to finish the sentence anyway; I see the guilt in his eyes for this pain he's inflicted on me.

"I am sorry I failed to protect you, mi hijo." He invites me in for a hug, but I step back onto the escalator, heading up toward the call center. He said before that I did all I could do with Harry Hope, but there are still twenty-nine Deckers counting on me, and I need to make up for lost time.

If this is my only shift as a herald, I will make sure Deckers don't die unwarned.

Even if that's the last thing I ever do at Death-Cast.

LOS ANGELES

PAZ

10:00 p.m. (Pacific Daylight Time)

Two more hours until Death-Cast hopefully calls and puts me out of my misery.

NEW YORK

ALANO
2:15 a.m. (Eastern Daylight Time)

A herald's one job is to make sure Deckers don't die unwarned, and I'm going to fail.

I have a hard enough time living with myself already. I can't let this happen too.

There's forty-five minutes until the outreach window closes on the East Coast, and I've made only twenty of my thirty calls. I deserve to be fired for not managing my time properly, but the other heralds are so backed up that we need all hands on deck, even mine. Roah Wetherholt has been forced to step in too if we're going to have any chance of getting this done.

Of the twenty calls I've made, Harry Hope remains the worst experience, but the other nineteen Deckers have become nightmares of their own. They've pleaded for time I can't give them and begged for answers I don't have on how they will die. The last Decker, Niall McMahon, even threatened to wait outside Death-Cast to kill me because I called him so late after midnight. Unless Andrea Donahue has neglected to tell me my name is on her roster, I don't have to take Niall McMahon's threat seriously, but I report him anyway so we're not held liable in case he has a violent spree on his End Day.

Before I can dial my next Decker, Andrea knocks on my partition panel. At first I think she's finally checking in on me after returning to my desk nearly two hours ago. You would think I'm not her daughter's best friend or a herald she's supervising or even her boss's son for how much she ignored me after my traumatic call.

"Why do I know this name?" Andrea asks, pointing to her monitor. "Is he an actor?"

I read the name on Andrea's screen and inform her that Caspian Townsend is an Olympic gold medalist. I understand how Andrea confused him for an actor, since Caspian Townsend rose to fame as the Olympic darling during the games and was hailed as the Michael Phelps of fencing. Hollywood is even making a movie about him. Now Caspian Townsend won't be around to see it.

"An Olympic gold medalist is a first for me," Andrea says like she's collecting prized Deckers. She calls him immediately. "Hello, I'm calling from Death-Cast to speak with Casper Townsend."

"Caspian," I correct.

"Caspian Townsend," Andrea says with fake remorse in her voice but not her face, which looks annoyed because his name is not what she mistook it to be.

I'm bothered by this, but I return to my desk. Eyes on my own paper.

My next Decker, Régine D'Aboville, is an au pair from Paris

who doesn't want to spend her End Day with her host family, so I'm suggesting the Last Friend app when Andrea gets up from her desk.

I'm expecting Andrea to do another lap like she did half an hour ago, when she scolded Honey Doyle for not speaking up when delivering the most devastating news in a person's life, Rylee Ray for crying on the phone with a Decker and making their moment about herself, and Fausto for spending eight minutes on one call because he was consoling a parent whose five-year-old is dying today. But Andrea doesn't talk to anyone. She just leaves the call center. I almost peek at her screen to see if she's done with her list, but I focus on my work.

After hanging up on Régine D'Aboville, I call the next Decker, Glenda Lashey, and I'm overwhelmed that I still have eight people on my list after her. Even if I get every Decker off the line in the desired five minutes, I'll still be five minutes short. I could do everything right and still fail. This wouldn't have happened if Harry Hope didn't shoot himself at the start of my shift. If I didn't walk away for half an hour. The memory of the gunshot is so loud that it's as if it's happening all over again. I can barely focus on Glenda Lashey as she talks about wishing her dead mother hadn't died when she was a little girl and that she knew where her father is.

"Hmm. I'm ready to move on to my End Day," Glenda Lashey says. "Do I just hang up now?"

"If that's what you'd like," I say. I hate myself for thinking it, but it's what I would like. We're five minutes into her call, seconds away from six. That's another Decker's minute.

"Actually . . ."

Glenda Lashey asks about special events happening today, and I'm silently cursing myself for not encouraging her to hang up when she asked. I tell her about the All-Night Market in Brooklyn for End Day–worthy meals; a boat tour around the Hudson and East River, where she'll have to wear a life jacket and be accompanied by a tour guide/lifeguard; and a new art installation at the Met of Valentino Prince on the deck of a ship to commemorate his status as the world's first Decker. None of that interests her, and she hangs up after taking another three minutes.

I'm losing this race against time.

I undo my tie, trying to breathe. My chest is tight again. This might be another asthma attack or even a panic attack. The latter can lead to the former. I still don't have my inhaler, because I rushed out of the wellness room to return to the call center so Deckers don't die unwarned. How could I forget my inhaler? Seriously. My father told me to not tease Death, and here I am, doing just that.

My parents don't answer when I call them from my desk phone, and I can't text them for my inhaler because personal phones are forbidden in the call center. Our phones remain in our lockers in the wellness room, where my inhaler also is. I stop wasting time and rush to get it. It's irresponsible knowing how far behind I am on my calls, but I need peace of mind and functioning lungs, so I don't drop dead while speaking with Deckers.

What if I am a Decker and my body is telling me I'm going to die since no one else has?

There would be justice in that given how much I've messed up.

I'm lightheaded when I arrive in the wellness room. I weakly open my locker, grab my inhaler, and pump the medicine into my mouth. I rest my forehead against the locker and inhale for five seconds and exhale for eight like earlier tonight, over and over as the harp music helps me relax. It's so nice that I wish I could stay, but Deckers need me.

I'm leaving for the call center when I hear someone talking in the quiet zone. I assume it's a custodian until I recognize the voice. Andrea Donahue. It seems hard to believe, but I wonder if Andrea experienced something difficult on her last call that required more privacy than the private booths in the call center. I can't blame her when I did the same thing. I slowly open the door so I don't startle her.

Andrea Donahue is sitting in the velvet rocking chair, laughing into her phone as if she's in the comfort of her own home. She should be upstairs speaking with Deckers. We both should, but Andrea especially. "You're never going to become the next TMZ if you don't loosen those purse strings," Andrea says mockingly. "If you're not willing to pay up, I'm happy to sell the story to a tabloid that can afford it."

I hide outside the quiet zone, listening even though I'm scared of what I'll overhear.

Andrea scoffs. "You paid four thousand dollars for the tip on that soap star last week, and I'm supposed to accept half as much for a beloved Olympic gold medalist? Have you no shame?"

I have to be misunderstanding something. Surely Andrea Donahue isn't keeping Deckers waiting for her call because she's too busy leaking her newsworthy contacts to tabloids. She's definitely not doing an illegal side hustle on company time.

"I'll settle for five, Gus, but I'm not happy," Andrea says, rocking back and forth in her chair. "Uh-huh . . . uh-huh . . . Well, there are no other exciting names on the roster tonight. . . . I do have another story, but I don't want to waste my breath on you when I know someone at TMZ will pay up. . . . Fine. How much would you pay for a story about Alano Rosa?"

Hearing my name is as shocking as that gunshot tonight but pierces harder. This is my best friend's mother selling a story about me. Andrea has watched me grow up during her entire employment here, and she's seen more of me these past three years as Ariana invites me over to her apartment. Did I say something while at Andrea's that she's now pitching to some tabloid? Did Ariana share my secret that only she and my parents know? Did Andrea somehow figure out my secret that no one knows?

"Add another ten thousand, and I'll come to you first with my next lead," Andrea says.

I should be downstairs, but I have to see what she knows.

"Now *that* deal I'm happy about," Andrea says. She relaxes into the chair and kicks her feet up on the beanbag while telling Gus about my first time heralding tonight. How I got so scared after my Decker killed himself that I hid under the table. How my father had to save me from an asthma attack. How my parents pulled me from the call center for thirty minutes.

"You can only be that bad at your job when your father runs the company," she says.

I almost think she's speaking directly to me. She laughs again.

"No, this won't get traced back to me. Everyone will suspect the new hires if anything." Andrea checks her watch. "I have to go break some bad news to four more Deckers, but I'll be in touch soon—"

She notices me watching her through the door and immediately hangs up.

I back away and head for the door, but when she shouts my name from the quiet zone, I freeze.

Andrea comes out of the room. "What are you doing here?" she asks, staring at me like I'm the suspicious one, a glint of danger flashing in her eyes.

What if this is how I die tonight? Killed by a head herald after catching her leaking company secrets?

I show her my inhaler. "I came to grab this, and I heard you talking."

"How much . . . What did you hear?"

The uncomfortable reality of not knowing everything Andrea shared settles in. "I heard enough" is all I say.

Neither of us know what the other knows.

Andrea stares, trying to figure out her next move, like when she's playing chess against Ariana. "You're a smart boy, Alano, so I won't insult you with any lies about that call not being what it looked like. Those tabloid reporters are vultures, always circling famous Deckers, trying to get that first bite so they can break the news of someone's End Day. I'm just feeding the scavengers."

"You're violating the trust of the Deckers whose privacy was promised."

"The world would've found out anyway, just like we do everything else about a celebrity's life. Why should their deaths be any different?"

"Exactly. They've had a lifetime of cameras in their faces. Let them live their End Day in peace."

"Do not overconcern yourself with the dead," Andrea says gently, like I'm some child who doesn't know better.

"Deckers are not dead yet. Neither am I."

The tension is tight between us.

"Why are you selling stories about me? I'm your daughter's best friend."

"Everything I do, I do for my daughter," Andrea Donahue says, as if that's a good enough reason to not treat people as people. "I've needed the money for her education, for her future. She doesn't come from a family of billionaires, so I saw an opportunity to make her dreams come true, and I took it. I'm not harming anyone."

These leaks can not only damage my position in the company, but they can damage Death-Cast's reputation, especially when the Death Guard is fabricating stories about us. We don't need real internal offenses supporting their narrative. On the other hand, if we were able to maintain trust with the public after the Death's Dozen, then I can survive a story about my reasonable reaction to a traumatic call. Especially if that money is supporting Ariana's future.

"What's your move, Alano?" Andrea asks.

I'm asking myself the same thing. I check the clock. There's seventeen minutes left before we close the outreach window. I have eight Deckers to call and Andrea has four—twelve Deckers total. A chill runs down my spine as I sweat over the risk of history repeating with the Death's Dozen. Everyone would know that a head herald and the heir are responsible for that catastrophe, even if Andrea has to leak that information herself. The pressure to save these Deckers by informing them of their fates is suffocating, and I'm scared I'll be forced to dehumanize them the way Andrea has for ten years in order to get through all the calls.

"We're going back to work," I say.

Andrea grabs my arm. "I'm not going anywhere unless I know where you stand."

If Andrea didn't have my best friend as her shield, this would look different. She would be fired and escorted out of the building by security before all phones were down in the call center. But I can handle some scrutiny from the media. "If you promise to never violate a Decker's privacy again, I won't tell my father."

The moment Andrea Donahue takes to think this over feels

like forever. "Don't tell my daughter either and you got yourself a deal," she says, as if she's doing me the favor for covering up her crimes. "Ariana's life shouldn't be ruined because of how much I love her."

There's finally something we agree on.

LOS ANGELES

PAZ

11:50 p.m. (Pacific Daylight Time)

Ten minutes until the Death-Cast calls begin.

If Death-Cast doesn't put me out of my misery, then I will.

NEW YORK

ALANO

2:59 a.m. (Eastern Daylight Time)

I'm on my last call.

I couldn't have done this without the assistance of the other heralds—including Andrea Donahue—who'd successfully gotten through their contact lists. My parents were almost forced to get involved too after returning from their last-minute meeting with security to debrief about the Death Guard threat from earlier, but it turns out that Fausto Flores is an excellent herald, even if he was too slow sometimes for Andrea's liking. I also had some tragic luck when I called one Decker, Leonor Pollard, only to realize his brother, Levi Pollard, was next on my list so I spoke to them both at once. They hung up on me by the third minute, ready to face their fate together.

Now I'm finishing my call with Morgane Kilbourne, a lovely young mother who I've aided in arranging urgent child care through a local shelter so her baby boys won't be left unattended should she die in the next minute. All I can think about is the alternate universe where Morgane Kilbourne dies without warning and the infinite tragedies that could have happened to her sons.

I speak our passing sentiment for the last time tonight: "On behalf of Death-Cast, we are sorry to lose you. Live this day to the fullest."

"Thank you, Alano," Morgane says before hanging up.

It's 3:00 a.m. The call center goes quiet as we close the East Coast's outreach window.

Heralds collect their things and follow Andrea Donahue back to the wellness room to decompress, but I stay in my seat, exhausted by this day where so much has happened. Strangers threatened my life while the Death Guard threatened Death-Cast. I discovered my best friend's mother is another threat to Death-Cast. I called twenty-five people tonight to tell them they're going to die and the first took his life before I could hang up.

I remove my headset, envying the Deckers I've called.

LOS ANGELES

July 23, 2020

PAZ

12:00 a.m. (Pacific Daylight Time)

Death-Cast better call to tell me I'm gonna die today.

12:34 a.m.

Death-Cast still hasn't called.

1:15 a.m.

What's taking Death-Cast so long to call?

2:30 a.m.

I'm starting to get nervous that Death-Cast won't call.

2:49 a.m.

Death-Cast isn't calling tonight, are they?

3:00 a.m.

Death-Cast didn't call, and it's so heartbreaking that I have to hurt myself.

I wanna boil in steaming-hot water like I'm cooking myself alive.

I wanna be in so much pain that I bite down on my lip and draw blood.

I wanna get as close to death as possible in this world that hates me but won't kill me.

I grab my thick journal out of the nightstand, which I've hollowed out to hide my knife from my mom and stepdad so they keep believing I'm doing better. I flip open the tacky cover, thinking about how this book was scarier when it was a 365-day journal instead of storage for a weapon. The inspirational quotes, the blank entries for my feelings, the hundreds of pages I needed to live through helped me realize how I don't wanna live long enough to have to get another journal.

I grab the knife, shaking, but I stop myself.

Fear makes me freeze, ever since childhood. But sometimes the fear gets so big that I unfreeze and do something terrible. Something life-ruining. So no matter how good it feels to hurt myself, I know it's not a good feeling.

I keep holding the knife, but I don't do the terrible thing.

I need to get past this impulse.

There's a million things I can be doing instead of this one thing that I'm not supposed to do. I could wake up Mom or Rolando and ask for help. I could call my therapist or even the suicide hotline and ask for help. I could return the knife to the kitchen where it belongs. I could throw out all our knives so they never find their way back into my bedroom or on my body. I could force myself to smile and laugh to trick my brain into thinking I'm happy. I could have a dance party by myself. I could reread my favorite book or watch another terrible comedy. Or I could just stay under this weighted blanket like it's a person holding me back from getting into a fight—a fight with myself. There's a million things I can do, but I wanna do the one thing I shouldn't because it's the closest I can get to doing the thing I can't do since Death-Cast didn't call.

I'm done trying to help myself.

Bad things should happen to bad people.

And I've been told for half of my life that I am one.

I roll the weighted blanket off me, but it doesn't put up a big fight to stop me from fighting myself. I guess it's more of a corpse than someone who cares about me.

I grab the knife, squeezing the handle so hard that my nails dig into my palm. It hurts, but that's nothing compared to what the blade's serrated edges will feel like. I can't think about that part. Reliving that pain turns me off; I just have to do my best to disassociate, that's the best way to both protect and attack myself.

The first time I self-harmed, I thought about my flashback scene in the movie that shows why Larkin Cano grew up to become Scorpius Hawthorne's soul-foe, the Draconian Marsh. Larkin had a troubled childhood that pushed him so far that he stopped using the shield spell to protect himself and started using violent spells to attack others. Something I used to go off about in therapy was how people around the world found it in their hearts to forgive a fictional villain who committed terrible crimes against innocent people, but not me, a real boy who killed my violent dad to save my mom's life. But now I see everything for what it is: Larkin Cano isn't real and I am, and that's why I deserve to be attacked by others and myself.

I think about the moment I became a killer, when I aimed the gun at my dad and pulled the trigger, and just as impulsive as that was, I start cutting myself.

I drag the knife along my inner thigh, where no one will see the damage I've done. My body twists as I scratch the scars that have been scabbing over from when I last hurt myself five nights ago. It's so unbearable that I squeeze my crying eyes shut, but I don't stop digging the knife into my thigh like I'm trying to make it part of my body, not even when blood starts sticking to my knuckles as I run the knife up and down, up and down. I show myself no mercy as I run the knife farther down my thigh, farther than I ever have before, carving my way through this untouched flesh instead of tripling down on my scars and scabs. I bite down on my shirt's collar to stop myself from screaming because if Mom and Rolando walk in now, then I'll never be able to do this again, and as unbearable as it is now, I know I'll need it again.

As my body fights the next breath I don't want, I set down the bloody knife.

That's enough for tonight.

And one day forever when Death-Cast finally fucking calls.

NEW YORK

ALANO
6:05 a.m. (Eastern Daylight Time)

I hug Bucky as I cry into his fur, haunted by the past I need to atone for.

Death-Cast saves Deckers, but it can also ruin survivors.

LOS ANGELES

PAZ
3:17 a.m. (Pacific Daylight Time)

I put on fresh clothes and bedsheets, hiding the bloodied ones in my closet.

Then I lie in bed, wishing Death-Cast called.

NEW YORK

ALANO

I love reading about other people, but I can't read about myself. It's too easy and unhealthy to absorb opinions that begin to feel like facts even when they couldn't be further from the truth. That's why I avoid reading that clickbait article from Spyglass, the tabloid press where Andrea Donahue sold the story of my first herald shift. I'm even angrier than last night because I didn't know this would be published by a pro-naturalist outlet, which is a bigger betrayal to the company. I can only imagine the facts that have been sensationalized into lies because I'll never read them.

But my father has.

We're in his home office, where he's working this morning. I'm taking the day off to try to rest, but he's woken me up after four hours of sleep to talk business.

"Do you know who did this?" Pa asks, holding up his tablet with the article.

I groggily stare at the plaque above his head, unable to face him. "No, sir."

119

He pauses for so long that I look back to find him gripping the tablet like he might try to snap it in two. "Was it that herald beside you?"

At first I think he's asking about Andrea Donahue, but he means Fausto Flores.

"No, sir. He was very nice."

"What do you mean he was nice? He took an interest in you?"

I hate that someone getting close to me is grounds for suspicion in our family. "He was just being polite and helpful."

"How can you be sure?" he asks.

Because I know for a fact who it was, but I can't say that. "I'm trusting my gut."

My father hurls the tablet against the wall, the shock of his violence waking me up. "Your gut is not good enough, Alano! We are employing a traitor who is leaking stories to people who seek to undo us. I've been receiving calls all morning from board members who are questioning your role, your strength, your future. All heralds will be summoned into the office this evening for interrogation. If the culprit hasn't been identified by midnight, then no one will enter that call center tonight, even if that means firing everyone to make every last call myself."

LOS ANGELES

PAZ

I'm home alone, planning my death.

An hour ago, I got Rolando to believe I was all good so he could go job hunt in peace, especially now that I won't be making that movie money, but really I just needed him out of the house so I could bleach all the clothes and sheets I've bloodied.

I'm in the living room, opening my laptop so I can go on my favorite website and plan for my short-term future. I'm immediately distracted by my messy desktop background. I used to be more organized when I didn't want any icons blocking my favorite still of the movie of me as young Larkin Cano holding the iron wand, but that memory started stinging too much, so I swapped it out for a picture of a rainy night, since we don't get enough of those in LA. Now there's just a storm of files and folders: fanfics that shipped Scorpius Hawthorne and Larkin Cano because I love enemies-to-lovers; steamy fan art that I preferred over porn whenever my dick was shouting for a quick release; the five final-draft files for the short films I wrote but never filmed; drafts of things I wanted to say to Dad before finally handwriting a letter to him on my birthday; and the biggest clusters are the dozens of media articles that reported on my incident over the years, including the ones that have been surfacing the past few months because of the docuseries and how close we are to the ten-year anniversary.

I'm tempted to delete every file because what's the point of cleaning this up? It's not like I'm ever gonna make these short films anyway. And what, is this fan art of Vale and Orson from *Golden Heart* kissing in a silver sky really gonna cheer me up? How about the fanfic where Larkin and Scorpius compete in a tournament but can't find the will to kill each other in the final round? No, all rereading that story is gonna do is remind me that killing is always a choice, even if it didn't feel that way when I shot Dad before he could beat Mom to death.

I almost slam my fists down on my keyboard, pissed that I can't even do something as simple as go on my laptop without being reminded of what a killer I am. Instead, I highlight every icon and drag everything into the trash, leaving nothing but a rainy sky.

My therapist wants me to have better control over my impulses. I can practically hear Raquel gently reminding me that there were other options instead of throwing everything away, like putting all my files in a folder so the chaos is out of sight and hey, who knows if I'm feeling sentimental down the line and wanna look at them later. She's doing all of this so I won't do anything rash, like swallowing pills, which is sorta working, but not how she would like.

The truth is that while the act of suicide was a lot more impulsive before the days of Death-Cast, it now requires premeditation to pull it off, which is why I spend a lot of time on Edge-of-the-Deck, an online forum for people who tried and failed to become Deckers, and I study where all their suicide plans went wrong so that when I go to kill myself at the end of the month, I won't find myself back here telling my own story.

After my suicide attempts, I unfortunately had all the time in the world, so I ended up on Reddit to see if other people felt like total losers for not being able to kill themselves. I definitely wasn't alone, just like everyone tells you whenever you mention you're depressed, but I really got the full scope when this Reddit user recommended Edge-of-the-Deck as a resource that even Death-Cast had begun promoting for those struggling with suicidal thoughts.

Edge-of-the-Deck is a really vulnerable forum where the survivors weighed in on what they tried: a young man who couldn't swim rented a Jet Ski and flung himself into the water, only for the owner to save him before he could sink, and he was ultimately so grateful for another shot at life; a stressed doctor jumped off a highway bridge, causing internal damage, but she was revived by her colleagues and lived to save others; and a boy was committed to dying after his sister got her End Day call, but when he tried suffocating himself, his survival instincts kicked in and he clawed open the plastic bag, and at first he hated himself for not going through with it, but he was now proud to be alive to write that message. There were so many other stories, some with methods so horrific that I couldn't keep reading, but for the ones I did finish, all the survivors had the same warning: Death-Cast is never wrong.

I go to Edge-of-the-Deck. There's a pop-up message saying to dial that new 988 number to reach the Suicide and Crisis hotline if I'm struggling. I click it closed because I'm not calling anyone for help unless they're trying to help me die. The site is very easy on the eyes, looking like a digital sky with its blue and white shades. There are audio options for white noise, gentle music, and meditations to calm visitors down, but I don't play any. I'm not here for vibes or breathing exercises; I'm here to make sure there's no flaw in my suicide plan. So far there hasn't been any story that suggests my idea is stupid, but I have no way of knowing if that's because no one who tried my exact plan survived then also shared their backfired experience here, or because they actually achieved suicide. I really hope they got their way, because if I survive what I'm planning, my life will become significantly worse.

I open a trending thread on the forum.

StillHere6790

WHAT IF I QUIT DEATH-CAST?

(Trigger warning: suicide)

I know it's probably stupid to put a trigger warning on a site where we all talk about suicide but a lot of you seem to have healed and like still being here on earth. I'm still here too, but I don't like it. I want to die so if you don't want to read about that then stop reading now. I have a question. IDK if it's okay to ask, delete this if not, but what happens if I quit Death-Cast? Would I feel braver to attempt suicide? Scared to try? IDK. I'm 30 years old so I remember what it was like growing up without Death-Cast, but I've also now had Death-Cast in my life for 10 years. It would be weird to quit. I keep thinking it would be like trading my iPhone for an old flip phone that can't tell me anything except who's calling. Anyway, I regret not trying to kill myself before Death-Cast existed. I only signed up because I thought I would get a call and it would bring me peace but they never call. Now I just feel trapped and I think quitting would give me freedom to try to die.

TL;DR: Did you quit Death-Cast and try to take your life? What happened?

I don't think about life without Death-Cast anymore. That was such a different time, where my dad was alive and I had a fear of dying instead of now, where my life has been defined by killing my dad and being desperate to die. If only I could go back to being that kid who was flying to Brazil with his mom, scared that the plane would crash before he ever made it to set to meet his favorite actors and film his scene in a movie. That fear is impossible today unless you opt out of Death-Cast like the OP—original poster—is aiming to do. I thought about canceling my Death-Cast subscription for the same reasons the

OP wants to, but I missed my opportunity. I should've done it when I was eighteen, before I ever attempted suicide instead of now at nineteen, four months after my first attempt. There's no lie Mom or Rolando would believe about me opting out of Death-Cast that wouldn't make them suspicious. I get a lot past them, but there's a line. I've made peace with keeping Death-Cast around, especially since there's still a window of opportunity for them to call when I execute my suicide plan, but I read through the many comments to see if anyone found quitting Death-Cast to be helpful.

StillHere6790 posted their question over an hour ago, and there's already thirty-something responses, which is a lot for a site where people usually trauma-dump or brag about how their lives are better and then move on. Most of the comments are words of encouragement to keep soldiering through life, and that's not surprising, but if this were my post where I was telling strangers how I wanna die, the last thing I would wanna hear are reasons to live. I'm sure they once felt that way too, but how can they forget that having so many people you don't know trying to save you can feel so suffocating?

I skim through the responses for the ones that actually answer the OP's question:

ThisIsMeTrying

I felt like Death-Cast was holding me back so I deactivated my account. I thought I was going to feel brave but I've never been more scared in my life.

OceanSayre

Duuuude don't do it. U know how ppl get so arrogant when deathcast doesn't call? Like they can do anything in the world? Guess what. You can't do anything. You can't even kill yourself when deathcast is out of the picture. I went sky-diving and jumped out of the plane without my instructor and I felt FREE plummeting to my death but the dude DOVE DOWN AND SAVED ME. It was like a spy movie. I'll tell u something. Ur time will come. Mine too. IDK when and I'll never know when because I never signed back up for death-cast, but I feel better not knowing. Quit Death-Cast, don't quit Death-Cast, that's ur choice. U can sign back up later if u want. Just give life another chance.

Christi_Jenkins

I lost my true love on the first day of Death-Cast. William was going to propose in Times Square but instead of becoming my fiancé he became the first Decker to die in the history of the world. Some masked man (WHO STILL HASN'T BEEN IDENTIFIED OR CAUGHT!!!) shot him in the throat and then William died in my arms. If you watched that TV show GRIM MISSED CALLS then you'll know William's story because the first episode was about him. I get that it was too late to call him, but William was only killed in the first place because his murderer saw Death-Cast as a sign of the apocalypse and went crazy. There's so much blood on Joaquin Rosa's hands. Beginning with William's. Some of mine too. Every way I could hurt myself, I did. Every day that Death-Cast was celebrated for not fucking up, I hurt myself even more. I hate Death-Cast with my whole heart and I've never looked back on canceling that piece of shit service. Do people really believe that Death-Cast has only failed twelve people in TEN YEARS? That they've had a PERFECT record and ONLY ONE DAY where things went wrong? COME ON! Open your eyes, people. The Death Guard is right that we can't trust Death-Cast. Look at how much freewill you've lost. I don't want you to die, StillHere6790, but I want you to live without Death-Cast. Set yourself free, get an old-school therapist (they're usually more pro-natural), and don't let Death-Cast get in your way ever again.

I haven't watched any episodes of *Grim Missed Calls*, but after reading Christi's response here, I'm not surprised that the woman whose life partner became the first dead Decker has now become a pro-naturalist.

I keep scrolling, stopping at a comment from a moderator, expecting her to shut this whole thing down, but she's actually weighing in.

DeirdreClayton (Moderator)
Hi, StillHere6790. I'm Deirdre Clayton, I created Edge-of-the-Deck as a resource for those who are struggling with suicidal thoughts. I encourage you to reach out to a professional or a friend or neighbor, but I understand that you may

not go that route so I just want to say that you can talk to us. I'm a survivor of multiple suicide attempts. I used to work at Make-A-Moment where I was tending to Deckers all the time and I was so jealous of them. There were many times I wanted to prove Death-Cast wrong, and one day, I removed Death-Cast from the equation so I could feel that freedom again. I wanted to make a choice without knowing that I would fail. I won't get into the specifics of how I was planning on taking my life, but before I could try, a woman saved me. All she did was listen, which knowing her now couldn't have been easy because that woman loves talking, but I finally felt connected to someone who heard how brokenhearted I was living in this world. Now I'm choosing to ground myself in this world. I signed back up for Death-Cast. I'm growing my life and nourishing my heart with a lot of self-love. I'm even build-ing a life with this woman who makes me happy every day I'm not a Decker. I'm spending my life saving others because no matter what dreams of ours may come true, I'm aware that we will still have those painful moments where we hope Death-Cast calls. Know that we will always be here to help you walk away from the edge of that deck. Sending you love, StillHere6790, and I hope your name is true for many years to come.

If StillHere6790 is anything like me, they're not gonna get any comfort about how they might discover the will to live once someone saves them. Why can't life just not suck so much that people wanna die? I don't know how many lives Deirdre Clayton and her site have saved, but I'm betting she just drove the last nail in StillHere6790's coffin after bragging about her love story.

I'm reading through other people's uncertainties for canceling Death-Cast when a loud buzz scares me. It's just the washing machine, but my antidepressants got me jumpy. I set the laptop on the couch and go down the hall to dry my load. Scratch that, I have to run another cycle because there are still streaks of red on the soggy sheets. The bloodstains are faint, but they're clear enough that Mom or Rolando will notice if they do my laundry. I'm pouring in extra bleach when the front door opens and Mom walks in. My heart is racing, like she's about to catch me cleaning up a crime scene. I'm quick to swap the bleach for detergent and pour it in, accidentally overflowing the little compartment.

"Hi, Pazito," Mom says as she sets down her tote bag and slides out of her Crocs.

I close the washing machine door and set it to start before walking out into the living area. "Hi, Mom. Why are you home so early?" I bet she wanted to check on me.

Mom sighs as she sits on the couch, right next to my laptop— my laptop that's still open to Edge-of-the-Deck. One look to her left and I'm caught. She'll get concerned and make sure I'm never home alone again. I already start prepping a lie about how I was reading up on people who started businesses for the Death-Cast generation and then decided to check out Deirdre Clayton's site.

But Mom doesn't look at my laptop because she's not looking at anything as she closes her eyes like she's in pain or something.

"My boss sent me home," Mom says.

"Why?" I ask as I sit between her and my laptop, shutting it closed.

"Not feeling well. I think I have food poisoning."

"What did you eat?"

"I brought leftovers from the other night, the tuna and egg salad."

I mean, that sounds like a risk on any day, but leftovers? Dangerous. I hate that Mom ate that salad to save money. Rolando better come home with a job so my mom can have only fresh food for the rest of her life. I really wish I was a movie star with a crazy bank account so I could buy Mom a bigger house and nicer car and hire her a private chef and just spoil her like she deserves.

I saw on the news today that Death-Cast is running a lottery on their ten-year anniversary, where entrants can win lifetime subscriptions to the service. All I could think about is how Mom will have to cancel my subscription soon. Between saving money on my mental health and not having to pay $900 a year for my Death-Cast subscription, Mom is gonna be able to buy the things that she needs: shoes that are as comfortable as Crocs but nicer, like the ones I've seen her looking at online; a new mattress so she won't wake up with back problems; dinner dates at decent restaurants; a gardener who can tend to the backyard, where she can grow fresh food; and a beautiful wedding dress that makes me sad to think about, since I won't be around to walk her down the aisle in December.

The best thing I can do for Mom is just die.

"Can I get you anything?" I ask.

"Do we still have ginger carrot soup?"

I check our kitchen cabinet, where we still have a ton of soup that Rolando panic-bought during the COVID lockdown. I find the last can of ginger carrot soup, and while it's heating up in the microwave, I can't help but sneak the can's sharp lid into my bedroom to cut myself later. I come back out and bring Mom a tray with her bowl of soup and water in her favorite tumbler.

"Thank you, Pazito."

"No problem. I'll be in my room if you need anything else."

"Keep me company? I promise I'm not contagious."

I remember all the times Mom has been at my side whenever I was sick. Not just the physical stuff when I had fevers and stomach issues, but the mental stuff too, like how she refused to leave my side when I was admitted to the hospital, even with the doctors warning her that a forty-nine-year-old like herself would have tougher odds surviving COVID if she caught it while hanging around. Mom was willing to die if taking care of me was the last thing she did. It's that kind of love why I should tell her that I need to be alone in my room or some other lie so I can keep severing our bond before I die. So that she can remember all the times that I wasn't there for her and she still turned out to be okay. But I just can't. Maybe it's the extra antidepressants working hard to suppress my self-destructive, go-break-a-heart impulses, but I can't leave Mom's side.

"Totally, Mom," I say, grabbing my laptop and sitting beside her on the couch.

There's a light in Mom's eyes, and it breaks my heart how happy she is to be near me. I try not to recognize the reality of what will actually happen once I'm dead at the end of the month—how Mom will mourn me for the rest of her life, even if the rest of her life is just days as she makes good on her promise to kill herself after I do.

NEW YORK

ALANO
2:53 p.m. (Eastern Daylight Time)

I'm at a Graveyard Sale with Ariana and Rio.

I wasn't able to get any more sleep after my father's outburst about the Spyglass leak, so I jumped at the chance to leave the penthouse when Ariana invited us out so we can find furniture for our future apartment. She's a regular on the Graveyard Sale app and usually knows which ones will be worth it. This estate sale in an Upper East Side brownstone was listed online as being run by the daughter of an auctioneer who died last month and spent her life collecting treasures. It's so busy that people either aren't recognizing me behind my sunglasses or don't care, but if that changes, my bodyguard is hiding among them and won't be shy about making himself known.

"You're better off not reading it, babe, it was madness," Ariana says while inspecting a beautiful stereo table that wouldn't fit anywhere in her apartment. She knocks on the wood before moving on to the plush velvet ottomans. "They wrote something

134

about you not having the right words to save that Decker, as if that was the reason he was always going to die."

"You just told Alano not to read the article and told him what's in it," Rio says.

Ariana pops up from the ottoman, hands over her mouth. "I'm sorry," she says, muffled.

"It's fine."

Not once have I thought about Harry Hope's suicide being my fault. He was always fated to die, but maybe he didn't have to die so soon. Would Roah Wetherholt have been able to calm Harry Hope down if they made the call? What about any of the other heralds? I believe they all could've done a better job than me except for Andrea Donahue obviously. She would've heard that gunshot, hung up, and called the next Decker without batting an eye.

"Did your mother read the article?" I ask.

"I showed her. She said that Death-Cast should sue Spyglass for those lies."

Death-Cast should sue Andrea Donahue for her lies. We would be well within our rights. It makes me sick that she's lying to Ariana about all of this.

"Who do you think snitched?" Ariana asks while testing the comfort of a lawn chair even though she doesn't have a lawn and we're not looking into units that do. "My mom thinks it was one of the newbies."

Every new lie that Andrea tells to cover up her tracks makes me angrier.

"I don't think it was," I say through gritted teeth.

"Then who?"

I take a deep breath while admiring the foyer's crown molding. "I don't know."

We go upstairs to one of the guest rooms, where there are tables of electronic relics. VCRs, DVD players, a Walkman, pagers, a bucket of Nokia cell phones, landlines, Dell computers, GigaPets, the first PlayStation, and more.

Rio's dark eyes lock on a dusty PS4 like it's a ghost. It sort of is.

"I know," I say, resting my hand on Rio's shoulder.

"You know what?" Ariana asks.

I wait for Rio to speak up, but I answer for him, as he's welcomed me to do so many times before. "This was the first gaming console Rio and Lucio shared as kids."

I've heard so many stories of how Lucio pushed Rio to play story modes at their highest difficulty and never let him win in any racing games so that Rio always felt the highest sense of achievement, something their own parents were never pushing them for.

"I wish I still had ours," Rio says, picking up the PlayStation. If that PS4 had been around before Lucio died, Rio would still own it, as he has never thrown away anything of his brother's.

I've read books on helping friends through grief specifically to help Rio. There was conflicting advice, so I've always gone with what feels right. I offered a listening ear, even when he wasn't ready to talk. I invited him out of his apartment because I knew how haunting his bedroom had become. There was some trial and error too, like when I offered to take Antonio to the movies to get his mind off things and Rio was upset that I was taking over his responsibilities as the new eldest brother. As if Rio was failing Lucio's memory. The most important thing has been never diminishing how he's feeling. That's why I don't tell him how I'm scared his grief is evolving into a hoarding disorder.

Rio sets the PS4 down. "It's weird that there's going to be games and objects that collect dust without Lucio ever even getting to try them when they were new." Time passing is a lot to stomach for him. "I'm going to get some air."

"Do you want company?" I ask.

"No, thanks," Rio says, leaving.

"Should we follow him anyway?" Ariana asks.

"Not unless you want to get yelled at," I say. I've been on the other end of that.

Ariana accepts defeat and looks at these old objects in a new light. She whispers, "Your dad's new invention will find itself on one of these tables in the future."

I'm grateful she made sure we're alone before whispering that. Ariana only knows about Project Meucci because I got her cast to be in the promotion we're filming next week. Unlike the original actor, who has now been recast, Ariana happily signed the NDA and has been forbidden from speaking about the product with anyone, including her mother. Hopefully Ariana doesn't take after her mother's disregard for sensitive information.

It is strange to think about my father's invention collecting dust in drawers around the world before being sold at future Graveyard Sales. I can only hope something stronger is in its place. I suppose that will be something I'm overseeing, assuming I don't get fired with everyone else tonight.

After going through all the guest rooms and not finding anything else of interest, Ariana leads us downstairs and into the dining area where trays of porcelain dishes sit on the long table. I keep my head low as there are other people in here too and I don't know where anyone stands on Death-Cast or me, especially after that Spyglass article. Agent Dane hovers around the table before positioning himself in front of a wall mirror, discreetly watching everyone who comes in and out.

Ariana leans over a set of vintage teacups. "Babe, look at these. They're gorgeous."

I peek over my sunglasses to admire the floral detailing. "They are."

"I'm delighted you both think so," an older woman says in this wise tone that makes me feel like Anna Wintour complimented my cotton jacquard jacket with mother-of-pearl buttons. The woman is so sophisticated in her white sleeveless turtleneck, black pleated jeans, and emerald festoon necklace that must live in a safe when not making her look like a queen. "I've loved those sets since I was a little girl."

Ariana lights up. "You're the seller? Chiara?"

"I am indeed," she says, shaking our hands before picking up the teacup with roses. "My mamma threw the best tea parties for me and my stuffed animals."

"Mine too!" Ariana says.

"As great mothers do."

Ariana also picks up a teacup, this one with sunflowers. "It's honestly so stupid, but pretending I was a waitress at a fancy tea shop who was taking my mom's order, overpouring apple juice into every cup, and bringing her the same Chips Ahoy cookie over and over was when I discovered how much fun acting is. I loved it so much that my mom signed me up for weekend classes when I was four. . . ." Ariana is tearing up while telling this story I've never heard before. "I thought she was just trying to get me to play with someone else since my dad wasn't around, but she sat in on every class and never stopped supporting my dream."

The tears fully run down her face as she fights to say, "And now I'm starting Juilliard in September."

I'm standing here stunned as Chiara embraces Ariana in a tight hug.

Every time Ariana shares an amazing story about her mother, it never makes sense in my head. It's like if I was staring at Van Gogh's self-portrait and Ariana said it's Pablo Picasso's. Factually she would be wrong, but maybe facts don't mean as much in relationships. Maybe relationships are more like art, where everyone sees something different. For instance, I see Andrea Donahue as a criminal, whereas Ariana sees her mother as a hero. Who am I to tell her what she sees? Who am I to tell Rio that he has to stop seeing Dalma Young as the cause of his grief? I need to be better at respecting other people's perspectives, especially my best friends'.

"You have to take these, sweetie. On the house," Chiara says, collecting the teacups for Ariana.

"No, I'm happy to pay for it," Ariana says while pulling out cash.

"Put that away." Chiara leads us to a gift wrap room where she carefully packs the teacups into a small box. "Have a tea party with your mother in honor of mine, okay?"

Ariana hugs the box. "Thank you, Chiara."

We leave the brownstone, and Rio is sitting at the bottom on the stoop. He doesn't like anyone asking him how he's doing when he goes away to get air, which is actually code for crying. I just help him up from the step, and Agent Dane escorts us all to the black Lincoln Navigator, where our chauffeur, Felix Watkins, is waiting to drive everyone home.

I usually prefer driving myself around the city, but I'm too tired and don't want to risk an accident where I hurt someone or kill a Decker, especially a Decker I personally reached out to. The public calls this "getting killed by the messenger," and as far as we know it's happened five times in our company's history. The most recent was an accident on Tuesday, September 5, 2017. That day was hard enough because after a summer of intensity with Rio, one-sided feelings were declared but not reciprocated. I had to fight for us to be best friends—nothing more, nothing less—so we wouldn't lose each other. As we parted ways, I received a call from my mother that she and my father were heading into the office because one of the newer heralds, Victor Gallaher, had run down a Decker, Rufus Emeterio (the very same from the *Time* magazine profile on Last Friends). He claimed it was an accident, but Victor Gallaher's recording of his call with Rufus Emeterio showed him conducting himself unprofessionally and emotionally, which was enough to get him fired and arrested since police investigated foul play. It's never been lost on me that just because you're not dying doesn't mean you can't ruin your life in a moment as quick as sudden death.

From the back seat of the car, Ariana hugs the box of teacups so close, like her arms are its seat belt. The entire ride home she shares more memories of the different characters she pretended to be growing up, like a nurse treating Andrea when she wasn't sick, a laundromat owner charging Andrea a penny to use her own washing machine, and a teacher stickering Andrea's old paperwork and telling her what a good job she did. I wouldn't give Andrea Donahue any stickers for her work as a herald, but there's no denying she deserves some as a mother.

After we drop off Ariana and Rio, I grab my phone and see a notification from the *New York Times*: "Olympic Gold Medalist Caspian Townsend Killed by Paparazzi." My head spins as I read about twenty-seven-year-old Caspian Townsend trying to make the most of his End Day with his twenty-nine-year-old pregnant wife, Eris Bauer, and their four-year-old son, Champion Townsend. From paparazzi camping outside Caspian Townsend's house as early as 3:15 a.m. to his family being hounded to his lawyers being bribed for details on the updated will to his fans crowding the street with memorabilia to get signed, it's no surprise that things got ugly when Caspian Townsend was denied privacy for half of his End Day. There are conflicting statements on who threw the first punch, only that Caspian Townsend proved why he brought home that gold medal as he fought off six aggressive photographers before having the back of his skull bludgeoned by two cameras . . . in front of his pregnant wife and son.

The phone falls out of my hand.

I'm so lightheaded. If I could speak I would ask Watkins to pull over, but I don't feel like I'm allowed to ever talk again after feeling some responsibility for what I just read—and what I didn't read.

That article is missing facts.

Facts are important.

The fact of the matter is that Caspian Townsend wouldn't have spent his End Day fighting and dying for his privacy if Andrea Donahue didn't feed him to the vultures.

9:35 p.m.

All the heralds have been summoned to Death-Cast early tonight.

Upon entering the building, every herald and their personal belongings were inspected by our security force with pat-downs, body scanners, infrared detectors for hidden cameras, and radio-frequency monitors for listening devices. Phones and electronics were confiscated and locked in a safe on the ground level. HR representatives questioned each herald with at least one of my parents present. Once cleared, security escorted the heralds to our briefing room, where no one was allowed to speak. All they could do was reread the NDAs they signed when originally interviewed and hired; my father tasked me with highlighting the consequences on all forty-four contracts so everyone, myself included, will remember what's at stake—fines, termination, imprisonment—when betraying Death-Cast.

Now, for the past thirty minutes, my father has been laying down the law on how we operate in this building.

"You never violate someone's death or life. No one, living or dead!" Pa's voice is growing raspy from all the yelling, but it's still powerful enough that he doesn't need the podium behind him. He rolls up his sleeves while stepping toward the heralds, who are either sweating, fidgeting, or petrified. My father points at me in the corner, where I'm standing with my mother.

"In case you are not aware, that is my son. His privacy was violated last night while doing the important work that only we here at Death-Cast can do. And yet, *someone*—one of *you*!—on *my* payroll decided to make a buck off his distress! To have lies spun about him. To make him look weak. If you are given the chance to continue working here, you will never violate my son's privacy. In fact, forget the name Alano Angel Rosa. If a reporter or anyone asks about my son, you say, 'What son?' Failure to comply with this human decency will find you on the other end of my inexhaustible power!"

I would hate to be on the other end of this speech.

Pa undoes his tie and catches his breath. "Do we understand?"

Some heralds nervously nod, but no one speaks up.

"DO WE UNDERSTAND?!"

Every last herald says they understand.

"Let's see if you do," Pa says. He walks up to Fausto Flores. "What is my son's name?"

Fausto is sweating. "What son?"

Pa nods before walking up to Roah Wetherholt. "What is my son's name?"

"What son?" they say.

He walks up to Andrea Donahue. "What is my son's name?"

"What son?" Andrea says.

Pa doesn't move on. "You know my son's name. What is it?"

Andrea is puzzled. "What son?" she asks, questioning if this is what she must say.

"You know what son. You've known him for years. He's best friends with your daughter. Tell me his name, Ms. Donahue."

Her heart must be pounding as hard as mine. "What son?"

"*My* son—Alano. Angel. Rosa." Pa crouches before Andrea Donahue and even though this is the softest he has spoken all evening, the room is quiet enough to hear him say, "That's my son's name, which you sold to my enemies last night while working for me."

Everyone is shocked, myself included. This afternoon I came clean to my parents about Andrea Donahue's violations after reading about Caspian Townsend being killed in front of his wife and son. I don't know how many times she has leaked the deaths of prominent Deckers, but I knew I couldn't let it happen ever again. My father was furious but insisted on still putting every herald through this investigation so they understand the lengths he will go to to find a culprit. Then he planned on confronting Andrea privately.

Plans change.

"I don't know what you're talking about," Andrea Donahue lies. She then points at me. "He's lying, and if you try scapegoating me for his negligence, then I will sue you for everything you have."

My father laughs, a sound as haunting as the silence that followed Harry Hope shooting himself. "Asking me to believe you over my son is as hopeless as your chances of beating me in court."

"Is that what you really think? You have no proof of these accusations, Joaquin."

He stands again, towering over her as she continues sitting, and he addresses the other heralds. "Inexhaustible power is what I've warned you all is at my disposal. Ms. Donahue here is smart to act innocent until proven guilty, but as sure as I am that the Deckers we call every night will die, I am confident that she will lose her day in court. We possess surveillance footage of Ms. Donahue vacating the call center at 2:20 a.m. after alerting Caspian Townsend of his fate to sell his story to Spyglass, an act that not only breaks the company's NDA and constitutes as an antitrust violation for trading information to a pro-natural competitor, but her scheme tragically resulted in Mr. Townsend's murder this afternoon." Pa stares down at Andrea. "You are correct that I do not have proof of these accusations yet, but I trust my lawyers to secure the necessary subpoenas for your phone and bank records to prove me—and my son—truthful."

Andrea Donahue rises. "You're accusing me of making money off the dead. Does that sound familiar?"

"It's time for you to leave, Andrea," Ma says, stepping forward. "It was time a long time ago, but we pardoned your negligence out of respect to our children. Enough is enough."

"I have been here since the beginning," Andrea Donahue says. "If you try to end me, I will tell the world everything I know about Death-Cast."

My heart is hammering. Is this a real threat? I'm going through all my past interactions around her and know I never said anything to her, but I'm very aware that not everyone has to be told critical information. Sometimes they simply overhear it.

Pa shakes his head. "You know nothing, Ms. Donahue. You would have long sold that information if you did. So I will not try to end you tonight. I simply will. You are fired. Never step foot in this building again so long as you live, and not even then."

Andrea addresses the other heralds—the heralds. "Be careful of every move you make. This tyrant has his spy watching you," she says while pointing at me. She approaches, and Agent Dane guards me as if Andrea might attack me; I'm not sure that she wouldn't. "You've ruined her life."

"No, ma'am. You did."

"Get out," Pa demands. "Do not speak to my son or say his name ever again."

Andrea scoffs, and as she's escorted out by my bodyguard, she mutters, "This isn't the end."

I already knew this wouldn't be the end, but hearing her say it sends a chill down my spine. I want to run and call Ariana before Andrea has a chance to reach her phone downstairs, but I wouldn't know what to say. How I would break the news about who her mother really is. If she will even believe me without real evidence.

Pa stands before the heralds. "I am eternally grateful for the critical work you all do here. You are the heart of Death-Cast, but let tonight be a warning that if I sense any sign of trouble, your removal will be swift."

The heralds are all dismissed.

I'm alone with my parents.

"What happened to doing this privately?" I ask.

"Threats are not loud and clear in private," Pa says. "If one person is willing to betray a contract as if the consequences are nothing but words on paper, then they all needed to hear it from me directly so they understand the force they are up against."

"This is costing me my best friend."

"A tragedy, but one worth paying to protect this company."

"Joaquin," Ma scolds. "Alano is your son before he is your employee."

"He is everything," Pa says, and it feels as empty as words on paper, even hearing it from him directly.

My destiny at Death-Cast is costing me the future I want.

10:14 p.m.

I've called Ariana four times, but she's not answering.

Has Death-Cast terminated our friendship too?

11:32 p.m.

There was no shortage of heralds tonight at Death-Cast, even with Andrea Donahue out of the picture, so I came home. Besides, last night's shift has ruined my life enough. Even my father isn't putting me through that again.

I'm in my bedroom, cuddling with Bucky and reading Dr. Aysel Glasgow's psychology book *What to Know About Those Dying Inside* about treating suicidal patients. I grabbed it from my father's office so I can identify signs should I find myself trying to save a suicidal person, even if it's just a Decker who I want to have a longer End Day. There are so many things I recognize about myself too.

There's a knock on my bedroom door.

"Come in," I shout.

Agent Dane steps in. "Ms. Ariana is here to see you."

I toss the book to the side. Arming myself with the skills to save a life is urgent business, but so is saving my friendship. "Send her in."

"She's downstairs."

"Have Mr. Foley send her up."

"I unfortunately can't permit that. Mr. Rosa doesn't want guests inside at this time."

"Any guests or Andrea Donahue's daughter?"

Agent Dane is quiet. "I'll accompany you downstairs."

I go down the elevator with Agent Dane, well aware he won't defy my father's orders, even though we know Ariana isn't the criminal.

The lobby boasts a diamond chandelier, white marble front counter, potted plants, and four black leather chairs on a burgundy rug, but no one is here except our doorman. Mr. Foley must be confused why Ariana was denied visitation since she's been at the penthouse so often the past three months that I've told him he doesn't have to call before sending her upstairs, but he continues to do so anyway because of my father's rules.

"Evening, Mr. Foley. Did Ariana leave?"

"I believe she is outside, sir."

I stop at the revolving door. "Mind staying here?" I ask Agent Dane.

"I have to keep an eye on you."

"You don't need to protect me from my best friend."

Agent Dane's eyes lock on the windows, manual doors, and revolving door. "Stay visible."

I go through the revolving door and find Ariana leaning against the wall.

"Hey," I say nervously. Going in for a hug feels stupid, but Ariana gives me a head nod.

Her hands are tucked inside the pocket of her big hoodie. She struggles with getting her words out. "I'm not allowed upstairs? Really? Does your dad think I'm going to kill you?"

"I'm sorry. My father is tightening security. I only just found out."

She kicks off the wall and steps toward me. "Why—why didn't you tell me?"

"I wish I had, but after not reporting Andrea's crime when

I should've, I needed to follow protocol." I don't need to tell Ariana about Pa's decision to make an example out of Andrea Donahue to ensure the other heralds won't repeat her mistakes, but she does need to hear the truth from me. I explain how I caught Andrea Donahue selling the stories to Spyglass and how we made a deal to let it go as long as she never did it again, but I couldn't in good conscience honor that after Caspian Townsend was murdered by the very paparazzi who paid Andrea for the story.

Ariana stares with glassy eyes. "Is there any proof?"

My word should be enough, but I reveal that the camera footage shows Andrea leaving the call center after alerting Caspian Townsend of his fate. My father's lawyers will obtain more evidence.

"If that's all true, what harm is it doing?" Ariana asks.

"She called a man to tell him he was going to die and then got him killed. All for five thousand dollars."

"Five thousand dollars toward my dreams."

"You don't want your dreams paid for with blood money. Do you?"

"No, but I've worked so hard for my dream, and now it's done. Not everyone has rich parents, Alano." Ariana puts her hands up like she's in trouble. "Sorry, am I allowed to use your name, or should I forget it too?"

This is a side I've never seen from her before. "Don't make me the enemy, Ariana."

"You got my mom fired!"

"Your mother committed a crime," I say calmly, hoping she'll settle down.

Ariana breaks down crying. "I know it was wrong for my mom to sell those stories, and I'm sorry, but should she really go to prison for telling the truth? She's all I have left."

"You have me. We'll get our apartment and—"

Ariana laughs sarcastically. "Babe—Alano, we're standing outside because Joaquin won't let me upstairs, but you think he's going to let you move in with me? Let me tell you, if we're about to have ten bodyguards for roommates and watching my every move around you, they better be paying rent."

"That's not what I want either."

Ariana wipes her tears, smudging her face. "Then it's too bad that our parents have decided our futures and ruined our lives."

I'm tearing up. I don't like crying in front of people because my father says that can teach people how to hurt you, but hurting my best friend is even worse. "We can start over."

"Alano, I *have* to start over because your destiny ruined mine."

"Then let's rewrite our destinies together."

"There's no forgetting that I'm a girl with no future because my best friend is the Death-Cast heir." Ariana cries so hard that she's clutching her chest. "You might not be able to have a different life, but I can. Goodbye, Alano."

Ariana walks away, ignoring my pleas to stay and talk, and she turns the corner, vanishing.

I want to hate Death-Cast for pushing Ariana away from

me, but Death-Cast is also what brought us together. Maybe Death-Cast will have the power to save us too. There are countless stories of friends, family, lovers who are at odds but then someone receives their Death-Cast alert and their first call goes to the person they haven't been speaking to for ages. On the other hand, there are tragedies where a loved one discovers someone died without making amends, even when Death-Cast gifted them with the time to do so. I hope Ariana and I have a better story.

I'm about to go back inside when someone calls my name.

There's a boy around my age. He's wearing dark denim and a black tank top beneath his jacket. His gelled black hair goes well with his outfit, almost like he might start snapping his fingers down the street and break out in song like he's in *West Side Story*. I personally would have gone with boots instead of the track sneakers, but he's attractive enough that most people are probably paying more attention to his face than his feet. He's not my type necessarily, but I see the appeal. Brown eyes, high cheekbones, rounded jaw, and kissable lips even if the bottom one is bloody, as if he's been biting on it. There's something familiar about him too, but I can't place it.

"Wow, it's really you," the boy says.

"Hi. How's it going?"

"I'm shocked. I never thought I would meet you or anyone in your family to tell you what Death-Cast means to me." The boy extends his hand, and Agent Dane comes busting out of my building and shields me.

"Step back," Agent Dane says forcefully.

There's a panic in the boy's eyes. "I'm sorry, I'm sorry, I'm sorry!"

"Don't sweat it, Dane," I say. This is code that I'm genuinely okay with this interaction. It's not only important that my physical health is protected but that my reputation is as well for Death-Cast's sake. Sometimes I'm uncomfortable around some fans—usually adults with strong opinions and no boundaries—that I want to get away without looking rude, so Agent Dane becomes the bad guy for me. But this is another teenager. Someone I've inspired. I could use that energy after the night I've had.

"I'm sorry," I say to the boy as Agent Dane eases up. "It's his job to look after me."

The boy nods. "Okay," he says while still staring at Agent Dane, this uncertainty in his eyes.

I turn to Agent Dane. "Could you give us some space? I'll be inside in a minute."

Agent Dane scans the boy while stepping back, looking like the building's doorman.

"What's your name?" I ask the boy.

"Jonathan," he says, reaching into his pocket. Footsteps pound across the sidewalk, and Agent Dane's hand is wrapped around Jonathan's wrist before he can pull whatever out of his pocket. "It's just my phone. I was going to ask for a selfie, sorry."

Agent Dane slowly drags Jonathan's phone out.

Jonathan looks uncomfortable. "Is that okay?"

"It would be my pleasure," I say, patting Agent Dane's fist to release Jonathan. "Would you like Dane to take a photo of us?"

The fear in Jonathan's eyes lives on. "I prefer selfies," he says, and I read between the lines.

"Mind waiting inside for us?" I ask Agent Dane. "I'll be in shortly."

"Only after an inspection, Mr. Alano."

This is ridiculous, and I'm about to say as much when Jonathan consents. That alone proves his innocence, but Agent Dane continues on with the full-body inspection anyway—having Jonathan raise his arms above his head, patting him down over and inside the jacket, checking the waistband, and then finally his legs, as if we wouldn't see a gun-shaped bulge in his tight jeans. Once Jonathan's cleared, Agent Dane returns inside, watching me from the lobby's window.

"I'm sorry about all of that," I say.

"It makes sense. You're *the* Alano Angel Rosa," Jonathan says.

There's something unnerving about hearing my full name, especially after tonight, when my father forbade our heralds from ever speaking it again.

"Death-Cast has done so much for so many people. My uncle was one of the first people to sign up for the service because of his intense thanatophobia. Do you know what that is?"

I nod. Of course I do. Cases of death anxiety range from minor to severe, but it would have to be intense for someone to categorize it as thanatophobia. It's no surprise he registered for Death-Cast to have some peace of mind. "How's he doing now?"

"Dead," Jonathan says, his eyes welling with tears.

"I am sorry for your loss."

"My father was never in the picture, but my uncle was. He was a role model for the kind of man I want to be. It's been almost ten years, and it still hurts like yesterday."

Almost ten years. "When did he die?" I ask, my heart beating faster.

He stares, seeing the recognition in my eyes. "The first End Day. Not that he knew what was going to happen."

I realize why he's familiar. It wasn't his appearance, which has changed since I last saw pictures of him online three years ago when he was scrawny and blond instead of the muscular brunette before me with a face that has filled out. The name Jonathan threw me off too, since his name is actually Mac Maag. But it's his voice that I recognize, that I remember from yesterday morning, when he called and threatened my life—"I'm going to kill you, Alano Angel Rosa"—a warning I don't deserve since his uncle died without his own.

Mac Maag said he wanted to tell me what Death-Cast means to him.

I think he means show me.

A switchblade springs out of his phone's case, shocking in and of itself. The blade almost reaches my neck when I swing my elbow to block as Agent Dane has trained me. No Muay Thai lessons could have prepared me for steel dragging across my forearm, tearing it open. The searing pain transports me back to my fourteenth birthday, when I was rock climbing for the first time and slipped, my thigh landing on a jagged edge, staining the mountain with my blood like I'm doing with the sidewalk now. It's one thing to be trained to fight and another to have to put it into practice. I hit him in the leg with a low kick before returning to my stance. I immediately regret it because this isn't a safe brawl, this is a knife fight. I should've powered a push kick to get him away or knocked him with my jump switch round-house kick because all I did was make him collapse to his knees, leaving my stomach open to be stabbed.

Mac Maag is driving the switchblade deep into my abdomen when Agent Dane flies out of nowhere and tackles him.

Fire is eating away at my wound, or that's what it feels like. I fall to the ground in pain, choking on my breath as I pull the switchblade—the phone with a switchblade—out of me. I only hear my heartbeat and my assassin screaming "Death to Death-Cast!" over and over, but as I stare at the bloody phone, I know I will be hearing my alert too.

LOS ANGELES

PAZ
9:52 p.m. (Pacific Daylight Time)

I'm doomscrolling when I see that the Death-Cast heir, Alano Rosa, is in critical condition after an assassination attempt by some crazy Death Guard kid. This world is so violent and unpredictable, even to the son of the man who created the company that predicts death.

Did anyone see this coming?

Alano Rosa was at my trial, but we were on different sides of that courtroom and never met.

I've envied the life he's gone on to have.

I now envy how close he is to death.

NEW YORK

July 24, 2020
ALANO
12:56 a.m. (Eastern Daylight Time)

Death-Cast is calling any minute now to tell me I'm about to die.

I've been fading in and out of consciousness, always waking up to a burning pain that makes me wish I was still asleep. The doorman, Mr. Foley, called 911 the moment Agent Dane barged outside to help me; I would be dead already if it weren't for the police's swift arrival to detain my assailant so Agent Dane could apply pressure to my wound until the ambulance came, but I have no doubts that I'll be dead soon enough.

My parents arrive to the emergency room before I can die, both of them grabbing at my hands and hair and face, letting me know that they are here.

"I love you, Alano," my mother says through tears.

"It's okay, mi hijo, it's okay," my father says.

He's giving me permission to die, to find out what happens after this life. This is for the best. I won't be able to ruin any more friendships. I'll be free of all my pain and the things I can't forget. Dying is also tragic. I've gone skydiving and mountain climbing and paragliding and deep-sea diving, but that's not living. Not really. I would trade all my adventures around the world for a loving relationship where someone becomes my world and every day with them is an adventure. But I will never live that life. Still, I thought the Death-Cast heir would at least get a proper End Day.

Thankfully I already left my parents a time capsule.

Last year on September 2, my family attended the opening day of Present-Time Gift Shop, a one-stop shop for Deckers who want to leave behind something special for loved ones but can't afford to spend their precious time shopping at different stores or waiting in line at the post office to send a gift across the country. The shopkeepers can engrave any of their timepieces and even upload recordings into some of their objects.

The first shop opened in Chicago, built across the street from Millennium Park, a high-traffic area where the rent was only affordable because of our investment. The founder, Leopold Miller, was a recipient of our End Day Enhancement grant, created to support new business ideas that would improve a Decker's End Day. We toured the shop while being followed by camera crews from ABC, CBS, CNN, and WTTW. The WTTW cameraman was so close to my face that my mother linked her arm through mine and pulled me away, like she has my entire life when my personal space isn't respected. That was right when Leopold Miller was telling my father about the time capsules.

"Present-Time isn't only for the dying," Leopold Miller had said, speaking up for the cameras as encouraged by my father, since Leopold in reality was an older man of few words who was posing as a salesman for a good cause. "While I encourage Deckers to make Present-Time one of their first stops on their End Day, our doors are open to anyone who would like to prepare time capsules for their loved ones in advance."

"Present-Time will save *you* time on your own End Day," my father had said, pointing at the camera for all the viewers at home.

I took Leopold's advice when a Present-Time Gift Shop opened in New York on December 1, the day before I went back to school. There had been a pretty aggressive campaign throughout the holiday season with subway ads and billboards saying *DON'T WAIT UNTIL THE LAST MINUTE. GIVE THE GIFT OF TIME TODAY!* and *MAKE YOUR GOODBYES LAST FOREVER.* I'd been holiday shopping with Rio for his little brother, but buying a time capsule was something I needed to do privately, so I went my own way.

I'd arrived at Present-Time after seven, and it was the busiest I'd ever seen any of these shops, which meant there were eight customers and two employees struggling to tend to everyone. The cashier either didn't know me or was too stressed to recognize me, so I was able to discreetly buy my time capsule with cash and raced home to prepare it.

My time capsule will unlock later tonight when I die, containing a parting message for my parents about how grateful I am for the life they've given me (something I'm rethinking here on my deathbed), instructions to let Bucky smell my corpse so he understands that I've died instead of thinking I abandoned him, and my confession for something I've sworn to myself I would take to the grave.

I hate that I'm not getting the chance to hug Bucky or scratch him between his ears one last time, but I also can't face my parents when they discover that I'm far from the perfect son they believe I am.

"What's his condition?" Ma asks a nurse. "He's so pale," she adds while sobbing.

"He lost a lot of blood, but all major arteries in his abdomen are intact," Nurse Yasi says.

"Where's Dr. Garcia?" Pa asks.

"I don't believe Dr. Garcia is on the schedule this evening."

"She was not until I personally called the hospital and requested your most senior surgeon. Find out where she is and arrange for my son to be moved to a private room," Pa says, turning his back on her. "It is outrageous he is still exposed like this."

"Please," Ma says to Nurse Yasi, who leaves immediately.

"Sir," I hear Agent Dane say.

"You," Pa says. One word breathed, and I already know this won't be the gratitude Agent Dane deserves. "Under no circumstances should my son ever be in a hospital under your care. He could have been killed."

"I apologize, Mr. Rosa. I inspected the assailant's person, but not his phone."

"That mistake almost got Alano killed."

"I understand. I'll never let it happen again."

"If it were up to me, you'd be fired, but Naya, for some reason I do not understand, wishes to give you another chance."

"Because you saved Alano's life," Ma says.

"I apologize for not trusting my instincts, Mrs. Rosa. I will not fail you or Mr. Rosa or Mr. Alano ever again."

My father grunts. "Should someone so much as cough on my son you will be fired. Now go keep watch outside the ER."

"Yes, sir."

I need to take the blame, since Agent Dane was only honoring my requests, or even pin some on my father for not letting guests up to the penthouse in the first place, but anytime I try speaking, my words get buried under my groaning.

"Relax, mi hijo, you will survive this," my father says. He leans in and whispers, "Today is not your End Day, Alano. This I know, already. This I know."

2:37 a.m.

Tonight my father broke code for me.

After learning that a Death Guarder tried assassinating me minutes before midnight, Pa ran straight to the Death-Cast call center, where Roah Wetherholt has taken over as head herald on duty after Andrea Donahue's termination. Pa demanded to see the full roster of Deckers. This privilege has never been awarded to anyone, not even the president of the United States.

Not until tonight, when my father scanned the list to make sure my name wasn't on it.

I'm special, apparently.

"You are to be protected at all costs," my father says after Dr. Garcia finishes stitching my wounds and returns home for the night.

We're in the comfort of a private suite, a bigger upgrade than we actually needed, but the medical field remains grateful for the advancements in their practices and preservations of resources that Death-Cast has allowed.

"Speaking of—Naya, any word from our team on reaching Carson Dunst?"

"No, Joaquin. We shouldn't expect anything tonight. Let's be present," Ma says, sitting on my bed with me and holding my hand.

"Why won't he take our calls? I just want to talk to him," Pa says. The murderous look in his eyes says otherwise.

"You need to calm down. Alano is okay."

"He sent an assassin after our son!" It's rare for my father to raise his voice at my mother. "How would he like it if I do the same with his daughter?"

More shocking than the thought of that threat is the fact that my father says it out loud. I've been raised to operate as if every room I'm in has been bugged because of my family's secrets. Secrets my father plans to tell me when I'm older. We've already been burned before, sadly, but despite all of that, my father is threatening to exact revenge on Bonnie Dunst, the daughter of the presidential candidate whose campaign has been built on undoing Death-Cast.

My mother catches onto my father's mistake too. "You don't mean that, Joaquin," Ma says out loud, but really speaks her true warning through her eyes. "You're just angry, as any parent would rightfully be."

"Of course I do not mean that, Naya," he replies, his clenched fists betraying him. "It is not as if we would have ever given them the martyr they are so desperate for."

I read between the lines. An eye for an eye, a child for a child.

"Don't worry, Pa. I'm still alive," I groggily say. I've been better mentally, but physically I'm okay because of Dr. Garcia's medical attention. Ever since learning I would be surviving and that my assailant missed all my major arteries, I've been more concerned about losing control over my upper limbs, but my brachial artery went unharmed, so all that's changing will be the new scar.

"Besides, if they had killed me, all they would've done was make me a martyr for Death-Cast."

"They would've done more than that," my father says quietly.

He never says what would happen, he couldn't, not even among family. But his murderous gaze says everything and lives in his eyes for the rest of the night, long past the Death-Cast call that we weren't supposed to know was never going to come.

4:25 a.m.

The doctor advised that we spend the night in the hospital, but my father trusts no one. All it takes is one worker or patient to expose our location and another assassin may arrive to finish the job. We know they will fail tonight, but there's only so much damage my body can survive.

Once I'm discharged, the full force of Shield-Cast is at my service, forming a barrier around me and my family as we go through the hospital and out into the cold night, where our car is waiting. My father is still so furious at Agent Dane that he allows only Agent Andrade to ride with us. It's outrageous, but I need my father's temper lowered before fighting that fight.

My mother withdraws my phone from her purse. "You have missed calls."

I scroll through the missed calls and I call the person responsible for each and every one.

"Alano?" Rio answers, like he's scared someone is calling to give him bad news.

"It's me," I say groggily.

"I thought you were dead. No one was telling me anything. I tried calling your parents and Dane—"

His voice sounds extra loud with my migraine. "Security is tight," I interrupt.

"Are you okay? Did Death-Cast call?"

"No. I'm going to live."

Rio exhales. "I need to see you. What hospital are you at?"

"We've just left the hospital. Going home now."

"No you're not," Pa interrupts, setting down his own phone.

Surely the drugs I'm on have me misunderstanding everything, but even Rio overhears my father and he's confused too. "What do you mean?" I ask.

"You don't survive an assassination attempt at home and then return there."

I want to argue that we have a highly secure panic room, but that only matters should we find ourselves running into any issues while inside the penthouse. I was attacked outside the building. "Then where are we going?"

"Elsewhere," Pa says, not saying more while I'm on the phone, as if Rio can't be trusted, when he's the only one who has called to check in on me.

Ariana not calling feels more devastating than if Death-Cast had.

"How long are you going to be gone?" Rio asks.

"I don't know." There's no point asking when I won't get any answers.

Once again, I'm not in control of my own life.

Not even when it comes to the one friend I need now more than ever.

LOS ANGELES

July 24, 2020

PAZ

3:03 a.m. (Pacific Daylight Time)

Death-Cast didn't call because I'm not dying today, and according to the news, Alano Rosa isn't either.

Sucks to be us.

NEW YORK

ALANO
6:07 a.m. (Eastern Daylight Time)

We've boarded our private jet, preparing for takeoff to Los Angeles, where we will lay low until it's time to return for the Decade Gala. I'm up front with many other Shield-Cast agents and my parents. Bucky is secure in the bedroom and being monitored by Agent Dane, which my father is treating like an insult, but I want my bodyguard taking care of my dog too. It's now July 24, exactly ten years since Bucky was adopted. I can't believe I was almost killed on this anniversary.

I can't believe I was almost *killed*.

Ma helps secure my seat belt. "Have you told Ariana we're leaving?"

"She doesn't care," I say while looking out at the runway.

"Of course she cares," she says, taking her seat next to Pa.

If she cared, she would've called.

"It will all work out, mi hijo," Pa says, nursing an ale instead of his typical whiskey.

I almost explode because he's not all-knowing, but that's

the last thing anyone wants on a plane, even one that has yet to take off, even on a day where we're as guaranteed to not crash as anyone can be since none of us have received alerts tonight. But I close my eyes instead and once we're in the sky, the last thing I think about before falling asleep is how easy my death could have been if only I'd left my neck open for the assassination.

LOS ANGELES

PAZ

2:45 p.m. (Pacific Daylight Time)

I'm unfortunately alive enough to tell my therapist how I wish I was as dead on the outside as I feel on the inside.

I usually don't tell Raquel when I'm having strong suicidal urges, but it's like my defenses are down after all of this week's self-harming and spiraling about my doomed future. At the start of every session, Raquel always asks how the week was, and I basically give her my "Previously On" recap like my life is some TV show. As we dive deeper into the *Golden Heart* rejection, I really feel like this past week was the penultimate episode of my life. One more week until the series finale, where there will be a funeral like most great shows.

Seven more days until I can kill myself on the tenth anniversary of Dad's death. I need to hold it together for seven more days, pretend like I'm Survivor Paz or some bullshit, who cares.

Raquel is sitting across from me in her beige leather chair. She's like thirty-five or something with streaks of pink in her blond hair and a sleeve of bunny silhouette tattoos hopping along her light brown skin. She always has this welcoming smile, which I don't get because don't people come into this cozy office all day with their heavy baggage? I used to wonder if she was dead inside like me and smart enough to make money off other people's pain without being affected, but I'm sure she's just got her shit together.

"I'm proud of you," Raquel says.

"Why, I didn't do anything."

"Exactly. It would've been so easy for your suicidal thoughts to result in destructive behaviors, but you didn't hurt yourself at all. Did you feel any temptation to do so?"

I didn't tell her about all the vicious self-harming. "Yeah," I say, because even I'm not a good enough actor to sell the lie that it wouldn't have come up at all.

"That's understandable. You should be as proud of yourself as I am for being gentle with yourself. What are some of the ways you self-cared this week?"

I spent more time hurting than caring, but I did do some. "Little things. Hung out with the fam. Took my meds. Talked about my feelings. Stuff like that."

Raquel nods. "All great things."

"But that's not enough to save someone in the long run, right? I mean, I did all that stuff before and still tried killing myself."

"No, but you chose to show love to yourself anyway."

That advice pisses me off. Anyone can tell me to love myself, this isn't something Mom should be wasting her money on. "I hate that I have to work so hard to love myself," I say through gritted teeth, which is one of the most honest things I've told my therapist. "Everyone else has it so easy, they just wake up and live their lives, but not me."

"You're not alone in this pain, but I know how it must feel that way," Raquel says, which she must say hourly to all her other suicidal clients. "There's something I've been meaning to speak to you about that I hope will provide some clarity. A diagnosis, if you're open to it."

I scoff. "What, like you think I'm crazy or something?"

"I absolutely do not think that, and you shouldn't either."

"I don't think I'm crazy, but everyone else does."

"This is all connected, Paz. Are you familiar with borderline personality disorder?"

Never heard of it, but it doesn't sound great. "What is that, like multiple personalities?"

Raquel shakes her head. "People with borderline personality disorder—BPD for short—are known to struggle with impulsive behaviors, severe mood swings, and managing their emotions. It's often misdiagnosed as bipolar disorder, even by other therapists, but bipolar comes in waves of episodes whereas BPD is always present and even more delicate. Something small can be emotionally devastating, and even if logically you don't think it warrants that reaction, it can be difficult to settle down. There's a chance this could've been passed down through your family, possibly your father's side given everything you've shared about his upbringing, but I believe your BPD stems from childhood trauma. Not just the incident with your father, but all the abuse you witnessed that led up to you killing him, and everything that has followed you ever since."

This feels like the moment in a fantasy novel when someone is told they've been gifted with magical powers from their ancestors, except I'm being told that I've been cursed with a mental disorder thanks to my dad and trauma.

My breath gets caught. "Is it bad?"

Raquel is smiling for some mysterious reason. "Of course it isn't bad. Some of my favorite people have BPD. I specialize in working with clients who have it too."

"You were recommended because of suicidal stuff. We didn't know that I— Wait, does my mom know that I got BPD?"

"No, this is as confidential as everything else in our sessions. Regarding our relationship here, as we were working on addressing your suicidal ideation, I was searching for the root of it all. Everything falls in line with BPD."

"Then how long have you known this about me?"

"Within our first month working together," Raquel says casually, like it's totally okay that she's been keeping a secret about me and from me for three months.

I'm about to have one of those severe mood swings. "Why are you just telling me now?"

"A diagnosis like BPD can be a lot for someone to stomach, so I needed to trust that you would be able to take care of yourself outside of this office. The way you've been self-regulating despite your many struggles showed me that you were ready to receive this information. What I would really like to address moving forward are your challenges with loving yourself. This disorder is the cause of many sensitivities that interfere with a sense of self. An emptiness and hopelessness brought on by others' perceptions of you. Fears of abandonment, which might sound strange, but would have been born out of your father's death. And the suicide attempt, of course. Everything you feel because of BPD is bigger. Your highs are higher and your lows are lower."

My highs are higher and my lows are lower.

"Is this why I sometimes feel too much . . . and feel dead inside?"

Raquel nods. "We can work together to better protect you moving forward."

"Protect me from what?"

"A pull toward other reckless behavior such as self-harm, drugs and drinking, unsafe sex."

In other words, protect me from myself and some impulses I've already given in to.

Maybe I should tell Raquel all about my self-harming and sex with two guys from the Last Friend app and even my second suicide attempt. But if everything about this diagnosis is true, what's more important is asking her how she's gonna save me from this so I can escape all these spirals that led to those behaviors. "What's the cure?"

"There is no cure for BPD."

And it's cruel fates like this that make me feel dead inside and on the verge of tears. "No cure?"

"There are only treatments. If you're willing, I'd love to

get you involved in DBT—dialectical behavior therapy. It's a six-month program designed to give you the tools you need to self-regulate during the most extreme of circumstances. The group meets once a week, which could reduce your feelings of loneliness as you navigate this diagnosis. I'm also one of the two counselors leading the program, so we can always discuss how you're feeling in our individual sessions." Raquel leans forward with a small smile. "It's beautiful witnessing how people emerge from DBT feeling so much more in control over their lives, but I can't force you to do this, Paz. It has to be your choice."

I've already been counting down to my desired End Day, struggling with how far away seven days feels. There's no way in hell I'm choosing to live for six more months, all in the hopes that I can live an even longer life with an incurable mental disorder.

The clock strikes three, and I get up from the couch.

"You don't have to decide today," Raquel says. "Call me if you have any questions or concerns. I'm here for you."

"Sure. Thanks," I say, and I mean it. She really tried.

"I'll see you next week," Raquel says.

No, you won't, I wanna say.

I lie one last time instead. "See you next week."

4:15 p.m.

The entire walk home, I'm questioning who I am.

I don't feel real, it's like I'm some fucking puppet whose

strings are being pulled by emotions and there's nothing I can do except hang there and go where they take me. This diagnosis has got me second-guessing everything. Whenever I got depressed or pissed off and self-harmed, was it even that serious or just my BPD blowing something out of proportion? And yeah, what about Dad? Did I have BPD back when I killed Dad? Was that an impulse beyond my control?

Or was that just me?

I drag my feet up to my front door but don't go in yet. I don't know how to bring this up to Mom. She already feels guilty for not leaving Dad sooner, she'll just spiral when she discovers that I'm sick in the head because of him. I'll keep this to myself like everything else that would break her heart.

I walk inside the house and find Mom and Rolando hugging on the couch. At first I think Mom is laughing, but I realize she's crying into his shoulder. She gasps when the door closes behind me and she looks at me like I'm a ghost.

"Pazito." Mom wipes away her tears. "Hi, my son. How was therapy?"

Something is happening, but watching Mom trying to play it down makes me feel like a kid again during all those times when she had just been arguing with or hit by Dad. I look at Rolando, trying to read any guilt on his face because if he broke his promise to never hit my mom I would kill him—

It's just a thought.

People think it all the time, even if they would never actually kill someone.

But I've actually done it, and my out-of-control impulses might make me do it again.

"What's going on?" I ask, my heart pounding in my ears.

"I still wasn't feeling well, so I visited my doctor," Mom says, then she's quiet.

This is gonna be bad. Death-Cast will be calling Mom soon, but when?

Rolando squeezes Mom's hand. "Do you want time to think first?"

I snap, "What, no! Are you dying, Mom? You gotta tell me now, you can't—"

Mom gets up from the couch, shushing Rolando as he urges me to calm down, and she holds on to my arms as I'm shaking. "I'm not dying, Pazito." She has a soft smile as she looks at me with her teary red eyes and brushes my cheek. "I'm pregnant."

There are so many thoughts swirling around in my head plus one emotion that's growing in my heart, but I don't know if it will show its face, if it's even true, but I feel it. "Are you messing with me . . . ? Is that what the doctor said? Are you sure because . . . ?"

"Because I'm so ancient?" Mom says with a laugh, like she knows how ludicrous this is. "I'm forty-nine. It's rare, but it's possible for me to carry a child."

"But it is scary," Rolando says. "That is what we were discussing just now. The many complications."

"It's scary, but life is scary." Mom squeezes my hand. "I was scared to bring you into this world, and you have been my greatest joy." She leads me to the couch and sits between me and Rolando. "This was the last thing I thought the doctor was going to tell me, so there's a lot for us to discuss as a family."

"It's whatever you want, Mom," I say.

"I raised you right." Mom playfully elbows Rolando. "Didn't I raise him right?"

There are a lot of people online who won't agree with Mom, but Rolando does. "Yes, Glo, of course, but we have to be certain this is what is best for the family. I have loved you for thirty years, and I used to dream about having a baby with you. It still is a dream, but I am concerned we will lose you to the pregnancy." He puts his hand on her belly. "Both of you."

I can't believe that life is growing inside Mom this very moment.

"We'll do early screenings. Many of them," Mom says, wanting this so badly, it's like when I was a kid who begged for a dog but Dad said no. "I wish Death-Cast could predict miscarriages, but we'll have to do this the old-fashioned way. If the doctors advise that the pregnancy is too risky, then I will get an abortion. It will be difficult, but I would do it. Know that I love you both too much to leave you."

"Good because I want to love you for many more years," Rolando says, resting his hand over her engagement ring.

Mom faces me. "What do you think, Pazito?"

"You love being a mom," I say.

"I will always be a mom thanks to you. How do you feel about being a big brother?"

I don't know how to feel about being a big brother because I don't know which feelings are even mine and which feelings belong to my disease. Maybe this pregnancy is life's way of asking me to stick around. To go through dialectical behavior therapy to treat my borderline personality disorder. To get better so I can look after my little sibling. This kid is gonna be so lucky to have Mom and Rolando as parents, my life would've been so much better if Rolando was my dad.

This pregnancy also feels like another signal, one that's only making that emotion in my heart grow and grow and grow.

"Everything about this makes me happy," I say.

Mom tears up with the biggest smile and pulls me into a hug. "We could all use some more happiness, don't you think?"

I'm happy for Mom.

I'm happy for Rolando.

Most important, I'm happy for me because now that Mom will have a new baby to look after, I can go kill myself in peace.

Tonight.

ALANO
7:54 p.m.

I don't deserve this life. I've always known it, but I feel it after surviving an assassination attempt.

How can I not when I'm afforded the privileges of boarding our family's jet to leave New York and fly to Los Angeles to recover (and hide out) in this gorgeous mansion in the hills with eight bedrooms, a home theater, panic room, tennis court, infinity pool, a garage with a rotating platform, and a view of downtown that makes you feel like a god in the sky. The fact that we don't live here full-time is despicable, an egregious waste of resources, criminal even. This isn't a home, not really. It's more of a prison preventing me from living my life when I should be behind bars in a tiny cell for the things I have done when no one was looking.

I'm out by the infinity pool with my legs in the water and Bucky's head in my lap as I stare out into the city. The dark hills beneath us, the back of the Hollywood Sign miles away, the countless buildings as far as the eye can see. I've asked to be alone as I try processing every horrible thing that has happened in the past forty-eight hours but I hear someone approaching. I'm expecting it to be my parents, but it's my bodyguard.

"Sorry to disturb you, Mr. Alano," Agent Dane says.

"Does my father want you to protect me from Bucky?" I ask.

Bucky perks up, and I scratch him between his ears.

"No, I've come to apologize for my negligence last night. I shouldn't have left your side. You could have been killed."

I look at my bandaged arm, reliving the burning pain of that slice and getting stabbed in my abdomen. "No one could've known that boy was secretly an assassin with a blade hidden in his phone."

"It was—is—my responsibility to anticipate any threats. I will be more diligent in the future. Even if that means carrying around garlic and holy water and poking everyone's gums in case they're secret vampires."

Any other night I would've laughed, but my head is too loud with all the recent chaos replaying like an unstoppable loop: hearing Harry Hope's cries of relief and the gunshot that took his life; telling Deckers they would be dying and the grief of knowing they're all now dead; catching Andrea Donahue committing crimes and getting her fired; and fighting with my best friend and fighting off an assassin. All of it, over and over and over, enough to have me thinking about how badly I want to climb into a dark place I've only ever been once before.

"Are you okay, Mr. Alano?" Agent Dane asks.

I can't say what I'm itching to do because it's in my bodyguard's job description to protect me from all threats, including myself.

"Not really."

"Would you like to talk about it?"

"You do enough. You don't have to be my therapist too."

"I don't feel like I did enough last night. Let me make up for it."

When I was first assigned Agent Dane as a bodyguard, I thought we wouldn't ever talk about anything personal, only security matters. I'm happy that's not been the case. I know he grew up here in Los Angeles and was in a long-distance relationship for two years before moving to New York in 2016 to be with his girlfriend, only for her to break up with him after two months. I know he was planning on spending his twenty-first birthday in Las Vegas, but it was on Thursday, March 19, during the lockdown, so he played poker online with friends instead. And I know he has a great ear that he uses to listen out for everything, not just danger.

"I'm struggling with who I'm supposed to be," I say. I'm staring out into the city as if the answer will be in one of those buildings, or someone inside them. I'll never know.

"Are you struggling with something in particular?" Agent Dane asks.

"You know what," I say, turning to him. "It's the reason you're sworn to protect me."

Agent Dane nods. "It's a big responsibility. It will take up your life."

"Even more than it already has. I really envy the children of presidents. They don't have it easy during active terms, but eventually their parent leaves office and they get to slowly slip into obscurity again like every other former First Family. I will never have that. I'm growing up to become even more powerful, more recognizable. My father expects me to raise my kid the same way, as if I'm ever going to be able to start a family of my own when you're being paid to tackle anyone who says hi to me."

Agent Dane stifles his laugh, like he does when he's on the clock, which is technically anytime I'm in his proximity. "I'm sorry about that."

"I deserve to have a life of my own before telling people how to live theirs before they die."

"You're definitely in need of some soul-searching, Mr. Alano. This week we can hike up to the Wisdom Tree. I would go whenever I needed to reflect. There's even a box of journals waiting by the tree that people contribute to, but you might want to bring your own since you lose all anonymity when writing about being the Death-Cast heir."

I can't even be part of a community of strangers on paper because of who I am.

Enough is enough.

"Soul-searching at the Wisdom Tree is a great idea," I say. I won't be going later this week, though. I'm hiking the trails to the Wisdom Tree tonight.

Alone.

PAZ
8:44 p.m.

I open *Golden Heart* and stare at Orion's message:

Keep living.

I rip the page out of the book, shredding it in two.

ALANO

8:45 p.m.

I am going to start seizing life when I want, as I want.

One of my biggest mistakes has been acting as though being someone's son means behaving like I'm a child who needs permission for everything. Even when I was a child I didn't get to properly be one because I was forced to grow up sooner than most. Now I'm nineteen, but it feels like the horrors this week have aged me by years. I want to grow older with happier memories that can silence the gunshot that will echo forever in my mind, the pleading cries of strangers and friends, the switchblade springing out of an assassin's phone to kill me.

Those tragedies are among many that have inspired me to undergo my biggest change, just as the losses my parents faced trying to conceive me is what led to the creation of Death-Cast. My father wanted to protect the world from the unbearable pain of unexpected grief. In doing so he's had a suffocating hold on my life that has forced me to adapt for my freedom.

I finish filling out a form on the Death-Cast app and read the message that pops up:

Death-Cast is sorry to lose you as a member, Alano Rosa.

As long as you live, we are always here to remove the unknown of your death should you seek to reactivate your service.

That's it.

To ensure I forge my own destiny, the Death-Cast heir is now living pro-naturally.

PAZ

9:09 p.m.

I'm writing my suicide note.

It's my first one ever. I didn't have the time before my first two attempts because they were so impulsive, but this note is flowing out of me like I've been working on it my entire life. I sorta have.

Mom, I love you. There is a lot I've lied about, but that's true.

I'm sorry I didn't say goodbye in person. I just couldn't risk changing my mind. People like to run their mouths and tell me that I'm just young and things will get better when I'm older, but that doesn't make sense to me.

If I'm so young, why does life feel so long?

I think I finally have my answer. Today in therapy I was diagnosed with borderline personality disorder. I know it's a disease, but it feels more like a demonic possession that prevents me from making good choices. The worst part is there isn't an exorcism to set me free so I'm doomed to raise hell wherever I go. The demon is born because of trauma or genetics or both, IDK, but this isn't your fault, Mom. This is Dad's fault like every other bad thing. He's already ruined my life completely, but I won't let him ruin yours anymore.

I'm happy you and Rolando will have the baby to keep you company. I'm just sorry the baby will be an only child. It's for the best, Mom, trust me. The baby will get to live the life I never got to have because they'll have Rolando's angel genes instead of Dad's demon genes.

This is your fresh start to have the life you always deserved.

You're a survivor, Mom. I'm sorry I didn't inherit that from you. I take after Dad and just like Dad I have to die to make the world a safer place.

Thank you for the best parts of my life. I love you, Mom.

Yours forever,

Pazito

I fold up the tear stained letter and tuck it inside my copy of *Golden Heart*. I know this suicide note will break Mom's heart when she finds it, but at least she'll fully understand that mine has been broken for ages and I couldn't keep living like this.

I wanna go into Mom's room and give her one last hug, but I'm scared I'll see her and think about the future with the baby and trick myself into thinking things are gonna get better when they're only getting worse and worse. No, the best thing I can do for Mom is die so she can have her life back. And the best thing I can do for the baby is make sure they don't grow up in a home with a gun like I did.

I go into my closet and grab the gun I've been hiding and leave home so I can make tomorrow my End Day.

PART TWO
The End Day,
Whether Death-Cast
Likes It or Not

Death-Cast is never wrong.

——Joaquin Rosa, creator of Death-Cast

Death-Cast is never wrong.

——Death-Cast heralds

Death-Cast is never wrong.

——All survivors on Edge-of-the-Deck

PAZ
11:42 p.m.

Edge-of-the-Deck taught me that no matter how much some-one wants to kill themselves, there will always be some X factor that keeps someone alive. That stops Death-Cast from calling.

My first intervention was Mom waking up from a night-mare to find me drunk and drugged out on my bedroom floor and rushing me to the hospital before near death became death. Then for my second suicide attempt—at the same place I'm headed to right now—I had an accident that made me nervous I would survive with injuries that would make my life extra unlivable if I tried again. This time I'm pretty damn sure I've got my suicide down to a science. The only thing that might stop me before I even get to try is what I'm hoping will ulti-mately take me out: the gun.

Just because I used a gun once doesn't make me an expert, and I didn't exactly ask the black market seller for a tutorial when I bought the gun off him while downtown on the day Mom and Rolando thought I was having fun at an arcade I've never been to (and now never will). Even though I removed all the bullets and put them in a separate pocket in my backpack, I'm still nervous that this unloaded gun with the safety switched on will still somehow shoot me in the back and paralyze me. It sounds stupid, I know, but if I'm not destined to die soon, then that means something is destined to save me.

I'm doing my best to make sure nothing can.

Instead of calling an Uber and risking getting pulled over or ending up in a nonfatal accident, I walked for over an hour and a half to Griffith Park. I avoided everyone on the streets, scared they might rob me for my backpack and get away with the gun. I read on Edge-of-the-Deck that a suicidal man was going home to shoot himself with his new gun when the police stopped him because he fit the description of another man who had just murdered a Decker nearby. The night he spent in jail while being investigated gave him a change of heart once he was freed. Good for him, but that's not my story.

Griffith Park is a popular site for hiking—it's also where I impulsively tried killing myself last month on my birthday and where I will succeed tonight. The park has been closed since six, but that didn't stop me from stomping out my last cigarette ever, climbing the gate, and hopping over; I was relieved when I landed on both feet without snapping an ankle, that would've been a stupid way to get caught. I used my phone's light as I climbed up through the steep, uneven dirt trails, tripping more times than I could count, but over an hour later, I've made it up here.

The Hollywood Sign. This is where I'm gonna kill myself.

There's a gate behind the sign that's warning trespassers away. I'm about to hop over when I hear something—someone?—

behind me. I turn around, staring into the darkness of the path that leads up to the Wisdom Tree, but I don't see anyone. I exhale in relief that it's not some security guard appearing as my death's X factor. I hop the gate, which, on my birthday, I thought was gonna electrocute me or something, but nothing then and nothing now. Not even an alarm when I walked down to the sign as the sun was setting. The city claims they have security on the job, but no one ever knocked on my door to fine me or arrest me. If someone is watching this time, I'll hopefully be dead before they reach me. I skid down the steep hill and fall on my ass, scared that I might tumble past the sign and into the darkness. I dig my nails and sneakers into the dirt, trying to brake, and I bump against a rock that kills all momentum. Of all the saves that could happen tonight, that was a good one.

I wipe the sweat out of my eyes at the base of the forty-five-foot-high Hollywood Sign and start climbing the workman's ladder up the letter *H*. My heart is racing, just like on my birthday, but this time I don't fall at the halfway mark, scraping and bruising my legs and arms and getting the breath knocked out of me. This time I keep climbing, rung by rung, until I get to the platform on the very top. I've pictured myself standing up here fearlessly and leaping to my death, but it's so windy that I'm scared I'll be blown back down the ladder, banging all the way down again, and only getting gravely injured. I cling to the platform and crawl across until I get to the center, sitting on the ledge.

This is a beautiful view of Los Angeles. The City of Dreams.

Everyone has a dream, even those of us who've given up on them. I look up at all the glittering stars, wishing they could've made my dreams come true, but I'm the only one in this world who can give me what I want.

I unzip my backpack and grab my gun. It's a black pistol, the same model I used on Dad, according to various news reports. That's why it felt so fated when I started devising my suicide plan on the night of my birthday and ended up on a black market site selling this exact model. I sold books and video games and even an old autographed headshot to someone on eBay to afford the gun. I've even wondered if somehow, in the almost ten years since I held it last, this could be the exact gun I used on Dad. I inspect the gun again, like I'm gonna find my fingerprints or my signature or something. I'll never know if this is the gun I used on Dad, but it's definitely the one I'll use on myself.

I review my suicide plan in my head.

If there's a cruel world where I survive this, then Orion and his asshole producers can say goodbye to their movie because who's gonna want a story about a fictional nineteen-year-old immortal when a real nineteen-year-old immortal exists? Luckily for them, that won't happen. They'll have their movie with some inferior actor playing Death and I'll just be dead. Maybe I should've written a suicide note or recorded a Last Message for everyone in Hollywood who wouldn't give me a second chance. But Hollywood won't need a suicide note. They already know why my blood will be on their hands—and sign.

I keep a tight grip on the gun as I stand, my legs shaking. *Don't look down, don't look down, don't look down.* I focus on the night sky even as I feel my gaze trying to shift downward, like my body is going into survival mode and trying to scare me from doing this. I'm sweating—no, I'm crying. I hate that I got cursed with such a painful, doomed life. I wish things were different, but they're not.

I grab my phone and check the time: 11:59.

I'll pull the trigger in one minute, right at midnight.

Maybe I'll hear Death-Cast calling a millisecond before the gunshot.

I bring the gun up to my head while staring at my phone.

My finger grazes the trigger, ready to pull.

"Don't jump!" someone shouts—someone up here with me.

I swing the gun away from my head and toward the voice.

A boy.

I wipe the tears with my phone-carrying hand and cast the light on him.

This isn't just any boy interfering with my End Day.

This is the Death-Cast heir.

TWENTY MINUTES AGO

ALANO

11:39 p.m.

Life has already been so much more thrilling in the three hours since deactivating Death-Cast.

Once my parents went to bed early to get some rest before my father heads into Death-Cast's Los Angeles facility tonight, I snuck into my car and took off when no one was looking. I should be able to come and go as I please, otherwise what was the point of them buying me this BMW for my eighteenth birthday? I understood that security would've been forced to report my leaving the premises, so that is why I timed my getaway with their patrolling the hills. I drove for twenty minutes with the windows down, the wind blowing my hair back as I screamed into the night.

I parked a block away from Griffith Park, which is closed for the night, but I didn't let that stop me from crawling under the gate. The hike up to the Wisdom Tree wasn't easy in my condition, but determination (and a few breaks along the trail for my aching abdomen) got me up here safely. I stood on the rock by the billowing American flag, admiring the gorgeous views of Los Angeles lit up at night, and felt a childhood joy gazing down at Universal Studios, where the Milagro Castle from the Scorpius Hawthorne movies stands proudly, but the real stunner is the majestic Wisdom Tree itself. On the surface it looks like any other big pine tree that's standing alone on this peak, but knowing it is the lone survivor of a wildfire makes it that much more powerful. This must be why it has so many other names speaking to its power, like the Magic Tree, the Wishing Tree, the Giving Tree, and the Tree of Life. There's a rebellious spirit about that tree not dying that I relate to tonight.

For the past thirty minutes I've been sitting against the Wisdom Tree's trunk, reading through the journals stored inside a green ammunition box. Some strangers kept it simple by only writing the names of their hiking party while others wrote love letters, poems, secrets, life advice, and even drew pictures. (My favorite picture is of this blue owl that reminds me of Duo, the green Duolingo owl who has celebrated and judged me many, many times since I started picking up languages after the platform opened to the public on June 19, 2012.) I paid most attention to the life advice, especially now that I'm charting my own path: Anonymous recommended starting a gratitude journal, but I've never had much of a need for journaling; Persida and Carlos scribbled a reminder that the best lovers are also best friends, which I've grown up believing from watching my parents; D'Angelo says to "read, read, read" and learn something new every day, which I already strive to do; someone known only as A says to never give someone too much power over you, which hits so hard that it's as if Future Alano time-traveled here to write and sign this before my arrival tonight; Lena tearfully encourages those in love with someone to seize it while they can along with a postscript about how she still loves a man named Howie who died, all of which makes me wish I knew more about who they were so I could find out if Lena and Howie ever got to be together before his passing; and another anonymous writer says to choose your friends wisely, which made me freeze and stare into the night because I thought I had done just that with Ariana.

I might be a survivor like the Wisdom Tree, but that doesn't mean I want to be alone. I also have no proof that I'm going to be okay in the long run. I check my watch, and it's twenty minutes to midnight. These are my very last minutes where I know that I will not die. It doesn't mean someone can't try to kill me again, right here, right now. But it can also mean what every other day has meant: living.

This grand feeling inspires my contribution to the journal: *Forge your own destiny in the unknown.* I hesitate at signing my name because whether I like it or not (and I don't) I am the most famous Alano in the world. This could trace back to Death-Cast and cause bad press. Actually, that consideration makes me sign my name. Proudly. I'm done letting Death-Cast run my life.

I return the journal in the ammunition box and begin my journey back to my car, going down a narrow path for a few minutes. I'm thinking about grabbing something to eat, or maybe visiting some other tourist landmark, when I hear movement. First I'm expecting an animal, which does scare me because I don't know how effective Muay Thai is against a mountain lion. Then I see a boy from behind—light hair, on the skinnier side—wearing a backpack. Him I can probably take in a fight, but I'm nervous anyway, so I duck behind a bush right as he's turning around.

My heart is pounding as I watch him through a small gap between the leaves and branches. He stares back but doesn't see me. Instead, he hops a gate and vanishes.

I don't have a good feeling about this. I should turn around, but I creep toward the gate, watching as the boy climbs a ladder up the Hollywood Sign. It's unlikely he's only planning on sightseeing this close to midnight. This dread in my chest is screaming that this is a suicide in the making. Then there's a gunshot, and for a moment I believe the boy has already killed himself when I realize it's only the powerful memory of Harry Hope's suicide. I wasn't able to save him, but I can try to save this boy.

I *will* save this boy.

I conquered my fear of heights, but now that I'm entering the uncharted territory of my own unknown fate, climbing this gate and then the ladder feels like it's against my better judgment, but I can't be haunted by another memory of someone dying because of something I didn't do—or something I did.

Once I'm on top of the Hollywood Sign, I shout, "Don't jump!"

If I live long enough, I will never again question anyone who accuses me of knowing my End Day when I have done something so reckless that a suicidal boy is now aiming his gun at me as if we share a death wish.

NOW

July 25, 2020
PAZ
12:00 a.m.

Death-Cast will call me tonight, but what about the Death-Cast heir?

Will he die too?

Will I kill him?

This can't be real; this has to be a hallucination. There's no other reason why Alano Rosa of all people would just magically appear on top of the Hollywood Sign right as I've figured out a surefire way to game suicide in a Death-Cast world. My therapist didn't mention anything about hallucinations being a side effect of BPD. Maybe that's what this is, maybe it isn't, maybe seeing things is some other illness in my sick brain. I could pull the trigger and find out if this phantom is real. If Alano isn't a hallucination, then maybe I should kill him as a middle finger to Joaquin Rosa for all the ways Death-Cast trapped me in this life when I wanted to be dead.

No, this isn't my dad trying to beat my mom to death. This

is an innocent boy, my age. I wouldn't kill someone for revenge, that craving must be coming from my BPD. But what do I know about my own life, I was wrong about how my own head works, maybe I'm lying to myself about being a cold-blooded killer.

"Please don't shoot," Alano Rosa says.

Alano has gone from telling me to not jump to my death to not shooting him to his. He's holding his hands up and trying to keep his balance as a strong wind picks up around us. He doesn't wanna fall . . . he doesn't wanna die. How fucking nice it must be to appreciate life.

I lower the gun. "Get out of here," I say, my voice trembling. Alano doesn't retreat down the ladder. He keeps standing there. "What are you doing? Alano, go!"

"No." Alano takes a few steps closer. "What are you doing up here?"

"What does it look like?" I ask, waving the gun.

"It looks like you're trying to kill yourself." Alano leans forward, squinting, almost like there's a chance he's got this all wrong, like I've climbed up the Hollywood Sign to gaze at the stars, maybe shoot at them too. "Wait. Paz Dario?"

I almost don't say anything, but my name will be all over the news tomorrow anyway. "Yeah."

"Your blond hair threw me off," Alano says, taking another step toward me. "But I never forget a face."

"We've never met," I say.

"That didn't stop you from knowing me."

That's ridiculous, of course I know who he is. He's famous because of Death-Cast. But I'm being ridiculous too, of course he would know who I am. I'm infamous for killing Dad.

That's not how I wanted to be known, but that's all I'll be remembered for.

The gun goes back against my head like magnetism.

"Please don't shoot," Alano says again, this time for my well-being. "Talk to me, Paz."

"You don't know me!" I shout.

"I know I don't know you, but . . ."

Alano stops speaking, and he's so still that I can't tell if he's breathing. I stare at him, really feeling like I'm seeing him, since that first glance that told me who he was. I didn't give a shit to take all of him in before, still don't, but I can't help it. It's too dark to make out the color of his eyes, but there's something familiar in his gaze as he looks at me like I'm a ghost. His dark brown hair is brushed up, holding its own against these winds that have Alano trembling in his ripped blue jeans, but the crystal earring dangling from his left ear keeps swinging. He's a few feet away from me, but he seems to be a couple inches shorter. I've got height on him, but he's got muscle on me. His arms are lean with veins bulging on his left arm while the other is wrapped with a white bandage; that's from that Death Guarder's knife. But I feel most drawn to Alano's T-shirt, which has a graphic of a skeleton smoking a cigarette. It reminds me of killing myself.

The gun is still pressed against my temple, and I wanna pull the trigger.

"You don't know me, but what?" I ask, snapping him out of his trance.

"But I do know what it's like to wish it was your End Day," Alano finally says after what feels like forever. Then time freezes again when he adds, "I've tried killing myself too."

ALANO
12:03 a.m.

Death-Cast cannot call me, but I don't need them to anyway: it appears today is my End Day. Paz's too. The only difference between us is that I want to live, even if it hasn't always been that way.

"You tried killing yourself?" Paz asks. The gun sinks to his side.

I'm not surprised Paz is questioning that someone with a seemingly glamorous life would try to kill himself, but it is one of the reasons I've never told anyone about my attempt. Actually, that's not true. I've technically told a lot of people. Last Halloween, Rio threw a blackout party in his basement for his eighteenth birthday. The first two hours were devoted to everyone showing off their costumes, but once the lights went off, people began shouting secrets throughout the night. One girl admitted to cheating on her boyfriend. A boy lied about crying Death-Cast. Rio came out of the closet, which I obviously already knew. Ariana confessed to missing the ex-girlfriend she ghosted. I shouted that I tried killing myself the week before. Someone nearby asked if I was okay while someone else rushed to turn on the light as if I was an active danger to myself, so I shoved my way across the room and acted like it wasn't me.

But now, up here on the Hollywood Sign, Paz Dario sees me for the survivor I am.

"Yes," I answer. The confession feels like releasing a deep breath. But I'm still scared that all I've done is share a secret with someone who will take it to his grave any minute now. "Will you come down with me? We can talk about whatever brought you up here."

Paz shakes his head. "No, this is it for me."

"Not yet. Just sit with me."

I carefully crouch down. One wrong move and I'll plummet to my death. I sit on the beam and hold on to the sides as my legs dangle, sending an awful chill down my spine. I might have a new rebellious spirit, but I'm no daredevil. Being up this high is absolutely terrifying, especially without knowing what destiny of mine has been written in stone, and even though this is resurrecting my fear of heights, I'll sit up here with Paz for three hours until I know Death-Cast hasn't alerted him.

Paz keeps standing. "How did you try killing yourself? Was it like this?" He stares at the gun while choking on his cries. "Or like this?" he asks, turning toward the dark depths below. He flinches. Fear is a good sign. If he's scared to die, then there's hope to get him down alive.

"Sit-with-me-and-I'll-tell-you-everything," I quickly say, almost like it's one word because time is of the essence.

It's the best I can offer. My psychology book about treating suicidal patients got left behind in New York before I could read more of it. That wasn't my fault, since I was busy recovering from getting stabbed, but I am mad at myself for grabbing that Vincent van Gogh biography off my father's shelf instead of the crisis-negotiations guidebook I remember seeing and thinking I would never need. That would've been a lot more helpful in this moment instead of offering up one of Van Gogh's many depressing anecdotes, like how despite how famous he is in death, he only managed to sell one of his estimated nine-hundred-plus paintings in life. The injustice would make any fragile artist put a gun to their head.

Paz looks between me and the darkness and decides to sit instead of leap. We're directly across from each other, several feet away. It reminds me of playing on the jungle gym seesaws pre-Death-Cast except none of those kids were holding guns.

"So?" Paz asks, wiping snot from his upper lip. "Tell me how you did it."

I don't actually want to relive my suicide attempt, but I'm scared that Paz will kill himself if I don't honor my word. "I was going to jump off a roof," I say. I don't tell him where. It's too depressing and personal and even if it wasn't, my chest is too tight from admitting this out loud for the first time. The memory is coming back to me in sharp detail like usual. October 24, a Thursday. The sky was clear, a beautiful send-off. "I got down and, ironically, almost died anyway because I was hyperventilating from how scary and close that was. I thankfully reached my inhaler before it was too late."

Paz's eyes narrow. "Thankfully?"

"Thankfully," I repeat. "I wanted to live, Paz."

"No. You never wanted to die, Alano."

I'm tempted to tell Paz everything bad about my life that led to me trying to jump off a roof, but fighting him for not respecting my suicide attempt isn't going to stop him from trying to kill himself. "I think suicide is less about wanting to die and more about wishing your life was better. I don't know why you're suffering, but I'm sorry you are," I say, trying to be as delicate as possible, like I'm disarming a bomb.

"It's not your fault," Paz snaps. He's maybe not fully defused, but he hasn't exploded.

"Do you want to tell me whose fault it is?" I gently ask.

"My dad's," Paz says.

I know plenty about Paz because of his court case, the documentary, and my own research over the years, so I'm about to ask more about Frankie Dario when Paz says, "Your dad's fault too."

It's both surprising and obvious to hear this. My father has been blamed for enough over the past decade that I can sense where Paz's anger is coming from. "Is this because of Death-Cast serving as a suicide prevention tool?" The words come out of me like I'm at some press conference. I hate it.

"I've tried killing myself before too," Paz confesses. He begins breathing faster as if the fuse has been lit. "I swallowed my antidepressants with alcohol and lived. Then I was gonna jump off this sign on my birthday, but Death-Cast not calling scared me away." Paz is hyperventilating, ready to explode. "If I shoot myself in the head and fall from this high up I'll die, right?" Angry tears flow down his sweet face. "Especially if I do it before the Death-Cast calls end, right? Please, Alano, please tell me I'll die."

It breaks my heart how Paz is begging for permission to kill himself. I can't give it to him.

"There's no guarantee you'll die," I say, even though I can't see how it wouldn't work. I'll never say it would because the truth could literally kill him. Besides, there have been many freak accidents from people who tried proving Death-Cast wrong. Hell, it could play out like Van Gogh's death, where he shot himself in the chest but missed all of his major arteries. It was ultimately the doctors' failure to retrieve the bullet that led to the infection that killed Van Gogh two days later. Paz himself could suffer a terrible miracle like that. "Take a deep breath and—"

My own words get swallowed by the loud whirring of a helicopter that is flying up the hill and toward us. Beams of light illuminate us like spotlights for troublemakers. The helicopter hovers near us, and its blades are blowing gale-force winds our way.

"This is the LAPD," an officer announces through the loudspeaker. "You are trespassing and must leave the premises now."

Paz rushes to stand, and at first I hope he's about to follow their instruction, but he stares at the vast, rocky drop below. I'm terrified he's about to go through with his suicide plan. I shout for Paz to stop, but he doesn't hear me over the helicopter. I quickly crawl across the beam and fight for balance against the winds as I stand. I'm tempted to grab Paz, but I'm scared we'll topple over and die together. I hold out my hand instead.

"Come with me!" I beg.

"Why?!"

"Because we didn't meet so I could watch you die! I believe we met because of . . ."

"Because of what?"

I say the only thing that makes sense. "Fate!"

PAZ

12:07 a.m.

Fate.

The Death-Cast heir believes fate brought us together on my End Day . . . on what will become my End Day if I shoot myself and fall to my death right now. But unless Alano Rosa is actually the grim reaper in disguise, there's no other reason we should be meeting. And if Alano is the grim reaper, he sucks at his job for trying to keep me alive.

The LAPD officer's voice booms over the loudspeaker: "This is your final warning!"

Pulling the trigger would be so easy, especially when I have the cops threatening me. What the fuck are they gonna do, throw my corpse in jail for trespassing? But Alano said there's no guarantee I would even die. How is this not a fucking guarantee?

Alano is reaching out for me, and I grab his hand. Together, we slowly walk across the beam, his hand squeezing mine the entire way, like he's terrified of falling or of me changing my mind.

Once we reach the ladder, Alano goes down first while I switch on my gun's safety and drop it in my backpack. There's a part of me that feels like a failure as I go down the ladder, rung by rung, like I can't win at death any more than I can win at life. Everything feels over and disappointing when my feet touch the ground, like I've missed my only chance to die.

The helicopter is still shining its spotlight on us, giving me a clear view of Alano's long-lashed eyes, which are two different colors. The left is brown, the right is green, like he's got the forest in his eyes. Beyond the colors, I see relief too. "You made a great choice," Alano says earnestly.

"No, that was stupid, that was so fucking stupid," I cry. "They're gonna arrest me for trespassing and possession of a deadly weapon and have me thrown in jail or a mental hospital."

I don't know which facility would be worse, all I know is that I won't get a fucking choice because of the fucking choice I made to keep fucking living.

"Maybe," Alano says. "But only if they catch you. Follow me."

Alano darts toward the darkness while the spotlight remains on me. I stand there, my heart racing even though I want it to shut the fuck up forever, but if I can't die, I need to run toward a less distressing life. My heart beats harder as I charge into the shadows, doing my best to outrun the light.

Ahead, Alano skids down a small slope and trips toward a boulder, giving me a chance to catch up. The light is zigzagging behind us, getting closer and closer so we keep moving. I've never been so far off the trail like this. We go deeper into the mountain's wilderness, panting as we hide beneath the trees that give us the most coverage, squeezing between bushes that prick our arms, and holding back low-hanging branches for each other as we continue paving our way toward the city. Something tiny—a lizard—scurries across my foot, giving me goose bumps. I hate how many more bugs and animals there are to be worried about out here. In New York, we really only had rats and roaches, but in LA, there's so many mosquitoes, lizards, and spiders roaming around our houses. Not to mention the snakes, coyotes, and mountain lions on and off these trails. The possibility of dying is still really real if one of those heavy hitters kills me.

I look up when I don't hear the helicopter anymore and the only light I see is coming from the moon. "I think we're good."

"Good." Alano coughs. He's leaning against a tree, holding his stomach, which I think is where he got stabbed. "Because I . . ." His hand slides down to his pocket but can't get in. "I can't b-breathe. Asthma," he wheezes.

I rush to his aid and wrench the inhaler out of the tight pocket of his jeans and straight into his mouth. I pump the medicine down his lungs. Alano inhales while looking me in the eyes. This whole thing is already so intense without his stare. The way he's fighting for breath makes me think about Alano's suicide attempt. He didn't tell me why or where or when, just the what: he was going to jump off a roof and then had an asthma attack after saving himself, just as he's having me save him now, giving him more and more pumps of medicine until he signals with a thumbs-up that he's all good. Alano rests his head against the tree, relaxing. My heart is still pounding. The last thing I need on my forever record is killing the Death-Cast heir. And the last thing Alano wants to do is die.

"Thank you," Alano breathes out.

In the ten or whatever minutes of knowing Alano, I've almost killed him twice. Meanwhile he's trying to keep me alive. He's better off staying away.

"Why do you think fate brought us together?" I ask.

"It's hard to imagine anything else. Someone tried to assassinate me and tonight that made me rebel against all the security measures put in place to keep me alive because I wanted to go live my life as I see fit, only to find you about to kill yourself. If that's not fate, then what is it?"

"I don't know, a huge coincidence or some story you're telling yourself."

"I'm not a writer, but I am a reader." Alano looks up at the night sky. "Something about our meeting feels written."

"Where, the stars?"

Alano returns his gaze to me. "Possibly."

I look up at the sky, searching for this constellation that's shaped like us, but I just see scattered stars. "I don't see it."

"Maybe you'll see things differently when I let you in on a secret," Alano says. He seems to be prepping himself to share this secret, or regretting bringing it up but knows he can't turn back now. "Tonight, for the first time in my life, I turned off Death-Cast."

"You're lying," I spit out.

Alano puts a hand on his heart, as if that means anything to me. "It's the truth."

"How the hell do you go from almost being assassinated by some pro-naturalist to living pro-naturally twenty-four hours later?"

"This has been more than twenty-four hours in the making. It's honestly as if my life has been building to this moment for as long as Death-Cast has been around. Being the heir has had many privileges, but it's also gotten in the way of the life I want for myself, so tonight I decided enough was enough. I will no longer be defined by Death-Cast, even if that means living the old way," Alano says. He takes a seat on a boulder and tells me all about his trip up to the Wisdom Tree, his first act of carpe diem. "I shouldn't have been up there, but I was, tonight of all nights, and when I saw you climbing that sign, I had two choices ahead of me: risk my life to save you or just let you die."

And I would've died. That much feels true now. "I wasn't even supposed to do this tonight," I say, proving Alano right. "I was originally gonna kill myself on the anniversary of my dad's death."

"The anniversary of the first End Day," Alano says.

One and the same.

"So who do I blame for my shitty life? Fate or Death-Cast?"

"Why not both?" Alano asks sincerely. "Your future got derailed on the first End Day. If Death-Cast didn't fail to call your father, then things would have gone differently."

I've imagined this before. I even wrote it out in my letter to Dad last month after surviving my attempt. "Sometimes I think it was for the best. My dad wouldn't have died quietly. Maybe if he knew he was gonna die he would've had more time to actually kill my mom and stepdad. Maybe even me, I don't know." I hate how much guilt I feel over killing someone who I can't confidently say wouldn't kill me too.

"Then maybe it was fate that Death-Cast didn't call," Alano says.

"So I should thank Death-Cast for my shitty life instead?"

Branches snap under Alano's feet as he gets up and walks toward me. "I'm sorry your life was thrown off course because of Death-Cast's error."

"I gotta ask you something."

"You want to know how Death-Cast works," Alano says, already shaking his head.

"No, I wanna know why Death-Cast *didn't* work on the first End Day."

Alano looks at the stars again like he's about to tell me it's fate, but instead he says, "I don't know."

"What, your dad never told you?"

"My father has never told me how Death-Cast works, let alone anything about the system error," Alano says, meeting my eyes again. "What I do know is that I'm happy you're alive, Paz. I'm hoping we can keep it that way."

Alano pulls me in for a hug, and I hate how good it feels to be held. He's like a walking, breathing weighted blanket, designed to calm me down when I'm feeling terrible. But I've been here before. I've been under the weighted blankets, I've squeezed the stress balls, I've talked it out in therapy, I've taken the meds, I've had strangers hold me—I've tried everything. I break free from his hug.

"No, nothing's changed. I always think it's gonna get better, but it never does and I'm tired, I'm just so tired," I say. My breath tightens. If I cared about living, I would snatch Alano's inhaler. "I feel too much and I'm dead inside, Alano. I gotta figure out how to die while there's still time."

Alano is quiet. He's accepting defeat too. I can't be saved.

"How about we make a deal?" Alano quietly asks.

So much for accepting defeat. "No," I say, turning away.

Alano grabs my wrist. "You'll want to hear this. Trust me."

"What?"

"You want to die tonight, but I want to keep you alive. Let's let fate decide what happens." Alano checks his watch. "It's twelve twenty. There's still time for Death-Cast to call you. If they do, then you'll get your way, I guess. If they don't, you hang out with me, and if I haven't convinced you that life is worth living before midnight, then I'll leave you alone."

"No deal, I don't have another day in me," I snap.

Alano's eyes dart around, like he's calculating something. "Fine. Give me until two fifty."

"Then you'll leave me alone?"

"I'll do you one better, Paz." Alano takes a deep breath. "I'll help you kill yourself."

ALANO

12:20 a.m.

Even if I wanted to, I'll never forget the first time I witnessed death.

It happened on September 6, 2011, five days after we moved into our Manhattan penthouse. My parents bought the place for just shy of twelve million dollars after Death-Cast's first successful year. From that high up with a view of Central Park and the reservoir, my father thought we should've been crowned as the city's royals. I overheard my mother saying how she would sleep easier at night knowing no one could break in unless they were spies rappelling the thirty floors. I used to be terrified of heights, but I was tempted out onto our rooftop garden because I wanted to stargaze with the telescope NASA gifted us in gratitude for how Death-Cast was better preparing their astronauts for missions.

That following Tuesday afternoon, my amazing tutor Mrs. Longwell had just left after our second homeschool session of the new school year. I returned to my bedroom and was unboxing my Transformers toys when a bird crashed into my window. I told my mother, and we ran out to the rooftop garden to investigate if the bird was okay. Bucky sniffed out the bird, finding it gravely injured beneath a bush. The bird's beak was hanging off its tiny bloody face, one leg was broken, and both wings were droopy, preventing it from flying away like it was trying to. I tried tending to the bird with my mother when my father rounded the corner, ending another call where the government was pressuring him to give advantages to the American military and withhold Death-Cast alerts to warring countries.

"What's all of this?" Pa had asked, his frustration from the call alive and well. He inspected the bird. "Poor thing. Let's take care of it."

I had thought we would bring it to a vet. My father dropped a brick on the bird.

I cried all night. "It could've lived, Papa," I had told him when he came into my room that night to apologize. "Your stupid job doesn't know about animal deaths!"

"No one deserves to live in pain. I showed mercy."

My father's lesson lives in me tonight.

"You'll help me kill myself?" Paz asks. In any other circumstance, I would love the hope in Paz's light brown eyes. Right now I hate it.

What I hate even more is my proposal, but desperate times call for desperate measures. "You're scared of surviving another attempt, right? I'll make sure you don't. It's the least I can do to make up for every way Death-Cast negatively impacted your life."

Paz sniffs back his cries and wipes his tears. "You're not just talking shit? If you are, I'll . . ."

I don't know what he's suggesting—or threatening—but it won't matter. "I hope you'll change your mind, but I mean it. This is a two-way street, though. You have to promise to treat me like a lifeline first."

Paz looks back up the mountain, like he's weighing his options between just returning to the Hollywood Sign now where he can try his suicide plan and risk surviving, or choosing to live a couple hours more with me so that he won't be left to live if he fails to kill himself. I'm relieved when he turns around and nods at me. "Fine. I promise," he says.

"Awesome. Let's get back to my car. I can drive us wherever you want."

I head downhill, but I don't hear Paz following me.

"Your turn," Paz says, holding his ground in the exact same spot. "Promise me."

The pleading in those two words is so strangled but alive. It's strange how people usually beg to not be left for dead, but Paz is begging to not be left for life. I think again about the afternoon of witnessing my first death and how badly I wanted that bird to be able to fly again. How I can try to nurture Paz back to life, but he might call on me to be his brick.

"I promise."

PAZ
12:50 a.m.

Two hours until I get to die by my hand or Alano's.

I honor my promise by telling Alano about my shitty life.

Recapping Alano on my heartbreaks and hardships feels like I'm back in therapy except instead of being in an office I'm going downhill on a mountain with a loaded gun in my backpack. Alano is a great listener, he's definitely acknowledging how much shit sucks as I go on about how unwelcomed I've felt in life these past ten years, and after sharing everything about the painful rejection from Orion's producers, Alano straight up stops in his tracks.

"But they loved your work!" Alano says.

"Not enough to give me a shot."

"I would've cast you," he says, carrying on as we finally clear the mountain's wilderness and reach the trail that will return us to the street.

"You didn't see my audition."

"But I've seen you act. I used to be a big fan of the Scorpius Hawthorne movies. I was actually watching the last one on the first End Day." Alano looks over his shoulder and grins. "Fate?"

"It's not fate for a nine-year-old to watch a Scorpius Hawthorne movie."

"Maybe not, but I did think you were great in it."

"All three minutes of it?"

"Three minutes where you're running around the Milagro Castle and casting magic."

That scene took all day to film, and the magic got edited in later. "I guess."

I used to have Alano's attitude about filming the movie. There was this childlike wonder where the Milagro Castle didn't feel like a set and my wand wasn't a prop. I was chosen out of three thousand kids to become young Larkin Cano, even if it was just for a day. That day felt fucking magical, but now I'm just fucking powerless.

"I'm sorry you didn't get that other role," Alano says once we hop the gate.

"It's fine," I say, shrugging it off.

Alano stops right under a streetlamp and gets in my face. Sweat is sliding toward his right eye, the green one. "Our time together might be limited so you can't dismiss your feelings. Tell me how it actually makes you feel."

"Okay," I say, thinking we'll keep walking and talking, but Alano stands here, waiting. "If there was ever a movie I felt destined or fated or whatever to star in, it was that one, but it's not, and I can't believe I was so stupid to think my comeback story would be one written by the guy who lost his boyfriend because of my dad. Now I'm just fucking hopeless." I catch my breath. "Is that what you want?"

"I don't want you feeling this way, but I'm glad you're being honest about it." Alano continues down the street toward the lone car that's parked outside an apartment building. "Knowing you won't be in the movie makes me happy I never read the book. I'll ignore them both out of solidarity."

"No, it's fine, I'm sure they'll cast someone great."

Alano stops outside the driver's door of his car. He raises his eyebrow.

"The movie won't be as good without me," I say, telling my truth.

"There's a lot more than a movie that won't be as good without you."

I don't say anything. I just feel something—something *good*—that I don't deserve to feel.

Alano gets into his car and pushes open the passenger's door when I don't let myself in. It's been a couple months since I've gotten into a stranger's car, something I was raised to believe was End Day behavior, but I was doing it anyway because it made me feel alive on my Not-End Days. My heartbeat was pounding in my ears when I got into the car of the man who sold me the gun. I get into Alano's car now, knowing this won't be as risky. He drives a white BMW that's black on the inside. It's so damn luxurious, unlike my family's shitty Toyota Camry. There's that faint new-car smell in here. Our Toyota reeked of cigarette smoke covered up in air freshener, which is how Mom and Rolando were able to get it at a good deal.

"Seat belt, please," Alano says. I glare. "You're not dying on my watch."

"Until it's time to watch me die."

"Until then."

I put on my fucking seat belt.

This car has got everything from tinted windows to seat warmers to cameras to subwoofer speakers, but it has zero character and tells me nothing about Alano. Say what you want about our busted Toyota, but there's no denying we've made it ours: hanging from our rearview mirror is a wooden ornament of the coquí—a frog that's super loved in Puerto Rico—a seat cushion on the driver's seat because Rolando kept complaining that his ass hurt, and we used to have an Oscar statue bobblehead that my mom bought to inspire me, but I asked her to take it down, and she replaced it with a President Page bobblehead. See? Character.

"You should vibe-up your car," I say. "Get an air freshener or plush dice for your rearview mirror. Just something."

Alano switches on the ignition, the engine running smoother than our car. "Apart from it being illegal in California because it can obstruct your view when driving, my family's security has always prevented it. They don't want our cars easily identifiable. I originally wanted a red car for my eighteenth birthday, but my parents bought a white one because most cars are white, so I have a better chance of blending in if I'm being pursued. I got over it. I only drive this car when we're in Los Angeles anyway."

I don't envy the security threats Alano faces, but I do envy his gifts. For my eighteenth birthday Rolando got me a mono-grammed wallet for all the money I don't have and Mom gave me a new camera and ring light for all the self-tape auditions that go nowhere. I try not to think about how much Alano's car costs to just sit in some garage while my family has a shitty car that could break down any day now when Mom needs it for work—and her new baby.

It's still wild that Mom is pregnant. I'm trying to not wonder about that too much, like if the baby will take after Mom's looks this time since I took after Dad. If Mom will honor my loss by using my name for the baby's middle name or something. And if she'll add more character to the car with a *BABY ON BOARD* sign.

I'm so lost in thought that I don't realize Alano is already driving. "Wait, we never figured out where we're going," I say. If I were along for the ride with any other stranger, I would probably be concerned that I'm about to get murdered, but it's not time for Alano to kill me yet.

"I just want to get you far away from the Hollywood Sign before you can become the next Peg Entwistle," Alano says, putting the mountain in the rearview mirror.

"The next who?"

He bites his bottom lip. "Oh. I figured you knew who she was. Never mind."

"Who is she?"

"It's probably better if we don't talk about her."

"Fine, I'll just look her up," I say, grabbing my phone.

"Don't . . ." Alano sighs.

"Who is she?" I ask one last time.

"The Hollywood Sign Girl. Peg Entwistle. She was this successful Broadway actress who moved to Los Angeles in 1932 to try to transition from stage to screen. She didn't have any real luck. She waited around all summer for an opportunity, but the phone never rang. Then she gave up in September. She climbed the Hollywood Sign and jumped to her death."

That story feels made up, I'm tempted to google it anyway, but why would Alano lie about this? If anything, I see why he thought I knew about Peg Entwistle already. I've also dreamt about becoming a Hollywood star. I've also waited around for calls that never came (in more ways than one). And most chillingly, I was about to meet her same fate. I can imagine the headline if I died: "Paz Dario, the Hollywood Sign Boy."

"How old was she?" I ask. If he says nineteen, I'm going back to that Hollywood Sign and jumping because that would actually be fate written in the stars.

"Twenty-four."

That doesn't make me wanna live anymore. "See, it doesn't get better. I don't have five more years in me."

We stop at a red light. This is my chance to break my promise.

"I'm not asking for five years. I'm asking for two hours," Alano says.

"Like that's gonna change anything."

"Living through one more day could be what changes everything," Alano says.

The red traffic light glowing on his face switches to green, but he doesn't drive. There are no cars ahead blocking us or any behind honking. I don't know if Alano would care if there were.

"There's a Hollywood legend that the day after Peg Entwistle killed herself, a letter arrived in the mail offering her the lead role in a movie about a woman driven to suicide. There's no evidence, but it could be true. We'll never know."

"So what, Orion is gonna call tomorrow and tell me the producers had a change of heart?"

"Only one way to find out," Alano says. He drives forward.

This Hollywood legend sounds like some bullshit Alano has made up to keep me alive, but I look it up on my phone, and it's true, everything else about Peg Entwistle too, down to the timeline.

"How do you know all of this?" I ask.

"I like learning about the world. I watch a ton of documentaries, but I mostly read. Usually a book or two a week."

"Then why haven't you read *Golden Heart*, is it too long or something?"

"No, I'm a really fast reader. I'm just more into nonfiction. But maybe you and I can have our own *Golden Heart* book club?"

I get what he's hinting at. "Yeah, I'm game. Let's see if you're a fast enough reader to read a nine-hundred-page book before I die in two hours."

"If that's how you want to spend our time together, I would honor it. It wouldn't be the worst thing in the world to get to know you through your favorite book."

I'm seriously considering my hallucination theory about borderline personality disorder again because there's no way someone like this actually exists in the world. There's a real chance I'm still up on that Hollywood Sign, imagining all of this.

"Is that how you want to spend our time together?" Alano asks after I don't answer him.

If I was trying to live, maybe I'd start a book club with Alano, but I'm not. "No, I just . . . I've spent more time thinking about how to die than what I would do before dying."

"Then how should we start this possible End Day of yours?" Alano lifts a finger, silencing me before I can answer. "You can't suggest anything that will ensure it definitely becomes your End Day."

"Damn."

I've always thought about performing, but I did that for my dream role, and it got me nowhere. And I hung out with my mom and stepdad. That's all I got. I try drawing inspiration from what my Last Friends did on their End Days. I'm not religious, so I'm not going to church or any other houses of worship like when I accompanied my first Last Friend, Amos, to his childhood synagogue. I had a lot of fun with my third Last Friend, Darwin, at this 8-bit arcade in Hollywood where we got priority playing because of his End-D8te-bit pass, but I'm not in the mood for video games.

"I don't know," I say.

"I have an idea. Do you want to know or be surprised?"

"I don't care."

Alano types in a location on his car's touchscreen. When he looks at the rearview mirror, I secretly hope he'll do a U-turn and take me back to the Hollywood Sign, but he keeps driving straight.

I'm spiraling again about Peg Entwistle and read about her on my phone to find more parallels between us that will keep my eye on the prize. That's when I see a transcript of her suicide note:

> *I am afraid, I am a coward. I am sorry for everything. If I had done this a long time ago, it would have saved a lot of pain. P.E.*

I've lived so long feeling dead inside, but never when someone is speaking about their struggles with life. I'm fighting back tears after reading Peg's note, confident that no matter what Alano has got planned for us, I will trust Peg's pain and save myself from my own.

1:14 a.m.

Yeah, Alano is out of his goddamn mind if he thinks bringing me to Hollywood Boulevard is gonna save me. "I know we're strangers, but you should know me better than this."

Alano parks the car. "Hear me out."

"Why would I come to Hollywood on my End Day?"

"To be fair, I met you on top of the Hollywood Sign."

"To kill myself! Did you bring me here to kill myself?"

"No. I brought you here for inspiration."

"Okay, cool, I'll look out for a different way to kill myself."

Alano gestures to take a deep breath with him. I don't.

His exhale is loud, frustrated. "Maybe it was stupid to bring you here, but your pain runs really deep, and I don't want to waste time dancing around it. I'm reading this psychology book *What to Know About Those Dying Inside*. In the first chapter, Dr. Glasgow shares this beautiful visual about treating negative thoughts as weeds that need to be raked from the ground and planting positive seeds in their place. There are always going to be weeds in your garden as long as the root remains, but you can grow and nurture flowers too." He takes another breath, this one for himself, breathing it out more evenly. "I'm not trying to dig you a deeper grave, Paz. I'm trying to give you a helping hand out of yours."

I look out the tinted windows, imagining Hollywood Boulevard as my wasteland of weeds, dead flowers, browned plants like the one in my bedroom. Trying to turn that into a garden feels exhausting, like I could spend the rest of my life yanking weeds, sweating and sunburnt and straight-up sad, and still never salvage this field. But Alano isn't asking me to do a lifetime of cleaning up. He's just hyping me up to make space for one fucking flower.

I unbuckle my seat belt and step out onto the curb—out into Hollywood.

Alano is cautiously smiling as he joins me. "We're doing this?"

"What exactly are we doing?"

"The more light you give a closed flower, the faster it opens."

I glare at him. "I will walk back into that car."

Alano laughs. "I'd like to know more about you and your acting journey."

"For someone who doesn't wanna waste time, you should've just said that."

He laughs again. I'm not even trying to be funny, I'm just keeping it real.

I can't believe Alano is putting up with me. How hard he's working to not have to honor his promise. I gotta get it together and do my part in this arrangement, even if my opening up is just a performance. That's why I crafted Happy Paz in the first place.

"I moved here last summer. We thought it would be a fresh start," I say, light and airy, like I'm already potting plants in my garden, but really those weeds are scratching and squeezing my heart. "But *Grim Missed Calls* ruined my life again."

"I'm sorry," Alano says.

I can't accept his apology—it's not his fault, it's his dad's if anyone's. "I'm sure that show sucked for your family too."

Alano is quiet. I'm sure he's about to give me nothing, like his family affairs are too private or something, but he opens up. "My father wasn't concerned about people turning on Death-Cast. The company has had a clean record since the first End Day. Still, he met with the filmmakers in the hopes of shutting down the project to protect the families whose wounds would be unnecessarily reopened." At the crosswalk, I see the guilt on Alano's face. "Families like yours."

"My mom and stepdad hoped my episode would remind the world I was innocent. It just put a bad spotlight on me again, like I was a risk. No manager or agent wanted to rep me. Acting studios rejected me. I was desperate to act in something to prove that no one would actually care if I was attached to something. I sent in self-tapes for anything. Student films, commercials, even a Sharknado sequel."

Alano cringes. "Yikes. Do you really want a Sharknado movie on your IMDb page?"

"I don't want my last credit to be myself in a documentary about how I killed my dad."

The deeper we walk into Hollywood, the harder it is to be here. I haven't been in this area since last year, though I almost got dragged here recently by a Last Friend, Marina, to Madame Tussauds of all fucking places before she changed her mind. Whenever my family has to drive through here I close my eyes. It hurts too much seeing all the billboards and theaters and stars on the Hollywood Walk of Fame.

We cross the street, and to our left, between Hollywood Boulevard and La Brea, is the Four Ladies of Hollywood sculpture, which I visited with Mom and Rolando when we first moved here. I tell Alano all about how we started our Hollywood Walk of Fame tour there because Mom wanted to see the bronze statue of Marilyn Monroe on the spire of the sculpture's gazebo and Rolando wanted a picture with Elvis Presley's star. That picture was the first of a hundred because Mom and Rolando kept freaking out whenever they saw stars for their favorite actors and actresses, as if they were there in flesh and not just names inscribed into brass.

"I dreamt about how amazing it would be to have my own star," I say, resisting the jealous urge to stomp on the stars of others. "Not even for me, but for my mom. She would be so damn proud, probably camp out on the streets to tell anyone passing by that the star they stepped on belongs to her son." I've struggled with how much I've lived because that's what my mom wants, but there are also times where I've lived because I wanna make my mom proud. "I'll never get a star."

Alano stops, pointing at a star with no name. "How about this one?"

"That's a placeholder for someone else."

"You could be that someone else, Paz!"

"Yeah, I don't think a committee is gonna throw a star my way for one scene as Larkin Cano when they still haven't even given Howie Maldonado a posthumous star for playing him in eight movies."

"Not for Scorpius Hawthorne—not just that, at least. For the body of work you'll create," Alano says. I start protesting because he's not understanding me, but he asks to hear him out, and I do this time instead of fighting. "You're right that you just need someone to give you a chance and then you can prove everyone wrong. Look at Robert Downey Jr. He was arrested for possession of cocaine, heroin, and an unloaded .357-caliber Magnum. Do people talk about that or the fact that he's Iron Man? How about Tim Allen? I grew up knowing him as Buzz Lightyear, not a drug trafficker. Don't get me started on Hugh Thompson running for vice president when he has cried Death-Cast multiple times, even though he's never been registered for the service. You're always going to see the shadow of the first End Day, but I believe with time you'll make everyone remember you for who you actually are."

I wonder if Alano is still planning on taking over Death-Cast, but if not he would make a great life coach, maybe even a therapist. He reminds me of my sessions with Raquel, where she's really encouraging me to keep pushing through, but it's even more meaningful coming from Alano because he's this stranger who isn't being paid to talk out my shitty life with me. It also isn't costing my mom for once. If anything, it's buying her more time with me.

"Okay, but Hugh Thompson isn't some Hollywood star. He also doesn't have one."

"You're right. I actually don't know if the others have stars either," Alano says sheepishly.

"Sounds like you should read up on that instead of spreading misinformation like Hugh."

Alano's sharp jaw drops. "Look it up on your phone."

"Look it up on yours."

"Mine is currently off so my parents and bodyguard can't track me."

I'm not risking him getting pulled away before it's time to die, so I google the actors. "Okay, so Tim Allen has a star, but Robert Downey Jr. doesn't."

"That feels as criminal as you not having one," he says.

"Nope, don't try to suck up, you're not getting my write-in vote."

"I'm just happy you'll be alive this fall to not vote for me," Alano says, his green eye winking.

I throw a smile his way, like I've practiced a million times as Happy Paz, but part of it feels real too, and I really hate that part because it's hope, and hope is as dangerous as a nine-year-old with a gun. I remind myself that Alano believes the real stars above predict fate, that they tell stories. But Alano is giving me abridged versions that leave out the messy parts. Like how Robert Downey Jr. was in his forties when he became Iron Man, and I don't even have twenty more hours in me, let alone twenty years. Or how Hugh Thompson could build a political career lying about Death-Cast being wrong because of Death-Cast's real historic error. That's the unabridged truth.

I keep walking on the stars knowing I'll never get my own.

We approach El Capitan, one of Hollywood's premier theaters that has a dazzling marquee promoting *Black Widow*, which came out last month after a slight delay caused by the coronavirus scare. I saw videos online of Scarlett Johansson and Florence Pugh surprising moviegoers here at opening night. It made me jealous of everyone—how easy it was for the actors to move in and out of a theater to applause, how lucky the attendees were that an ordinary viewing experience became extraordinary, a gift for being here in Hollywood.

But nothing hurts more than what I missed out on twelve years ago. "The world premiere for *Scorpius Hawthorne and the Immortal Deathlings* was held here," I say.

"Wow," Alano says, taking in the theater like it's some fun fact. "Did you have a good time?"

"I didn't go. The studio invited us, but my role was too small for them to fly us out and put us up. We couldn't afford the trip, so my mom had to pass." This is a reminder that my life had its limits before my incident, that the only good thing that has ever happened to me was booking a movie that I couldn't celebrate with all the other actors.

"That sucks. Did you get to see the movie in theaters?"

"I did. . . ." I pause, feeling some flowers bloom in my mental wasteland. "My mom felt bad that we couldn't go to the premiere, so she planned one for me opening weekend. She invited my entire class. I don't remember a lot, just that we all went to a Saturday morning screening dressed up in wizard robes with clip-on ties to make it fancy. Oh, and my mom brought gift wrap from the ninety-nine-cent store and rolled it out in front of the theater like a red carpet." I stand under El Capitan's marquee, no longer feeling as bad about missing the movie premiere. "Wow, I haven't thought about that in forever. It's so funny how memories get lost like that, right?"

"Right." Alano looks up at the marquee too, like he also sees that my memory is better than what I've imagined. "It sounds like your mother really loves you," he says, his gaze returning to me as we keep walking down the block. "I take it she always supported your dream of acting?"

"Oh yeah, for sure. Even when our acting class just had us messing around, pretending we were eggs being scrambled and stupid shit like that. My dad's the one who didn't take me seriously until I booked the movie. He was treating me like a kid who wanted to be a knight or dinosaur. My life would be so different if my mom didn't take me to those weekend classes, the auditions, Brazil to film, all of that. Maybe I would be happier."

It's a sad thought, but it's true. I could've grown out of my dream the same way kids grow up and stop pretending they have T. rex arms. I could've settled for any job, like a cashier or busboy, just so I could get some money. Maybe colleagues would've turned into friends. Maybe friends would've turned into more. My life could've looked so different.

"It's not your mother's fault for helping you follow your dream, Paz," Alano says gently. "She's just doing her job. It's beautiful how much she believes in you."

He must think I'm some monster who blames my mom for everything. I don't. I never blamed Mom for not leaving Dad, no matter how many times she apologized for it. I never blamed Mom for how poor we were, because I've seen her many sacrifices to make ends meet. But there is something I do blame her for. Something that I don't know how to say without sounding even more monstrous. It's not until we walk over another block's worth of stars, past a man trying to sell us weed, and a woman getting high, that I spit it out. "Sometimes it's hard to live for someone who loves me so much."

Alano is quiet, and I'm expecting him to judge me because wow, how hard my life must be to have a mom who loves me. "I understand."

"Really?"

"It took nine years of trying and twelve miscarriages before my parents had me. They've never said this, but sometimes I think my mother was willing to die trying and my father was willing to let her. I never understood how they could love each other so much but be willing to let death get in the way for someone who didn't even exist." Alano is shaking his head, like even he thinks his own existence was not worth those risks. "My parents call me their miracle. They would probably die from heartbreak if they ever found out I was almost their tragedy."

I stop in my tracks, right on top of another placeholder star. "Your parents don't know you tried killing yourself?"

"No. My attempt was so impulsive. It would've surprised them as much as it was surprising to me. I don't know how I would even start talking about that with my parents after knowing everything they went through to have me. So I don't talk about it with anyone ever . . ." Alano shrugs. "Until now."

"No one knows?"

"No one except you, Paz."

"Not even a therapist?"

"I'm not in therapy right now, but I like to think I would trust them with my secret."

"Don't worry about your secrets, they'll die with me."

"I'd rather my secrets live with you. Your secrets can live with me too." Alano's gaze is intense. I wanna look away, but I can't, it's like he's hypnotizing me to tell him everything. "You can trust me," he says in a whisper or shout, I don't know, I'm so sucked into how he's looking at me that blood is rushing to my face.

"My mom threatened to kill herself," I spit out. It immediately feels like the fist around my heart is opening up. "It was after I tried killing myself."

"Which time?" Alano asks.

I forgot that I told Alano about my second suicide attempt while we were still high up on the Hollywood Sign. That was one of my secrets, one I kept from my therapist too, but he's getting to know the real me, and there's something comforting about someone knowing my truth before I die.

"It was after my first attempt."

"Overdosing on your antidepressants," he says, not a question. Alano listens.

"After my stomach got pumped, my mom was so relieved but also so upset. Not angry-upset, she was heartbroken-upset. She's always been a planner—Halloween costumes, that premiere party, shit like that—but she told me that she would not plan to live in a world without me. I've kept that a secret, even at home. I don't want my stepdad knowing he's not enough for her and I don't have it in me to tell my mom how unfair that was." I'm breathing so hard, panting, like I'm out of air, and my face is wet with sweat and tears. "I love my mom so much, Alano, but I hate life even more."

Alano's two-color eyes are tearing up. I can't watch him. I just look at his T-shirt with the skeleton smoking a cigarette, thinking about how soon enough I'll be nothing but bones. "It sounds like your mother can't stand the idea of living without you, but that is a lot of weight to carry . . . to drag around, really. What changed tonight that you're ready to . . . ?"

"Let her die too? She's not gonna kill herself anymore."

"Why not?"

"She's pregnant," I say. I'm still surprised this is something that's true and not a lie I'm telling to get my way. "I found out today."

Alano looks confused.

"It's not impossible for my mom to get pregnant apparently."

"No, I understand that. A sixty-eight-year-old woman gave birth via IVF in April, and a woman who was rumored to be somewhere between seventy-two and seventy-five had a natural birth last October, but . . ." Alano closes his eyes and squeezes his hands into fists, like he's about to fight himself for getting carried away with this absolutely random trivia. "I know all of *that*, but I'm confused why you think another child could ever replace you."

I shrug. "My mom just needs to be someone's mother."

"She wants to be your mother for as long as possible."

My mom probably has another thirty years in her, maybe forty if she's lucky, but I don't even know what thirty years feels like, and I never wanna find out. "I gave her nineteen years. Maybe the new kid will give her more." I'm struck with this thought that my little sibling will one day grow up to be older than I ever was. How they'll be able to look after Mom and love her so much that she'll forget about me.

"What if she loses the baby too?" Alano asks. "There are more risks for advanced-maternal-age pregnancies—"

"Stop!" I shout, shutting my eyes and covering my ears. I'm not trying to hear the reality I've tried so hard not thinking about.

Alano's hands wrap around mine, gently pulling them away from my ears. "I'm sorry. I just want to make sure you're thinking this through."

"I don't wanna think it through," I say, sliding my hands out of his. "I don't wanna think about my mom having a miscarriage and losing both her kids, okay? She won't be strong like your mom was, she will absolutely take her own life, and I can't think about that."

I also can't help but think about it now.

When I spent those three days in the psych ward, I was haunted by Mom's threat. My imagination was running wild, picturing how she would kill herself if she actually made good on her promise. At first I thought she would imitate my suicide, in this almost sick way of wanting to be close with me in death. Then I pictured her putting herself in danger, like rolling out of the car while speeding down the highway, or setting herself on fire. But I don't think it would ever be that fast. I bet Mom would stop taking care of herself—refuse to eat, only drink alcohol, leave Rolando—and eventually her body would get the point and die. That slow, miserable death is how my life feels, and I really don't wish that on my mom.

"Don't you want to meet the new kid?" Alano asks, snapping me out of my spiral.

In the same way I don't wanna live long enough to see who gets cast as Death, I'm better off not knowing more about the child replacing me. But I can't help it. I fight back tears as I think about holding the new kid, making stupid faces so they laugh, teaching them bad words, and everything I can do to protect this kid's life from being derailed like mine.

"I'll never let myself die if I gotta be that kid's big brother," I say.

Alano slowly nods. "You're helping me understand my parents better, Paz. It's really amazing how much we're capable of loving someone who doesn't even exist yet. So much so that you want to die now because you know you'll put their life over your own."

I can't bring myself to lie out loud or even to myself, because Alano is dead right. "I love this kid enough to not ruin their life. They'll be better off with me gone."

"If that's how you really feel, then we should make sure they know you loved them," Alano says, dropping that cryptic cliff-hanger before we continue down the block.

This walk down memory lane turned into a guilt trip real fast.

1:45 a.m.

"Have you ever been to the World Travel Arena?" Alano asks.

He still hasn't told me where we're going, but this is his third attempt at making conversation since our talk about the new kid. He first asked me about my favorite non–Scorpius Hawthorne movie, but I didn't answer. He told me he's a fan of everything Christopher Nolan does, but especially *Memento*, which I think is the movie that's told backward—I don't know;

I haven't seen it. Then he pivoted to asking me if I've ever traveled anywhere outside of New York or Los Angeles or Brazil, which I haven't. Now here he goes again, segueing into a conversation about those arenas that are basically high-tech versions of Disney's Epcot theme park.

"I went once," I say. I don't wanna get into it. "You?"

"I've been a few times with my parents for Death-Cast media tours, and I think it's great in a pinch for Deckers, but it isn't an intimate introduction to any foreign city. That would be like someone visiting Times Square or Hollywood and going home thinking they saw New York or Los Angeles when really they just had a tourist's experience. What did you think?"

"It wasn't my favorite day ever," I say.

"What happened? Did you . . . Oh. I'm an idiot. I assumed you went for fun. Most non-dying people do these days, outweighing Deckers by eighty-four percent according to the division manager. Did you go with a Decker?"

I'd planned on taking this pathetic secret to the grave, but who gives a shit. "I went with a Last Friend," I confess.

"That's really admirable of you."

"Not really. I was just so lonely that I was counting on those Deckers being so desperate for a friend too that they would hang out with a killer."

"You're not a killer, and they knew that. How many Deckers?"

"Six."

"Wow."

"Is that a lot?"

"It's subjective, obviously. *Time* magazine published this fascinating profile on Living Last Friends for the app's upcoming five-year anniversary. There were all these stats on how often Living Last Friends assist Deckers. Most Livings do it once, if ever. Your buddy Orion Pagan has never used the app even though his love story inspired it, but the app's record holder, Teo Torrez, has served as a Living Last Friend over one hundred and thirty times in honor of his son, who lived his best End Day thanks to his Last Friend."

"Did you say—"

"One hundred and thirty times? I did."

"Okay, so that's a lot! Six is nothing."

"Six is a lot for someone who struggles with his life."

I don't deserve this credit, I'm not noble. "I was lonely."

"You don't have to be anymore. You'll always have me."

"Always isn't a long time."

"Then I'll be your Last Friend until the end," Alano promises.

I never even thought about signing up for a Last Friend because I've had such rough experiences on that fucking app, especially my sixth so-called friend. I believe Alano will be better than the Deckers I befriended, but I've been wrong about a lot before.

"What happened during your visit to the Travel Arena?" Alano asks.

"I went with this girl, Robin . . ." I feel bad that I don't remember her last name. "She died in Paris—the arena's Paris, obviously."

"Were you there?"

That's a sore spot. "No. We'd been hanging out for a few hours, and I was keeping her spirits up, but around two or three in the afternoon she got nervous, suspecting that maybe I was gonna kill her after all. She asked me to leave, and I did. I found out online that she died a few minutes later. There was some malfunction or something on the arena's Seine River simulation and—"

"And she got sucked into an unsecured part of the pool, right?" Alano finishes. "Robin Christensen."

"Wait, how do you know all of that? Did you know her?"

"I read about her in an article. Maybe the same one as you."

I couldn't remember Robin's last name even though we spent five hours together, but Alano could off one article. "You like reading about death?"

"I like reading about real life," Alano says. "Especially the lives that ended because of Death-Cast affiliates. My family pays attention to all of those, as well as anyone affected by Death-Cast."

"Like the first End Day," I say, weighed down by the trauma that I swing my backpack off my shoulder and reach inside. Alano comes at me so quickly that I think he's about to tackle me, but he just grabs my arm.

"Don't do it," Alano pleads.

"Don't do what?"

"Shoot yourself."

I almost—almost!—laugh in his face. "That's not what I'm

doing," I say, shrugging him off and pulling out my cigarette and lighter.

Alano exhales in relief. I'm just about to inhale the lit cigarette for my own relief when he smacks it out of my hand.

"Okay, are you trying to get me to reach for the gun?"

Despite the death threat, Alano laughs. "I'm trying to keep you alive."

"A cigarette won't kill me tonight."

"It could in a few years."

"You're only keeping me alive for another couple hours."

"I have an ulterior motive to keep you alive a lot longer," he says, taking the cigarette carton and throwing it in the trash.

I point at the smoking skeleton on his shirt. "For someone who doesn't want me smoking, you're sure as shit teasing me."

Alano looks down at himself. "Kop van een skelet met brandende sigaret," he says, continuing down the street, like he doesn't realize he's just spoken to me in another language.

"Cop-van-and-what-what-what-cigarette?"

"It's Dutch for '*Skull of a Skeleton with a Burning Cigarette.*' Van Gogh painted this while studying at the Royal Academy of Fine Arts, but he dropped out—"

"You speak Dutch?" I interrupt, more interested in that than Van Gogh's life story.

"Een beetje," Alano says, and then sheepishly translates. "A little. I study languages before we visit countries for business and pleasure."

"How many languages do you speak?"

"I'm fluent enough in French, German, Portuguese, Italian, Thai, Russian, Chinese, and ASL. I've also been studying Japanese, Farsi, and Dutch."

I thought he would list three languages, maybe four. "That's it?"

"And English and Spanish, obviously, because of my parents. I'm guessing you do too."

"No, I'm a bad Puerto Rican. My mom and stepdad know Spanish, but I only speak English."

"If you need a tutor, I know a good one." Alano raises his hand.

Is this what it's like to not have a brain that messes with your emotions and ruins your life? It leaves space to learn languages and facts about Van Gogh, Peg Entwistle, and Deckers you've never met? It makes me wanna hit a one-eighty and grab my cigarettes out of the trash.

"So why the shirt?" I ask, still craving that smoke down my lungs.

"No one really knows why Van Gogh painted it, but scholars consider it to be a vanitas."

"Vanitas? Is that more Dutch or one of the other languages you speak?"

"It's Latin, which I don't speak."

"Yet."

"Yet," Alano echoes, like he might actually take up a dead language. "A vanitas is a still-life artwork that uses symbolic objects of death. Usually skulls, sometimes wilted flowers. It's meant to remind the viewer of their mortality. It's a lot like memento mori, which means 'remember you must die' in Latin. My father almost named the company after that sentiment, but he wanted something original."

I don't really care about the Death-Cast fun fact, but after learning the meaning behind the smoking skeleton I really do feel like I'm staring into a mirror. "You don't think it's weird that you're trying to get me to live while wearing a shirt that's reminding me I have to die?"

"I'm not psychic, Paz. I didn't get dressed knowing I would be spending the night with a suicidal boy. I put it on tonight as my own reminder that I need to live while I can. But if it bothers you that much . . ."

Alano stops and takes off his shirt, half-naked in the streets while turning his shirt inside out. I stare at his body the entire time—his sculpted shoulders, the growing patch of hair between his flat but defined pecs, the bandage wrapped around his abdomen, and that famous V-line that trails down his jeans. I don't even care about the dried bloodstain on his bandage. I've seen worse on myself, but his body is just . . . better. I wanna die, but my heart is still pumping and it's pumping a lot of blood right now. It's like he's a lighter and I'm a cigarette. The fire starts at my head and is burning all the way down to my—

"Were you just trying to get me to take off my shirt?" Alano asks, smiling as he catches me staring at him. He slings the shirt over his shoulder. "Whatever makes you happy."

"Your body isn't an antidepressant."

"But does it help?"

I hate how Hollywood always forgives bad acting just because someone's hot. I've sometimes wondered if Hollywood would forgive me for killing my dad if I was hotter. It's depressed me then and depresses me now. "It doesn't help, if anything it makes me feel worse because I don't look that way."

"I'm sorry." Alano puts his shirt back on, inside out so I can't see the smoking skeleton.

Once my blood cools I ask, "How are you feeling? After the attack."

"Holding up. It's a miracle my stitches didn't tear open during all the climbing and running. Maybe they will when I fight you over how you're beautiful as you are."

Okay, he's definitely deflecting, but he's doing a bad job because a compliment isn't gonna save my life any more than his body will. "There's not gonna be another time, you have less than two hours with me."

"Well, maybe our next destination will change your mind. We're almost there."

Alano gives up on the flirting, as welcome as that would've been earlier in my life. Maybe even another life, where I don't have borderline personality disorder making me doubt my own feelings. I can't have anything good, I can't be happy. My mind is this minefield and there's nowhere safe for me to go without detonating more depression. That's why as thoughtful and beautiful as Alano is, the next time he takes off that shirt will be because it's been splattered with my blood.

We go down a street, and Alano finally stops. "Here we are."

We're outside a small shop that looks old with its wooden exterior and awning striped with brown and yellow. The window display has shelves of clocks paired with colorful gift boxes that are all wrapped with beige bows. There's an *OPEN 24/7* sign on the red door and a bigger sign above that reads:

PRESENT-TIME GIFT SHOP
NO TIME LIKE THE PRESENT . . . FOR A PRESENT!

"You're getting me a present?" I ask.

"You don't know about Present-Time?"

"Nope."

"They're fairly new. The first one launched in Chicago last September."

"This place looks old."

"The founder wanted the shops to feel inviting and cozy for Deckers."

"I don't get it, how is this a shop for Deckers?"

"It's your End Day, Paz," Alano says, winking as he opens the front door. A gentle bell rings. "Why don't you go inside and see for yourself?"

If we're gonna act like it's my End Day, I need to play the role of Decker Paz. I walk into the shop, which is warmly lit with lamps and smells like cardboard boxes. I've never seen so many clocks in my life: wall clocks, pendulum clocks, grandfather clocks, cuckoo clocks, digital clocks, and even sundials. They also have a glass cabinet of watches with dozens of unique bands. There's no one behind the counter, but there is a middle-aged woman speaking with an elderly man on the sales floor.

"I'll be with you shortly," the woman calls out to us.

"Okay," I say to her before turning to Alano. "I still don't get how this is a shop for Deckers."

"What do you think they're selling?" Alano asks.

"I'm gonna guess clocks."

"They're selling time." Alano flips a bronze hourglass and watches the red sand fall. "Deckers never have enough time to do everything they need on their End Days, not even the rare few who get the miracle of a midnight call and an 11:59 p.m. time of death. There isn't even always the chance to have meaningful goodbyes. Present-Time acts as a one-stop shop for Deckers who want to leave something special behind for loved ones but can't afford to spend their precious time shopping at different stores or waiting in line at the post office to send a gift across the country. They can engrave any of their timepieces and even upload recordings into some of their objects." Alano turns away from the hourglass and toward me. "I brought you here so you could leave a message for the new kid."

"Like what?"

"Anything you want. Big brother wisdom. It could even be a simple 'I love you.'"

Maybe I'll warn the new kid to never shoot anyone.

I browse the shelves, not feeling a real pull to anything until I spot this cuckoo clock that's painted orange, red, and yellow and carved like fire. I press a button and a porcelain phoenix shoots out of the tiny doors, screeching at me. It's a cute—slightly heart-jumping—idea for Deckers, especially those who believe in reincarnation, but I don't have any messages of rebirth for the new kid. Maybe I can recommend the Scorpius Hawthorne series since there's a cool ghost phoenix that haunts the Milagro Castle in the second book. That's stupid, is that really the message I want to leave from the afterlife? Go read a fantasy series that everyone will be reading until the end of time? And hey, while I'm at it, I should recommend watching the movies so they can see their dead big brother.

No, I gotta keep looking.

"What about these?" Alano asks, waving me over and showing me three grandfather clocks: the first is traditional with its wood paneling; the second has a steampunk vibe with its metal and exposed gears; and the third is whimsical with its green and gold tones and curvy shape, like it belongs in Wonderland. "You got a favorite? Maybe you can leave it behind for your family."

"No," I say.

"That's okay. They thankfully have more options."

"No, I don't wanna leave one behind for my family." How haunting would that be for my mom to have an hourly chime, reminding her that I'm not only gone but that I also took my own life?

"Do you want to get them something else?"

"I already left my mom a note," I say, turning away.

"A suicide note?" Alano asks, tailing me down the aisle.

"You should leave behind something more beautiful for her to remember you by."

I'm quiet for so long that I would swear time has frozen if it weren't for the pendulum clocks doing their thing. "What if I want my mom to forget me and move on?"

Alano's hand lands on my shoulder from behind, stopping me. "Your mother could live to be a hundred and never forget you," he says in my ear before turning me around to face him.

I love Mom enough that I stop fighting Alano on this. I search the shop, trying to find something for everyone in my family.

I go to the watch cabinet to see if anything jumps out at me. They have a shelf with character watches—Snoopy, Mickey Mouse, Homer Simpson, Scorpius Hawthorne (but no Larkin Cano), and Mario among many more—and I'm about to turn away when I see an analog Pac-Man watch with a retro silicone strap.

"My stepdad calls me Paz-Man all the time," I tell Alano while grabbing the watch. If Rolando was the one dying I would love for him to gift me this watch with a recording of him calling me Paz-Man to hold on to forever.

I keep it moving, finding a fifteen-minute hourglass with black and white sand. "This reminds me of Othello," I say.

"The Shakespeare play?"

"The board game. I've played it with my mom since I was a kid. Now the new kid can."

"That's really sweet," Alano says.

Finding something for Mom is the hardest, even though she would be happy to have anything from me, like a custom clock with my face or an alarm clock where my voice wishes her good morning every day, just to give her the strength to go on. A nearby table has a memory clock on display where you can type in as many beloved memories as you want, which will cycle through every few minutes, but unless Alano convinces me to live much longer, I don't have the time to write down every highlight I've shared with Mom. Then I remember Mom likes simple things that get the job done. Simple car, simple shoes. I choose a simple gold locket with a clock on its ornate case and space inside for one picture.

"My mom will love this," I say, thinking about how she'll wear it to her grave.

"It's beautiful. You're a good son," Alano says.

A good son would keep living for his mom, but at least I'm giving her something better to hold close to her heart that's not my suicide note.

I carry everything over to the gift station where there's all the colorful wrapping paper and beige ribbons from the window along with cards and these little white boxes that look like the smoke detectors at home.

"One more minute," the employee calls out to me as she finishes ringing up the elderly man at the counter. She tries returning his credit card, but he's not paying attention.

The man with a Knicks cap over his bald head clings to this pink box. "Is it too late?"

"I assure you this will arrive to your son by the morning. I simply have to wait until three before clearing a driver to make the trip to San Francisco."

"No, not the package." This man is tall, even while hunched over. He seems to be folding in on himself even more. "Is it too late to make things right?"

"If there was ever a time to try, it's now."

The man releases the box and takes his credit card, putting it back in his pouch. "Thank you, Margie."

"Honored to help," Margie says. "I'm sorry you'll be lost, Richard."

The Decker—Richard—is sniffling as he exits the shop. Whatever happened between him and his son, he sounded so haunted.

I can't help but wonder if there's anything Dad could've said to me in his final hours to make up for the trauma he inflicted on us. An apology? How he accepts me for who I am? A quick recording saying how much he loves me? I can't remember the last time Dad said he loved me, but how can I ever believe him anyway, since he told Mom he loved her and still treated her so horribly?

Maybe there are some things in this world that can't ever be made right, not even in a long lifetime, and definitely not on an End Day.

"How can I help you?" Margie asks, coming over to the gift station.

"Just this," I say, setting down the watch, hourglass, and pendant.

"Do you mind my asking if you're a Decker?"

"I am," I lie.

"I'm sorry you'll be lost."

I've dreamt of hearing those words said to me for so long, a sign that I would finally be dead soon. I could cry from happiness and sadness all at once.

"And you?" Margie asks Alano before squinting. She gasps loudly once she recognizes him. "Alano Rosa? Oh no, honey, are you dying?"

Alano shakes his head. "No, ma'am," he says even though he has no idea. "I'm here supporting my Last Friend."

"That's wonderfully generous. I was worried about you after seeing that Death Guard incident on the news. You be safe."

"I'll do my best, ma'am."

Pretty hard not to take it personally as Margie gets more worked up over Alano potentially dying when she knows—believes—I actually am. Just because I'm not the famous son of a famous man doesn't make me worthless. But Alano doesn't think I'm worthless. Having been a Last Friend six times, I know that these friendships don't always work out, and it's a really shitty feeling knowing that someone chose you to hang out with in their final hours and the chemistry is all off and you've wasted their precious time. But Alano isn't wasting my time—he's literally helping me buy some.

"You've selected some beautiful pieces here today," Margie says, remembering me. She eyes Mom's future pendant. "Good on you for getting here early. This is our last in stock. If you'd arrived around six or seven when most Deckers have grieved themselves enough to stop in, I fear it may have been gone already."

"His mother will love it," Alano says when I stay quiet.

Margie slaps her chest, like her heart is broken. "Aw, you poor thing. If you'd like to record a message for her, I can have it uploaded into the pendant so she hears your voice every time she opens it. Think of it like those recordable greeting cards, which we have too if you prefer," she says, turning around to her card section.

"The pendant is good, thanks," I say.

"Fill this out for me, sweetie," Margie requests, handing me a form.

The Present-Time Gift Shop form asks for my personal information, the name I want engraved on the presents ("Pazito" for Mom's pendant, "Paz-Man" for Rolando's watch, "Paz" for the new kid's hourglass), and the address for the recipients (everything is going to my house, which Mom hopefully doesn't find haunted when I'm dead). Then I'm given one of those white boxes, which is actually a voice recorder for me to use now and for Present-Time staff to later transfer into each object.

"I'll give you some privacy," Margie says, making her way to the front of the store.

"Same," Alano says, going to the corner with the grandfather clocks.

I'm left alone with the objects and voice recorders. My chest is tightening, and I want a cigarette so bad to relax, but I've gotta get through this. I start with the new kid, that'll be easiest. "Hey, it's your big brother, Paz. Play Othello with Mom.

Let her win whenever she's sad. She deserves to smile. I love you," I say, unable to picture this stranger-sibling, but believing I love them anyway. I set the first recorder down by the hourglass.

I'm working up the strength for Mom's message, so I do Rolando's next. "Hey, Rolando, it's Paz-Man. Keep Mom alive and make her happy. If you don't, I'll haunt you like those Pac-Man ghosts. I love you." I set the second recorder down by the watch, knowing that Rolando will get a kick out of me haunting him even though he doesn't believe in ghosts.

Now it's time for Mom's message, but instead of picking up the recorder, I grab the pendant, thinking about which picture I can use to make it special and what I can say to give Mom the will to keep living. She loves this picture of me as a kid where I was in a blue blazer and white shorts, but maybe she wants to see me as I am now, as old as I'm ever gonna be. Maybe in my recording I should apologize for not being strong enough, or just tell her I love her over and over until the recorder cuts me off. Then I realize that no matter what I choose, this is the one present I'll never see Mom open.

I pick up the recorder, planning on just speaking from the heart—or I was before the sound of glass shattering sends my heart racing so fast it's like I'm running into Death's arms. The security alarm blares as Margie screams, but nothing stops a man with a skull mask from entering the shop with a steel bat. I duck behind the counter, wondering if this is how I'm about to die; I can only hope one swing to the head takes me out.

"TIME IS RUNNING OUT!" the man shouts. "DEATH TO DEATH-CAST!"

I'm bracing to die, but I look across the shop to find Alano fearing for his life.

This Death Guarder is gonna kill Alano.

ALANO

I thought I was fated to save Paz's life, but maybe I'm fated to die with him.

I'm hiding from the Death Guard raider, crouched behind this mahogany grandfather clock, my face pressed so close to the panel door that I can hear the faintest of ticks in between the security alarm, Margie outside shouting for help, and the blood rushing to my head. Through the reflection of another clock I watch the raider smashing the shop's timepieces with his bat while repeatedly calling for the death of Death-Cast. There's no way I'm getting out of this alive.

Thankfully I already left that time capsule for my parents—

Oh no. The time capsule is connected to my Death-Cast identification number, meaning that since I've deactivated my account, it can't be triggered open. My parting messages and secret are going to the grave with me.

All at once, the clocks begin chiming, gonging, chirping, blaring, a cacophony of time that's louder than the Death-Cast call I should've been receiving tonight. The grandfather clock I'm leaning against is so loud and startling that I fall over, exposed. I get lucky because the raider is too busy pummeling the loudest grandfather clock. He's too big for me to fight, but I could sneak up and hit him with a mantel clock or that massive brick on the floor that has "DEATH-CAST IS UNNATURAL" written on it in chalk. That should give Paz and me enough time to escape and for the police to resolve this themselves.

By the fifth gong, I'm ready to move on the raider when I see Paz hiding against the edge of the counter, staring off into space. It's the same look from when I found him ready to kill himself on the Hollywood Sign. I don't trust Paz to not do something stupid, so I crouch-run to the counter and wave my hand over his eyes to get him to snap out of it. He looks at me.

"You okay?" I mouth.

There's a fury in Paz's eyes.

I need to be able to defend us. Behind the counter, there are extra light bulbs stored on a shelf that we could throw and Richard's wrapped present for his son that needs to be protected at all costs, but the tin toolbox under the cash register might be our best bet.

"Stay here," I whisper in his ear. My stitched-up wounds hurt as I crawl toward the toolbox. I'm nervous about making too much noise, so I time all my movements with the security alarm sequence—unlatching the toolbox, lifting the tray, grabbing the hammer and wrench for us to use on the raider.

Then I turn around to find that Paz has his own plan to save us: he's pulled out his gun.

PAZ

2:02 a.m.

My gun is loaded with three bullets.

The first for the Death Guarder.

The second for me.

The third for Alano to finish me off if I don't die.

Alano may have been right that we were fated to meet, but he was wrong about why. This isn't about getting me to live. It's about giving me a better death. Instead of just killing myself and becoming the Hollywood Sign Boy, I can take out this Death Guard son of a bitch too, and then Alano will live to tell the tale about how I saved his life. Who knows if saving the Death-Cast heir will finally get me called a hero or if I'll forever be remembered as a killer. Who cares. I won't be alive to see my name dragged online. I can only hope that my sacrifice makes Mom's life better.

I'm about to stand up and shoot the Death Guarder when Alano is suddenly in my face. He sets a wrench and hammer down on the floor. He's gotta know my gun is how he gets out of here alive. He leans in, his cheek pressed against mine, sweat on sweat, reminding me of the two times I've had sex, and how I feel more dead inside now than I did then.

"Don't do this," Alano whispers in my ear.

"I have to," I say out loud.

Alano pulls back in a panic, wincing as if the Death Guarder heard me, but all I hear is the sound of more discordant gongs and glass shattering. More noise. That's all these Death Guarders are good for, making noise. They run their mouths about how everyone should be pro-natural and scream for the end of Death-Cast. It's time to make this Death Guarder shut up.

I'm getting up, but Alano shoves me back down. He pins my shoulders against the counter as I try fighting free. I don't get why he's stopping me, I can put a bullet in this Death Guarder before he can hurt anyone.

Alano is tearing up, fear alive in his eyes, but he's no longer looking around, his gaze is locked on to me. He leans in, and I have this dumbass thought that he's about to kiss me during this life-or-death moment, but he moves past my face and his lips brush my ear.

"This is not who you are," he says, soft enough that it's for me and me only, but his words sit heavy in my chest, like catching someone I wanna trust in a lie.

"You don't know who I am," I cry.

"Please stay alive and tell me," Alano begs. He relaxes his grip on my shoulders, and his hands slowly slide down my body—my collarbone, my pounding heart, my rib cage—until his hands are wrapped around mine. He's trying to pry my fingers apart, but my grip on the gun is so tight that he's gonna have to use that wrench on me. "Give me the gun. I'll take care of you."

At first, I think Alano means that he'll shoot me, right here, right now. "No, just let me kill him, you'll be safe, just make sure I die, please—"

"No," Alano interrupts, pulling back so I see the tears sliding down his face. "If you have to die tonight, live longer so I know who I'm grieving."

For a moment, I swear I've died. It's like my brain and body have shut down. My hands relax open so Alano can take the gun, but I can't be dead because my heart and lungs are still pumping, keeping me alive longer for my Last Friend. Even with danger literally around the corner, Alano is still protecting my life, even above his own. He's seeing something in me, or not something, but everything. I thought I was catching him in a lie about him not knowing who I am when really I was the liar pretending to be nothing but a killer who deserves to die.

Heavy footsteps approach the counter, and glass shatters, raining onto us. This is the closest the Death Guarder has gotten to us. We have maybe a minute, but probably just seconds before we're discovered.

Alano stares at the gun in his hands, like he's trying to figure out if he has what it takes to protect us or if we're both about to die together.

I can't watch. I close my eyes, tears squeezing out as I imagine Mom and Rolando cradling their new baby. A happy life, like I never got to have. As destruction continues around me, I brace myself for death, knowing I'll find happiness there; I just hope happiness won't hurt too much.

Then I hear the sirens.

I feel heavy footsteps on the floor becoming lighter.

And I open my eyes to see Alano peeking over the counter.

"He's gone," Alano says, shaking glass out of his hair. He shoves the gun into my backpack, throws it over his shoulder, and stands up. "We need to go too."

I'm frozen. Is that it? We survived and now we're gonna keep living?

"Paz, come on, the cops can't find out we have a gun on us."

Just like when we were on top of the Hollywood Sign, I take Alano's hand. We run around the counter and through the shop that looks like it's been hit by a tornado with its flipped-over tables and glass sparkling on the floor. We jump over a disemboweled grandfather clock and run out the door, bumping right into Margie.

"Oh, you're both okay," Margie says, especially shocked to see me alive.

I'm still shocked too.

"We're okay, but we have to go," Alano says.

Margie points at the police car, a block away. "The police will need a statement—"

"He doesn't have time," Alano interrupts, holding up my hand. "Who knows how long the police will take to question him. Or worse."

The police might mistake me for the criminal. The criminal I would've been without Alano.

"Get out of here," Margie says with tears in her eyes, pushing us forward, giving us the present of time.

THE END DAY, WHETHER DEATH-CAST LIKES IT OR NOT

I don't feel innocent lying about my End Day or running away from the scene of the crime with a gun on us, but that doesn't stop us from returning to Hollywood Boulevard, where our feet pound the brass stars for blocks and blocks, my fingers locked around Alano's the entire time.

2:08 a.m.

After failing to catch his breath once we stop running, Alano finally lets go of my hand to use his inhaler. He's still standing there, but not being held on to makes me feel like I'm a balloon that's about to float away into the night sky. That thought is bullshit, and I know it. Not because I'm not a balloon, but because if I was, Alano would climb a building's fire escape and leap off the roof to catch me, even if I'm better off among the stars.

Once he's able to fully breathe, Alano pockets his inhaler and we walk off, farther and farther from his car. I don't know where he's taking me and if he even knows himself. He's asked me if I'm okay and doesn't push me when I don't answer. Other than that, we're both quiet, just keeping each other company. Every time we're crossing a street, there's an urge to be closer to him, maybe even reach for his hand again. If I told Alano that holding his hand made me feel secure, he'd give it to me in a heartbeat, but I can't give in, not when I'm so close to getting what I really want, and definitely not when I'm gonna need Alano to help me get it.

I check the time: 2:10. Forty minutes until I'm free to die.

Until Alano has to pop the balloon.

He sees me reading the time on my phone. "Any last thing you want to do?"

I don't answer.

"Do you want me to choose?" he asks.

I don't answer.

"Are you hungry?" he asks.

I don't answer.

I'm not trying to be difficult, and Alano must know this, because he's not pushing me to open up and be honest. That incident at Present-Time was intense and there's a lot I'm processing in my head about who I really am and what I really want. I bet Alano is already planning on activating Death-Cast again after all these close calls.

I follow Alano down some restaurant's drive-through and I realize he's brought me to the Hollywood DIEner, where the staff dress up as famous dead characters. I've never been before, but considering I started the night on top of the Hollywood Sign and then did the Hollywood Walk of Fame, the Hollywood DIEner feels like the perfect place to end my night and life.

The host is dressed like Death if Death bought his robes at CVS during Halloween season. "Welcome to the Hollywood DIEner, mortals," he says in some silly spooky voice. "If you do not wish to know the fates of certain famous souls floating around tonight, be sure to peruse my Scroll of Spoiled Souls before DIE-ning with us."

The scroll being pinned to a clipboard feels like bigger bullshit than the costume, but I read it anyway:

The Scroll of Spoiled Souls

Tonight's production will contain spoilers for the following movies:

Star Wars: Episode VI—Return of the Jedi (1983)

The Lion King (1994)

Armageddon (1998)

Avengers: Endgame (2019)

"We're good to dine," Alano says. He doesn't check with me, but there's no reason I should care about spoilers for any movie if I'm trying to kill myself.

Death hands us menus. "Go dig your own graves, a soul will haunt you very soon."

"Huh?"

Death drops the accent. "Sit wherever you like. A server will be right with you."

The dining area is lowly lit with plastic candelabras at every table. We pass a waiter who looks more like the Cowardly Lion than Mufasa as we get a booth in the back, close to the kitchen, where Iron Man comes out and delivers ice cream sundaes to a young boy and an older man. I'm guessing one of them has to be a Decker, there's no other reason you have a kid out this late unless someone is dying. I don't wanna think about which one is the Decker, but I can't stop my brain from obsessing over the intrusive thought that I hope it's the kid so he can be spared the misery of growing up in this terrible world where people kill for no good reason and people hate you when you kill for good reason.

"Anything look good to you?" Alano asks, reading his menu.

The top of the menu says "FOOD TO DIE FOR" but there's an all-you-can-eat special for Deckers at the bottom that says "FOOD BEFORE YOU DIE." There's also the disclaimer that Deckers must disclose all allergies and sign a waiver before being served any food.

Darth Vader approaches our table with a notepad. "The Force is strong with this table." He bows his head at Alano. "I am *not* your father, but I admire your father's work. You may share your order with me for I am your . . . waiter."

There's no way in hell I would ever be desperate enough to act that I'd work here.

"Impossible burger, sweet potato fries, and a Coke, please," Alano orders.

"Coke, not Pepsi? You belong to the Dark Side," Darth Vader says, writing down the order. "You?"

I don't answer and slide the menu away.

"I find your lack of appetite disturbing," Darth Vader says.

Alano hands Darth Vader our menus. "Sorry, Vader, my friend here is a Decker."

I can't see his eyes behind the helmet, but Darth Vader is definitely staring at me. "Sorry you will be lost," he says in his regular voice, breaking character. There's a time and a place for playing dead in the Hollywood DIEner apparently. Darth Vader leaves that waiver and a pen on the table before vanishing into the kitchen to get Alano's food ready.

Alano is looking around the restaurant when he says, "Halloween 2017. That's when the Hollywood DIEner opened. My family was invited to the grand opening, but my father thought it was too gimmicky. I was relieved we didn't have to go. Halloween is my favorite holiday. I can put on a mask and have a regular night with my best friends. Anyway, it was our first Halloween dressing up together, and we did a group costume. I was Spider-Man and Rio and Ariana were Venom and Black Cat. I even brought my dog, Bucky, and dressed him up with spider legs—"

"I was gonna kill that Death Guarder," I finally say, like I've been holding my breath forever, and it feels like coming out to my mom, who had already suspected I was gay.

Alano might already know this about me, but for all the shit he remembers, he seems to have forgotten this.

"Tonight is supposed to be my End Day, not yours. I would've killed that man to save you, but you stopped me. Do you have a death wish too?"

"No, I don't have a death wish. If anything, I have a life wish—life wishes for the both of us," Alano says. His brown and green eyes watch me as I vibrate in anger. "There are two reasons I stopped you from killing that raider. The first is not wanting to give the Death Guard a martyr."

"Martyr? But he was no one," I say.

"Martyrdom would've made him someone. A household name. The Death Guard lies enough, but if they could point to a martyr that was undeniably killed by one of us—the Death-Cast heir or a boy known for killing a man who never even signed up for Death-Cast—it could threaten the election this fall." Alano takes a deep breath and softly adds, "Maybe even Death-Cast forever."

I'm about to ask how one death can have that much power when I remember the unforgettable bloodstain on my life. One death can change someone's life. The death of a martyr can change everyone's lives. I'm so tainted that I can't even save people right. I would've killed that Death Guarder and then shot myself, thinking I was dying a hero, but really I would've ruined the world that Mom and Rolando will be raising their kid in.

"What's the other reason you didn't let me kill him?" I ask. I wait to hear why I'm an even bigger fuckup than I realize.

Alano eyes my hands from across the table. "For as long as you live, even if you die soon, I don't want you to get any more blood on your hands."

I reflect on him holding my gun. "What about your hands?"

Alano tenses. "What about them?"

"Were you gonna shoot him?"

"If I had to, but I wouldn't shoot to kill."

"See, you're not a killer."

"I'm one because of you," Alano says sadly. He stares at the ceiling, unable to face me. "Or I will be soon."

"Don't make me feel guilty for honoring your deal. I gave you hours to turn my life around, but I still wanna die," I say, ready to break down and cry. I definitely have to look away from Alano because I can't watch his eyes keep filling with tears. "Look, you might not even need to kill me. Maybe I'll get it right. But if I don't, just lie about shooting me in self-defense or some shit like that. No one would doubt you. My legacy is killing."

I hate this world and everyone in it. Except Mom and Rolando. The new kid.

And Alano.

I definitely hate Darth Vader as he returns to our table with a tray of food and soda. "I'm sorry, but I need that waiver signed before setting this down," he says in his regular voice. "Restaurant policy."

I'm about to sign the waiver so Alano can get his food when he stops me.

"We don't need it," Alano says, waving Darth Vader anyway. "You can eat, I don't care."

"We have twenty minutes before we're supposed to leave. I know how we're spending this time."

"How?"

Alano flips the waiver over where it's blank on the back. "Write the obituary you expect to be published after you die tonight."

"What, why—"

"Time is ticking, Paz." Alano hands me the pen. "Write."

271

ALANO
2:30 a.m.

I might not be able to save Paz.

I'm tempted to betray my promise and inform a server to call the police to detain Paz. I don't want to hurt or kill Paz any more than I want Paz to hurt or kill himself, but there's only twenty minutes left before he's held up his end of the deal and he'll be expecting me to do the same. I won't have to if he's sent to a medical facility to receive the proper help. I obviously didn't get far into that psychology book, but in the first few pages, Dr. Glasgow speaks about the importance of not betraying the trust of a suicidal person. If I betray Paz's trust, then he'll be alive, but what kind of life will he have if he only sees this world as one filled with liars and traitors?

This exercise has to work.

Paz is writing furiously, angry tears falling over the obituary before he slides it across the table. "There. That's what some asshole is gonna write about me."

I pick up the obituary and rip it in half without reading a single word.

"What the hell?"

"I don't care what strangers will say about you," I say, hailing down an astronaut and getting another waiver. I flip that one to the back. "Here."

"You want me to write my own?" Paz asks.

It's not uncommon for Deckers to write their own obituaries so they can control what's published about them, but I want Paz to go deeper. "I want you to write the obituary that you would love for the world to read about you if you live to be one hundred."

"One hundred?!"

I hand Paz the pen. "If you're not going to live it, I'd love to know what your dream life could've looked like."

PAZ
2:34 a.m.

Writing the obituary for my dream life is more heartbreaking than writing my suicide note.

In my first obituary, I wrote about how I'll be remembered more for picking up a gun instead of holding a wand, how I was proven innocent and still treated like a threat, how I'm leaving behind the mom and stepdad everyone was mad at me for saving, how they have a new kid on the way who will be better than me, and how police are still investigating the suicide, but let's face it, once a killer, always a killer, and everyone will be happy that I only killed myself this time.

Now I'm being challenged to imagine a future where everything went right for me, and every line feels like a lie, but the more I write, the more I wish it was true.

I slide over the tear stained page when I'm done.

Alano hands it back. "Read it to me."

It feels stupid, but I read my obituary: "'On June 21, 2101, I finally received my Death-Cast call on my one hundredth birthday. My life used to be hell, but I ended up having one hell of a life. I've loved acting since I was a kid, but my career slowed down after I killed Dad on the first End Day to save

Mom and Rolando. The public mistreated me for years, but it was Hollywood that derailed my destiny when I wasn't cast in Orion Pagan's film *Golden Heart* because producers viewed me as a box office risk. Guess what? I didn't give up. I kept auditioning and auditioning, and I got cast in a mega-hit franchise that turned me into a box office hit.'" Yeah, that's petty, but I would love the chance to flip off Hollywood. "'Later, when I was in my thirties, I wrote a film about my childhood trauma called *The No-Plan End Day* where I won an Oscar after my heartbreaking but healing performance as my dad. And in my fifties, I was honored with a star on the Hollywood Walk of Fame.'"

Alano's sniffles distract me, but he urges me to keep going. It's getting harder and harder as I keep imagining how vindicating and fulfilling this future would be.

"'On my deathbed, I'm surrounded by my loved ones, including my husband, who I never harmed and who kept me safe from myself; my children, who grew up in a house without a gun; my grandchildren, who I still can't believe exist even after all this time; my younger sibling, who reminds me so much of Mom and Rolando, who I still miss every day; and my Last Friend, Alano Rosa, who encouraged me to live when I was desperate to die,'" I say, full-on crying.

This obituary feels too real, like I got cast in this role as Old Paz and am now filming my last scene. I finish with my final lines.

"'I smiled when Death-Cast called, but not because I was

free from all the pain but for the peace I was named for, and the peace I finally found with my long life.'"

I'm inconsolable after imagining my dream job, dream family, dream life, and even dream death.

"I'd love to meet one-hundred-year-old Paz," Alano says, tears flowing down his face too. "Would you like to become him?"

I want that life as badly as I've wanted a Death-Cast call.

I check the time on my phone: 2:49. One minute until we're supposed to put me out of my misery. And my misery is still here, beating me down, telling me that I will never act again, I will never fall in love, I will never be happy. That I'm in for a life of pain and need to get out while I can.

"That obituary is a fantasy. I'll never be Happy Paz," I cry.

Alano scoots closer to me in the booth, taking my hands in his. "But you want to be. Maybe it won't be as easy as writing it down on a piece of paper, but it won't be impossible. I'm here to help you become your happiest self."

I watch the time change. "Look, it's two fifty; it's time to go, just help me die," I beg, like a tired kid whining for something that'll make him feel better until he can rest.

"Hold on, stop and think about this—"

"No!" I shout, yanking my hands out of his.

Everyone's staring at us. It's stupid to feel embarrassed before I'm about to die, but I do. I only like when Alano is gazing at me, not these strangers whispering under their breaths like they've figured out who we are. What am I saying, they probably only know Alano. Even if I wasn't blond and more recognizable with my dark hair, I fall somewhere between a nobody who never actually rose to fame to win an Oscar and someone only famous for killing his dad. I'm tired of thinking these thoughts and feeling these feelings. I'm tempted to whip out my gun and scar all these people by blowing my fucking brains out right here, right now, but instead I grab my backpack and run for the door, getting the hell out of here to go die my way.

It's a bad sign that Death-Cast hasn't called yet, but there's still time to die.

ALANO

2:51 a.m.

If I stay, I won't be responsible for Paz's suicide, but if I go, I might be charged with his homicide.

No, I don't accept that this ends with Paz's death.

It's a good sign that Death-Cast hasn't called yet. It means there's still time to save him.

I chase Paz down the drive-through, and he turns a corner, vanishing. I run as fast as I can, the stitches in my abdomen threatening to burst open as I go into an alley that reeks of garbage and piss. There's a shadowy silhouette very familiar to the one I found earlier tonight on top of the Hollywood Sign.

A boy with a gun to his head.

PAZ

2:54 a.m.

This might not be the Hollywood Sign, but I'm gonna die in Hollywood.

Growing up, I swore every inch of Hollywood would be glamorous, but this city is as covered in makeup and injections and expensive dresses as the stars who benefit from it. There's the high rent that no one can afford, but if you don't sacrifice everything to make it work, you're told you don't wanna be here enough. There are celebrity names on brass stars to distract you from the homeless person on the curb asking for help. There are all the unspeakable favors to make your dreams come true. And there are doors to dreams that can never be reopened once shut, no matter what you do, no matter what you believe.

My gun is pressed to my head, and I'm ready to die in this dream-killing city.

"Paz, please don't do it," Alano says, slowly approaching.

I back up. "I'm sorry," I say, switching the safety off.

One pull of the trigger and it will be over, but my finger is frozen.

"Give me the gun," Alano says, his hand reaching out. "I'll do it."

"No you won't, you're gonna run away or something."

"You honored your word, and I'll honor mine," Alano says, turning up to the stars.

Does he still think we were fated to meet? Has he accepted he's meant to kill me?

Alano slowly approaches, and I don't move away. He's close enough that I see the pain in his eyes, the sweat running down from his forehead to his lips. I can feel the many breaths he's still catching and the brushing of his fingers as he takes my gun for the second time tonight. He doesn't run away. He takes one step back and puts the gun between my eyes. My heart is racing so fast it might give up before the bullet can leave the chamber.

"Close your eyes," Alano whispers.

I take one last look at Alano before closing my eyes. I stare into the darkness and wait for that to vanish too.

Any moment now I'll be dead, maybe even this moment, or this one.

"I'm proud of you for choosing your life tonight," Alano says.

I don't open my eyes, I just listen to his voice, wondering if he's telling me a story to make me feel less alone, like Mom would when putting me to bed.

"You not only saved your life when you climbed down that Hollywood Sign, but you protected your life when you relinquished that gun and didn't kill that Death Guarder. You could've ruined everything, but you didn't because you're not a killer at heart."

I begin to wonder if he's eulogizing me since I'll never get a funeral.

"After hearing your beautiful obituary, I have to beg one last time for you to choose life." His voice cracks as he fights to get his last words out. "Don't make me stand over your body tonight when I can be at your bedside eighty years from now."

I can't believe a stranger wants me alive this badly, that he sees someone that's worth being alive, but it releases lifelong tension in my body.

I don't know what time it is, if it's too late for me to die today, if I even have the choice to survive, but I don't wanna know. I just need to know that tonight, Alano's desperation to see me in the future is inspiring me to choose life.

I open my eyes, my vision still crossed because of the gun until I grab it. Alano doesn't let go. "It's okay," I say, slowly taking the gun away, switching on the safety, and setting it down on the ground. "I'm okay." That's the best way to describe myself. I'm nowhere near happy, but more important, I'm nowhere near hopeless.

Alano breathes out all the air in the world and clutches his heart and falls to his knees. I swear he's dying until he lets out the happiest sob. "Oh my— Ugh! I want to thank God or someone, but I'm not religious. I really thought you . . . that I was going to have to . . ."

Now that the gun is on the ground, I can't believe how much Alano and I have been through tonight with that damn thing. I also can't believe that he was willing to go through on his crazy promise.

I kneel down and squeeze his shoulder. "I'm sorry I put you through that."

"Better this than the alternative."

I picture Alano standing over my body. Then I picture both of us old. "Look, I'm not sold on this faraway future, but I wanna try . . . I'm gonna try."

"All you have to do is take it one day at a time. Eventually you'll get there."

"And you'll help me?" I quietly ask.

I don't tell him that I can't picture living without him.

His help, I mean.

"I'm all yours," Alano says, which doesn't slow my heart down at all. "Anything to make the life you wrote in your obituary a reality. I know where we should start."

ALANO
3:42 a.m.

Saving Paz makes me feel as if I've broken a curse that's been plaguing me, one where I send the grim reaper to people's doors. Maybe that was inevitable as long as I was devoting my life to Death-Cast.

The entire time we're driving to Echo Park, I'm still in disbelief that Paz is alive. He's sitting shotgun, mostly staring out the window. I don't force him to speak. I think he's still processing that he's alive too.

I park the car a couple blocks away from a homeless encampment. Death-Cast has received a lot of criticism over the years for not being accessible to the unhoused community, but that will be corrected after Project Meucci is unveiled. I take note of this encampment to make sure it's on the radar of our director of product management before remembering that my position at Death-Cast is unclear. I haven't formally resigned yet, but my father might outright fire me once he discovers that I deactivated my account. That's a problem for later; I'm being present with Paz.

We walk down to a trail that's empty except for one jogger. The lake is dark and beautiful under the moonlight and there are swan boat rentals gently rocking by the dock, but that's not why we're here.

"Do you know about Edge-of-the-Deck?" Paz asks.

It's nice to hear his voice again, though it does make me sad that it's because he's talking about that platform for suicide survivors who tried proving Death-Cast wrong. "I'm familiar. Are you on it?"

"I've never left comments or anything like that, but I was studying every survivor's failed suicide plan to build my own. I learned from everyone's X factors that prevented them from suicide, but there's no way I could've predicted that the Death-Cast heir would appear out of nowhere like some guardian angel or superhero to save me. I doubt anyone would believe me if I shared that story on Edge-of-the-Deck, but I don't care. I know the truth and"—Paz keeps walking with his head hanging low, like he's unable to meet my eyes—"and the truth is that your parents are right. You really are a miracle, Alano."

After rocky moments with my best friends, it's beyond nice to have a stranger show me such profound appreciation. No, not a stranger. My new friend. "That means a lot," I say as we stop by the lake. "I needed to hear that."

Paz digs into his backpack and pulls out his gun. I'm not nervous. I trust him to do what we came here for. He empties the gun and the three bullets roll around in his hand.

"I'm sorry I pointed the gun at you," Paz says.

"Thanks for not shooting it," I say.

"Thanks for saving my life."

"I'm sorry I wasn't around sooner."

"You're here now."

"I'm here now."

I take the bullets and throw them into the lake like I'm skipping stones.

Paz is left with nothing but the gun. "It's not that scary now that it's empty."

"Please don't keep it as some twisted souvenir."

"Definitely not. I'm using that obituary as the compass for the life I want. That means no guns in my house ever again. I don't want my future kids repeating history, or having easy access to a gun the next time things suck."

Paz throws the gun into the lake.

I'm proud of how hard Paz has just made things for the grim reaper.

"How do you feel?" I ask as we walk back toward the car.

"Safe from myself. How are you feeling?"

"Proud of you."

"No, I mean about not knowing your fate."

It's well after 3:00 a.m., which means that while we know Paz isn't dying today, there is still no indication whether I will. The adrenaline of tonight's intensity is certainly fading now that we've gotten rid of the gun and I'm able to look more inward. "It's an adjustment after growing up with that security blanket Death-Cast provides. I have to keep reminding myself that something bad could happen at any moment. I also don't want to be ruled by that fear any more than I wanted to be ruled by Death-Cast, so I'm focusing on living my life instead."

"You make that sound so freeing. Maybe I should quit Death-Cast too," Paz says.

That thought concerns me. Paz is a frequent visitor on Edge-of-the-Deck who has planned on killing himself three times already without a Death-Cast alert. "It's ultimately your life, but I'd like you to really give it some thought. You're feeling safe from yourself tonight because you know you can't kill yourself. I worry about you becoming a greater threat without Death-Cast holding you back."

Paz nods. "Yeah, you're probably right." He sounds bummed.

"I hope one day you feel healthy enough to quit Death-Cast if that's what you still want."

"And I hope quitting Death-Cast is everything you want it to be."

I do too. Truly.

PAZ

4:13 a.m.

"Paz, wake up."

For a moment, I wonder if I've dreamt everything, like I fell while climbing up the Hollywood Sign and got knocked out, but I open my eyes to find Alano Rosa behind the driver's seat and my house outside the window. Everything really happened.

"Sorry," I say, my eyes still fluttering. "How long was I asleep?"

"Not long. Twenty minutes, but it's after four. You should go to bed."

"Okay, yeah." I take off my seat belt, but I don't leave. I'm scared of what happens the next time I wake up and Alano isn't there. "When do you go back to New York?"

"I think Wednesday morning. We have to be back for our Decade Gala on Thursday."

Today is Friday—no, it's after midnight, so Saturday. He leaves in four days. It already doesn't feel like enough time. But he's here now and there's something I wanna ask, but I'm not sure how I'll live with myself if he rejects me.

"I wish I could read your mind," Alano says, leaning against his headrest.

"No, you don't. It's really sad and scary up in here."

"I still want to know what you're thinking. That hasn't changed because our deal is done."

I can't look him in those eyes when I ask, "Do you wanna hang out later today?"

"I really do," Alano says, making me so damn happy. "But—"

"It's all good," I say, not selling that line at all. I open the car door when he grabs my shoulder.

"But I have to speak with my parents in the afternoon about my decision to deactivate Death-Cast and figure out what that means for the rest of my life," Alano finishes. "I'm free in the evening, though. Want to hang out then?"

I'm so embarrassed at how quick I was to judge that I can't even face him.

"Paz? Please look at me," he softly says.

I turn to find a grin on his tired face.

"I meant it when I said I'm going to be there for you."

Knowing I'll see Alano later makes waking up less scary, but I still can't reach that same happy high I was on before, it's like I've been blocked off.

"I have a mental disorder," I spit out, half hoping Alano won't be scared away, half sabotaging to scare Alano away. "Border-line personality disorder. I only found out yesterday afternoon. I get these mood swings and shit like that, but you probably already know everything about it."

"I'm actually not all that familiar with borderline personality disorder, but thank you for telling me."

I start taking deep breaths, hyperventilating, and I'm so pissed at my brain for messing with me. "I'm not trying to pressure you to hang out with me, I know how hard it is. I actually have to live with myself, and yeah, my life sucks."

Alano is quiet. He's probably regretting not letting me run out of the car just now or even helping me down the Hollywood Sign because I'm too much to deal with. But that's my brain talking for him because Alano actually says, "I would've found myself trying to make today my End Day too if I went through everything you did, but we're both alive and we're committed to living. In fact . . ." He reaches over my knees and opens the glove compartment, fishing around for a black marker. "Let's make this official with a contract." Alano signs his name on his bandage. He offers me the marker. "We can heal together. No more trying to live our End Days. Let's promise to live our Begin Days."

Very early on in therapy, Raquel mentioned the importance of reframing negative attitudes in our heads. She recommended that I always find the positive, and if it felt hard, all I had to do was flip how I was feeling. So instead of saying "I wanna give up on life" I could reframe that as "I wanna live." That felt like a cheap trick, but I only had to act like I was doing it one hour every week. Tonight I'm promising to actually commit to life, in and out of therapy, with or without Alano.

My Not-End Days will be my Begin Days.

I take the marker, holding Alano's bandaged arm as I gently sign my name next to his.

"To beginnings," Alano says.

"To beginnings," I say.

I like seeing our signatures together.

"What's your number?" Alano asks.

"Seven-one-eight-two-four-five . . ." I stop because he's just staring at me. "Aren't you gonna write it down?"

"Phone numbers are easy. I'll remember," he says.

I tell him my number, and Alano immediately repeats it back. He takes my phone and types in his number. "Just in case."

I can't believe I just exchanged phone numbers with Alano Rosa, or that we've created a contract to heal together, or anything about this night.

"I'm excited to see you later," Alano says.

"You too."

This world I'm entering feels new, uncharted. It's one where I won't find myself chasing Death and will now outrun him. That's all thanks to Alano, who has brought me here so I can reach for the stars and stop and smell the roses and other shit like that. But I don't know how to trust myself in this new world when I'm dragging my old world with me, like my borderline personality disorder that can make me fall hard and fast for someone or just make me think that I am. I'm feeling so much tonight, but I don't know how to tell what's real. Like how looking at Alano makes me like breathing. How Alano is so beautiful that I wanna paint his portrait and wear it on a T-shirt. How I wanna reach for Alano-shaped stars and smell Alano-shaped roses. How when I say good night I wanna kiss him like I'm dying. And how much I miss him already when he drives off and how happy I'm gonna be when I see him again.

How do I know if any of that is real?

I don't know, but I now have time and Begin Days to figure that out.

ALANO

4:38 a.m.

Why did fate wait so long to bring Paz and me together?

We're the same age. We grew up in New York. I know for a fact that we were supposed to meet on August 15, 2010, because my father wanted to apologize for Death-Cast's error in person like he had other affected families, but Gloria Medina canceled at the last minute because she didn't think it was the right time and she never rescheduled. The closest Paz and I have been around each other before tonight was during his trial. My mother originally didn't want me to go, but I overheard my father saying that it was good for Death-Cast's case to appear as a family. All I wanted to do was help out Paz, who looked so scared on the stand, just like he was tonight on top of the Hollywood Sign.

The stories you hear about End Days are phenomenal. Deckers fall in love before dying. Extraordinary sacrifices are made so others can live. The stories that have always moved me the most are the ones where people have spent their lives orbiting each other, only to finally connect at the end thanks to Death-Cast. It reminds me that for all the harm that's been caused by the company, so much beauty was created too.

Tonight was not the end of Paz's story. It's the start of a new chapter for him—for us.

I'm proud of Paz for choosing to live and myself for helping him get there. Though if he had called on me to kill him, I would've done it, as unfortunate as it would've been.

If people are this terrible to Paz for killing one person, what would they do when they discover I have far more blood on my hands?

PART THREE

The Begin Days

The beginning is always today.

—*Mary Shelley*

PAZ

12:00 p.m.

Twelve hours ago I tried making today my End Day. Now I'm waking up to my first Begin Day.

I turn off my alarm, which has been going off every ten minutes for the past hour. I'm still groggy, and my phone's brightness is hurting my eyes but lights me up inside when I read a message from Alano: To beginnings, he texted at 5:02 a.m. I'm tempted to reply with an entire text block of smiley faces, but I play it cool. To beginnings 😊, I text.

As I begin my day, I'm still surprised that I'm alive. I wasn't supposed to sleep here last night or make my bed this morning or open my curtains to bask in the sunlight. I'm supposed to be dead at the bottom of the Hollywood Sign; I wonder if my body would've been discovered yet.

The moment I open my bedroom door, Mom calls me into the living room, where she's on the couch with Rolando, watching the news.

"Morning," I say.

"It's your morning, but our afternoon," Mom says, sipping her herbal tea.

"Then good afternoon," I correct with a smile. "How are you feeling?"

"Still nauseous, but at least we know why." Mom rests a hand on her stomach.

I'm gonna be alive one day to feel the baby kicking. To hold the baby when they're born. To look after them as they grow up. And everything else that leads up to the new kid becoming an old-but-younger-than-me adult at my bedside when I die at a hundred.

"Glo and I were wondering something," Rolando says seriously. He's definitely about to ask what I was doing out so late. "What is the point of an alarm if you are going to ignore it for an hour?"

I laugh, not even just laughing it off, but actually laugh. "I just needed more time to get it together," I say.

"Are you okay?" Mom asks. It's funny how she's more suspicious of me when I'm kinda happy versus when I'm performing happiness.

I tell the truth. "I'm good."

"Were you up late?"

Here's where I can fully lie about being home all night and bingeing some new show, but I wanna tell the truth—some version of the truth, at least. I just can't open up about my suicide attempt without causing a panic. "I was hanging out with someone last night."

Rolando turns away from a commercial about a new lawn mower. "Who?"

I'm torn between whether I should say, but I can't help myself, it's like saying his name is a serotonin rush. "Alano Rosa."

They're both quiet. It's funny watching them process this.

Mom's eyes widen. "Alano Rosa? You were hanging out with Alano Rosa? H-h-how? Why?"

This is where I gotta get creative. "We met online," I lie.

"Online? Like a dating app?" Mom asks.

I've been out to her and Rolando forever, but apart from a couple crushes during freshman year, I haven't really had a chance to talk about any real prospects. "We were just hanging out, but he's only in town for a few days, so we're seeing each other again tonight."

I can't wait. I already wanna fast-forward through this entire day.

"His father is a piece of work," Rolando says, looking like he wants to spit on the floor. "Alano have a better head on his shoulders?"

"Yeah," I say, while thinking about Alano's beautiful head—his long lashes that try but thankfully fail to hide his striking green eye and brown eye, his thick brows that fan out in the inner corners, his bow-shaped lips that form the most breathtaking smile, and his brain that knows everything, including how to save someone who is seconds away from killing himself. And then I think about the body his head is resting on.

"Pazito?" Mom calls me back.

I apologize through a smile.

"You're old enough to make your own choices, but I still wish you'd told us you were leaving the house that late."

"Yeah, sorry."

"Did you have a fun time?"

"Rough start, but we got somewhere good."

"What did you do?"

Then, a news report comes on that might answer that question for me. The anchorwoman is speaking about Present-Time's break-in last night. Panic swallows my happiness like a black hole. I should distract from the news, but I'm frozen. My focus has only led to Rolando increasing the volume, and they're about to clearly hear my and Alano's names.

A grainy picture of the Death Guarder attacking a grandfather clock appears alongside the anchorwoman.

"The suspect can be seen wearing a skull mask, identical to the ones worn by many violent offenders on the first End Day. A brick with 'Death-Cast Is Unnatural' was found on the crime scene, which police have collected for their investigation. Death-Cast has issued a statement cautioning everyone to be extra mindful around Decker-friendly businesses, especially after the Death Guard attack on Alano Rosa in New York two nights ago. The Present-Time shopkeeper, Margaret Hunt, says no one was harmed last night, but most of her property has sadly been damaged."

I'm relieved that Alano's name has come up only as a past incident and not because we were in the shop when this all went down, but Present-Time might still bite us in the ass. Me especially. If there's footage of the Death Guarder, there will be some of us too. Including me with my gun. And what about the presents I was preparing for my family? Are they still being sent here? I never even got to pay for the gifts. Maybe they got destroyed. I don't know, but if I go in person, the shopkeeper is gonna swear I'm a ghost.

"Paz." Rolando snaps his fingers. "You okay?"

There's no hiding my panic behind some fake smile, they'll see through me. "Scary times."

"How is Alano?" Mom asks.

I'm thrown off at first, but she's only asking about the assassination attempt. The problem is we spent so much time talking about me that I realize I don't know that much about him. It makes me feel stupid or even straight-up wrong over everything I'm feeling for him, like it's nothing but physical attraction or my BPD warping my sense of reality.

"He's fine, just bandaged up," I say. I remind myself that I signed his arm bandage to seal a promise that I would keep beginning, even when it's hard, even when I'm sinking into depressive holes like now.

"That's good to hear he's okay," Mom says. She gets up from the couch.

"Mom, sit. What do you need?"

"It's what you need." Mom goes into her bedroom and returns with my Prozac bottle. "How are you feeling? One pill, two pills, three pills?"

"Is that a new Dr. Seuss book?" Rolando asks.

Mom fights back her laugh. "We don't joke about mental health."

"Sorry, Paz," Rolando says.

"Don't be, it's funny."

The pills rattle around the bottle. There's a part of me that doesn't want any because I feel better than usual, but I wanna be good and functioning to enjoy my time with Alano, to get to know him better without spiraling over my trauma.

"I'll take two."

I swallow them down with a smile.

And then I give Mom the hug I didn't get to give her last night. "I love you, Mom."

"I love you too, Pazito."

This Begin Day is off to a great start, but it's only gonna get better once I see Alano.

ALANO

"You did what?!"

This isn't the first time my father has shouted at me today.

Before leaving for Death-Cast last night, Pa had gone into my room to check on me but found only Bucky in bed. He personally searched the mansion's grounds, but couldn't find me in the home theater or spa or by the pool. He called my phone and held on to hope that it was only off because I'd forgotten to charge it. Then he went into the garage to discover my car was missing. That's when security reviewed the cameras to find me driving away and not returning home until after five, when police were waiting for me.

At first I thought the police were there to aid in any search, but it was actually because the LAPD recognized me—and only me—on top of the Hollywood Sign. I spent the morning speaking with the officers, cooperating with their investigation in every way except revealing the identity of the "blond boy with the gun." All I said was I stumbled on a troubled boy and managed to talk him down safely and that he's now alive. I had the privilege of getting away with a warning because I'm my father's son. Death-Cast has reduced nonfatal police shootings by 72 percent since 2010, now that officers can confidently work to de-escalate situations without fear of being killed. America is still behind other countries on this front, but President Page has highlighted this progress in his reelection campaign. If Paz and I didn't escape Present-Time when we did we could have threatened that statistic.

Once the police left at 7:10 a.m., I was so exhausted that I could barely keep my eyes open, but I snapped awake when my father called our bodyguards into the living room. He scolded them all for letting me out of their sight, but things tensed when he got in Agent Dane's face.

"Do you have some ulterior motive to get my son killed?"

"No, Mr. Rosa."

"Am I not paying you enough to protect my son?"

"You are, Mr. Rosa."

"Then why have you failed my son two nights in a row?"

"I wasn't aware that Mr. Alano left the premises."

"Your ignorance could have gotten him killed. I won't allow it again. You are fired," my father said.

Agent Dane could be stone-faced during many interactions, but he couldn't mask his shock here. "Sir?" He turned to my mother as if she were going to defend him. She remained quiet.

I wasn't. "This isn't his fault. Dane wanted to accompany me to the Wisdom Tree later in the week, but I snuck out."

My father snapped toward me. "And if you had died you would have paid the price with your life, but I am done paying him to keep you alive when he is so incompetent at his job."

"I'm alive, Pa! I would've been dead if Dane didn't stop the assassin."

"An assassin who should have never gotten as close as he did," my father said, turning to our head of security. "Ariel, escort Dane out of the mansion."

I tried protesting, but Dane accepted his fate, showing himself to the door before I could even apologize. Getting Andrea Donahue fired when she was actually guilty was bad enough, but it was a hundred times worse getting Dane fired all because I went rogue.

I refused to speak with my father again, even though he chased me down the hall to my bedroom, yelling outside my door until my mother forced him to give me space and let me rest. Despite how exhausted I was, my guilt made it hard to fall asleep. I just cuddled in bed with Bucky and cried over the cost of how saving one person's life got another fired.

I got three hours of sleep before I woke up from a nightmare where I was pouring gasoline over Dane Madden and set him alight. There was no going back to bed after that.

Now I'm seated at the dining table with my parents, eating lunch prepared by our private chef. I redeliver the news that I knew would cause another eruption.

"I deactivated Death-Cast last night," I repeat, keeping my tone even.

My father taps his ginger beer, practically willing Mezcal into it. He's on the verge of exploding again when he turns to my mother. "Naya, he is out of his mind, yes?"

"Do not speak of Alano as if he is not in this room," Ma says.

"I do not believe he is. No son of ours would do something so stupid."

I stop myself from shouting, wanting to rise above my father. "No son of yours gets to live his life as he pleases," I say.

Pa's eyes narrow. "How is it possible you are forgetting about the life you have?" He doesn't wait for an answer. "You sky-dived in Dubai. You climbed a frozen waterfall in Canada. You braved sharks in Australia. Those are some of your many ventures, all of your choosing, all of which we arranged on your behalf. If that is not letting you live your life, then what is?"

There's no way I can forget any of this. I conquered my fear of heights by jumping out of that plane over the Palm Islands in Dubai and climbing Helmcken Falls in Canada. Then I took on my childhood nightmare of being eaten by sharks by traveling to the Neptune Islands Conservation Park in Australia to swim with great white sharks. I was able to confidently do all of this thanks to Death-Cast, but I may never have that peace of mind again unless I reactivate my account.

"How do you not get it, Pa? All of that is not living. I was almost killed and had regrets on my deathbed."

My mother's brown eyes well with tears. "That may very well be the worst thing I've ever heard in my life," she says, reaching over to squeeze my hand. "How can we help change that?"

It's clear that my father is about ready to try to crush the glass in his hand, but he's biting his tongue to hear me out instead.

"I need independence to explore my life as I see fit. I'm tired of being treated like I'm a child who needs around-the-clock protection while also having to be a company man who must conquer every last expectation projected onto me as if I'm inheriting Death-Cast tomorrow."

Pa runs a hand through his graying hair, ready to rip it out. "You could not have chosen a worse time to act on these urges, Alano. It's bad enough that you are evading protection exactly one night after surviving an assassination attempt, but have you given thought to the severe ramifications around the world should anyone find out you deactivated Death-Cast?"

"I can't be expected to live my life by the bottom line of your company. The internet didn't collapse when Bill Gates forbade his children from using it and iPad sales didn't plummet when Steve Jobs banned the device in his own home. Your empire doesn't live and die by me," I say.

The hurt in my father's eyes swallows his anger for a moment. That moment is enough to haunt me. "If it helps, I don't plan on speaking about this openly with the public."

"Did you tell the mystery boy last night?" he asks.

My silence is loud.

"Reckless, absolutely reckless. What is stopping that stranger from selling this secret?"

I understand the concern after Andrea Donahue. "That's not who he is."

"You don't know him!" My father's fist slams on the table. "You seek to be treated like an adult, but you are behaving like a child. The politics at play are not a game. If this gets out, you do not get privacy. You become the face of our enemies' campaign for why our services must be so unnecessary and harmful that the heir himself has rejected his destiny. Your choice will single-handedly secure the presidency for Carson Dunst who will work tirelessly to undo everything I have built, everything I have built so that you may never suffer from the same heartbreaks your mother and I have known."

He gets up and begins walking away, which is probably for the best, but my father spins right back around. "Your life may not look as you desire and now your death will not fit our desires either. The unknowing of your death is a punishment to us and us alone and perhaps you do not care because you will not have an End Day to grieve yourself, but your death would haunt your mother and me for the rest of our lives." My father puts a hand on his heart. "All I want in this life is to never meet your ghost, mi hijo."

Then he walks away for good.

I sit here, thinking about how if this is how my father reacts to the news that I might die unexpectedly one day, he wouldn't be able to function if he knew that I tried killing myself. It has me thinking about what Paz said about his mother threatening suicide if he succeeded in his. I believe that my parents would try to live for each other, but the possibility of either of them attempting to take their own lives breaks my heart too.

"I'm being selfish," I admit.

My mother squeezes my hand. "So is your father, but everyone has the same goal of wanting the very best for you. He isn't ready to listen to you, but I am. I didn't fight to bring you into this world only for you to not love your life."

Her ability to always show me grace is why I came out to her first.

I talk about how difficult this past week has been between the tensions with Ariana, the trauma of my first herald shift, almost being assassinated outside my home, and managing to save a life last night simply because I was in the right place at the right time.

"I don't approve of you sneaking out, Alano, but you are correct that it is your right to leave the house as you wish and that if you had asked us for permission, we would've said no. Do you still have it in you to recognize why we are upset? Why we are having trust issues? You didn't deactivate Death-Cast and go to bed. You left the house without your bodyguard, trespassed a canyon, illegally climbed the Hollywood Sign, and hung out with an armed stranger. This doesn't instill trust in your choices and instead leaves me concerned about your mental well-being."

Her parenting has always been gentle and firm. I never want to fight back, and I'm always willing to listen to her say the hard thing.

"What do you mean about my mental well-being?" I ask, nervous.

My mother picks up on my nerves. "I've witnessed what vicarious trauma has done for many of our heralds and how distress has affected you in the past. I fear you're on the verge of a psychotic break."

I immediately have the urge to deny that a psychotic break is on the horizon as if that undoes my pleas for freedom before remembering psychosis runs on my father's side of the family. My grandfather had Alzheimer's disease, which caused him to lose his grip on reality in its later stages.

"It was devastating to see him that paranoid and unpredictable," my father had lamented.

It has affected him too, in ways he is opening up about in his memoir. All of that led to me researching everything I can, especially the likelihood of it passing down to me. If someone was actually diagnosing me with a psychotic break, they could argue that my fight for independence is nothing more than the result of not thinking logically, disruption of sleep, intense feelings, impulsivity, and a distorted view of reality. I want to resist this warning so bad, but it becomes harder to deny when I remember that psychotic breaks can be triggered by trauma and physical injuries, and that my own reality has been challenged many times over the years because of my brain.

"Okay." That's all I can say.

"Do you think that's a possibility?"

"People having psychotic breaks don't usually recognize when they're having one."

"How do you feel?"

"Powerless," I say. Also empathetic to Paz, who is struggling with his own diagnosis, which I was studying in bed before lunch today. "I quit Death-Cast to regain control of my life and now it's as if everything I have done was also out of my control. You would think my brain has given me enough trouble, but . . ." I choke on my words.

"You're brilliant, Alano, but you're not untouchable. We will always want to protect you, even when it feels overbearing. That has to mean protecting your sanity too. Your father and I will work together to lighten the load we have placed on you."

I breathe a sigh of relief. "Thanks, Ma."

"I'm still not happy about your night out, but all's well that ends well and you saving a boy's life and coming home alive yourself means this ended very well."

"The boy called me a miracle, like you do."

My mother smiles. "I'd like to know more about this boy," she says before digging back into her spicy rigatoni.

"He's had a hard life, which is why he's so strong today, but I believe he's going to be happy. He just needs some help."

"We all do," she says in between bites. "What's his name?"

I look at Paz's name signed alongside mine on my bandage. "Paz Dario."

She stares down like usual whenever she's trying to remember something, as if she will find the answer written before her. "Why do I know that name?" Then she snaps up. "That boy from the first trial."

"Who lost his father," I say.

"Who killed his father," she says, concerned. "That's whose life you saved?"

In the months leading up to the trial I overheard conversations between my parents and their lawyers. Everyone agreed

Paz was an innocent who'd killed his father in self-defense, but my parents were advised to focus on Death-Cast's successes since the first End Day's errors. Now I'm worried about Paz's character being judged by my mother just as strangers have his entire life.

"Yes, I saved Paz and I would do it again."

My mother picks up on my defensiveness. "I'm sorry. Of course I'm relieved that you saved Paz's life. I was just caught off guard and concerned that he might not be the best company for you."

"Paz isn't a threat. He only killed his father because he was nine and scared. He has more self-control now."

"Last night he was planning for self-destruction, Alano. If you're not careful, he'll destroy you too."

I don't like this slander. "Paz could've exacted revenge against Death-Cast, but he didn't."

"If you believe you are safe from Paz, then I trust you."

"I do. He even threw away the gun because he's committed to living. I'm going to help him."

"You have plans to see him again?"

"Tonight."

She squirms. "I will not get in the way of your seeing him because it sounds as if Paz needs your touch in his life, but . . ." She begins tearing up and squeezes my hand. "Guard your heart in case you cannot save this boy forever. You may be our miracle, but you are not a miracle worker."

My mother's word of advice feels more like a threat. I want

to believe in the Begin Days, I have to, for my sake and Paz's, but what happens if I don't guard my heart and Paz breaks our pact? What if psychosis is making me delusional into thinking I can save someone who may be destined to destroy himself? Why does that thought make me want to go up to the rooftop and stand on the ledge?

PAZ
4:12 p.m.

Later, when Alano asks how my first Begin Day has been, I'm gonna make him so proud.

First, I treated myself with a lot of love, even when I got undressed to shower and felt bad that my body didn't look like Alano's. I took a nice cool shower, never switching to the hot water that I use to burn myself. I cleansed and moisturized my face and lotioned myself from neck to toe. I applied petroleum jelly to the scars on my thighs to help them heal. I made a quinoa salad with toasted tofu and veggies. And when I was done caring for myself, the house was next. I not only cleaned my room, I mowed the backyard so Mom can have her garden again. I thought it would give her some peace during her pregnancy so she can read outside or plant seeds for more flowers that can grow with her. Last night the idea of tending to a mental garden felt exhausting, but there I was, getting my ass kicked by the very real sun for a very real garden that made my mom cry very real happy tears.

While Mom and Rolando are enjoying their iced teas in the backyard, I call Present-Time to tell Margie to cancel my order since I never died and am trying not to anytime soon, but the call goes straight to voice mail:

"Hi, you've reached Present-Time on Hollywood Boulevard. The shop will be closed for the next few days as we undergo repairs after tragic vandalism. For local Present-Time needs, please visit our locations in Malibu and Los Feliz. Thank you."

The call drops, so I can't even leave a message.

I'm exhausted after all that work and sun, so I lie down in my bed, itching to text Alano again, maybe send him a selfie so he can send one back until we see each other, but I'm trying to play it cool. That doesn't mean I can't go look at his face online.

I go on Instagram and find his verified profile— @AlanoRosa—and even though he has only thirty posts, he has 3.4 million followers. There are Scorpius Hawthorne cast members who were in all eight movies and don't even have half of Alano's following. I scroll through his most recent posts: Alano inside a museum gift shop while holding a print of a sunflower field painted by Van Gogh (caption: *Plant something. Paint something. Create something. Just make it say something.*); Alano's shadow interlocked with two others (caption: *A.A.R.: Alano + Ariana + Rio*); and Alano holding a beautiful rust-orange memorial urn at Urn Your Keep, a pottery studio and spiritual experience where those choosing cremation can craft the final resting place for their ashes (caption: *Knowing I'll live on in my own art after my End Day made this a true labor of love. EDITED TO ADD: Today is not my End Day! I decided to be proactive. I'm sorry to those I alarmed.*). I scroll through more posts, aching to ask Alano what it was like skydiving in Dubai and how he even heard about climbing frozen waterfalls because that's news to me and why he risked his life or at least limbs to swim with sharks.

Before I can go any further, I exit out of his profile. I don't wanna learn about Alano from @AlanoRosa. I want him to tell me about his life himself.

I can't hold off from texting him any longer:

What time do we begin tonight? 😁

ALANO
4:34 p.m.

I'm playing fetch with Bucky in the backyard when Paz texts me. He's asking what time we will begin tonight. Hearing from him is a much needed endorphin rush. I don't know when I'll see Paz yet, but I know no one will stop me. My father might try, but that's why my mother is currently speaking with him about my plans because I'm not interested in arguing over Paz's innocence. She's hoping—I am too—that she can talk some sense into my father so I can live the life I deserve without fracturing the family.

Bucky returns with the tennis ball, but he doesn't drop it. Ever since he was a puppy he's always wanted me to wrestle the ball out of his mouth before throwing it again. At least he's not making me chase him around as much in his old age. Between Bucky panting harder, my abdomen aching, and my nondominant arm tiring, I toss the ball as far as I can for one last throw.

I'm about to text Paz when Agent Andrade walks across the backyard. He must be coming to summon me to my father's office. I'm still sick and angry over Dane's firing. He ignored my calls, which is understandable. His livelihood has now suffered because I went rogue for my life. I don't think I would ever get away with anything like last night under Agent Andrade's watch.

Before becoming the head of security of Shield-Cast, Agent Ariel Andrade was a police officer who made nation-wide news after tracking down the creators of a snuff channel called Bangers where Deckers desperate enough to leave behind money for their loved ones killed themselves in unique ways for entertainment. The perverse viewers contributed to the daily jackpot, but only the Decker who was voted as going out with the biggest bang got to secure those fortunes while the others died in vain. (I hate to think about Paz signing up for that cruel competition if it still existed today.)

Two months into his investigation, Andrade's partner, Officer Remy Graham, received his End Day alert on July 4, 2017. Officer Graham bravely chose to work, seeing it as a sign that he and Andrade would work together one last time to put an end to Bangers on the very day that fireworks would be banging throughout the sky. The two followed a lead where traffic had built up on the Williamsburg Bridge because a competing Decker, Carmy Castellon, set up two cameras, installed a ramp for his motorcycle, and strapped fireworks to his chest. Graham tried stopping Carmy Castellon, only to get knocked off the bridge where he drowned. The Decker was awarded top points for his killing of a cop and his phenomenal timing as he flew off the bridge and detonated the fireworks, dying in a horrific explosion and securing the jackpot.

On Christmas Day, Andrade posed as a Decker and infiltrated

the competition, uncovering the source. My father always hated how Bangers exploited the power of Death-Cast, so right as Andrade was determining his next move after getting justice for Graham, he convinced Andrade to be his personal bodyguard and head up his new security force, Shield-Cast. He has served our family loyally since January 17, 2018.

"You have a guest, Mr. Alano," Agent Andrade says.

No one knows we're here. "Guest?"

"Mr. Rio Morales."

I almost drop my phone. "He's here? Now?"

Agent Andrade nods. "Yes, sir. He's out on the porch. Your parents are preparing to greet him too."

If I'm not fast, my father's greeting will quickly turn into banishing. I rush through the backyard and house with Agent Andrade and Bucky following. I get to the front door right as my parents step through it. I go outside, moving past my parents and Agent Chen to find Rio is actually here. Bucky shoots past me and runs straight to Rio.

"Hi," Rio says, petting him.

"Has he been searched?" Pa asks, shielding me.

"Yes, sir," Agent Chen says.

"Thoroughly," Rio says, tucking his Luigi shirt into his jeans. "Makes me miss Dane. Where is he?"

"Former Agent Madden no longer serves this family," Pa says.

"I'm guessing that's code for you fired him," Rio jokes.

"No one messes with my son," he says pointedly.

Ma asks, "What brings you here?"

"Unannounced," my father adds. He turns to me. "Uninvited too, correct?"

I reluctantly nod. "Can you cool it?"

Rio tears up as he notices my bandaged arm. I'm certain he's about to excuse himself for a walk so no one can see him cry, but he fights his way through those feelings. "Alano never said where he was, but I went to that creepy Twitter account that tracks your private jet. Here I am." His neck is craned as he takes in the mansion. "Nice place."

My father turns to Agent Andrade. "Speak with Twitter."

I hope he's not implying that he's going to have all of Twitter terminated.

My mother goes and hugs Rio. "It's lovely to see you, and I appreciate your dedication to checking in on Alano, even if it does cross a line," she says, pinching Rio's cheek. "I know it was all out of love, but in the future, please respect our privacy. Okay?"

"You got it, Naya," Rio says.

"We'll leave you to talk outside," Ma says, a slight raise of her eyebrow to tell me that Rio is not welcome inside. I don't like that he's being treated as if he has knives for fingers and cameras for eyes, but I'm just so happy to see him. Ma hooks her arm through Pa's. "Let's finish speaking inside."

My father holds strong in his spot as he tells me, "You will remain under Agent Andrade's supervision. We will talk after my call with—" He stops himself, not wanting to reveal in front of Rio that he's scheduled to speak with President Page. "We will talk after my call."

My parents go inside, Agent Chen returns to her post by the driveway, and Agent Andrade stands by the fountain, watching Rio through his shades.

"Am I going to get shot if I hug you so hard that I might squeeze the life out of you?" Rio asks.

"No. Just don't ask for a selfie with any phones that have hidden switchblades."

"How about hidden poison darts?"

"How about you just hug me?"

Rio barrels into me with a big hug, picking me off my feet. I groan in pain, but I wouldn't have it any other way. This closeness is so familiar and needed. When he sets me down, he doesn't let go. Our faces are buried in each other's necks.

"I needed to see you alive again," he says.

"I'm alive."

"You look like shit, though." Rio stares into my eyes. "Some red has found its way into your green and brown."

"I haven't gotten a lot of sleep," I say, going to the dusty patio table where Bucky rests his face on my foot as he hides from the sun. "This whole affair has been haunting." I don't elaborate on how my mother believes I'm on the brink of a psychotic break because I'm not ready to admit that to myself either, but I give him the full account about Mac Maag.

"This was after everything with Ariana?" Rio asks.

I nod. "Ariana walking away would've been one of my last memories."

"Has she called?"

"No. Have you spoken with her?"

"She was relieved that you were okay. She was supposed to reach out by now."

The longer she takes, the more unforgivable it is. "Ariana should be here too."

"Am I not enough?" Rio asks jokingly.

"Our friendship was never in danger." I sigh. "I guess we're not getting that apartment."

Rio leans in, his hands pressed together. "We can still get our own place, Alano. I would really love that. I can be your new bodyguard and . . ." He inspects my bandaged arm. "Are we signing this? It's not a cast. Who's this? That a P-name?"

I'm hesitant to bring this up, but I can't dismiss this without making it a bigger deal. "That is indeed a P-name that belongs to someone I met last night."

Rio's thick brows meet in the middle. "Is this someone a boy? A boy-boy? A no-homo boy or yes-homo boy? I flew out here because I was worried about you, but you went and had a meet-cute after your assassination attempt? That's grounds for killing you."

I hold back my laugh. "Calm down. There's nothing to tell."

Well, not nothing. I share the bullet points of last night's events. It only leads to more questions:

"You climbed the Hollywood Sign? Is it because he's cute?"

"How did you talk him down?"

"What's his name?"

"You ran from a helicopter?"

"Did you kiss him?"

I answer all of Rio's breathless questions.

"Why are you being so secretive about who he is?" Rio asks.

For the same reasons my mother is speaking to my father about this instead of me. "I don't want you to judge him."

"I won't."

I brace myself. "It's Paz Dario."

It takes a moment to register who he is. "The killer?"

"He's not a killer."

"He killed his dad. Didn't they do a whole documentary about him?"

"It was one episode in a docuseries, not a whole documentary, which was created by pro-naturalists, by the way. The millions of people who watched that show may not have seen that Paz was declared innocent in court, but I witnessed that ruling with my own two eyes." I might not be able to change everyone else's mind, but I can keep my best friend accountable. "Paz killed his father in self-defense, and being treated as a cold-blooded murderer is one of the reasons he found himself on the Hollywood Sign last night."

Rio seems as if he's about to tap out, but he leans in again. "Paz is lucky to have been saved by you, but you're hanging out with a victim of the first End Day after being almost assassinated by a victim of the first End Day. Are you that arrogant about Death-Cast that you think you're so invincible?"

Would Rio ask that question if he knew I was living pro-naturally? Or would he be even more alarmed that I'm hanging out with someone he calls a killer?

I remember the gun aimed at me. "Paz had a chance to kill me, and he didn't take it."

"That's dark and doesn't make me feel better."

"Paz is committed to living, which is why we turned my bandage into a contract for the Begin Days," I say, giving him a closer look.

"You signed it too . . . ," Rio points out.

I'll open up one day that I tried killing myself last year, but that time isn't now. "I signed the contract as a promise to help Paz," I say, which is partially true. "I'm seeing him again tonight."

"So it's a date," Rio states.

"No." Not officially, at least.

"But you like him." Once again, it's not a question.

Sometimes Rio thinks he knows how I think. He doesn't even know everything about me. Everything I've done and everything I can do, but I would be lying if I said Rio is absolutely wrong here.

"It wouldn't be fair to say I like Paz when I don't really know him yet."

"You might not believe in love at first sight," Rio says confidently. "But maybe Paz does."

"Paz didn't fall in love with me when he was about to shoot himself."

Rio shrugs. "How can you know that if you don't really know him yet?"

I've never had a real boyfriend, but sometimes it felt like Rio was my first. We were so infatuated with each other that my parents and the Moraleses didn't believe us when we said we weren't dating. I think we would've been amazing boyfriends before we agreed to only be best friends so that we could guarantee we would be lifers.

"I'm going to get to know Paz," I say delicately.

"Then be careful that you don't lead him on," Rio says, bold enough to look me in the eyes. "I don't want you turning up as a corpse because you trusted the wrong person who wasn't right in the head."

Like his brother did.

I hate the suggestion that Paz will become dangerous like the Last Friend killer all because of his mental health. I remind myself that Rio is only talking about Paz's suicidal urges and not his borderline personality disorder. He doesn't know about Paz's diagnosis, and he's not going to unless it comes from Paz himself. It doesn't matter that he's my best friend. Secrets belong between the person who owns it and the person they're trusting to keep it. Just as Paz would be rightfully upset if I talked about how his brain functions, I would feel betrayed by Ariana if she shared the secret of how my brain functions, something I told her in confidence on Christmas Day in 2018 for the two-year anniversary of our friendship. Outside my parents and my childhood doctor, who's now dead, no one else knows, not even Rio.

"I'm going to be careful," I tell him firmly. "Thanks for being a friend."

"Anytime," he says.

I hope he's telling the truth. I'd hate to lose my best friend over matters of the heart that I can't control.

"Do you have plans tomorrow?" Rio asks. "I got two tickets for Universal Studios as a pick-me-up. That was before I knew you were making friends on the Hollywood Sign."

I ignore the dig. "That's really generous. Let me speak with my father. Things have been tense obviously." I also have legitimate concerns about existing in a public park without any certainties that I would survive. "Universal sounds like a lot of fun, though."

We stand and hug while Bucky slaps our legs with his tail.

"Don't get killed by the cute boy," Rio says, kissing my cheek. "I want to see you tomorrow."

Tomorrow isn't a guarantee. I could be living my End Day right now, and that's as unknowable as what it means that Rio's lips lingered on me longer than usual or what's actually written in the stars between me and Paz. All I know is that I'm finally getting excited about the future again, and I'm dreading my father getting in the way of that.

PAZ

5:02 p.m.

Begin Days are bullshit, nothing but a lie Alano told me all night and a lie I told myself all day.

I should've known better, to be honest. Promises are bigger lies than Begin Days. My dad vowed he would love my mom through sickness and in health and then he tried killing her. Orion claimed he would back me up with his producers but didn't put up a fight. And Alano had me sign a contract on his bandage that I knew wouldn't be legally binding, but I still thought he would keep his word anyway.

Except Alano hasn't given me any words since his first text.

To beginnings, he had texted at 5:02 a.m.

Exactly twelve hours ago.

I don't get it, did I do something? Say something? Not say something? I wondered if my messages weren't going through, so I texted Mom and Rolando pictures of them lounging in the backyard and they received them immediately.

I came up with other excuses for why Alano hasn't reached out. Maybe he's still sleeping since we were out late and he was jet-lagged. Maybe he lost his phone and didn't memorize my number like he thought he did. Maybe he got in trouble for sneaking out or for saving a lost cause like me. Or maybe Alano is dead.

I hope I'm wrong about Alano being dead, almost as much as my other heartbreaking theory that Alano isn't ghosting me but has actually been a ghost all along.

These spirals got me reading up on borderline personality disorder while curled up under my weighted blanket, and my fear has been confirmed: people with BPD experience hallucinations. It can be brought on by stress (check) or social isolation (check) or medication (check) or trauma (check) or physical injuries (brought on myself, but check). Ghost Alano said it himself, the timing for his appearance on top of the Hollywood Sign was a huge coincidence. He called it fate. I'm calling it a breakdown. A last-ditch effort from my body or brain or soul to survive.

I relive the night in my head—the Hollywood Sign, Hollywood Boulevard, Present-Time, the Hollywood DIEner, Echo Park—and I try to fill in the blanks on who I was talking to if not Alano and how I got around the city if not because of Alano and whose hand I held when running from danger if not Alano's.

Then I throw the weighted blanket off me and rush to my closet to check something.

My gun isn't in my chest. I didn't imagine throwing it out, but I do regret it.

No, I don't regret throwing away the gun. I regret not pulling the trigger.

JOAQUIN ROSA

5:15 p.m.

Death-Cast did not call Joaquin Rosa because he is not dying today, but he fears the Death Guard may soon bring that alert into his life. Or worse, his wife's and son's. Well, his son has frustratingly chosen to opt out of the service, but the threat of death lives on regardless.

Joaquin is currently speaking on the matter with the president of the United States.

"It is not that simple," President Page says over the phone's secure line. "Alano's assailant was seeking revenge because of the first End Day. There is no proof that he has any connection to Dunst."

"Would you still need proof if someone attacked Andrew, Mr. President?" Joaquin asks, making it personal. Let President Page imagine someone slashing and stabbing his son. "The answer is no because you are smart enough to know that there is no such thing as a random act of violence when it comes to the president or their family, no such thing as coincidence when you have enemies who hate what you stand for. Investigate the matter all you want, but you will not find any checks signed by Dunst or any promises for favors apart from the world he will restore for his pro-natural zealots."

A world where President Page is no longer in power.

A world where Death-Cast no longer exists.

A world where no one knows when they will die.

As President Page reiterates his campaign strategy—it is rude to interrupt people, but especially the president—Joaquin paces his home office, a large but simple room in the mansion. An oak desk and leather chair sit in front of a bookcase where one tug of volume 10 in his encyclopedia collection will open up to a decoy panic room designed to trap any intruders who get past Shield-Cast's defenses. A threat that feels likely more than ever, disturbingly, but that is why a formidable panic room exists elsewhere in the mansion.

The bar cart by the window tempts Joaquin with his favorite whiskeys and tequilas, none of which have been dumped or donated, seeing as he hasn't been in the house since going sober on his fiftieth birthday. One shot of Clase Azul and Joaquin would feel better, just one shot. That never made anyone black out. He grabs the bottle to pour his shot, but before that first drop can fall, he's drawn to Naya sunbathing by the pool per Joaquin's request to let him stress and her relax instead of them suffering together about Alano's well-being. The sun may not be as delicious as tequila, but Joaquin is inspired to choose the heat on his skin instead of the burn down his throat. Maybe he'll even remain outside long enough to watch the sunset with Naya, something they used to do regularly at their penthouse before life got too busy.

"Believe me when I say Death-Cast is a valuable asset to

our country," President Page says, concluding his long-winded speech where his voice spiked with that authoritative inflection, as if he were standing before a rally of voters instead of speaking with the individual who knows more than anyone Death-Cast's value.

"I am aware," Joaquin states.

"As you are about your company's shortcomings too," President Page says.

These bottles of whiskey and tequila may soon be undrinkable if Joaquin hurls them all across the room in anger. "Meaning?"

"The empire you have built is impressive, but it is not one everyone wishes to live in."

"The same can be said for the nation you are overseeing."

This isn't the first heated exchange between creator and president over the years, but Joaquin recognizes it is the most personal.

"Precisely, Joaquin. World leaders cannot create a utopia, no matter how much we devote ourselves to producing one for society. My intentions with this country are pure, just as yours are with your company. This doesn't negate our failures in shaping this new world. There are Americans and Deckers who are disappointed in our leadership, respectively. The difference is my supporters are alive to tell me I failed them."

Joaquin eyes the whiskey, desperate for a drink.

It has been impossible to live a life profiting off death without feeling haunted.

He's written about this in his memoir, *Life and Death-Cast*, which publishes on August 4, four days after the company's tenth anniversary. There's a strict embargo because of the many secrets his publisher has been teasing to stir up more interest. Joaquin is under no illusions that the secret readers are most hoping to discover is the method in which Death-Cast can predict a Decker's fate. The publisher begged for this book to be not only a moving celebration of End Days but the ultimate tell-all of the world's greatest secret and the man who created it. Joaquin read between the lines: skyrocketing sales if he shared with the public this secret that he hasn't even shared with his own son. He'd discussed the possibility with Naya, who has known the secret since she was pregnant with Alano, but she didn't let Joaquin give in to the pressure.

"Once that door opens, it can never be closed," Naya reminded Joaquin.

There are many doors Joaquin won't open for his readers, but he will do so for President Page right now. "You're wrong, Mr. President. The dead talk to me. They have since the beginning."

For almost ten years, Joaquin Rosa has been haunted by ghosts. He's tormented by the Deckers who were failed by Death-Cast, especially the Death's Dozen. Doctors believe these apparitions are nothing more than psychological disturbances brought on by the pressure and trauma of Joaquin's work, but no matter their reality, Joaquin sees these ghosts, and he wouldn't be surprised if they were exactly that, given everything else he's laid his eyes on that others have not. He has tried treating this disorder through therapy, psychiatry, counseling, and even an exorcism, and while those sessions helped with his depression—the exorcism gave him a nice laugh—the ghosts continue haunting Joaquin in his sleep and waking hours. Drinking was the most effective treatment. Now he's trying his hand at journaling, finding that, much like writing his memoir, there is this release that comes with putting words down on a page, but unlike the book, he will not be publishing these particular entries for the world. In fact, he burns them at the end of every session, never to be discovered by anyone, not even Naya and especially not Alano. One man's ghosts shouldn't become another's.

President Page doesn't take Joaquin literally. "I hope your ghosts can't vote because internal polling predicts a tight election given the recent surge in the pro-natural movement. It's important we don't outright condemn Dunst for his beliefs or we risk upsetting pro-naturalists who aren't overly concerned with Death-Cast and are otherwise happy to vote the party line."

A politician's ability to avoid accountability has always impressed—and disturbed—Joaquin. That trait is not in his nature. After the first End Day, Joaquin took the time to personally meet with the loved ones affected by Death-Cast's failure to predict a Decker's fate so he could apologize—or he tried to, at least, his presence rejected by three out of the twelve families. As hard as those nine meetings were, Joaquin endured because it was the right thing to do; he even hoped the man in Texas who put a gun to Joaquin's head ultimately found some healing in watching Joaquin beg for his life on a day that could've easily become his own unpredicted End Day like the man's young daughter.

"Focus on converting Dunst's supporters," Joaquin says. "Expose him for the crook he is."

"The unfortunate reality is that we could catch Dunst redhanded and his staunch supporters will still vote for him simply because he is anti-Death-Cast."

This system is broken when a man can commit a crime and still qualify for the presidency.

If Joaquin wants the world to evolve into a utopia, he may very well have to run for president himself to fix the system, just as he rebuilt the life-and-death experience.

Joaquin is no stranger to the responsibilities, having worked closely with President Reynolds on many matters, most famously ensuring workers in certain industries were mandated to be registered for Death-Cast for the safety of all. This ranged from pilots to city bus drivers, police to firefighters, stuntpeople to bodyguards, and every government official. Death-Cast predicted President Reynolds's End Day, but what no one saw coming was his Secret Service agent assassinating him because of his resentment for being forced to sign up for Death-Cast to make his living. This is why President Reynolds became one of Joaquin's ghosts.

That assassination set the stage for this year's election.

After President Reynolds was killed, his vice president was elevated to president, while the speaker of the house became the new vice president: Andy Page and Carson Dunst, respectively. Joaquin witnessed that pairing fracture firsthand as Dunst sought to undo the laws set by Reynolds. It was no surprise when Page parted ways with Dunst at the end of their term. With the help of his new running mate, Clea Paquin, Page secured his first official term as president, and together, they're seeking reelection for his last. All President Page has to do is beat his former vice president.

If Dunst wins the election, Joaquin will run against him in four years.

There's a knock at the door and Joaquin opens it to find Alano standing there. They have much to discuss, but he holds up a finger to wait before closing the door in his son's face.

"I hope I haven't lost your confidence," President Page says.

"You will have my vote this fall," Joaquin says.

"Enthusiastically?"

Joaquin is quiet, long enough that he's sure he's making the president sweat. "No candidate is ever everything we need them to be," he finally says. "If I must choose between the man sending assassins after my son or the man doing very little to stop it, then I will vote for the lesser evil, but make no mistake that any man showing lack of regard for my son's life is evil in my eyes."

Then Joaquin Rosa hangs up on the president of the United States.

Later, Joaquin will seek guidance from Naya on how best to navigate his frustrations and disappointment, knowing he cannot retract his support for President Page without tipping the edge in Dunst's favor, but for now, he takes a deep breath and calls Alano into his office.

"How was your unexpected reunion?" Joaquin asks.

"Really good," Alano says, taking a seat.

"Did you tell Rio about your secret?"

"No."

That's a relief.

"How'd the call go?" Alano asks.

"Fine." Joaquin doesn't want his son knowing that he isn't important to the president. "Private matters about the company."

"Is this your way of telling me I'm fired?"

"Are you even fireable? I was under the impression that your life outside of Death-Cast meant more than opting out of the service."

"I haven't officially decided, but feel free to add me to your list of terminations."

Joaquin hates how Alano speaks of him as if he is the grim reaper who delights in claiming the lives of every soul on his scroll. "None of this brings me any joy."

"How fast you are to fire people this week says otherwise."

"I fire them because I am furious!" Joaquin barks.

He hates yelling at Alano. He hates how his anger got the best of him at the end of lunch when he slammed his fist on the table. He hates everyone who has or could have a role in endangering his son.

"If I could fire Death for coming to claim you one day, I

would put him out of business and watch the universe implode."

"Even you're not that powerful," Alano says.

"Even I am not," Joaquin reinforces, hating the truth of it. "All that said, Dane's termination is for your benefit."

"You're not giving him credit for the times he has protected me."

"Maybe if you had not rebelled against your common senses then he would have been positioned to prove his worth when it mattered most."

Alano sighs. "I agree. That was my fault. He shouldn't be punished. I'd like for Dane to be reinstated as my bodyguard."

Joaquin rocks back in his leather chair. "Why would I agree to that?"

"You're right that I can't roam around without protection. I'll die before I can find the life I want. The only way I'll accept security detail is if it's Dane. I can either keep you and Shield-Cast in the loop, or I can pay his salary out of my pocket and you won't know when I'm coming and going or who is part of my life."

This negotiation is another moment of pride, Joaquin must admit. It shows that Alano does have some sense left in him. "I will consider this proposition," he says, wanting to be clear on the terms first, the top one being that should Agent Madden fail to protect Alano again that he will not be given any more chances. But Agent Madden's detail will never be the ultimate assurance. "Will you consider opting back into Death-Cast?"

"No," Alano says.

"No?"

"Not right now, at least. If I'm truly going to experience what my life looks like outside of Death-Cast, that means not living under its peace of mind. I meant what I said before, though. I'm never going public with this information, but I reserve the right to tell the people closest to me."

"The more you speak of this, the higher the risk that this news will spread to the media and the Death Guard, wait and see."

"My friends don't want me dead," Alano snaps. "They're not going to say anything."

Joaquin's trust issues run deep, the cause of much reflection on whether he is overly cautious or severely paranoid, but regardless, both paths lead to the same core thought: never fully trust anyone except his wife and son. The caution—or paranoia—has only grown stronger as of late, even bleeding into whether Naya and Alano are to be fully trusted, but especially Alano.

How is Joaquin to share the extraordinary and life-changing secret behind Death-Cast's power with Alano when they are at odds over things so ordinary and life-threatening?

Perhaps he may never need to.

"Tell me something, mi hijo. Do you still foresee yourself inheriting Death-Cast?"

Alano sits with this long enough that his tone changes, going from snapping and defensive to soft and thoughtful. "I honestly don't know, Pa. I have other desires, but I question if anything I do will ever be more important than what Death-Cast does for the world. Almost as if I should sacrifice all my needs. Professional, personal, even romantic."

Joaquin wishes he could relax too as his son's rising flames are fanning out, but this talk of romance only ignites bigger concerns. Earlier, Naya spoke with Joaquin about how Alano's mystery boy was none other than Paz Dario. With that came the warning to not express the very concerns burning through him now about how his son's life may be threatened by this boy whose impulses have led to death before and may lead to death again. Joaquin has already ordered Shield-Cast to perform a background check, but the biggest red flag they have returned with so far has been Paz Dario's patricide of that horrible domestic abuser and murderer, which anyone with Google or a Piction+ subscription can find out.

"Are these romantic feelings about the Dario boy?" Joaquin asks.

"I don't know. Maybe."

"Naya said you intend to see him tonight, but I do not believe this is wise," he says, hoping his son will see reason.

Of course Alano does not. "Your whole business is built on carpe diem, memento mori, all of that, but I guess that's only for people buying into your services."

"You have never paid a cent toward Death-Cast," Joaquin reminds because Alano has a lifetime membership—*had*.

"I'm not talking about money. I mean belief."

Failure to make his own son believe in the mission sits heavy in Joaquin's throat and he wishes to wash it down with some whiskey. "It is a tragedy that you do not believe in Death-Cast, but nearly three billion people welcome our reminders to live before they die. However, my job as your father is to keep you alive for as long as possible."

"How about happy, Pa? Is that part of your job as my father?"

"Of course it is," Joaquin says earnestly. "But I would rather you be alive and angry at me than happy and dead."

Joaquin has long considered the risks of overparenting, especially when observing how much Alano already gravitates toward Naya for personal conversations—such as his coming out, which Joaquin welcomed fully when told, and now this matter of Paz Dario—but all Joaquin can think about is how much darker this dark world will be if his son is dead. If one day Alano were to stop speaking with Joaquin and carved out a life where he was happy with his partner and children, then Joaquin will have done his job right. A job Alano will then intimately understand himself and perhaps let Joaquin back into his life.

Alano looks as if he might cry, something that has always broken Joaquin's heart, but also enlightened him on how much Alano feels, going so far as to teach him that crying could be perceived as a weakness that is weaponized against him. "Why are you keeping me away from someone who needs a friend?" he asks.

A thought—a fear—strikes Joaquin over why Alano is so connected to this stranger. "Do you have a death wish?" Joaquin watches his son closely, knowing Alano's tell for when he lies. It hasn't changed since he was a child lying about childish things, such as Bucky eating all the snickerdoodle cookies, or blaming the expensive vase he broke on the maid. He is fixed on Alano, who remains still as he stares back at Joaquin.

"I don't have a death wish," Alano answers honestly. "Why?"

"Then why are you insisting on putting yourself in danger? Why are you not living for your preservation as I am?"

"I don't find my life valuable and worth protecting. If today was my End Day, I would die unfulfilled—and it would be your fault."

There's one impulse to fight back, another to down a bottle of whiskey, but he absorbs the weight of what his son has said: if he died today, he would not die happy. Joaquin will have failed as a father.

Everyone wants something to live for, there is not a soul that does not; even those who wish to kill themselves would stay alive for the right reasons.

Joaquin must know what will get Alano's heart pumping.

"Tell me, mi hijo. What does your dream End Day look like?"

It's been a while since Joaquin has asked Alano this question, the last time during his seventeenth or eighteenth birthday, if memory serves him right, and while Joaquin's own vision of his dream End Day has not changed since Death-Cast began, that does not mean his son wouldn't grow up to want more.

"I want a life worth remembering." Alano's eyes light up like he's picturing his End Day now. "I don't want my highlights to be all the cool things I did. I would trade skydiving anywhere in the world in a heartbeat for a walk in the park with my soulmate. I want to grow up and grow old with someone who will hold my hand as I die on my End Day."

Like father, like son.

Joaquin's dream End Day is simple, where everything has already been said and everything has already been lived. There is no need for the World Travel Arena or Make-A-Moment or Present-Time. No need for the Last Friend app because Joaquin will be on his deathbed, holding the hands of the two people he loves more than life itself.

Alano wants a love like that too. A love that no business can sell.

Joaquin senses he should hug his son, but he is unsure that Alano would be willing to embrace him. But they can continue speaking. "Let's discuss how best we can keep you alive so you can have a life worth remembering."

Joaquin Rosa will do anything to ensure his son does not become a ghost who haunts him.

PAZ
5:58 p.m.

I no longer have a gun, but I still have my knife.

Hours ago, when I was on my self-care streak, there was this dumbass voice telling me to return the knife to the kitchen, that I wouldn't need it anymore, but I was smart enough to not listen. I open my drawer and grab the knife, pulling back my shorts, and the scars on my thigh look like the scratched-up floor in a horror movie from someone trying to claw their way to freedom; I can relate. I'm about to run a new line across all of them, like a tally, but I'm ready to move on to a new spot. Like the bottom of my foot. Yeah, that's even better, I can hide the scars and every painful step will remind me to never believe in stupid-ass lies again. My heart is pounding as I take off my sock and bite down on it so Mom and Rolando won't hear my screams. I press the knife against the sole of my foot, wincing already; this is gonna hurt, it's gonna be so bad, I know it, but I have to do it, and I have to do it now.

Hurting myself is how I'll get better.

I'm a millisecond away from that first slice when my phone rings; I almost don't hear it over the sound of my blood pumping. And I can't believe my eyes when I see Alano Rosa is calling.

343

He's saving me from myself again.

"Hello?" I answer immediately, like I'm scared he'll vanish again if I take too long.

"Hey, Paz. It's Alano." Four words. Just four words from Alano and I can breathe again. "I'm sorry it's taken so long to get back to you. It's been a day. How are you?"

How am I?

"I'm okay," I say, returning the knife inside my journal and shutting the drawer. "What's going on with you?"

Alano sighs. "It's been a very eventful day of fighting with my parents."

"Did you win?"

"Everyone won and lost," Alano says sadly before perking up. "Long story short, I can still hang out, but I have to be home before midnight. It's very Cinderella of me."

That's a funny thought, but my mind doesn't let me laugh, it takes me somewhere dark. "Why before midnight, do your parents think I'm a threat to you?"

There's a breath-long wait. "You're no threat to me, Paz. Others are, especially now that my fate is up in the air. The compromise is my newly reinstated bodyguard has to accompany me everywhere I go."

"So your bodyguard is coming on our—" I stop myself from calling this a date, since that's not what this is. "He's coming to hang out with us?"

"Is that okay? Dane will keep his distance."

"Yeah, that's okay."

"I understand if it's not."

"No, no, it's fine. Seriously," I lie.

I want Alano to myself, but between his bodyguard tagging along and Alano having to be home before midnight, I'll take what I can get.

"Thanks for understanding. I'm going to leave in a few and text you my ETA. Then we can enjoy some Begin Day fun."

After we hang up, I stare at my foot, picturing what it could've looked like. I wince. From saving my life to saving my body, Alano has magical timing. Death-Cast calls people to live before they die, but Alano calls me to keep me alive and well.

And that scares me.

GLORIA MEDINA
6:39 p.m.

Death-Cast did not call Gloria Medina because she is not dying today, which she does not take for granted because she is planning on living a long life.

It has been a decade since Gloria secretly signed herself, her ex-husband, and their son up for Death-Cast without even knowing if it truly worked. She had spent so long bracing herself for an untimely end at the hands of Frankie that she simply had to know for sure when her time was up so she could give Pazito a proper goodbye. Gloria did not plan on Pazito killing Frankie on the first End Day, an incident that haunts her family to this day but has allowed Gloria to keep her life, to watch her son grow up, and now, to grow her family.

Gloria Medina is now with the true love of her life, Rolando Rubio. She did not hand her heart over easily. She told herself over and over and over that Rolando would never hurt her, but still, she'd once believed the same of Frankie. And she believed Frankie when he said he would never hurt her again. And she kept believing and believing and believing even though her broken heart told her the truth: the man she loved was no longer her protector and was instead her attacker. But Rolando is different. He has always cared about her happiness, even at the expense of his own. It could not have been easy watching Gloria start her family and have her first child with a man he despised, but Rolando was always there for her, always there for Pazito. She knows he will make an excellent father to the child they are having together.

The child she hopes she is having, at least.

She's very nervous about this pregnancy, this fear living within her that something will happen to her baby, just like she felt when Frankie attacked her while she was pregnant with Pazito. There are so many moments that Gloria still reflects on today when she wishes she had left Frankie. One of the biggest is knowing Frankie got so mad at Gloria that he could have killed Pazito before he got to live. Rolando would never have done such a thing, and since Gloria once believed that of Frankie, she made sure she took her time to be certain that Rolando was truly the one.

One evening many years ago, during an argument over how best to fight back when Pazito was being demonized at that Catholic school, Gloria took note of how she didn't flinch when Rolando raised his voice because he was angry at the teachers, she didn't flinch when Rolando got up from the kitchen table upset, and she didn't flinch when he put his hands on her because he was only putting his hands inside of hers. That was when she knew she could start letting her guard down, that if she wanted, she could have even deactivated Death-Cast knowing she would be safe with her lover.

That night, Gloria Medina kissed Rolando Rubio, a kiss that was decades in the making.

They kissed for so long that Pazito came out of their room

and saw them. He had been in the bedroom they were all sharing, and when he spotted them in the kitchen, he was scared for
his mother, but also scared about what he would be called on to
do to Rolando if he was endangering her. That broke her heart,
but Gloria told Pazito that Rolando was helping piece her heart
back together. That they were safe.

In the days that followed, Gloria explained to Pazito that she
and Rolando were committing to each other as life partners.
That Pazito didn't have to keep calling him Uncle Rolando and
could even call him Dad if he saw fit.

"I don't want another dad," Pazito had said. "What if I kill
him too?"

Gloria has never shared this with Rolando.

"You won't kill him because he will never threaten our
lives," Gloria told her son.

"You didn't think Dad would," Pazito said.

That wasn't true, of course. She knew there was a chance
Frankie would end her life, but she chose to believe he would
get better. She was wrong.

Gloria was wrong about Frankie, but she is right about
Rolando.

Hours after discovering she was pregnant, she nudged
Rolando after kissing him good night and asked him if he liked
the name Armonía if the baby is a girl. "Then my children will
be named after peace and harmony," she said.

Rolando sat up in bed excited, the biggest smile on his face as
he entertained more names for their child. "What about a boy?"

Oh, how Gloria would love to raise another boy. "I don't know. What do you think?"

"I've always loved the name Ruben," Rolando said. "Ruben Rubio."

"Ruben Rubio-Medina," Gloria corrected. She has already decided that when she weds Rolando, she will be keeping her name, but she is okay with Rolando's last name in front of hers for their child, especially since it's so delightful to say Ruben Rubio aloud.

Still, she's scared to fall in love with any name right now, before she knows if this baby will even survive. Death-Cast can't predict that fate, but Gloria can serve her child best by taking care of herself.

The doctor encouraged a nutrient-rich diet, staying hydrated, and most important, told Gloria to manage her stress. It's easy enough to eat and drink well, but leading a stress-free life is its own challenge. Gloria hates checking the mail, knowing there will be bills waiting for her. She needs to lessen her workload, but she can only do that once Rolando secures a full-time job that will allow her to take leave from the shelter knowing that the bills in the mailbox will be paid. But that won't be the end of her stress. Truth be told, there aren't enough soothing songs or nature walks or warm baths to keep Gloria from stressing about her firstborn.

Gloria knows more about Pazito than she has let on. Her son is a wonderful actor, but that doesn't mean she can't see past his performance and know that he is struggling. That Pazito is unhappy.

A mother knows.

As Pazito comes out of his bedroom, dressed for his evening with Alano Rosa, Gloria senses a shift in him, a genuine excitement that she has missed in her son.

"You look good for your date," Rolando says.

"It's not a date," Pazito says.

He isn't being defensive, just cautious, something Gloria appreciates after his dangerous behavior months ago. But Gloria can tell that Pazito wants tonight to be a date. "I hope you have fun," Gloria says, getting up from the couch to walk her son to the door.

"Don't watch me walk out, Mom," Pazito says.

Again, not defensive. Gloria can tell he doesn't want to be embarrassed, though she misses the days when Pazito would smile back at her when he left the house, a genuine smile because he loved being watched after. "Of course, Pazito." Gloria pulls her son in for a hug and kisses his cheek. "Be safe."

"Okay, Mom."

"I love you."

"I love you too," Pazito says. He waves at Rolando and leaves.

Gloria can't help herself. She peeks out the window, watching Pazito walk toward Alano Rosa, who is standing outside his car. She hopes this date-that-is-not-a-date goes well.

"Please don't break my son's heart," Gloria whispers, hoping Alano can somehow hear her.

Gloria knows how dangerous love can be.

PAZ
6:44 p.m.

I leave the house to find Alano leaning against his car. The fact that he's here makes me catch my breath. I suck in the crisp air, loving it more than I have in a good minute. It has everything to do with Alano, which I really gotta figure out because he doesn't live here and he's gonna leave soon, and I don't know what will be left of me, if anything, when he's gone. But for now I close the space between my house and his car, and he closes it even more by pulling me into a hug.

I hate when there's space between us again.

"Happy Begin Day," Alano says. "I almost wished you a Happy Begin Night, but it doesn't look like night at all. Your sky might be broken."

The sky is still mostly blue, with the pinks and oranges of sunset creeping in. This is what summer in Los Angeles looks like. But I'm more focused on what Alano looks like. He's wearing a baggy black hoodie and even baggier sweatpants.

"Forget the sky, why are you dressed like that? Are we going somewhere cold?"

Alano looks down at his outfit like he's forgotten what he's wearing. "I opted for plain clothes. No vanitas that might trigger you."

I like how thoughtful he is. I really need someone like him in my life. And then I remember him taking off his shirt, and I think about how I really, really, really need someone like him in my life.

"I hope this is okay," Alano says after I keep staring at his hoodie.

I hate that you're wearing anything, especially baggy clothes that hide your body is what I wanna say. But I actually say, "It looks cozy." I have to stop undressing him in my head. "So where are we going?"

"I've planned a surprise to help relaunch you back into your life," Alano says before turning and waving at a black car parked down the block. "First, you should meet Agent Dane."

The car pulls up behind Alano's and out walks his bodyguard. He's wearing all black too, but he's way more formal and fitting in his suit. He's younger than I expected, like right around our age.

"Pleasure to meet you, Mr. Paz," Dane says. His words are nice, but his gaze is intense. "Mr. Alano has requested that I give you both space, but if there's any sign of trouble, be sure to alert me. Call or text or shout." He reaches into his jacket and pulls out his card, but I don't take it because in the flash of his jacket opening I saw a holstered gun.

Less than an hour ago I was in my room missing my gun and seeing one so close to me reminds me why I missed mine in the first place. I wanted to die because I should've been dead already, but Alano convinced me to live, and now I am, but it's not enough, it's not gonna be enough, nothing will ever be enough. I'm not strong enough to fight Alano, let alone Dane, who is like three times more muscular, but maybe I could get lucky, snatch the gun, and shoot myself and bleed out on my front yard and die after midnight.

Alano squeezes my shoulder. "You okay?"

I snap out of it. "Yeah, yeah, I'm good."

I take Dane's card, which has nothing but his phone number, not even his name.

Dane looks between us, lingering on me like I'm unstable. He's got a great eye.

"We'll take off in a minute. Thanks, Dane," Alano says, dismissing him. Once Dane is back in his car, Alano asks me what's going on. "Don't say you're okay when you're not."

I won't lie, especially when he knows I'm lying. "I saw his gun, and I spiraled over how I still wanna die." There is no life in my voice. "I suck at Begin Days."

"You don't suck at Begin Days. First of all, this is the first one. We're figuring it out as we go." Alano lifts his sleeve and shows me his bandaged arm that we signed last night. "More importantly, our contract is for *living* our Begin Days, not acting as if they won't be hard. You might not like what you're feeling, but you should be proud of yourself for opening up. I truly believe that honesty is how we keep you safe."

Alano then grabs my gunless hand and squeezes away my will to die.

"Thanks for giving a shit about me. It makes me give a shit about me," I say.

"As you should. I've known you for less than twenty-four hours, and you're one of the strongest people I know."

"Strong? You met me giving up on life."

"You chose to survive. That took strength." Alano rubs my arm, like he's feeling for how strong I am, which if we're judging by my arms, I'm not, but his touch makes me feel powerful anyway. "Your borderline personality disorder is what's tripping you up the most right now, but you'll get steady once you go through dialectical behavior therapy to target your traumas and better regulate your emotions during times of distress, or schema-focused therapy to disrupt unhealthy behaviors that are adding fuel to the fire."

Alano reads the massive confusion on my face because last night he didn't know anything about BPD and tonight he's an expert? I don't even know what schema-focused therapy is, and this is my thing.

He sheepishly adds, "I've been researching borderline personality disorder."

"What? When?"

"I listened to a podcast episode while driving home last night and read a few essays this afternoon before lunch. I ordered some books too."

Alano must be a liar because there's no way any of this is true. "You're joking."

"Not one bit."

"Why did you look that up? Are you trying to be some walking encyclopedia that knows everything?"

"Encyclopedias don't know everything." Alano smirks.

I roll my eyes. "Okay, but why?"

"Because I like getting to know you."

"Even the stuff that makes me scary?"

"All of you," Alano says, his gaze strong. "I don't want to be one of those idiots who treats you like someone you're not. Like someone scary. I want to understand the real you. What makes you tick, what makes you laugh, what makes you sad, and even what makes you climb up the Hollywood Sign with a gun so I can help make sure you never do it again. I want to be a walking encyclopedia about Paz Dario who reminds you of your potential so you can love yourself enough to live for yourself."

When I received my diagnosis yesterday afternoon, I swore it was worth ending my life over. BPD is ups and downs, dizzying turns, big highs and bigger drops, getting up to not only fall again but fall even harder than last time, no matter how careful I am. I have to remember that falling all the time isn't the point. It's making sure I don't stay down. And until I can learn to pick myself up, Alano is my helping hand.

As I learn to love myself, I can't help but freak out over if I'll fall in love with him too, and whether that will be heart-healing or heartbreaking.

ALANO

6:52 p.m.

How to be a friend to someone with borderline personality disorder.

This was one of the most important questions I sought answers for today. It can be difficult sifting through the range of opinions found across medical journals, blogs, and podcasts, but everything I've explored so far seems to be in agreement that the best ways to serve a friend with borderline personality disorder are to validate their emotions, identify their triggers, and encourage professional help both for their benefit and as a boundary to protect yourself.

It turns out the best way to be a friend to someone with borderline personality disorder is to simply be a good friend.

I have already endured the distressing trial of convincing Paz to live, but now it's time for the Begin Days to help him reclaim a future that felt so lost he was desperate to die. I hope my plan will help get his life back on track.

PAZ

7:22 p.m.

We arrive at our first Begin Day destination: the Santa Monica Pier.

On the drive over, I caught up Alano on how my Begin Day was going. I didn't get into anything about the self-harm since I haven't opened up about that yet—and I will—but I did tell him all about my self-care routine, doing laundry, and mowing the backyard for Mom. He was proud of me, as I hoped. I also told him that I tried reaching out to Margie at Present-Time, which he did too apparently, and he also got the voice mail. We're gonna try again to make sure no security footage of us with the gun will get leaked.

Then as we were parking, Alano filled me in on how his Begin Day began with the police showing up at his place because he was recognized on the Hollywood Sign. Even though he was doing the right thing, Alano's parents were pissed that he risked his life for me. "I'm lucky no one knows we were at Present-Time with that raider," he says as we cross under the Santa Monica Pier sign and walk downhill. "My father would've had the cops lock me up for my safety."

Instead, we have his bodyguard following us.

"I'm sorry I almost got you arrested," I say.

"Your life is worth going to jail," Alano says.

"So is yours."

"Thanks for believing that."

I still don't know everything that led to Alano wanting to jump off a roof, and I hope he opens up to me like I have to him, but for now, I'm giving him space. "So your best friend surprised you?"

"One of my best friends, yes. That's complicated. Do you mind if we get into it later? I'd rather have fun with you now."

"I won't fight you on that," I say, throwing him a smile.

We walk through the pier. The Ferris wheel is already lit up even though it's not fully dark yet. The sky's blues and pinks have fused into this beautiful purple while the clouds glow orange like they're being burned away for the night. The smell of salty air is getting stronger as the ocean's waves get louder. Outside Bubba Gump is a snack cart, and we grab Sour Patch Kids, Airheads, and cotton candy for the world's sweetest dinner. We almost pop into the arcade, but there are so many live performances, like a breakdancing trio who have drawn a big crowd, a mime who recognizes Alano and mimics a phone call before playing dead, and a girl playing guitar and singing into a mic. The girl is covering Taylor Swift's "Lover" while two older women dance together and share a deep kiss. The thought of asking Alano to dance to this song as the sun sets has my insides breakdancing, but I'm as speechless as that damn mime. Alano places some cash into the girl's guitar case, and we continue down to my favorite part of the pier, where there's carnival games, a roller coaster, and the Ferris wheel. It might not be a romantic dance, but I wouldn't mind being alone in the sky with Alano. Instead, he stops in front of somewhere unexpected.

The Make-A-Moment station is a simple white-bricked building and a *NO-RISK THRILLS!* sign above the double doors. This VR company is built with Deckers in mind, but a lot of non-dying people come anyway because of safety, accessibility, and even affordability. Booking experiences at Make-A-Moment isn't cheap, but it's a lot cheaper to virtually scuba dive the Great Barrier Reef in LA than it would be to fly to Australia and get certified and rent equipment to do it for real—and you also don't have to worry about jellyfish stinging you to death.

"Am I really about to act like a Decker again on our first Begin Day?" I ask.

"I was thinking about a different kind of acting," Alano says, pointing to a sign.

HIRING!

Make-A-Moment is seeking to fill the following positions:
Front Desk Agents (full-time)
Show Guides (full-time)
Security Guard (full-time)
Actors (of all ages and backgrounds)
for new Make-Life-Moments Experience
Training begins in August (part-time)
Preference to those who can work
overnight and early mornings.

Apply inside or online.

"Wait. They're hiring actors?"

"The Make-Life-Moments Experience is the company's effort to expand beyond safe thrills and create intimate milestone moments that the Decker might not have experienced in life. This could mean anything from exchanging wedding vows to winning a Pulitzer, all in front of friends and family so they can cherish the moment too," Alano says, turning away from the building to look me in the eyes. "But they need actors. This might not be your dream role, but the role you play for a Decker could make their dream come true."

I stare at the sign again, imagining the endless possibilities of who I can become for these Deckers. "What if it's too much to handle mentally?"

"I'm the last person on this planet who will judge you. I should've trusted my own instincts and not done that herald shift," Alano says, closing his eyes and shuddering like he's reliving that memory in high-def. He shakes it off. "In the spirit of Begin Days, I thought I'd show you another avenue to pursue acting until we get you back on the big screen. Also, you've survived personal experiences with Last Friends, so I thought you could handle more time with Deckers too. At the end of the day, you know yourself best."

Every breath I haven't wanted to breathe is slowly filling me up. Training starts next month, which means living past the anniversary of Dad's death—which means not killing myself. This job could be something to live for, something that gives me purpose on the hardest Begin Days. Not only would I get to act, but Alano is right that I've proven that Deckers are fine around me. Then I feel all the air leaving me because the dying aren't my problem. It's the living. "But they won't hire me."

"Why not?" Alano asks.

"No one is hiring a killer to hang out with Deckers every day."

"You were declared innocent."

"I also had my records sealed, but that hasn't stopped people from knowing who I am anyway." If only the Scorpius Hawthorne stuff came up when someone googled my name during background checks instead of everything about my trial. "It's okay, thanks for trying—"

Alano grabs my wrist before I can walk away. "What's the harm in trying? This is a place of no-risk thrills, right?"

"Yeah, the no-risk thrills that Make-A-Moment offers are more daring, like virtual skydiving and rock climbing, things you really shouldn't be doing on your End Day. I doubt we're gonna find a VR room for applying for a job."

"You forget that Deckers are also known to embrace the dangers of reality, even on their End Day. If they're willing to die doing what they love, why aren't you willing to live to get what you love? What's the worst thing that can happen?"

"Rejection," I softly admit. That's part of being an actor anyway.

"What's the best thing that can happen?"

"I could get the job."

That would change my life. Not just change my life—it could save it.

"Your call," Alano says.

"Okay, fine, but I'm gonna use my stage name to play it safe," I say.

Alano rests his bandaged arm on my shoulder, leaning in and coaching me. "You shouldn't hide who you are, Paz Dario. If they won't accept you, take your worth elsewhere."

It's hard when those people make me feel worthless, but I gotta stop giving them power over me. "You should give a TED Talk about motivating suicidal guys."

"Only if I can point to evidence that my little speeches work."

I smile, taking this Begin Day head-on and walking inside Make-A-Moment. It looks like a high-end arcade. There are four TV screens previewing the experiences, kiosks for booking, black leather couches, dimmed overhead lights with a neon yellow *MAKE-A-MOMENT* sign behind the empty counter.

"I kinda love it in here," I say, kicking sand from the pier on the rug.

"That's awesome, because it looks like they could use some help."

The door opens, and Dane walks in. "Mr. Alano, you know you're not supposed—"

"We're just grabbing an application for Paz," Alano interrupts.

"It's best that we step outside."

My heart starts racing. "What's going on? Are we in danger?"

"No, no," Alano says. "My father has recommended that I avoid businesses for Deckers after recent attacks by the Death Guard."

"That was an instruction," Agent Dane says. "Part of your agreement."

"We're fine. In and out."

"Mr. Alano—"

An older man in a yellow Make-A-Moment polo comes down the hall, and Dane immediately shields us—shields Alano, really.

"Hi," Alano says from over Dane's shoulder.

"Welcome to Make-A-Moment," the man says cautiously, like we might be the threats. Then he squints and makes out Alano. "Alano Rosa? Wow! It's a pleasure to meet you. I'm Ross, the manager of this location."

Alano comes out from around Dane and shakes the man's hand. "Hi. It's a pleasure to meet you, Mr. Ross."

Ross's eyes now widen. "You're not dying, are you?" he asks, no longer starstruck.

Just like last night at Present-Time, Alano assures this Make-A-Moment manager that he isn't dying and that he's here for a friend. "We saw the job openings."

Ross looks at Dane, hopeful someone of his build is here to become a security guard, and then he turns to me, where he's no doubt picturing me behind the counter and checking in guests. He doesn't know that I'm a killer. Not yet.

"It's for me," I say. Then I second-guess and third-guess myself before adding, "I'm Paz."

I wait for Ross to recognize my name, but he just opens a folder. "Which position are you interested in?"

"Actor," I say. It feels nice owning this again.

"He's fantastic," Alano says.

I smile at the compliment, even if he's working off a performance from when I was six years old. (I still look back at that movie and think my acting really holds up.)

Ross hands me the application. "I take it you're familiar with our forthcoming Make-Life-Moments Experiences. There's a lot of roles someone young like you could play: a first date, a friend at graduation, or a son playing catch with his father."

I flinch at the idea of playing catch with Dad—of knowing I'll never be able to when it's time for my own End Day.

"Paz," Alano says.

I snap out of my trance. "Yeah, sorry, I'm just imagining all the possibilities. I'm your guy, I can adapt to any role you need me to."

Ross nods. "Great. Apply as soon as you can so we can review your résumé and schedule an audition. We're getting a lot of interest." Then he mutters, "I think some of these Disneyland actors are tired of dressing up as Mickey and Elsa."

There's this mischievous glint in Alano's green eye. "Would it be too much trouble for Paz to do his audition tonight?"

Before Ross or I can weigh in, Dane does. "Mr. Alano?"

"I want to help give Paz the edge over the competition," Alano says, like Dane is an older brother who needs to loosen up instead of a bodyguard sworn to keep him alive.

Ross scratches his head, thinking. "I would love to make an exception in gratitude to your family, but I'm unfortunately short-staffed tonight and don't have someone for Paz to act with. I just lost an employee this afternoon who found the job too . . . difficult."

I'm sure "difficult" means "devastating." It takes a lot for someone to face the dying, especially for minimum wage. I would be doing it for my survival and happiness.

"Thanks anyway," I say. I wave the application. "I'll go fill this out—"

"I can act with Paz," Alano volunteers.

"That's okay," I say, nervous that he's gonna blow this.

"What if Paz and I book an experience? Could that double as his audition?" Alano asks.

"That depends on what characters you're playing," Ross says.

"How about two boys on a first date?" Alano says, and I'm now nervous for different reasons. "You said it yourself that Paz could pull that off. I could be the Decker and Paz could be my date. Assuming that's all cool with Paz?"

Fuck yeah I'll go on a date with you is what I wanna say, but I just say, "I'm down." If only Ross knew how well I sold that line he would hire me on the spot.

Ross smiles. "Our company exists to make moments like this happen."

Agent Dane approaches the counter. "For Mr. Alano's security, I will need to know if there are any other people in the building or if you have any upcoming appointments with Deckers."

"No one else is here. Walk-ins like yourself are always

welcome, but it's rare for Deckers to appear in the evening, you know."

It's chilling how most of today's Deckers are dead or will be in the next few hours.

"I'll keep watch," Agent Dane tensely tells Alano.

Alano rejects Ross's offer for a complimentary booking and leads me to the kiosk. We click our way through the eight-page-long waiver, wondering which Decker reads this thing and changes their mind. The thing is, for all we know Alano isn't just playing a Decker, he might actually be one. He better not die on our date, fake or not, or that's a wrap on the Begin Days. Alano swipes through the selections, looking really cute as he squints, reading the descriptions for rafting through the Grand Canyon, climbing Mount Everest, volcano boarding in Nicaragua, and orbiting the moon.

"I've had a lot of real-world adventures," Alano says. "Anything catching your eye?"

You, I wanna say, but the only thing scarier than getting rejected by Make-A-Moment is getting rejected by Alano.

I swipe and discover that Make-A-Moment now offers fantasy/sci-fi experiences, like a wizard heist where you get to throw fireballs and cast lightning bolts at all the orcs guarding a stolen treasure. "We can do a fantasy world if you're tired of the real world," I say.

"As cool as it would be to act like a wizard with a Scorpius Hawthorne legend such as yourself, maybe we shouldn't be fighting for our lives as we get to know each other," Alano says, leaning in to whisper. "We sort of did that already last night."

How can someone speaking so quietly make my body wanna scream?

This date isn't gonna require a single second of acting.

"How about horseback riding?" I ask.

"Anything to do with a certain Oscar-winning film about gay cowboys?" Alano asks.

"Yeehaw."

I freeze when we get to the payment screen. My ticket alone is gonna cost four hundred and thirty dollars. That'll only leave me with seventy bucks in my bank account. Not sure I should really be putting a price on a date, except I would be spending real money on a fake date that we're only doing so I can maybe make back real money.

Alano swipes his card, covering us both. "My treat since I asked you out," he says, linking his arm through mine.

I can tell all the lies I want, but my body always tells the truth: my face flushes with heat, my heart races because of something good for once, and these happy nerves spreading everywhere inside me make me wanna jump up and down, like the first time my mom brought me to an audition—like I'm so much closer to the world I wanna live in.

We're guided down the hallway where there are three mini-screens above each open door, previewing the differ- ent experiences that can be found inside. The set designs are so amazing that I feel like I'm teleporting across the world every time we pass a room: mounds of sand that lead to a four-foot-high water tank with a surfboard; props of medieval weaponry and glowing sconces and a throne with suits of armor for Deckers to really immerse themselves as knights defending their dark castle; a projection of outer space, astronaut costumes, and a shuttle the size of a tank; a rock climbing treadmill blends in perfectly with the 3D Mount Everest, all of it surrounded by high-quality faux snow that big-budget movies use; and then our trail, complete with animatronic horses, foam boulders, artificial bushes, and a projection of a bright red sunset.

We're given VR glasses, a haptic feedback vest so we can feel vibrations within the realm, and gloves so our avatars will move as we do. I breathe in the scents of grass and river, filtering in from the gray diffuser that's blending in with the foam boulders, before climbing on top of my fake horse's very real, very uncomfortable saddle.

Once we're both strapped in, we switch on our VR glasses and I select my avatar—a light-skinned, curly-haired guy in a blue plaid shirt and jeans—and I don't waste time accessorizing beyond that.

A white light washes over me. In acting class, we're trained to create our own fourth wall when facing the camera because staring directly into it will break the illusion for the audience, but thanks to the VR glasses, I don't have to imagine anything: I'm surrounded by the greenest of trees that shoot up into the clear blue sky, and the trail ahead has hoofprints that create a real sense of history in this virtual world. And then out of nowhere, Alano appears on a horse—sorta. His avatar has long brown hair that falls down the back of his black plaid shirt, and he's accessorized with a cowboy hat and handkerchief; I wish I was looking at the real him.

"Try not to mind me," Ross says, which pulls me out of this world even more, like an audience member's phone going off during a live theater performance. "We always have guides present to tend to our guests. Just forget I'm here and enjoy your first date."

The stereo switches on, playing sounds of birds singing and squirrels scurrying and hooves clopping at a steady pace, which are perfectly in sync with the gentle swaying of our robot horses. No, not robot horses—real horses. I don't love Sanford Meisner's acting method, but I do love what he said about how acting is about living truthfully under imaginary circumstances. That's what I would do on a real movie set and that's what Make-A-Moment will be expecting once they cast me to be a character actor for their Deckers. I ignore everything that you wouldn't find in a real forest—the diffuser, the stereo, Ross watching us like a casting director—and I pretend like I'm not auditioning and act as if I'm on an actual first date with the real Alano and not this CGI stand-in.

"I'm happy you asked me out," I say. That's not scripted.

"I'm happy you said yes," Alano says. I hope that's not scripted.

It's a good thing that our narrative is that we're two boys on a first date because I've never been on a real date, so all my clue-lessness will work in my favor. But now I can't help but wonder if Alano has been on real dates.

My body starts telling a harsher truth, like it actually was lying before when I thought everything was good: my face goes warm again but this time out of embarrassment for being stupid enough to believe Alano wanted this date because he's inter-ested in me, my stomach twists like I'm gonna be sick, and my breath tightens like I've just been thrown off the horse and had my heart trampled over. I will only ever get close to the world I wanna live in, but I'll never actually arrive.

I stop myself, recalling my therapist's advice about what to do when I'm making upsetting assumptions. Raquel says that if I can't identify the story in my head with one of my five senses, then it isn't real. In this case, I haven't heard Alano say that he's only doing this out of pity. I haven't seen him look at me in disgust, like I'm nothing but a killer who deserves to die alone. And I haven't felt him push me away, like I'm not worth saving.

If there's something I wanna know, I can ask Alano, but fuck my senses, I don't need to hear all Alano's stories about going on real dates as he travels the real world, or see pictures of the hot guys he's used to dating.

"How long have you known you were into boys?" Alano asks.

I try to calm myself down and remind myself of the facts: Alano asked me out. Alano said he was happy I said yes to the date. And Alano wants to learn more about me now. Just because we're in a virtual world doesn't mean it can't be real.

"I kinda started cracking the code I was gay when I was nine. I think it was on Fourth of July or some other summer barbecue, but Mom was taking me to the park, and I saw some boy wiping away his tears on the street. I don't even remember what he looks like, just that I got that butterfly feeling that told me it was different." It's weird reflecting on this perfectly normal coming-of-age experience, knowing that it all goes to hell a few weeks later, when I was dealing with being a killer instead of gay. "What about you?"

"I feel like I should take that answer to the grave," Alano says lightly.

"Oh, come on. It's me."

"That's kind of why I shouldn't say anything!"

"I've come all this way for you," I say as our horses go through a clearing that brings us to this open valley where the sun is slowly sinking behind a mountain. "You gotta give me something."

Alano laughs. "You promise you won't ride off?"

"I promise I won't ride off."

"I had a crush on you," Alano says.

Thank fuck I'm strapped onto this horse because I almost fall off. "You're kidding."

Alano's avatar is facing me. "Look at me. For real." I remove my headset to find that Alano has already done the same. It's so great to see the real Alano with his real smile, to see that he's so close I could reach out and hold his hand. "Remember how I told you that I was watching the last Scorpius Hawthorne movie on the first End Day? I really should've said I was rewatching because of you."

Even with our headsets removed, how sheepish Alano is being still feels like a performance, maybe one he's putting on for Ross so I better play along too. "So it was love at first sight?"

"I don't believe in love at first sight," Alano says, throwing me off.

"Really? Because Kid Alano was rewatching a three-hour movie to see Kid Paz in a three-minute scene."

"I like the journey," Alano says, beaming. "The concept of falling in love at first sight isn't foreign to me. Deckers do it all the time, though I've often wondered how many of those couples would've survived outside of an End Day where there wasn't an undercurrent of desperation to get life right before you die. No one can know one way or the other, which is probably for the best; it's comforting to believe someone found their soulmate while there was still time."

"Then what do you believe in?"

"Friends first to make sure we like each other as we fall in love."

I can't help but imagine myself as part of that *we*.

"It worked for my parents," Alano says. "They met on August 15, 1988. Both eighteen. My father heard my mother laugh in a coffee shop and knew deep down that if he didn't know the girl behind the laugh that he would regret it for the rest of his life. Everyone thought he was insane for believing in his gut like that and for not giving up when my mother took her sweet time as friends—eighteen months exactly—before they dated. Before agreeing to a Valentine's Day dinner, she gave my father one rule: no asking her to be his girlfriend on Valentine's Day because she thought that was too cheesy. At midnight on February 15, 1990, my father didn't waste another minute asking to be her boyfriend, and they've been together ever since."

It's a dope story, but it's kinda infuriating that Joaquin Rosa got to meet his soulmate at eighteen and have a normal life, meanwhile I've been suicidal forever because of Death-Cast's fuckup. I guess if things work out between me and his son, I can move past it.

"My mom and stepdad were friends first too. She just married the wrong person."

"Thankfully they made it right before it was too late," Alano says.

My incoming little sibling is proof that Mom and Rolando are still making up for lost time.

"Now that I've opened up, it's your turn to tell me if you ever found me cute," Alano says.

"You never called me cute," I point out.

"Did I have to? I wasn't charmed by all your demonic magic spells. Kid Alano thought Kid Paz was cute just as nineteen-year-old Alano thinks nineteen-year-old Paz is cute."

This fake date is starting to feel real.

"Have you ever thought about me?"

I feel like Alano is all I think about since meeting him, but it's still weird that we sorta know each other because of the spotlights we grew up under. "Kinda impossible not to think about someone as famous as you. I honestly envied you a lot. You had it all."

"No one has it all. Every person has their smoke and mirrors, especially if they're famous. It's the only way to survive in a world that's always watching you," Alano says, acting as if his robotic horse rocked him hard, but he discreetly nods at Ross as a reminder that he can't say everything he might wanna.

I'm so used to growing up with people not trusting me that I don't understand how hard it must have been to grow up not trusting everyone around me.

Alano continues, "It's always greener on the other side, but I wish I got to grow up as a normal kid."

"Same," I say, even though we're on different sides of that famous kid/infamous kid coin. "I hope it wasn't all terrible."

"Of course not. I've gotten to live in ways people dream about their entire lives. Global travel, the finest dining, the coolest parties. It's been a really privileged upbringing, but there are moments you can't buy. Or I guess you can now," Alano says, gesturing like we're linked because of Make-A-Moment. "But I would trade so many of those extraordinary adventures alone for ordinary moments with a boyfriend. Sitting on the couch and bingeing the new season of the show we've been watching together for years. Taking turns applying sunscreen on each other's backs. Learning something new every day. Waking up and talking about our dreams."

All of that sounds extraordinary to me.

"You know what else I want?" Alano asks.

I hope he says me. "What?"

He grins. "I'd like to know if you think I'm cute before I die."

I laugh, a genuine I-can't-believe-how-good-this-feels laugh. "You still have some time to find out," I tease.

Through the rest of our simulated journey, we share fun facts, almost like we're actually boyfriends learning something new about each other: he once dyed his hair purple when he was fifteen and wishes he could scrub those pictures from the internet, or even just his own mind; my favorite mode of transport is the train, though I'm not mad at these robot horses; he went skydiving in Dubai, which I obviously knew from his Instagram but don't voice; I wanna visit Puerto Rico badly; he once auditioned to play clarinet in his elementary school band, but wasn't good enough; how I wouldn't survive in a postapocalyptic landscape unless my group needed an actor for entertainment; and we both love everything about the rain, how it feels, how it looks, how the world smells different when it's done.

"I like flowers," I say. "But I've never gotten any obviously."

"What kind of flowers do you like?" Alano asks, like he's about to ride away to grab some. "Roses? Tulips? Dahlias? Irises?"

"I legit don't know."

"You can steal my favorite flower. The lily of the valley. It symbolizes rebirth. Kind of perfect for the Begin Days."

"And a generous parting gift on your End Day," I say, right as our horses slow to a stop and the stereos fade to silence.

Our first date is over.

Ross claps before helping us get unbuckled from the saddles. "Paz, you were fantastic. Inquisitive, charming, quick. I'm sure I'll be seeing more of you around here. Let's get that application filled out."

Alano gives me an air five across the room, but I wish we were much closer and touching for real.

We return to the front, where I fill out the application on the spot as Alano proudly watches. The form asks if there's any criminal history to disclose. I say no because my records are sealed. I hand the application to Ross and look around the lobby, envisioning myself here a lot, becoming a chameleon who meets the needs of every Decker's dreams.

After Ross gives me his phone so I can take a picture of him with Alano, we leave Make-A-Moment, moving back out onto the pier where Dane shadows us again.

"That was so much fun," Alano says. "Way better than when I did *Vogue*'s seventy-three questions."

I definitely wanna look that up later. "How honest were you in there?"

"A hundred percent." Alano bats his eyes then looks up at the Pacific Park sign before we enter the pier's play area. "I have no reason to lie to you. Everything was true. The first date. Favorite flower. Childhood crush. Everything."

"Okay, that's wild. Why didn't you say anything about the crush last night?"

Alano gazes back at me, raising one eyebrow. "We were a little preoccupied," he says, which only now reminds me that the top of the Hollywood Sign wasn't exactly the time or place to confess his childhood crush. "I had my priorities straight last night, and I have new priorities now. Including living my life as I want. That means memorable first dates with my new cute friend."

Okay, okay, okay, okay, okay, I think this is going okay? Like, Alano might actually be hitting on me? I was spiraling before because I thought there's no way he could actually like someone like me, but he's not just dropping hints, he's straight-up calling me cute. And yeah, he called me a friend too, but he wants to be friends before boyfriends. It gives me enough courage to get to the bottom of his romantic history. "I'm still shocked you haven't been on a date."

"Why is that so shocking?"

"You're you. Alano Rosa. The Death-Cast heir. All that living, but no dating?"

"Being the Death-Cast heir is precisely why I haven't been on a date. My life has made it easier to climb mountains and skydive than fully trust someone."

"Have you gotten close to trusting anyone?"

He nods. "The stars ultimately didn't align," Alano says, a discomfort on his face before he switches it up on me. I wonder who broke his heart, or whose heart he broke. "The same can be said about you, by the way. No dates?"

"Nope. Boys aren't exactly rushing to hang out with the psycho dad-killer."

"There's no way anyone who meets you believes that."

"I'm not in college, I don't have a job, and I can't even get into an acting class. Guys don't get to meet me unless I'm on the Hollywood Sign."

"And you're never going back up there," Alano says, firm but lovingly. "The old ways of how you've accepted your treatment are in the past now. We're moving into the future, one Begin Day at a time."

For the first time in forever, I'm no longer counting down to killing myself but instead to the day when Alano and I will grow from friends into boyfriends.

ALANO
8:32 p.m.

We're at the end of the pier, watching the sun set beyond the dark ocean.

"You're a really calming presence. Like these waves," Paz says.

"I do my best."

It's great that Paz sees me this way, but it takes a lot of work to maintain this calm composure, especially since the night I made Death-Cast calls. At any given moment I'm trying to stay afloat from a flood of memories that threaten to drown me. It's so hard to focus on my life knowing everything I know and shouldn't know and everything I've done and shouldn't have done. I've been able to anchor myself by learning as much as I can about the world to trick my brain into focusing on the random trivia I've cataloged instead of my many traumas. The oldest and darkest of those traumatic incidents keeps creeping in tonight.

Paz turns away from the ocean and stares at me. "I like your earring."

I'm grateful to have something else to think about. "It was a coming-out gift from my father," I say, running my finger up and down the inch-long crystal that I've worn since June 10,

2016. "My parents already knew without me telling them, but I originally only came out to my mother because I was scared of disappointing my father like every other time I've gone against his vision. I needed to protect my coming-out experience to have at least one good memory. Thankfully I was wrong about my father. He was hard on himself for not making me comfortable enough to tell him earlier and promised to be better. That night we were all at dinner, and I expressed wanting to explore some new looks like painting my nails, getting my ears pierced, maybe trying on a dress to see if any of it felt right. The next morning, I woke up to nail polish, an old dress of my mother's, and this earring, all personally selected by my father with a note saying he loves me."

Paz looks like he might cry. "That's really beautiful."

"It really is. It makes me regret not trusting him."

Paz reaches for my earring, and I lean in, allowing him to run his finger up and down the crystal like I did; his fingertip brushes my earlobe and sends a shiver down my spine. "I bet Joaquin worked harder to show his acceptance because you didn't open up right away."

"He did. It's especially touching when you consider that my father grew up at a time where most men wouldn't have been caught dead wearing a single earring if they didn't want people thinking they were gay since that was more of an insult back then. I like to think of this earring as a personal invitation from my father to rebel."

I'm sure Pa wishes I would rebel less these days.

"I think my dad would've tried to lock me in the closet," Paz says. An intrusive thought slips in that I'm grateful Frankie Dario is dead before he could've tormented Paz for who he loves. "I honestly think if my dad were still alive, he would've bought into enough conspiracies that he would've become a Death Guarder."

I stop myself from flinching at the memory of the assassination attempt and shift my attention to the many conversations I've had with my parents about Death Guarders. We of course never villainize any pro-naturalist for not choosing Death-Cast, and we do our best to not believe every Death Guarder is villainous too. That cult is mostly made up of people who are susceptible to the many lies told about Death-Cast. There are also followers who have genuine reasons to hate us, even if Death-Cast's intentions have only ever been to make the world better.

It's this thinking that reminds me that people have dimensions. My father gave me that beautiful memory and has also given me one of my very worst. Maybe Frankie Dario had another layer to him too.

"Do you have any happy memories of your father?" I ask.

Paz's face goes from neutral to angry.

"I said happy memory. You look like you want to fight someone."

"Yeah, I wanna fight my dad, but I . . ."

But Paz already fought Frankie. And he both won and lost.

It was too soon to ask Paz to tell me something good about his father. If I'm not giving Paz the complete Alano Rosa

Encyclopedia, it's only fair there will be some pages missing in the Paz Dario Encyclopedia too. I apologize for bringing this up.

"No, you're fine. I was remembering the time where he took me to the movies to see *Marley & Me*, which I thought was gonna be fun because—"

I gasp. "Because the trailer makes it look like a comedy?"

"Yes! Nowhere in that trailer do they even hint at that dog dying. I obviously left the theater crying, and instead of my dad telling me to man up or something, he carried me home. He could've easily passed me over to my mom when we got back, but he held me until I stopped crying. It's so stupid to give him points for that, or even think about this as a happy memory, but I remember feeling so safe with him . . . and I'm angry that he didn't give me more memories like that." Paz rocks back and forth as tears start spilling. "Maybe if my dad had made me feel safer then I wouldn't have shot . . . I would've thought twice . . . I, I—"

I pull Paz into a hug, and he cries into my neck. "You deserved better."

"Or I got what I deserved," Paz wails.

Holding Paz as he grieves the life he truly deserved is making me die inside.

PAZ
8:53 p.m.

I don't know how much time passes while I cry over Dad, or when we go from standing at the end of the pier to sitting on a bench that overlooks the beach, or how long I've been quiet. I only know that Alano won't leave my side.

"Do you want me to take you home?" Alano asks.

Okay, scratch that, Alano *wants* to leave my side.

I shrug out from under the arm he's wrapped around my shoulders. "Yeah, no, I'll go home," I say, walking down the pier, pissed at myself for flirting with Alano, for opening up to Alano, and most especially for meeting Alano. I could've been dead instead of dealing with more shit like this. Maybe I should go jump into the ocean since I can't swim.

Alano chases after me and blocks my path. "Whoa. Time-out. What did I say?"

"It's what you're being too nice to say. You're trying to get rid of me because I'm too much."

"Paz, I'm definitely not trying to get rid of you, and I don't think you're too much. I'm having a great night with you, even when things get heavy. That's part of getting to know the real you without all the smoke and mirrors. I offered to take you home because you've been so quiet, and I thought you wanted to be alone but were stuck with me."

It's absolutely psychotic that Alano thinks he's stuck with me and not the other way around.

"I'm sorry," I say, hiding my face behind my hands.

"No, I'm sorry for bringing up your father and then trying to leave you. Abandonment rage is a clear issue for borderline personality disorder, and I violated that. I promise I'll be more careful."

This is my dumbass brain telling my heart to take things personally.

I hate BPD.

It's horrifying to remember that this is me on Prozac and that this is me embracing new beginnings. Even with antidepressants and good intentions I almost self-harmed today and I've had freak-outs that I'm still trying to figure out if they're justified or triggered by my disorder.

I hate being a mystery to myself, but I'm lucky that Alano is trying to solve me too.

"Don't apologize, this isn't your fault, it's all mine," I say, desperate to win back Alano's charms. I try turning on Happy Paz. "Let's go play some games."

"No," Alano says firmly. "Your disorder isn't your fault."

"Okay, but come on, let's do something fun—"

Alano grabs my hands. "Tell me your disorder isn't your fault."

"It kinda is, right? BPD is created by trauma, and I shot my dad, that was a choice I made—"

"Your disorder isn't your fault," he interrupts.

"I gotta take some blame—"

"Your disorder isn't your fault."

I stare into Alano's beautiful eyes, promising myself to try to see myself as he does. To always be honest and show him who I am so he forgives me whenever my disorder takes over like some demonic possession. "My disorder isn't my fault," I say, voice cracking.

"No, it's not," Alano says, wrapping his arm around my shoulders again, proving that he isn't trying to get rid of me. He only wants to hold me close.

9:47 p.m.

After playing a bunch of games in Pacific Park, we go on the Ferris wheel.

We get into the passenger cabin, and once the door is shut and bolted, we're lifted away from everyone, even Alano's bodyguard.

"I used to be terrified of heights," Alano says as we slowly glide toward the sky. "It wasn't acrophobia, but close. I refused to go into my father's office at Death-Cast unless his blinds were down. I avoided roller coasters. I begged my parents to avoid bridges because I was sure we would roll off and die, even though we didn't receive Death-Cast alerts. It didn't help when we moved into a penthouse when I was ten. The slow ride up the elevator made me so aware of how high we were going. It was torturous, but nothing was worse than flying."

"What made you get over that fear?"

"I was more scared of missing out on life," Alano says, completely cool as we get higher and higher, even though it's a real possibility that he can fall out of this cabin and die. "If I couldn't handle great heights, I wouldn't be able to travel or go on hikes or be at peace in my own home. Exposure therapy helped. It's hard to be scared of flying after you've dived out of a plane."

"Or climbed a frozen waterfall," I say.

"Yeah—" Alano looks up, blinking, like he's processing. He smiles. "I never told you about Helmcken Falls."

Oh, right, I'm not supposed to know what I know from Alano's Instagram.

"Wow, look how high up we are," I tease, looking down onto the pier.

Alano laughs. "Were you checking me out online? Maybe because you think I'm cute?"

I stare at his *Gotcha* smile. "I don't know what you're talking about."

Alano stands, and the cabin rocks. I tell him to sit down, but he's still smiling. "Do you really want me dying without knowing the truth?"

"Okay, fine, I think you're cute, Alano."

My heart is pounding so damn hard as Alano howls triumphantly. It definitely doesn't calm down when he finally sits, because now he's sitting next to me, the balance shifting.

"I can now die happy," Alano says.

"You should know that your face is cheating."

"My face is cheating?"

"Yeah, you got two different color eyes. That makes anyone hot."

"Now I'm hot?" Alano says.

How high is too high before a person is not getting enough oxygen? I'm gonna guess it's as high as we are now.

"Honestly, Paz, that means a lot. Kids made fun of me for my heterochromia. They called me an alien with weird eyes who could foresee how people died. That eventually spun into this stupid theory about Death-Cast shackling an alien to a bathtub to predict End Days."

"That's definitely dumb, but not liking your eyes is dumber." I remember being at the foot of the Hollywood Sign when the helicopter beams lit up Alano's eyes. They were so striking then, and they're so striking now. "Your psychic alien eyes are dope. I wish I had them."

"I don't. Then I wouldn't be able to look at your eyes."

"There's nothing special about my eyes."

"Are you kidding? They remind me of this plant—"

"Let me guess, a dying plant that needs to be watered?"

Alano laughs. "No, a cymbidium orchid. My father gave some to my mother on February fifteenth for their thirtieth dating anniversary. The shade was so beautiful. A color trapped between brown and bronze."

"That's a really poetic way of saying light brown," I joke.

"Nothing wrong with poetry."

We're now at the top of the Ferris wheel, and instead of

taking in the dark sky or ocean, Alano stares at me with his psychic alien eyes, the right eye as green as bright leaves, the left as dark as tree bark. (There's some poetry for you.) Alano might not be seeing the End Days, but maybe he's seeing the future, or imagining one. And I don't just hope, I believe he's seeing me in his future, just like I see him in mine. And why wouldn't I? There's no future without Alano.

His psychic alien gaze shifts to my lips before returning to my eyes.

Yes, my cymbidium orchid brown eyes answer for me.

Our eyes close as we lean in, and the Ferris wheel suddenly thrusts us down, and we grab on to each other's hands to stay upright, laughing and screaming with the other passengers as the ride picks up speed, cold winds whipping our faces, and after two more rapid spins, we slow to a finish.

I hate that we didn't get to kiss, but that was so fun. The best part might be how Alano still hasn't let go of my hand.

"Hey," I say, bringing us to a stop as we cross the pier. "I'm really happy you got over your fear of heights before climbing up the Hollywood Sign."

Alano flinches slightly, like he's imagining what would've gone down—*who* would've gone down—if he hadn't been there. "I like to think I would've chased after you anyway."

"A total stranger."

"A stranger whose life was worth saving. You're more than a stranger now."

My heart is pounding even harder than when we were suspended in the sky. "Who am I?"

"Someone I hope I get to know forever," Alano says, and instead of leaning in for a kiss, he pulls me in for a tight hug.

It's unspoken, but I read between the lines: *Don't kill yourself.*

This isn't like Mom's threat. This is Alano pleading. He doesn't need to.

I can't think of any better reason to keep living than having a life with Alano.

ALANO

I still don't believe in love at first sight, but I do believe it's possible to fall for someone in one day.

On the ride back to Paz's, I was quiet as I focused on the road. I would hate for everything between us to end so soon because I wasn't careful. It's also given me the chance to process all of these big feelings. The elation I experience whenever I earn Paz's trust during his lows, knowing it will only lead to some incredible highs. The confusion over whether to kiss Paz since we aren't in the best headspaces and how much I want to live like I might not get another chance. And now the grief of our first Begin Day ending as we pull up to Paz's house.

"Here we are," I say.

"I rate this ride three stars," Paz says.

"Three stars?"

"I got here safely, but the driver was too quiet."

"Most passengers prefer quiet rides."

"Maybe when the driver isn't interesting."

"Was he cute at least?"

Paz grins. "He was pretty hot."

"Your driver would like to apologize for not filling the

silence with interesting tidbits. He was very interested in keeping you alive as well as being frustrated with his bodyguard."

After the Ferris wheel, Agent Dane insisted that it was time to go so we could be back at the mansion before midnight. I already broke one rule tonight by going to Make-A-Moment, and I would've happily broken another to keep hanging out with Paz.

"Dane was only doing his job, right?"

"A job he's already lost once because of me. My father would fire him for good if he ever messes up again."

"Your dad is also doing his job." Paz taps my crystal earring. "He loves you. Remember?"

I nod, but all I'm thinking about is how badly I want Paz to touch me again. It could be another finger tap or our hands holding. Lips meeting. I just need more.

"Do you have to swap that out?" Paz asks. He points at my bandage, signed with our names. It's seen better days.

"I do, actually. Every twenty-four to thirty-six hours."

"Isn't that—"

"Tonight."

The silence sits between us, and I wonder if the universe is about to answer my plea for Paz's touch. For a second chance at a first kiss.

"I have some gauze and ointment inside." Paz breaks our eye contact.

I can't tell if he's shy or ashamed or nervous.

"I can run inside and grab you some. Or you can come inside, and I can help you," he offers quietly, like he's bracing himself for disappointment as if this invite doesn't have my heart racing even faster. "I'll just bring it out, I know you gotta get going—"

"I'd love your help," I interrupt.

My only roadblock will be my bodyguard. We exit my car, and I walk over to Agent Dane's as Paz waits by his front door. Agent Dane lowers his window and asks if everything is all right.

"Please don't say no to what I'm about to ask," I say with pleading hands.

"It sounds like you already have your answer."

"I'm going inside Paz's house quickly. He's giving me a new bandage," I say, extending my arm so he can see that the threads in this one are coming undone. "I'll be out in ten minutes. Fifteen tops."

Agent Dane shakes his head. "You know I can't allow that, Mr. Alano. Background checks have already been performed on Paz's mother and stepfather, but we haven't surveilled the house."

"Did your background checks hint at his parents being dangerous?"

"No, but—"

"I'm going to be okay. If Paz was going to kill me, he would've done it last night when he had a gun."

"How do you know he doesn't have another gun inside?"

"Because he doesn't."

"Did you know the assassin had a switchblade in his phone?"

I stay quiet. It's unfair to compare Paz to Mac Maag, but from an outsider's perspective, especially a bodyguard's, it's more than fair. Both Paz and Mac Maag lost family unexpectedly on the first End Day. If one boy cozied up before trying to kill me, what's to stop another? Rio raised the same concern.

Agent Dane exits the car. "While I don't personally believe Mr. Paz is a threat, it is my job to assume he is. I've been fired already for trusting your instincts and for letting you out of my sight. Now you have had me reinstated to serve as your protector. I intend to do this right."

I'm used to treating Agent Dane more like an overprotective big brother instead of utilizing him as a bodyguard, and it's clear that his reinstatement won't ever let me forget his position again. "My time with Paz is limited, and I won't be able to know if there's more in store for us if I can't connect with him. I accept the risks if it brings me closer to what I want out of life."

Agent Dane peeks over at Paz like he's assessing him. "You might be willing to take some risks, but if anything happens to you from this night on, it will cost me this job and my entire career. No one will hire me if the Death-Cast heir dies on my watch. That's why I can't let you out of my sight."

"I understand," I say, turning so I can go say good night to Paz.

"But if Mr. Paz were to invite me inside and allow me to

conduct a search, then I can grant you limited time with him before returning you to the house," Agent Dane says.

I turn right back around with the biggest smile. "You're the best bodyguard ever."

"Your compliance is what will make you the best client. Now let me do my job so you can live your life."

PAZ
10:34 p.m.

I can't believe Alano Rosa is inside my house—and that his bodyguard is searching for weapons.

Yeah, this is definitely not how I pictured bringing a boy home for the first time, but it is what it is.

Before inviting anyone in, I knocked on Mom's bedroom door and alerted her and Rolando that we would be having guests. Mom was pretty damn cute about Alano popping in, which I don't take for granted because some parents would totally suck in this situation, but they definitely have some uneasiness over Alano's bodyguard wanting to rummage through our house. At the end of the day, we have nothing to hide and make peace with it. Alano needs these precautions. Mom and Rolando are changing into something more presentable than her nightgown and his tank top and boxers and then they'll be out any minute. I can't be more embarrassed by anything they'll say than I already am about what our house says about us.

Even though I cleaned the house today, I'm still so damn self-conscious. There's no way I did as good a job as the housekeepers Alano's family must employ. I'm also well aware that can't be a one-person job in their mansion here or their pent-house in New York. Our house is so small that Dane is almost done inspecting our living room, since we only have space for a TV, three-seater couch, small dining table, smaller coffee table, and an arched cabinet with family pictures. He opens the cabinet and only finds our extra throw blankets.

More than anything, I feel stupid about inviting Alano inside. I was so desperate to keep hanging out that I thought we could go straight to my bedroom, rebandage his arm and stomach, and maybe kiss in peace. I didn't think we would have to watch his bodyguard search for weapons that aren't here, or scan for cameras with his infrared detector, all so we can have a few minutes of privacy.

Alano isn't hanging by the door as ordered. He's conducting his own inspection of the framed family pictures on the cabinet's shelves. "May I?" he asks.

"Go for it."

He examines a throwback photograph of me on Halloween where I was dressed up as Scorpius Hawthorne in his crimson robe with the fiery emblem and the scar painted on my fore-head. I was trick-or-treating with a skull-shaped bucket.

"This is so cute," he says with the biggest smile that makes me forget about all my insecurities, even as Dane goes through our drawers in the kitchen. "That robe is amazing. Did you get to take one home from set?"

"Nope, this was before I even got cast. My mom made my costume."

Alano brings the photograph closer to his face. "It looks so real."

"I bet you've had some kick-ass costumes made for you."

He nods. "Sure, but nothing made by my mother. This is really special."

I might not live in some multimillion-dollar mansion that probably has secret passageways, but I do have an amazing mom who goes all out for me.

"Maybe your mother can make Halloween costumes for us this year," Alano says.

I have to fight against every instinct that is screaming that I'll be long dead before Halloween, but that's easier than usual when I imagine Alano and me in matching costumes—in a couple's costume.

There are footsteps down the hall as Mom and Rolando approach in their bathrobes.

"Hi," Mom sings. "Welcome to—"

Dane moves so quickly from the kitchen counter to the hall that he seems more like a threat than a protector. Rolando immediately shields my startled mom.

"Slow down, Agent Dane," Alano says—commands. "They're greeting us."

This doesn't make Dane any warmer. He asks Mom and Rolando if they'll agree to personal inspection, which honestly pisses me off, but they both do it, and they're doing it for me. I can't believe they're being patted down in their own home as if they're dangerous.

"I'm so sorry about all of this, Ms. Medina and Mr. Rubio," Alano says, truly embarrassed. He mouths an apology to me too.

"Don't be," Mom says once cleared. "You need to take care of yourself and allow people to take care of you." She opens her arms. "It also means I'm safe to hug, if you'd like."

Alano smiles as he steps into Mom's arms. "It's wonderful to meet you, Ms. Medina."

"Call me Gloria, please," Mom says.

"My parents would kill me," Alano says.

"Your bodyguard will stop them," Rolando says, shaking Alano's hand. "Or scare them, at least," he adds, looking back at Dane, who is continuing his sweep of the kitchen. "Anyway, it's good to see you. You won't remember me, but we met briefly before the first End Day. I was a herald—"

"I remember you, sir," Alano says. "I'm sorry to interrupt. That was rude."

Rolando waves off the so-called rudeness. "You actually remember me?"

"It was after the first simulation training for all the heralds. There was supposed to be an entertainer to cheer everyone up, but she no-showed, so my mother brought me into the rec room to color with all the heralds because she thought seeing a kid having fun could be a good reminder about how life goes on after the distressing practice calls. You complimented the ball gown and tuxedo I drew."

Rolando smiles, beaming with pride. "I can't believe I made such an impression. I definitely like you more than your old man."

"Rolando," Mom scolds. "Show some respect."

"It's okay," Alano says. "I've heard far worse about my father. In your defense, Rolando, it is pretty common for heralds to quit after their first shift. I had my own this week. I thought I knew what I was getting myself into after almost ten years of secondhand stories, but it's been impossible to recover from how difficult that was." His eyes glaze over, and I'm sure he's reliving the moment that Decker shot himself. He shakes it off. "I commend you for enduring through the very first End Day without knowing the true weight of that work."

Rolando shakes Alano's hand again and pats his back. "Maybe I'll give Death-Cast another shot when you're running that place," he says with a laugh.

"You would be welcome," Alano says.

I hope Rolando isn't holding his breath for a job at Death-Cast, since Alano won't be inheriting the company anytime soon, if ever.

"Can we get you something to drink?" Mom asks. "Tea? Water?"

I catch Alano as he looks past my mom and stepdad. Dane shakes his head slightly as if Mom and Rolando have eyes in the backs of their heads.

"I'm not thirsty, but thank you," Alano says, and pivots into a compliment about our pretty basic chandelier. I bet Alano actually does want a drink, but his bodyguard won't risk us poisoning him. It's no shit why Alano is struggling with Death-Cast's interference with his life.

"Anyway, I'm gonna help Alano clean up his wound in my bedroom," I say.

Dane blocks the hall. "I need to perform an inspection first."

This is pretty ridiculous, but I throw Dane a thumbs-up. It wouldn't have been a hard code to crack on which bedroom is mine, but I point it out anyway.

"I'm sorry," Alano says.

"Don't sweat it."

I'm gonna make this invasion of privacy worth it because once Alano and I are alone, I'm gonna confess that I like him. We were gonna kiss in Santa Monica, that's not in my head. Yeah, we got interrupted, but if I'm supposed to take that as a sign that it shouldn't have happened, then that means I gotta climb that Hollywood Sign again and kill myself like I was gonna do before Alano intervened.

Right? I legit can't tell if I'm talking myself into heartbreak or not. I also won't know if I'm losing out on love if I don't take a leap.

A good leap.

"Congratulations, by the way," Alano says to Mom and Rolando. "Paz told me the wonderful news that you're expecting."

Mom smiles through her surprise. "I suppose we aren't keeping this a secret, Pazito," she says.

"My bad, Mom. It just came up."

Alano muffles an apology behind his hands. Mom calls him adorable and says that her pregnancy is only a secret right now because she's nervous about the risks. I have Alano redeem himself by rattling off those stats he shared with me last night about women older than Mom who've had successful pregnancies. I watch as Mom and Rolando grow impressed with Alano and hopeful for their baby.

"Any chance you're a psychic who can predict life?" Rolando asks, laying a hand on Mom's stomach, which we all hope grows and grows.

"Unfortunately not," Alano says apologetically.

If Mom loses that baby, I don't know how any of us will survive that. The fear has me thinking about self-harming and—

Oh shit.

My knife.

My knife that's hidden in my nightstand.

My knife that's hidden in my nightstand in my bedroom.

My knife that's hidden in my nightstand in my bedroom where Dane is looking for weapons.

This is bad, this is so fucking bad. If Dane finds that knife he'll mark me as a threat to Alano, and Mom and Rolando will mark me as a threat to myself. I could lose Alano, and Dane could help detain me until I can be transported to a suicide prevention facility.

"I'm gonna check on Dane," I say while rushing toward my bedroom. I don't doubt that Alano will be fine with Mom and Rolando; he can talk to anyone about anything, but I won't be able to talk to him about everything and nothing if I get caught.

I stand outside my bedroom. The closet door is open, and my trunk where I hid my gun is closed. Dane is lifting my mattress, right next to my nightstand where *Golden Heart* is placed under my lamp.

"Hey, you need anything?" I nervously ask. I should be Play It Cool Paz or Totally Innocent Paz right now, but I'm sweating.

Dane drops my mattress back onto the frame. "Almost done, Mr. Paz."

He opens the nightstand, and I shut down my scream before it can blast out. This is where I gotta become Play It Cool Paz. I almost ask what he thinks about my room, but he's smarter than that, he would see right through the Totally Innocent Paz act. Dane would take a closer look and find my knife and he wouldn't believe my performance as I Only Have That Knife to Hurt Myself Paz even though it's true.

"That's my journal," I say, hoping he respects my privacy. I don't know if granting Dane access also allows him to read through my journal to make sure I haven't written down any master plans to assassinate Alano.

"My mom got it for me because I'm suicidal," I say before Dane can pick up the journal and realize the weight doesn't match that of an ordinary book, since I tore out all the pages to store my knife because I knew my mom and stepdad would actually respect my privacy.

"It has all these inspirational quotes. Most of them are pretty dumb, but some hit home," I lie. Not only about there being no pages in there but all the quotes actually pissed me off.

"I'm sorry to hear that you're struggling," Dane says as he closes the drawer.

I feel the intense relief that I only know from giving in to a self-harm urge. I hope I can find a healthier relief in a future Begin Day. Maybe even tonight when Alano and I kiss.

Dane inspects for hidden cameras before nodding. "Thank you for your cooperation, Mr. Paz."

"No problem."

Once Dane steps out, I take a moment to compose myself with some deep breaths. I can't believe how close that was.

There's a knock at the door. I spin around, and my heart races again.

"Hi," Alano says. He's standing in the doorway and already looking around my bedroom. "Your parents are lovely."

I always struggle with considering Rolando my parent. It has nothing to do with him because he's an amazing stepdad and the loving partner my mom deserves, but it's this psychological hurdle I can't get over. Almost like I don't wanna mentally slot Rolando into the same place Dad was in because of what I did to him—and what I would do again if Rolando ever became a threat to my mom. I don't get into this with Alano, I just say thanks.

"Are you going to invite me in?" Alano asks.

"Yeah—wait. How do I know you're not a vampire needing an invitation?"

"Well, the lore is about vampires being invited to the house, not bedrooms. Though the Eden family in the Nightlight Saga don't need an invitation. They're also beautiful and wealthy. I could be one of them," Alano says, stepping inside as if to prove his point. My heart is pounding because a boy has finally come into my bedroom, and, you know what, he might be a vampire like Edgar Eden. His human love interest, Zella Raven, sure as shit didn't know that she lived among vampires and werewolves and faeries. She didn't even have Death-Cast in her world, however the hell that works. For all I know Alano and his family are magical beings. "How much fun would we have if I turned you into a vampire?"

"Probably a lot, but immortality is my biggest nightmare."

"Only because you don't have someone who will stop you from stepping out into the sun."

I don't get into how the vampires in the Nightlight Saga glow like fireflies under sunlight instead of combusting in flames. I'm too caught up thinking about my favorite fantasy world. The Immortal's story in *Golden Heart* made me grateful that for as long as I have to be alive it won't be forever, but watching him fall in love with Death showed that eternity could be worth it as long as you have the right someone by your side—like Alano just said. I hope—no, I'm sure—that Alano is suggesting that he could be that someone.

"Now that I'm here, can I have a tour?" Alano asks.

"Sure, but the tour will be over really fast." I point out my dying Zebra plant and the camera I used for my self-tape and my collection of novels, plays, and games. "There you go."

Alano glares. "I'm giving you one star for that terrible tour."

"What else do you need, a tour of the bed?"

He grins. "That would definitely increase the rating."

I tell him to shut up when I really wanna say *Let's do it.*

"Can I please have a proper tour? I need to do research for my Paz Dario Encyclopedia."

"It's just a tiny bedroom."

"Even the smallest exhibits in a museum contain worthwhile history. Your 'tiny bedroom' can say a lot about you. I'd love for you to tell me what everything means."

"Not all my history in here is good."

"We all have history we're not proud of," Alano says. "It's still worth telling."

Most people's bedrooms are their sanctuaries, and I guess my bedroom has been too, but instead of nights of face masks and journaling and prayers, I spent mine waiting for Death-Cast to call and self-harming and desperate to die. Instead of depressing Alano, I show him my Scorpius Hawthorne collection: my hardcover of *Scorpius Hawthorne and the Immortal Deathlings* signed by Poppy Iglesias; the Polaroids with the cast, especially my forever favorite one where Howie Maldonado and I are holding the famous iron wand; and the framed pages of the sides I had on set.

Alano wants to know what's up with the monochromatic decor. Bright colors were honestly pissing me off so I stuck to black and white, especially after my therapist suggested that an absence of warm colors might be contributing to my bad moods. The big Zebra plant was supposed to help, though that's more brown than green these days, and we'll see if it makes a comeback as I keep tending to it during these Begin Days.

We go through my wardrobe, video games (his best friend Rio has been playing the *Dark Vanishing* sequel), plays, books, and I show him the binder on my desk of the short films I wrote and printed as if I would do something with them one day. Maybe now I will.

And as we approach my bed, I almost point out the knife in my nightstand or the spot on the floor where Mom found me after my first suicide attempt, but I hold back.

"That's my weighted blanket," I say instead. "It's supposed to feel like a hug or something."

"I take it you don't feel that way."

"It's just not the same."

"I fully agree. It's nice, but nothing beats a real cuddle."

I've had sex twice, but I wonder how many times Alano has—and with who. That's a bridge we're bound to cross as we discover more and more about each other.

Alano picks up my hardcover of *Golden Heart* from the nightstand. "Can I see what Orion signed?" he asks, opening the book.

Two pieces of paper fall out. I rush and pick them up.

"What are those?" he asks.

I remind myself I don't have to be ashamed of my history. I hand over the ripped autograph where Orion told me to keep living. "I tore it out the night I met you."

Alano studies the torn page like a historian. "I'm happy you're following his advice."

"I'm not living because of him."

"Still. It's really great advice. What if we taped it back inside?

I'd love for you to have this reminder the next time you reread this book."

I was torn on whether I would keep it, but something in me clearly couldn't get myself to throw it away when I was cleaning. I don't know if I'll ever have it in me to reread this book, especially whenever they announce the cast and set photos get leaked and the actual movie starts hitting theaters, but this might be the reminder that saves my life. I grab tape from my desk and stick Orion's autograph on the inside cover.

"It looks scarred," I say.

"Or like it's healing," Alano says. He points at the other page sticking out of my pocket. "What's that?"

This I don't hand over. "My suicide note."

Alano's overprotective mode comes alive. "Why are you keeping that? You're not planning on needing it again, are you?"

"No, I'm not planning anything like that, but . . . I don't know what the future holds. If nothing changes and I can't survive, then Mom will know that I loved her enough to not leave her in mystery over my struggles. Or maybe the Begin Days work out and this suicide note will be a reminder of how far I've come."

"I hope more than anything it's the latter, Paz."

"Me too, Alano."

He offers a sincere smile before looking around my bedroom. "Well, thank you for the five-star tour. I learned a lot about you."

"You gotta invite me over to check out yours."

"My parents are currently not allowing guests, not even my best friend who flew out here, but you're honestly not missing much. My bedroom back home is more representative of who I am whereas the one here needs more personal touches."

"Are you doing anything tomorrow? We have this dope flea market every Sunday that has lots of cool antiques, jewelry, clothes."

"I'd love that. Does it open early by any chance? I'm supposed to go with Rio to Universal Studios tomorrow."

I'm bummed that his Sunday is booked with a best friend he'll see back home considering he goes back to New York on Wednesday, but I just have to take what I can get—again. "The market opens at ten, it's on Melrose. Maybe you can pull some Death-Cast heir strings and get in earlier."

Alano laughs. "I don't want to abuse any privileges if I'm not embracing the role. I'll make ten work and can head to Universal at eleven. Do you think an hour is enough?"

I don't think it is, but I can't risk Alano backing out completely. "Yeah, we'll move fast."

There's a knock at the door. It's Dane. "It's twenty-three hundred, Mr. Alano. We need to be leaving."

"Ten more minutes," Alano says, showing off his old bandage. "Paz still needs to wrap me up."

"Ten minutes," Dane says as he returns to the living room.

"Only ten minutes?" I ask Alano. Suddenly an hour doesn't seem so bad.

"I'm sorry. It's only so I can keep the peace with my parents.

Believe me, I wish I could stay over. I could talk to you all night."

"You can if you want," I say so fast it's like I'm talking over another actor's line. "I mean, you could hang here with me, and we can make the couch nice and cozy for Dane."

Alano laughs. "That's a very tempting offer, but my father would probably fire Dane for allowing that in a house that didn't get to undergo a full inspection. Maybe another night?"

"Maybe another night," I say hopefully.

I go into my closet, where I hide my bandages, gauze, wipes, and petroleum jelly so that Mom and Rolando can't question why we're going through the supply so quickly. Alano and I sit on the edge of my bed. I wish I had time to lie down with him, to tell him how much I like him, but that's gonna have to wait until tomorrow morning at the market, I guess. For now I carefully unwrap the bandage from his arm and I fight back a gasp. There's dry, crusty blood and bluish-purple bruising around his stitched-up wound. It's one thing to inflict this kinda damage on myself and sickening to know someone caused this on the boy I care about.

"Let me know if this hurts," I say as I carefully wipe down his wound's perimeter before lathering on the petroleum jelly.

"You have a gentle touch, Nurse Paz."

My thighs would disagree.

I press down on his wound with gauze and rebandage his forearm.

"Is it disgusting to offer you my old bandage?" Alano asks.

"I mean, yeah, but it's a legally binding contract. We can't throw it away."

"Maybe you can store it somewhere safe with your suicide note."

I think I know just the place.

I'm about to put all my supplies away when Alano calls me back.

"Paz? You missed a spot." Alano gets up from the bed and lifts his shirt high enough to show me the bandage wrapped around his abdomen. "It's okay if you don't want to help—"

I'm back at his side so fast it's like I teleported. "What's the best way to do this? Do you wanna hold your shirt up?"

"It'll bother my arm. Do you mind if I just take it off?"

"All good," I say.

Alano takes his shirt off, and seeing his bare chest again makes me wish he was staying the night even more. I would close my door if I weren't scared of Dane kicking it down, but I'm gonna need it up for the next time Alano comes through.

I circle Alano as I unwrap the bandage around his abdomen, like a little dance. It requires more delicacy this time since the tape is clinging to his skin for dear life. Alano winces in pain, especially around his stab wound. He lets out little breaths, telling me he's fine, but I know it hurts like hell to remove tiny Band-Aids from knee scrapes and scabs, and it hurts even more to peel off bandages from bigger cuts like the ones on my thighs. I can only imagine the pain from being stabbed.

I rest a hand on his shoulder, steadying myself before I remove the final patch. "This is gonna suck," I warn.

"Just rip it off. I don't want to drag this out."

"Are you sure?"

"It's going to suck either way. I'd rather it be quick."

Together, we take deep breaths while staring into each other's eyes. My hand squeezes his shoulder, and I love the feel of his skin so much that I almost pull him closer. Instead, I put him out of his misery and rip the bandage off, his body tensing under my grip. He bites down on his lip while stomping in pain. I almost angry-cry looking at his horrific wound, but I quickly clean the blood and apply the jelly to provide some relief.

"I'm sorry, I'm sorry," I keep repeating.

"It's not your fault."

"I just hate hurting you."

"You're only hurting me to heal me."

Those words echo in my head as I do three laps around Alano with the new bandage so it's nice and snug. I end right in front of him. Everything changes in an instant. Alano's brown eye and green eye look between my eyes and lips. He rests a hand on my hip and pulls me closer. This is all I want, and I should be smiling or pressing my lips against his but instead I blurt out, "I self-harm."

Alano straightens as I back up. "You what?"

"I'm not some healer, I hurt myself. A lot. It's how I get through the Not-End Days—how I've been getting through them this year before meeting you," I say quietly. "No one knows."

Alano stands there, not moving a muscle until he puts his shirt back on. I wonder if he's about to leave because it's one thing to hang out with a suicidal boy with borderline personality disorder and another to hang out with one who's also self-harming. But Alano isn't a piece of shit. He climbed the Hollywood Sign to save a suicidal stranger. And now he walks right up to me and gives me a hug that makes me feel so safe from myself.

"Thank you for trusting me," Alano whispers. "I'm sorry you've been alone with this."

I half expect Alano to confess that he's self-harmed too, since he's also attempted suicide, but that never comes. I feel relief and guilt. "I'm sorry for putting this on you, I just don't wanna lie to you and I wanna put an end to it."

"Your history is worth telling, and I asked for all of it," Alano says, relaxing his hold to meet my eyes again. "The next time you're tempted to prove Death-Cast wrong, I'm here for you. Even if I'm on the other side of the world, I'm here for you."

"I believe you," I say, which is maybe the most powerful thing I've ever felt in my life. Even though Alano won't physically be in LA, I trust that I can call him at any time, almost like he's my personal suicide prevention hotline but even better because the other person on the line cares about me more than any stranger will. "I promise I'm done with self-harming. Tonight I'm gonna put my knife back in the kitchen."

"Where is it now?"

"In my nightstand."

"Didn't Dane check . . . ?"

"I turned my journal into a secret compartment."

Alano stares at the nightstand like there's a great evil inside.

"First phones hide blades and now books. Dangerous world we live in."

"Sorry. I'd put it back now, but Dane would probably shoot me if I go out there wielding a knife."

Alano flinches at the thought. He grabs my hand. "I'm really proud of you, Paz. This is the best way to end our first Begin Day."

I'm not sure it's the best way, but it's pretty damn promising. I just have to follow through, day by day, night by night.

"Are you going to be okay tonight?" Alano asks.

"Yeah, I think so." I believe myself for once. "If something changes—"

"You call me."

"I'll call you."

We hug for a long time, but not long enough because Alano's bodyguard is back to guard me from Alano's body again. To be fair, it would never be long enough. Not even if we were vampires.

Alano and I walk out into the living room, where Mom and Rolando welcome him back anytime before saying good night. I watch Alano as he walks to his car, waves one last time, and drives off. I don't realize that I'm doing exactly what my mom does whenever I leave until she teases me about it. That's when I realize that this is her way of showing she cares about me and my way of showing I care—really, really care—about Alano.

Last night, Alano stared up at the night sky and suggested

that our story was written in the stars, and I didn't see it take shape then, but the constellation is glowing bright as fuck now.

Before midnight, when I'm the only one awake, I honor my promise to Alano and remove the knife from my nightstand and put it straight into the dishwasher. If I'm ever tempted to hurt myself again, I'll open up my journal to find my suicide note and the Begin Day bandage instead of the knife. And I can call Alano, obviously, which is more than enough reason to keep breathing.

For now, I hug the journal to my chest as I fall asleep, not waiting up for Death-Cast to call.

July 26, 2020

ALANO

10:36 a.m.

Death-Cast still can't call me. My father finds that upsetting, but I don't. I wouldn't go so far to say that I've been living my best life ever since opting out of the service, but I would say that I'm on the right path. Mostly thanks to Paz.

The Melrose Trading Post—better known as the Melrose Market to locals like Paz—is a really impressive flea market outside Fairfax High School. I'm really happy I didn't miss out on visiting during this trip to Los Angeles. Nothing has caught Paz's eye yet as we bounce between booths, but I've already bought amber incense, reusable candles, an art print of the Santa Monica Pier (in a style reminiscent of Pierre-Auguste Renoir), a 3D flower bouquet that will survive in my absence, a Y2K Three Bats shirt, and a green quartz crystal that is said to be good for emotional stability. One hour definitely won't be enough time to get through all these booths, let alone spend meaningful time with Paz before I have to meet Rio at Universal Studios, but I'm making the most of it.

We're in a booth after the vendor invited us in, saying, "Come claim your name!" I thought it was going to be some unique experience, like an aura reading, but the woman is simply selling small objects with people's names. I already know I won't be buying anything here.

Paz spins a rack of name magnets. "Always Pat, never Paz."

"Always Alan, never Alano."

"My mom has had some luck, but Rolando hasn't."

"I've seen Joaquin magnets, but never Naya."

"That's so stupid, Naya is a beautiful name. We probably don't see it more because parents know their children would be disappointed at these racks."

I politely nod at the vendor as we leave the booth—followed by Agent Dane, who has likely seen his fair share of Dan magnets while searching for his own name—and search for our next stop.

"I've decided what I'm going to do instead of running Death-Cast," I say.

"What's that?"

"I'm starting a secret club for those who have suffered the indignities of never seeing their names personalized on objects. On Day One everyone will be welcomed with magnets, key chains, pencils, journals, mugs, water bottles, backpacks, and anything else."

"Can we get Beyoncé to join?"

"It's a fantasy. Beyoncé can perform before every club meeting."

"Okay, I'm all in. What do we talk about?"

"Nothing special, but we keep it secretive anyway so all the Common-Namers know what it's like to be excluded."

"'Alano' must mean 'genius' because this is brilliant."

"In Old German origins it means 'precious,' which honestly tracks with how I've been treated my entire life," I say, casting a quick smile back at my personal bodyguard. "My name is the Spanish cognate of 'Alan,' which means 'handsome.' Sadly my name doesn't translate to 'genius' in any language."

"I think you're a precious and handsome genius, Alano," Paz says while avoiding eye contact, as if the ice at the bottom of his empty lemonade cup is more fascinating than directly flirting.

"And I think you're living, breathing peace, Paz."

"Even all those times I was about to kill myself?"

"No, not then, but definitely the moments after where you chose to live," I say, remembering the heart-racing intensity when Paz had the gun to his head on the Hollywood Sign and in the alley. I push it away with the relief from both times Paz lowered the gun along with when he threw it away. "You're living up to the peace in your name, Paz. Maybe I can find a peace sign around here to send you home with until I get my club up and running."

"I actually hate the peace sign."

"You can't hate the peace sign, Paz."

"I hate the peace sign, Alano."

If Paz were anyone else, like Rio for example, I would joke that he's hopeless. The last thing I want is Paz remembering that I've said that, even kidding around. It's too easy for someone to believe there might be truth behind humor. "Fine. You hate the peace sign, but do you like gifts? I want to get you something."

"Why?"

"To thank you for bringing me here."

"You don't have to do that, I'm good."

"I want to. Is that okay?"

Paz seems hesitant. I almost retract the offer, but he says, "Only if I can get you something too."

I have plenty already from the market, but I agree. We plan to meet at the exit at 10:55. I should honestly spend these ten minutes hanging out with Paz instead, but I'd like to get him something to hold close when I'm not here.

Agent Dane watches Paz run off, alarmed, and I explain the situation. He obviously stays close as I browse through the booths. Even behind my sunglasses, I've already been recognized three times this morning. First at the food truck where Paz and I bought frozen lemonades, then by the artist who sold me their print of the Santa Monica Pier, and lastly when I was shopping for crystals. I happily obliged as the vendors asked for pictures and spoke about how Death-Cast has been meaningful to their lives, but the entire time I could feel Paz and Agent Dane watching them, unsure if these strangers were being sincere or luring me into a false sense of security so they could stab me with an ice pick or sharpened pencil or an obsidian knife.

There are so many booths and not enough time, so I go down my lane of Paz memories to come up with some options. His stress and depression are obviously at the forefront of my brain, but I don't think stress balls, coloring books, and fidget toys would be enough to keep Paz off the Hollywood Sign or that kitchen knife off his skin (something I still can't help but think about since I'm not sure where Paz was even self-harming and I can only rule out his unscarred arms, neck, and face). He suggested that I decorate my car with an air freshener so I can always get him something for his car. Then I realize that I don't know if Paz himself even drives or if he's only driven around by Gloria Medina and Rolando Rubio (and now me). I pass a booth that's selling frames and consider getting one for Paz's dream eulogy, but he won't be able to showcase that until he speaks about it with his parents. Another booth is selling stickers, and in another world this shiny yellow heart would have been a cute gift to celebrate his favorite book and casting in the adaptation, but if we lived in that world, Paz and I wouldn't have met when we did. Thankfully Paz and I did meet, but this sticker might be a sore spot, so I move on. There's a small bookshop selling language books and I think it would be really fun to learn a language with Paz, or tutor him in one I already know, like Spanish, so he'll feel less like a "bad Puerto Rican." This will have to do because I only have three minutes left. Right before I can step inside, something catches my eye outside the neighboring booth, something so perfect that I buy it fast before anyone else can because this is so destined for Paz that it may as well have his name on it.

I hurry toward the exit, where I see Paz running toward the gate while hugging a big brown paper bag to his chest. There's no time to guess on what it might be before we reunite.

"Hey," Paz says, wiping the sweat from his forehead.

I take a deep breath when my chest feels tight. "Any chance you got me new lungs?"

"Are you okay?" Paz asks. "Do you need your inhaler?"

"No, I'm fine, but thanks for caring."

"Back at you."

After spending last night learning more about Paz, meeting his parents, exploring his bedroom, and almost kissing, I went home thinking about how much I like him. We're good for each other as friends, and I'm confident we would be really good together as boyfriends, even if it has to be long distance. If that went well for a few months, what's stopping me from spending more time out here in Los Angeles to be with him? Certainly not Death-Cast. I only want to make sure that I'm genuinely in the right headspace to care for Paz as much as I do myself. If my mother is right about this psychotic break, I'll have to reassess everything, no matter how true it feels now.

To be clear, it feels very true now.

"Close your eyes," I tell Paz. Once he does, I pull his gift out from my tote bag and unroll it before his feet. "Take two steps forward and open your eyes."

Paz does what I said and looks down—no, he stares down at his yellow star-shaped rug.

"I was inspired by our stroll down the Hollywood Walk of Fame," I say.

"How—what—where the hell did you find this?"

"An Old Hollywood booth that sells set pieces. The vendor said this rug was for some TV pilot that never got made."

Paz gets self-conscious as he realizes everyone is staring at us since we're blocking foot traffic to the exit. He starts stepping off. "We should move—"

"You should get used to people staring at you," I interrupt, and center him back onto the star. "You're going to be famous one day, Paz, for all the right reasons. Just bask in the peace of them not hounding you for autographs and pictures right now."

A smile creeps up as quickly as it vanishes. "No one's ever gonna cast me in anything ever again, Alano. Definitely not anything star-worthy."

"Time will tell, Paz. Until then, put this rug by your bed so you wake up and go to sleep remembering that you're a star. On the days that are hard, know that I believe this won't be your last star—and the next one will have your name on it as Hollywood finally celebrates you."

Paz's smile comes back to life, but stays longer. "This is really sweet, seriously. I hope you like yours, I couldn't afford the super nice things I saw, but I think it's cool—"

I take the brown paper bag out of his hands. "I'm going to love it."

"You don't have to, you can hate it."

I pull out the gift, and I don't know how Paz ever thought that I could hate a brown ceramic vase shaped like a skull.

"It's a vanitas vase, though I don't know if this counts because you said vanitas are still-life artwork, but this is art and someone spent their life working on it," Paz says nervously like he wasted his money. "But you also said vanitases—is that even a word?—are usually skulls and dead flowers, so I thought you could put your new 3D flower bouquet in there. And I really liked it because then you got the brown and green like your alien eyes." Paz stares at me, trying to gauge how I'm feeling. It's honestly cute how much he feels the need to keep selling it. "I just thought it would be really fitting because now more than ever you need to remember that you will die since Death-Cast can't warn you."

I hug the skull to my chest. "This is honestly the most thoughtful gift I've ever received."

Paz exhales. "Really? You don't have to say all of that."

"Are you kidding me? This can't stay here in Los Angeles. This has to go everywhere I go."

We stand there and as much as I'd like the world around us to disappear, I also become very aware that everyone's watching us and that more people are beginning to recognize me. Paz picks up his star-shaped rug, and we exit the market.

"This is the best gift ever and best start to a morning," I tell Paz as he walks me back to my car. "No roller coaster is going to top this."

"Maybe a cool glass of tartsun from the Milagro Castle will top everything," Paz says as he fans himself with his star-shaped rug.

Tartsun is the signature beverage that all the demonic witches and wizards in the Scorpius Hawthorne series drink at the start of every school year to wake up the powers that have been slumbering from underuse. It's said to be sweet, sour, spicy, and not for the faint of heart. I'm excited and nervous to see how I fare against Rio.

"Is tartsun good?" I ask.

"I don't know. They didn't have any on set."

"You didn't drink any at Universal Studios?"

"I've never been."

I stop in my tracks, a few feet from my car. "What? How come?"

Paz shrugs. "It's always been too expensive to go to the park only to risk getting booed or kicked out if someone recognizes me."

I roll the skull around in my hands, feeling the same way about this gift as I do Paz. "Please come with me."

He laughs. "No, this is your time with your friend—"

"You're my friend, and I want more time with you."

"I want more time with you too, but . . ."

"But what?"

Paz's head hangs. "I don't really have Universal money. I wouldn't have cared as much about blowing it all during my Not-End Days, but I gotta think differently for Begin Days."

"I'll get your ticket."

"No, I can't accept that, it's too much—okay, maybe not for you, but still."

Even though my family has enough money to reserve the entire park to ourselves, I really appreciate Paz not taking advantage. "I understand. My family doesn't like accepting complimentary gifts, no matter how well-intentioned they may be." This is tricky because now that I've got this idea of Paz joining me at the park I can't imagine having a good time without him. "How about this? Rio bought me a ticket already that wouldn't be right to accept when I can afford my own, so I could give that one to you?"

"You don't even know that he wants me tagging along."

"He's going to love you." I'm not confident it's the truth, but it's not technically a lie. I'm sure Rio will need an adjustment period given how he reacted after hearing about the romantic possibilities between me and Paz in the first place, but Rio will see that Paz is innocent.

"Please come," I say, sure that I've almost got him. "We could really use another one of your five-star tours. Who else knows the Milagro Castle better than you?"

Paz rolls his eyes and smiles. "Fine. But only so you don't get lost in the dungeons."

I may have lied to Paz.

The vanitas vase is actually the second-best gift I've ever received. The first has to be all the time I've gotten to spend with Paz since he's chosen to live.

PAZ

Death-Cast didn't call, so I get to live it up with Alano, who better not die on me.

This is only the second Begin Day, but life is already feeling more promising, even after yesterday's BPD freak-outs (we're at zero so far today), all thanks to the most thoughtful person in the world. Opening up about the self-harm has honestly made me feel lighter. I believe I can commit to my promise to never self-harm again as long as nothing crazy-bad happens, like someone hurting Alano. Or worse.

I don't think I could survive Alano's death.

That's not the only thing I'm on edge about.

The entire ride to Universal, I was battling anxiety over how I might get treated in the park. If I'm recognized, will I get harassed? Attacked? Would Alano's bodyguard help out if something is going down? Or will Alano fight for my life and get killed in the process? I don't know, but to get out of the spiral I kept asking questions about Alano's best friend Rio to get up to speed. I got the basics, like how Alano met Rio and even what went down with their other best friend, Ariana, before the assassination attempt.

We park in the E.T. parking lot and go through the CityWalk, where there's all these shops and restaurants, on our way to meet Rio outside Voodoo Doughnut. The promenade is packed with people decked out in fandom shirts and gear, including crimson Scorpius Hawthorne robes even though it's so hot out. I'm getting anxious again, but nothing is beating the electrifying nerves once I see the sign for Voodoo Doughnut. I can't believe I'm about to meet one of Alano's best friends. That I'm crashing an afternoon that was planned for the two of them (plus Dane, I guess). It's either a good sign for how Alano feels about me or a test for how I would fit in his social circle.

A guy walks toward us. I'm about to take up a religion so I have a god to pray to because I hope this isn't Rio—he's so breathtakingly, intimidatingly beautiful. He's got an Alano vibe, but like Alano's messier alter ego. Unbrushed dark curls like he just rolled out of bed, a wrinkled Luigi T-shirt, and patchy stubble. It all works, like when a celebrity is photographed in nothing but an undershirt and sweats and still looks hot. That's why it sucks when Alano says, "Hi, Rio."

"Hi," Rio says, giving Alano a quick hug before finishing his éclair and licking his fingers clean. He turns to me. Rio's eyes are so dark, I think they might even be black. "Nice to meet you, Paz." He goes in for a handshake before remembering he just sucked up all the chocolate off his fingers, so we bump elbows instead.

"Thanks for letting me tag along," I tell Rio.

"No worries." Rio reaches into his drawstring backpack and

pulls out a red Mario T-shirt that he tosses to Alano. "I got this for you," he tells him.

"This is awesome," Alano says.

As Alano quickly swaps his plain white shirt for the Mario one, Rio turns to me. "I didn't know you were going to be here."

"It's all good," I say.

I'm trying not to read into this. It's just a T-shirt. I mean, they're Super Mario Bros., not Super Mario Boyfriends. If there was something going down between Alano and Rio, then Alano would've filled me in, or not invited me at all, so I can't risk getting into anything with Rio over nothing. If Alano has to choose between me and his best friend, I already know what's going down.

Dane comes over, going through his protocol of what his supervising will look like through the park. Basically, where Alano goes, Dane goes, which we figured, but he'll allow for some exceptions, like select roller coasters and dining. If we go our own way, that's on us. "If you see anyone suspicious, alert me."

"How do we know if someone is suspicious?" Rio asks. "We didn't go to spy school."

"Weren't you an aspiring detective?" Dane asks.

"Key word is 'aspiring.'"

Dane swallows a sigh. "Suspects will have tells. It can be anything from a disingenuous smile to lure you into a false sense of security, saying too much to distract you from a threat, excessive fidgeting or sweating, avoiding eye contact or downright staring—"

"What if they're staring because we're all beautiful?" Rio interrupts.

Dane glares at him.

"You're included in that!"

Dane keeps glaring.

"Now you're staring for a really long time, so do I report you to yourself or just run away?"

"Run away," Alano says, laughing.

I like their dynamic. Today's gonna be fun.

Dane finishes going through other tells someone might possess before advising that Alano keep his sunglasses on at all times, even indoors, which Rio jokes won't be suspicious at all. It definitely makes sense, though; I haven't even known Alano that long and I've personally witnessed him getting recognized a lot.

"Very last thing," Dane says. "Guns are prohibited in the park, so I am not and will not be armed."

Any doubts of whether Rio is familiar with my past have been shot, and he's looking at me as if I might shoot him next. I hope he's not a fan of the docuseries. I try ignoring the weight of his gaze, but I can't. My spiral is sucking me in, triggering memories of shooting Dad and aiming my gun at Alano and how ready I was to kill that Death Guarder even without being sure that I would die too. I'm telling myself over and over that I am the biggest threat in this group and Rio is right to fear for his life, even after we walk through the theme park's metal detectors that prove I'm unarmed. I still don't feel innocent even though I know I have no bad intentions.

My heart races when Alano grabs my hand, pulling me aside.

"You're in your head," Alano says. "Come back to me, Paz."

His voice and touch brings me back and grounds me. "H-how did you know I was in my head?"

"You have a tell."

"I do?"

"Avoidance. Instead of expressing how you feel, you keep it to yourself. I've observed a couple times when you're so deep in your head that you can't even hear me calling you."

I've noticed this about myself a lot, especially this year, but I never thought of it as a tell. I try to frame it in my head that Alano knowing me so well is a sign of our connection, but then I look over to find Rio and Dane staring at me too, and it only makes me think of myself as some mentally deranged boy with a dangerous past who must look like I'm plotting my next attack.

"Breathe with me," Alano says, holding my hands.

I stare at my reflection in his sunglasses, wishing I could see his eyes instead of myself. I squeeze my eyes shut, remembering the green in Alano's right iris and the brown in his left, how they're calming like nature, how happy he was when I gave him the vanitas vase I chose because it matches his eyes, how he said it was the most thoughtful gift he ever received, and how happy that made me because I'm sure he's received some amazing presents growing up with rich parents but the twenty-two-dollar vase I bought at a flea market won anyway. And maybe I'm stupid to believe that, but unless I can figure out Alano's tells for any lies the way he has figured out mine for when I'm lost in my head, then I'm just gonna believe every damn word he says because he's never done anything to make me doubt him. I exhale and open my eyes, finding Alano smiling. My reflection's too.

"Thanks-slash-sorry," I say.

"You're welcome—slash—don't apologize," Alano says.

"Is Rio gonna think I'm a freak?"

"He might not know your tell, but we all have dark pasts and can recognize when someone is being haunted by theirs."

ALANO

12:19 p.m.

I'm happy that my worlds are already coming together.

As we were making our way through Universal Studios, my friends were chatting about things to do in Los Angeles until Rio stopped for coffee, since he's still jet-lagged, which led to Paz admitting that he's starving, since he didn't have breakfast. We stop at the Jurassic Cafe. Rio and I have claimed a booth while Paz is in line ordering his Herbivore Salad.

"How was last night?" Rio asks.

I tell him the same thing I told my parents this morning: "One of my favorite nights ever."

"No red flags?" Rio asks, as if that's an appropriate response.

Unfortunately, my research has revealed that many people will consider borderline personality disorder a red flag. It was especially upsetting to learn some psychiatrists and therapists won't even treat patients with borderline personality disorder because their behavior can be too complex and unpredictable. There were certainly moments last night where Paz was sensitive because of his disorder, but I wouldn't dare write him off because of his trauma.

"No red flags," I say.

"That's good. I've been freaking out since watching *Grim Missed Calls* last night."

I stare in confusion. "Why did you watch that?"

"I couldn't sleep."

"Was that the only thing available?"

"No. First I watched this B movie on YouTube called *Canary Clown and the Carnival of Doom*. It was as low-budget as it gets."

"And *Grim Missed Calls* is as dishonest as it gets. You know that was made by pro-naturalists who are so clearly campaigning against Death-Cast and for Carson Dunst."

Rio gestures for me to calm down. "I watched that docuseries because you're my best friend and I care about you. You've been there for me, and I'm literally here for you." He nods at Agent Dane, who's keeping an eye on us at a nearby booth. "You were almost killed, Alano, by someone who had a secret switchblade in his phone, and Dane hasn't bothered to inspect mine. I suspect he hasn't inspected Paz's phone either. What if we wanted to hurt you?"

It's like I'm falling back through the memory of my assassination attempt. I relive the searing pain of Mac Maag's switchblade dragging across my forearm and stabbing me deep in the abdomen. I'm on the sidewalk outside my building, bleeding out. The trauma is so painful that I work hard to float back to the present.

"Do you want to hurt me?" I ask even though Rio already did by triggering that memory.

"Of course not."

"Do you believe Paz wants to hurt me?"

"I don't know, but I'll be keeping an eye on him. Has he been patted down?"

"No."

"Why not? You do it for me and Ariana, and we don't have his criminal record."

"Correction: my father makes the agents inspect you before entering our home. I trust you both otherwise, just like I trust Paz." Though, if I'm being honest, I trust Paz more than I do Ariana right now since she not only hasn't reached out to me since my assassination attempt, she's also ignored my texts and calls. "I'm glad you're getting this opportunity to meet Paz so you can see once and for all that he's not the criminal that internet strangers make him out to be."

"It's worth investigating the facts—"

"How's the hotel?" I ask, interrupting Rio.

He's confused until he sees Paz return, scooching in next to me as he sets down his tray with his salad, fries to share, and waters for all.

Rio picks at a fry and says, "The hotel is fine. I couldn't sleep, so I was up most of the night watching TV."

"Anything good?" Paz asks.

Rio eyes Paz suspiciously when he's not looking. "Nothing good."

"There's a lot of garbage out there," I say.

"And I can't get booked on any of it," Paz jokes. "What were you watching?"

I glare. It would make a really bad first impression if Rio admits to watching *Grim Missed Calls*, as it continues to disrupt Paz's life.

"*Canary Clown and the Carnival of Doom*," Rio answers. He calls it unspeakably bad and proceeds to speak about how bad it is for a few minutes. "Hopefully you're auditioning for better material."

Paz sighs. "Yeah, I actually had a chemistry test last week, but I didn't get it."

"For what?" Rio asks.

"The adaptation of *Golden Heart* by Orion Pagan."

I can practically see Rio calculating how Orion Pagan plus Valentino Prince equals a love story that gets divided by Frankie Dario, who gets subtracted from the mathematical problem because of Paz Dario, which means that adding Paz into any movie based on this equation isn't the right answer.

Rio thankfully bites his tongue.

"Last night Paz auditioned for a cool job at Make-A-Moment," I say.

"Alano was my scene partner," Paz says with a big smile.

"Scene partner?" Rio asks.

I explain the new Make-Life-Moments Experience and the need for actors. "We performed a scenario for the manager," I say, trying to avoid what it was specifically, but of course Rio asks and I won't deny the truth. "A first-date simulation."

Rio is naturally confused as anyone would be upon hearing about a first-date simulation, but I'm sure his confusion is coming more from my saying that I wasn't going on a date with Paz. "What does simulating a date look like?"

"Getting to know each other," I say.

"Proving we have chemistry," Paz says.

"But it was just a performance," Rio says.

Paz shrugs. "Felt like a real date to me."

"Me too," I say. I hope that doesn't come off as disrespect-ful to Rio, given our past, but when we had our conversation about how we needed to commit as friends and nothing more, we agreed that our many date-like hangouts weren't technically dates since we never defined them as such. "That's one example of an experience Paz might perform at Make-A-Moment."

"Unlimited roles I can play," Paz says.

Rio stares off into the distance, his dark eyes watering before he blinks the tears away. "There are definitely limits. No one could ever be my brother," he says.

Paz looks horrified and immediately apologizes. "That's not what I meant."

"That job isn't about replacing anyone," I say. It's safe to assume there will be Make-A-Moment clients using this service in relation to their grief, as is their right, but Rio will not be one of those people, as is his right. "The best actor in the world will never be your brother."

I'm expecting Rio to go cry privately, but he collects him-self with a deep breath. "The job sounds really cool otherwise," he says, moving on. "We should let Ariana know about the job opening. Did Alano tell you about our best friend who's pursuing acting?"

Paz nods. "Broadway, right?"

"She's really talented," Rio says. "Right?"

Ariana is very qualified to be a Make-Life-Moments actress. "Feel free to inform her," I say.

"What if you tried? It could be a nice gesture all things considered."

"I'll leave that to you," I say.

It would be a nice gesture, but no matter how guilty I feel in having done the right thing, I still recognize it was indeed the right thing to do. Morally and professionally. I'm upset that my father firing Andrea Donahue has interfered with my and Ariana's friendship, but I refuse to invest in Ariana's future when she's not even interested in what I survived. Every minute that passes where Ariana doesn't reach out, the more I believe that my best friend wouldn't have cared if I had died.

After some small talk as we finish the food, Paz clears his tray and runs to the restroom.

"I feel like you hate me," Rio says the moment we're alone.

"I definitely don't hate you."

"Then why are you fighting me on everything?"

"I'm sorry if it seems like I'm fighting you. I really appreciate you looking out for me, but I'm entering an era where I need to embrace what I want. I'd rather not obsess over Ariana when I can be present with you, who've proven you care about me. The same goes for Paz."

Even saying Paz's name stirs something beautiful inside me. I want to nurture this connection so that it blossoms, but I don't feel comfortable sharing that with Rio after his lingering kiss on the cheek yesterday has me questioning if that was his way of saying goodbye to the intimate moments we've been sharing as I make space for someone new or if he was trying to reclaim his abandoned throne, so to speak.

"Friends can't turn off our concerns for one another," Rio says.

"Pass that memo to Ariana."

Rio doesn't take the bait. "I'll try and relax and let you live your life."

"Pass that memo to my father."

He laughs. "Paz seems cool, by the way. *Grim Missed Calls* has gotten a lot wrong."

Coming from Rio, who carries many unfavorable opinions, this endorsement from my last standing best friend not only means the world to me, but grows my own world exponentially so that I don't have to risk losing Rio to begin something new and beautiful with Paz.

Choosing to live pro-naturally might actually give me the life I've always wanted.

PAZ

While walking through the theme park, no one has been making me feel like a killer—not Alano, not his bodyguard, not his best friend, and not even any strangers, but I'm tensing up as we finally approach the Milagro Castle.

I stop in my tracks.

"Are you okay?" Alano asks, his hand on my lower back.

"I'm just nervous about getting recognized," I say.

"Does that happen often?" Rio asks.

"It's happened a lot, especially since that shitty docuseries."

"Maybe someone will recognize you as your character and not your—" Rio stops himself.

"Myself?"

"That's not what I meant. I'm sorry," Rio says.

Alano's gaze is hidden behind his sunglasses, but I'm pretty damn sure he's glaring at Rio, who apologizes again. "Here are the facts, Paz. If anyone knows you from *Grim Missed Calls*, they're unlikely to detect you because you dyed your hair. The chances of you being recognized by casual movie viewers is also slim since you're, you know, older than when you starred in my favorite scene in the entire franchise." I doubt that part is really a fact, but it's sweet. "You're safe with us."

438

I take a deep breath. That perspective does help a lot.

"Okay, I got this."

"You got this," Alano says.

"And if you don't, Dane will make your harasser disappear," Rio says.

Dane doesn't deny that.

Throughout the first Scorpius Hawthorne book, Scorpius wrestles with being the chosen one because he doesn't think he can fulfill the prophecy to win a war against demonkind, but he soon learns that being the chosen one doesn't mean fighting alone. That's all thanks to the psychic demonic witch, Diolinda Souza, and the wealthy demonic wizard, Magnus Moguel (who we later learn in book six is Scorpius's soulmate, but only if Scorpius wins the war to keep Magnus's soul, which is absolutely not the pressure he needed at ten years old). I have spent so much of my life not having any real friends, or even a future to be excited about, but I do now thanks to Alano. There is no evil that can bury me in an abyss as long as I got friends backing me up.

We walk through the iron gate, officially entering the battle-scarred kingdom from the Scorpius Hawthorne franchise. We cross a drawbridge over the red pond known as Devil's Tears, pass a shaded playground that looks like the Seven-Legged Monster Spider's cave, animatronic water dragons that breathe mists to help keep guests cool, and, of course, there's the pathway of backward footsteps of the Curupira, a demon that I thought the author Poppy Iglesias invented but was actually adapted from real Brazilian myths, but instead of scaring away hunters who steal from the rainforest, the Curupira terrorizes those without magic blood, only providing safe passage for the demonic witches and wizards to the Milagro Castle.

And there it is.

The Milagro Castle is built out of four gray cracked spire towers leaning toward each other, like a clawed hand trying to pinch the sky, just like the series lore. The castle is actually the claw of Fera the First Demon, who became hexed between the underworld and the overworld after trying to rip apart the universe over its outrage of demons mating with witches and wizards. The Founders then straight up turned the ancient demon's hand into a school to prepare future witches and wizards for the day Fera is unleashed, which Larkin Cano plots to do in the final book/movies.

Seeing the Milagro Castle this close is mind-blowing; it's something I didn't even get to experience on set because the studio was just renting a different castle for its interiors, but that obviously didn't look like a demon's claw on the outside. I legit could cry from nostalgia, the happy memories I have of reading the series with Mom, and experiencing the movie magic in person.

"What do you think?" Alano asks, wrapping his arm around my shoulders.

"I don't wanna say it's magical, but . . ."

"But it's magical."

"Legit."

I've seen at least a billion photos online of people proposing in front of the Milagro Castle, always captioning that the biggest miracle of all was finding their soulmate, and while I've always thought that was stupid and cringey I'm wondering now if that's only because I was so bitter and had no one in my life that made me happy, powerful, and yeah, magical.

Alano claps. "First round of tartsun on me. Paz, how spicy do you want yours? Mild, medium—"

"Spicy-spicy. I've been handling the heat from my mom's kitchen all my life."

He smiles. "Noted."

Rio stares at the sign on the cart. "I'll have—"

"You'll have no spice," Alano tells Rio. "I don't want you having another coughing fit."

"Fine," he says as Alano and Dane walk off.

"Did Alano just ban you from spices?" I ask.

Rio laughs. "We had gone to dinner and I choked on a spicy salsa so bad that my coughing blew out the candle. This was years ago, but he's got that stored away in his Rio Morales Encyclopedia, so he'll never let me live it down. Anyway . . ."

I'm suddenly running so hot and my chest is tightening like I'm choking on spice too. I thought I was special in Alano's eyes with the Paz Dario Encyclopedia he's keeping about me, but I guess he does this for other people too? Like Rio? Like superhot Rio? Like superhot Rio who is dressed like the Luigi to Alano's Mario? Did Alano also give him some speech about how he wants to know the real Rio? I don't know, I don't know, I don't know. Alano did mention last night that he got close with trusting someone, but it didn't work out. Is that Rio? Wouldn't he have told me if we were about to hang out with someone he has feelings for? I'm trying to get out of this spiral because this might not even be romantic except that they were at a candlelit dinner together. I guess some restaurants set down candles even if you're not on a date, and Alano said last night was his first date.

I'm spiraling, spiraling, spiraling.

Rio waves his hand in front of my face. "Paz?"

I shake it off. "Sorry, was thinking about the spices. That's scary."

He looks at me suspiciously. "I asked if you're still in touch with the Scorpius cast."

"Nope. I met them when I was six."

"You haven't seen them since?"

The last time I saw anyone from Scorpius Hawthorne was during my trial, not that anyone would know this from watching *Grim Missed Calls*, since the filmmakers left out any mention of my high-profile character witnesses. First there was Poppy Iglesias, who had written to my mom and offered to fly from Brazil to the States to advocate for my innocence in person. Then there was the franchise's leading hero, Sol Reynaldo, who spoke about the pressures of being a child actor and how impressed he was with how I'd conducted myself during the intensity of filming a blockbuster movie with a three-hundred-million-dollar budget. But what meant the most to the jury—and me—was the testimony from Howie Maldonado since out of everyone on set he spent the most time with me. Howie was known as a villain on-screen, but in person he was a hero of mine, and I cried so much when he died in that car crash three years ago.

I don't wanna get into all this right now, so I just tell Rio it's been a few years since I've seen anyone. It's true enough.

Alano returns with three cups of tartsun. I thank him for mine even though I really wanna ask if he's hiding history with Rio because it means nothing or because it's something to hide. This spiral is souring my mood, and the drink sours my tongue. I only get more annoyed when Rio suffers from a brain freeze after chugging his tartsun for some fucking reason—actually for a clear fucking reason. Attention. Alano rushes to Rio's aid with every tip in the book to combat brain freeze and a hand on Rio's lower back. I almost chug my drink too to steal Alano's attention back.

I wander off to the school's garden that doubles as a cemetery for the students killed in the castle. "I'm a survivor," I breathe out as suicidal thoughts reach for me like the First Demon's claw.

"I'm a survivor," I say as I think about how much easier life would be as a corpse in a cemetery.

"I'm a survivor," I whisper, even though I don't wanna be.

Alano appears at my side. "Is this everything you imagined?"

"No," I almost snap, but Rio walks up. "It's just the start," I lie when it really feels like the end.

"Can we check out the castle?" Rio asks, his lips red from the spicy juice.

"Lead the way, tour guide," Alano tells me.

I'm not really in the mood to be the tour guide, but it has to be me since I'm the only one in the group who has read all the books—Rio gave up by book five, and Alano doesn't read fantasy—and because I'm obviously the only one who has been on the actual movie set. Dane upgraded everyone with VIP passes as a security measure, but we still wait in the torturously slow standard line because the express path will rush us through the castle, denying us the full experience. I'd rather this be over sooner anyway, but I try burying my rage by putting on my Happy Paz mask.

Happy Paz fools everyone, but every smile hurts me. I'm not actually happy when we finally get into the castle because now there's no escape, no wandering off. I'm not actually happy when we pass the crystal ball lanterns that predict small prophecies ("Danger ahead," it warns, as if I don't know that shit) because all those glowing crystal balls do is illuminate how Rio and Alano are pressed together, shoulder to shoulder. I'm not actually happy when the ground vibrates from under us as if the First Demon is flexing its claws because the fright only causes Rio to grab on to Alano as if they were about to die from a real earthquake. I'm not actually happy when we spend the next hour going through all the iconic rooms like the elixir lab, the training chamber, or even the goddamn library that looks so identical to the one from the scene I starred in because all of this is fake, as fake as a movie set, as fake as playing a character, as fake as boys who pretend their words are truth instead of lines from a script.

"A round of applause for our tour guide," Alano says as we go down the last flight of steps into the dungeon for the ride that will bring us out of the castle.

"You should work here," Rio says.

I fake a laugh and say yes even though there's no way in hell I'm going from a character in the movie to a theme park employee.

While we're waiting our turn, we watch the video of Scorpius Hawthorne, Magnus Moguel, and Diolinda Souza—portrayed by the original actors as they reprised their roles for this bonus footage—telling us that they're gonna need our help to stop Larkin Cano, who is trying to fulfill his prophecy as the Draconian Marsh to unearth the First Demon and undo the castle's many miracles. People of all ages, ahead and behind, are so excited, but I couldn't give a shit.

"Next!" the employee calls in a very North American accent instead of literally any of the other South American accents in the series.

The ride's vehicle can seat parties of four with the backs of all seats shaped like the wings that Milagro students grow in their final year. We can feel like we're flying too as this robotic arm carries us through the simulation. I've heard this ride is even more epic than most of the virtual offerings at Make-A-Moment.

"Let's ride up front," Rio says, dragging Alano by his arm.

Alano looks behind at me, trying to say something, but Dane interrupts with some security shit and next thing I know I'm in my seat, restrained under an over-the-shoulder harness, next to

Dane. Being separated from Alano sucks enough, but he's seated directly in front of me so I won't even be able to see his reactions, only Rio's, who's diagonal from me.

Why the hell did Rio have to grab Alano's hand? Is that something they do as friends? I guess Alano has done it with me ever since the night we met. But does Rio only see Alano as a friend? Does he still have feelings? Does Alano? I don't know a damn thing except that I wanna get off this ride and go cry, but the ride begins, slowly carrying us into the darkness where fans blow down on us, making it instantly chilly.

We follow the Trio as they creep through the castle. It's eerily quiet until I see a real ghost projected on one of the screens: Howie Maldonado reprising his role as Larkin Cano. He swoops down with his wings of fire and some unseen radiator blasts us with heat. "*MALTRATAR!*" he shouts, but his curse misses the Trio. "The First Demon will end you all," he says before flying away.

The ride accelerates, thrusting us through the four towers, where Larkin Cano's unearthing spell is blowing apart the ancient binding that has trapped the First Demon. The Trio fight off three-eyed giants, acid-breathing hydras, and skeletal dragons, often calling on us to shout spells and curses too to help them. Rio thinks he's funny by shouting made-up curses like "Fuck-him-up-uh-tis!" but the worst sound is Alano laughing at that dumb shit. Then we're up against Fera's fanatics, the Hex Breakers, who cast so many spells that blind us with a lightshow, flip us upside down, spin us around really fast, and then drop us into the abyss, where we come face-to-face with the First Demon, but all I'm staring at is Rio holding on to Alano's hand as if his life depends on it—like my life has.

I try pushing this harness off me so I can actually drop into the darkness, but I'm too fucking secured. The best thing I can do when Scorpius Hawthorne rescues us from the abyss, shooting us up so fast and high that our eyes water, is scream with everyone else, the way I can only ever scream when I'm home alone and self-harming.

I don't give a shit about this final battle where the Trio hex Larkin Cano into a gargoyle that now lives forever outside the Milagro Castle, bound to the master he failed to free. Everyone else is clapping at the victory, even Rio, who has managed to finally let go of Alano's fucking hand.

Once I'm unbuckled, I return to the platform where Alano is waiting.

"Did you have fun?" he asks.

"Yeah."

"I wish I got to sit with you," he says on the way out. "Maybe the next ride?"

"Yeah," I lie again. As much as I don't wanna leave Alano, I also don't wanna hang around for any more of this shit.

We exit into the gift shop, and Alano wants to treat everyone to wands and crimson robes. Rio grabs Magnus's wand, and Alano grabs Scorpius's, like they're soulmates. I'm the odd one out who needs to either get my shit together or curse out Alano for being a dick. I just grab an iron wand and robe instead of making a scene. At least everyone being in robes means I don't have to look at their stupid-ass Super Mario shirts anymore.

Outside the castle, Rio calls us in for a group selfie. Alano gets in the center, wrapping his arm around me, pulling me close. It's got me thinking that I'm turning nothing into something. Then in real time on the camera's mirror I watch Alano wrap his other arm around Rio. That kills any shot of a real smile from me. If Alano zooms in on the picture later, he'll see the truth of how I'm actually feeling because my eyes can't lie the way my mouth can.

We round the corner, and Alano excitedly stops me. "Check it out."

There's the gargoyle of Larkin Cano, Howie Maldonado's face frozen forever. Someone has dropped flowers underneath the statue. I've gotten so mad in the past about how people forgive Larkin Cano for his crimes all because of his terrible upbringing and not me for killing an abusive man, but I'm touched that people still grieve Howie, who was a great guy in real life.

I'll never know what it's like to be grieved by millions of strangers.

"Do you want a picture?" Alano asks, whipping out his phone.

"It's fine."

"Dude, you were the guy," Rio says. "You should get a picture."

"It'll be a cool full-circle moment," Alano adds.

I almost snap and shout at them to shut the fuck up, to stop ganging up on me, to run off and leave me alone, but I've had enough strangers in this lifetime looking at me like I'm dangerous, they're not about to catch me unhinged.

I give in, trying not to crack as I stand next to the gargoyle. Happy Paz smiles for the camera.

ALANO

4:14 p.m.

After working up an appetite in the laser tag arena where we battled with wands, we're now finishing lunch at the park's most popular Scorpius Hawthorne–themed restaurant. The Inferno Inn is yet another incredibly immersive replica where every dining table has cast-iron cauldrons to keep meals warm and the spicy foods range from low-heat to supernova-hot.

Rio has been talking a lot, especially to Agent Dane about investigations, and Paz has been on the quiet side.

"Are you okay?" I ask Paz.

He doesn't look me in the eye. "Tired. I miss the End-ergy Drinks."

Rio spins away from Agent Dane enthusiastically. "Me too!"

Early last year, End-ergy Drinks were manufactured and sold to Deckers needing more energy so they weren't tired on their End Days. The makers used so much caffeine to give Deckers their ten-hour rush that toxicology reports proved that's why these otherwise healthy individuals died of heart attacks. I kept begging Rio to stop drinking it for night school.

"For the sake of both your hearts, I'm glad the CDC shut it down," I say.

"I ordered a case online but got scammed," Rio tells Paz.

The Inferno Inn manager, Mr. Fabian, returns to our table, just as he has every few minutes to make sure we're comfortable ever since the host alerted him of my presence. "How are we doing over here?"

"Full," I say. The mashed potatoes and spicy roasted broccoli that Paz and I enjoyed were exceptional by theme park dining standards. Agent Dane was chugging water to keep up with his spicy wings while Rio ate two baked potatoes. "Everything was delicious, Mr. Fabian."

Mr. Fabian chuckles. "Ah. I hope you can find room for some spiced devil's cake." He adds, "Dessert is on the house, along with your entire tab, Mr. Rosa. We're all grateful for the great work Death-Cast has done."

There's an uneasiness because Mr. Fabian doesn't know that I have deactivated Death-Cast for upsetting reasons. It goes to show that no matter how much I distance myself from the duties of Death-Cast, I will forever be seen as the heir until I publicly renounce the title.

Until that day comes I will play the part. "That's very generous, but my parents will personally call me from Death-Cast's call center if they found out I accepted a free meal," I say, recycling the same joke I've used for years, since it always plays well with these well-meaning managers, as it does now.

"But we will take that dessert," Rio says.

"No dairy for Paz and no spice for Rio," I remind Mr. Fabian. "And the check, please."

Paz closes his eyes, sinking deeper into his seat. I've been tracing backward to see if I've said anything upsetting. Even now I want to invite him to go home if he's this tired, but I know from last night there's a chance he might misread that gesture as my not wanting him around when it's the opposite. I wonder if there's something else he's misreading.

"I spoke with Ariana this morning," Rio says, cutting through the silence, slashing me by surprise like my assassin.

"Lucky you. She's ignored all my calls, including this morning."

"She's hurt."

"*She's* hurt?" I repeat, slightly mocking.

Ariana's ability to be so dramatic is what makes her an incredible actress.

"I don't mean to keep score, but our friendship has always been imbalanced. I was there for Ariana when she ghosted Halo. I was there for Ariana when her father faked his End Day to make amends." Those were tricky events to navigate, especially pretending that Ariana was in the right when she persuaded her ex-girlfriend Halo to date her only to then ghost her two months later. I'm vibrating in anger all over again about how her father cried Death-Cast to prove that she still loves him, as if the company isn't combating abuses like this. What isn't tricky is how I have felt since the night of my assassination attempt. "Do you know what hurts more than getting stabbed? Knowing my best friend doesn't care whether I lived or died."

Paz is shaking his head, like he's as disgusted by Ariana's antics as I am.

Agent Dane continues surveilling the restaurant, but I can see he's tuned in too.

Rio seems frazzled, caught in the middle of this fight just as he was with his brothers. "Ariana cares about you, but she never believed you were in real danger of dying."

"Because I didn't receive an alert? That's pro-natural rhetoric right there." I remember my decision to live pro-naturally and how that sets me apart from the real danger. "That's Death Guarder talk. Did she also say that the devil was keeping me alive to be a soldier in an unholy war? That my soul has been poisoned by Death-Cast? Or the classic about how my family bargains with Death himself to target our enemies?"

I'm suddenly concerned that Ariana might take this so personally that she joins the Death Guard movement.

"Ariana only said you must know when you're going to die," Rio says.

That is so unbelievably frustrating, especially since I've trusted Ariana with a secret I haven't even told Rio. "I don't know when I'm going to die, and I've never known when I'm going to die, and that's truer than ever now that I've deactivated Death-Cast," I say in a rage, keeping my voice low so no one overhears.

Rio stares. "You did what?"

In the heat of the moment, I forgot I was keeping this secret from Rio too.

"This isn't to be repeated," Agent Dane says, like he would make Rio disappear right now.

Rio ignores Agent Dane. "Are you serious? When did you deactivate?"

"Keep your voice low," Agent Dane says.

I answer the question. "The night after the assassination attempt."

"The night you both met," Rio says, turning to Paz. "Are you pro-natural too?"

"Nope," Paz says.

I maintain it's not a good idea for Paz to opt out of Death-Cast's services right now, but maybe one day.

"I'm sorry I didn't tell you," I say. There are some secrets I must keep, but I hoped to be able to let Rio in on this once he stopped viewing Paz as a threat.

Rio leans forward, hands pressed together. "I'm sorry I didn't tell you I deactivated Death-Cast too."

It's as if he's shoved me over. I'm sure I heard this right because Paz's and Agent Dane's eyes have widened too. "You deactivated Death-Cast? When?"

"June nineteenth," Rio says. The fourth anniversary of his brother's death. Over a month he's kept this a secret. "Ever since Lucio's murder I've been wrapping my head around the good and the bad about Death-Cast. On the one hand, Death-Cast allowed me to say goodbye to my brother. On the other, Death-Cast killed my brother."

"H. H. Bankson killed your brother," I say.

"Lucio only signed up for a Last Friend because Death-Cast told him he was dying."

This is the great paradox of Death-Cast. There would be no Last Friend serial killer if there was no Last Friend app, and there would be no Last Friend app if society wasn't expanding cultures around people who are dying and we wouldn't definitively know people are dying without Death-Cast. Who's to say that H. H. Bankson wouldn't have still been a serial killer known for something else, still claiming the same set of victims, including Lucio Morales? But who's to say that all his victims wouldn't be alive and well?

If Death-Cast didn't exist, then Rio could still have his brother.

If Death-Cast didn't exist, then Ariana's mother couldn't have been fired.

If Death-Cast didn't exist, then my life could've been innocent.

Fortunately or unfortunately, no matter your view, Death-Cast does exist. This is something I've wrestled with too for more than half my life. I've seen firsthand the good that Death-Cast has done as well as the bad, but to pin every death on the company would be like blaming the Wright brothers for every plane crash. I know better than to challenge Rio on his choice knowing it was born out of grief.

"Why didn't you tell me?" I ask.

"I didn't want to defend my decision against the company you're set to inherit. I figured you were never allowed to have another life as the heir, but look at you," Rio says proudly. There's almost a sparkle in his dark brown eyes. His enthusiasm reminds me of Harry Hope receiving his Death-Cast alert. They're both free from the life they were living. "Welcome back to pro-naturalism."

My life has always been divided in two halves, Before Death-Cast and After Death-Cast, but both pieces are fusing into something new, where my death is a mystery once again even though it doesn't have to be. "Does living pro-naturally feel like the right choice?"

"I'm finally shedding anger I've been carrying for years. This path feels right and freeing."

"What about Antonio? Should something happen to you, don't you want him to know?"

"Knowing I'm going to die won't keep me alive," Rio says.

"It will help prepare him, as Death-Cast prepared you both for Lucio's death."

"It was too late for Antonio and Lucio to get close, but we're spending more time together now that my fate is up in the air. We're stronger brothers today than we could ever become on an End Day."

There's no arguing with those results. There have been studies that show people will wait until the last minute before they act on their personal relationships, believing they have all the time in the world until they discover they don't. Rio is actually living as we all should.

"I'm happy for you," I say.

"Thanks. What about you, what made—"

"Wait," Agent Dane says.

Mr. Fabian personally delivers spiced devil's cakes for us and raspberry sorbets for Paz and Rio. "Are you sure we can't comp your bill?"

"I am, but thank you so much for the offer." I pay with my Amex Centurion card and leave a generous tip.

"Good eye," Rio tells Agent Dane as Mr. Fabian walks away.

"You have to learn how to watch without your eyes," Agent Dane says. "It could keep you alive."

It's one thing to know the tells of my friends—Ariana's lip biting when lying, Rio's leaning forward when sharing unfiltered truths, Paz's avoidance and disassociating when hiding his feelings—but another to identify a stranger's. Especially one who might be a threat. How do I know if someone is sweating profusely because their body runs hot or because they're working up the nerve to hurt me? How am I supposed to detect deviations in someone's speech when I've only just met them? I don't know, but I plan on ordering the appropriate literature about body language for research and having deeper conversations with Agent Dane on this fascinating subject. Especially now that I know I don't even have the read on my best friends like I thought I did.

"I have to alert Shield-Cast about this development," Agent Dane says.

"Hold on. That's Rio's personal business," I say.

"Your safety is my actual business. I would have coordinated backup had I known we were spending the day with an unregistered civilian, increasing our chances to attract unpredictable danger. The force has to be alerted," Agent Dane says. He steps away from the table while watching the patrons as if someone might run up on us with dining knives. It's not an impossibility if we're actually a magnet for danger.

"I don't care who he tells," Rio says.

I do. My father is going to be pissed. He might have friends and associates who are pro-natural, but I'm sure those relationships are under scrutiny after my attack.

"Why did you deactivate?" Rio asks.

I don't feel comfortable saying anything more than I've already said in a public space like this. Our table could be bugged. Eavesdroppers and lip readers might be paying attention. "I needed a change," I say.

Rio scoffs. "You have a tell for when you're lying."

I tense up. "What's that?"

"You lie, and I can just tell. See? I also have a magical spy eye."

It's good that Rio doesn't actually know my tell. "I'm not lying. I did need a change after the attack. I just don't want to talk about it out in the open."

Rio nods, understanding. "Life shouldn't be lived like this, Alano. I've been digging deep and uncovering a lot of information to help reacclimate to the old ways and seeing what trajectory we're on if things don't change soon. There's real potential for an apocalyptic threat. If one local serial killer could exploit Death-Cast, what's going to happen when the military abuses that power? There's going to be a world war. Does Death-Cast have enough heralds on staff for the ultimate End Day?"

This information Rio claims to have uncovered isn't hard to find. All anyone has to do is turn on the news and watch Carson Dunst share these same conspiracies at his rallies.

"Are you voting for Dunst?" I ask.

"I'm undecided," Rio says.

Paz rolls his eyes. "No, you've definitely decided."

"There's a lot of time between now and November."

"But if you had to vote today, you would vote for . . ."

Rio pauses and admits, "Dunst. He's the candidate who will break the mandates on professions like law enforcement that require employees to be registered for Death-Cast."

"This is why you returned to night school," I realize. "You believe Dunst will win."

"I believe he should. Why should my dream to be a detective so I can solve crimes and make the streets safer in honor of my brother be restricted by the company responsible for his death?" He then turns to Paz. "Hasn't Death-Cast ruined your dreams too?"

Paz's leg begins bouncing under the table, and he digs his nails into his palm. I don't know if this is self-harm, but I slip my hand into his, stopping him from hurting himself.

"I got this," I say.

"I want to hear what he has to say," Rio says.

"You're going to listen to me first. It's one thing to deactivate

Death-Cast and another to vote against it when you know it's done wonders for millions of people."

"It has cost lives too. How many more people have to die before we recognize that Death-Cast is a failed experiment? If we don't go back to the old ways we might evolve too far to ever recover."

I've grown up asking my parents why people hated and feared Death-Cast so much.

"No one wants change when they like their lives as is," my father had said.

"And those hurt by the changes wish to return to a simpler time," my mother had said.

"A time that is forever lost," my father said.

There is no telling someone that the death of a loved one isn't enough of a reason to undo the world, but my heart is breaking that Rio has fallen into these conspiracy holes. I want to reach in and pull him out. To save him.

"Can you confidently say you no longer fear death?" I ask.

"Once I'm dead, I'm dead. Nothing I can do about that, but I'm scared about losing another brother." Rio tears up and looks at my bandaged arm and takes my hand, locking my fingers in his. "I'm scared of losing you, Alano."

All at once, I'm filled with gratitude for the friends who care so deeply about my life, including both boys holding my hands, and I'm also dreading the bomb that's been detonated the moment Paz saw Rio touch me.

PAZ
4:33 p.m.

I'm tired of Rio's shit.

"It's okay," Alano says, trying to calm me down, which good fucking luck because I'm not about to sit here saying nothing while Rio is hyping up radical pro-naturalism as if those people didn't screw up my life.

I let go of Alano's hand and go in on his best friend. "I got no problem with you living a pro-natural life, and I'm sorry about your brother, for real, but you can't act like you're scared about Alano dying when you're backing the assholes who have Death Guarders trying to kill him. Death-Cast ruined my life on day fucking one, and even I'm not saying all this stupid shit."

Rio's eyes look darker than before as he says, "Is killing only okay when you do it?"

That's a fucking low blow, and I'm trying so hard not to deck him.

"You need to stop," Alano tells Rio.

"What about him? He's dangerous, just like they said in *Grim Missed Calls*."

I laugh. I can't believe he's using that stupid-ass docuseries in his defense. "You think that shit is real? Yeah, I feel bad for anyone counting on you to be their detective when your fact-checking is that fucking bad."

"If you murder my best friend, I promise you won't get away with it this time," Rio says.

Alano presses down on my thigh, like he's trying to hold me back from fucking up his best friend, and he's got no idea he's putting so much pressure on my scars. "You don't know what you're talking about," he tells Rio.

"And you do because you've known Paz for two nights?"

"That's right," Alano says.

"Tell him how I was about to save you," I say.

"That's not necessary," Alano says.

"I think it is. He thinks I have it out for you when really it's his people coming for you."

"What's he talking about?" Rio asks.

Alano closes his eyes, rocking back and forth. "Please, you're both stressing me out. Let's take a breath."

"What people?" Rio asks.

"The same ones killing for pro-naturalism," I say, loving the look on his shocked face as he realizes I was the one backing up his best friend when Alano was still just a stranger to me. "You can give me all the shit you want for killing my dad to save my mom, but don't act like you wouldn't have done the same thing for your brother." I hate making it personal, but Rio started it. "What I did was self-defense, just like the other night when I was ready to risk my life to save Alano's."

Rio's dark eyes fill with tears as his face reddens. "It's not risking your life when you're also trying to die."

I can't catch my breath, it's like I've been shoved off the Hollywood Sign. No one has ever used my suicidal struggles against me. I get up with ready fists to make sure no one ever does again.

"Please stop!" Alano cries, holding me back.

Dane rushes to the table like I'm the danger. "What's going on?"

"That dickhead won't shut his mouth," I say, glaring at Rio. "I'm gonna go before I kick his ass."

"Don't you mean kill me?" Rio says.

Death-Cast didn't call me, but if Rio doesn't stop fucking with a suicidal killer, he might find out that living pro-naturally means dying pro-naturally too.

ALANO

4:39 p.m.

I wanted harmony when bringing my worlds together, not this collision.

"No one say another word," Agent Dane commands under his breath. "Civilians are watching and recording. Leave now in an orderly fashion."

Paz breaks free of my hold and rushes out of the restaurant.

I keep my head low, ignoring all eyes and cameras. If I thought my father was going to be pissed before, he's going to lose it when that footage emerges. How long were patrons recording? I hope no one captured mention of the second Death Guarder threat.

We all regroup outside a sour-candy shop.

"What happened in there?" Agent Dane asks.

I don't even know where to start. I also don't want to relive this.

"Politics," Rio jokes, but no one laughs or even speaks.

Agent Dane reads everyone's body language and draws his own conclusion before moving past. He informs us that Agent Andrade has advised that we remain in the park until additional security detail arrives. He'd like to move us somewhere more discreet in the meantime.

"I'm not going anywhere with him," Rio says. He doesn't even look or point at Paz.

"*Rio*," I scold.

"No one's trying to be around you anyway," Paz says.

"*Paz*."

"Is that what you think?" Rio flashes a petty grin.

"Yeah, that's what I think."

"I am begging you both to stop," I say, grabbing their hands when the last thing they need is to be closer. In a fight between Paz and Rio, I'm the only one who stands to lose. "You're both so important to me. I would like you to be friends with each other, but I will not force that. I do need you to be cordial." Apologies seem unlikely. The same goes for more fun at the amusement park. "Can we do that?"

Paz won't look at Rio but says, "Yeah."

"Fine, but he's not invited to our place," Rio says. "I don't feel safe around him."

Paz's light brown eyes darken with tears. I'm certain it's because Rio continues to treat him like a threat until he asks, "You live with him?"

I tense up.

"Not yet," Rio answers.

I've never had more of an urge to use my Muay Thai teachings against a friend because one quick throat stab would get Rio to shut up. I don't need anyone recording me getting violent.

Paz looks nauseous and furious and defeated. "I'm done," he says, ripping his hand out of mine again and storming away.

What is Paz done with? I hope he doesn't mean me. Most important, I hope he's not giving up on life. Fear of abandonment is one of the most common symptoms of borderline personality disorder, and I have no intentions of abandoning Paz. Him thinking otherwise might trigger an urge to self-harm. Or worse.

"It's for the best," Rio says, watching Paz vanish into the crowd.

"Are you going to say that if he dies?" I ask.

"I'm more scared of him being the death of you."

He steps toward me, and I not only back up, I turn the other way, running after Paz to save him and our own future.

PAZ
4:46 p.m.

Alano is calling my name, but I ignore him now like I should've when I was on the Hollywood Sign.

I run past Milagro Castle and through the iron gate, slipping out of the Scorpius Hawthorne robe along the way because I don't want a damn thing of Alano's. Once I'm home, I'm gonna burn our Begin Day contract and myself.

I'm pissed off at my stupid-ass lungs for breathing and my stupid-ass brain for making me miss Alano already even though he's why my stupid-ass heart is broken, but I'm super pissed off at my stupid-ass self for believing a life as scarring as mine could ever be healed.

Footsteps pound the pavement behind me and like we're in a race, Alano takes the lead. He blocks my path near the Jurassic Park ride. He's holding on to his chest as he catches his breath.

"Please stop," he wheezes.

I'm so mad at myself for not running away as Alano pumps his inhaler. Dane is right behind us, he can make sure that Alano is all good. But I don't go.

Why can't I let Alano die the way he should've let me?

467

Is it because of my stupid-ass brain? Or my stupid-ass heart?

Alano leans against a fence. "Talk to me."

I stare straight into his green eye and brown eye, not letting them enchant me or any shit like that. "I don't know what's happening between us, like, if we're friends or more, and I thought I knew how you felt about me, but maybe that's just my stupid-ass BPD brain telling a story that's not true or because you're the one not telling the truth, but I'm not gonna lie to you: I care about you in a big way, Alano."

I break down crying because this is the first time I've ever confessed romantic feelings to a boy—a boy who saved my life and made me wanna live!—and it's so damn heartbreaking. He tries to hold me, but I push him back because I only wanna be held if he means it.

"What really sucks is that I don't know if I'm even allowed to get upset over you and Rio being so damn touchy-touchy and moving in together since I'm not your boyfriend, but I thought our Begin Days were gonna take us to that future."

I wish I felt better getting all of this off my chest, but I don't, I just feel pathetic. I should have stayed home, missing Alano instead of being here and missing the Alano I fell for.

Alano is quiet, probably wondering how he can gently call me crazy for believing that I ever had a shot with someone as amazing as him. He slowly closes the space between us, and this time I don't push him away. He's tearing up as he wipes away my tears. He holds my hands in his—the same hands that helped

468

me down the Hollywood Sign, that took my gun away before I could kill a Death Guarder and myself, that signed a contract to live out his Begin Days with me.

"I'm focused on the future too, Paz." Alano's eyes gaze into mine. "A future for you and a future with us."

My heart races because I love these words so much, but I can't tell if they're bullshit.

"Then why didn't you say anything?"

"Timing. That might sound ridiculous coming from the heir to a company that promotes making the most of every single day, especially when I no longer know what's in store for me, but it's the truth," Alano says and I'm telling myself that he's not lying. "I also had to make sure that we are both in the right headspaces."

"Because you have feelings for Rio?"

"No, something else. I've only spoken about it with my mother, but I'd like to open up to you too. I think it's necessary."

I go from being pissed at Alano to swooning for him to being scared for him. "Are you okay?"

"I truthfully don't know," Alano says, which scares me even more. "I am sure about my feelings for Rio, though. He's my best friend who I love so much, but Rio was never my boyfriend, and he never will be."

I'm hit with relief and shame all at once. I acted this way over nothing. "Wow, my brain really is a stupid-ass liar—"

"No, I have history with Rio. It's sad and complicated and not always easy to talk about because it was one-sided, but I'm sorry for not trying. Your brain wouldn't have needed to fill in the blanks if I told you everything before putting you in this situation. Please believe that I invited you because I couldn't imagine being present with Rio without missing you. I'm sorry my carelessness made you feel unwelcomed, but you're the one I want. I'm here now with you, not him."

Alano has history with Rio, but he wants a future with me.

I gotta figure out what I'm doing now.

"Okay, but what about Rio? He definitely wants to be your boyfriend still."

"No, he doesn't."

"How can you be so brilliant, Alano, and so clueless?"

"I'm not clueless. I promise Rio doesn't want to be my boyfriend."

"You're not a mind reader! How do you know—"

"Because I asked Rio to be my boyfriend and he said no," Alano says.

His voice cracking breaks my heart because his pain is over some other boy. I thought it was one-sided because Alano rejected Rio, not the other way around.

"This was three summers ago. Rio was still grieving Lucio. I became his escapism, and he became mine. It turned intimate but never anything more because he didn't feel how I felt."

I'm gonna have nightmares about Rio in bed with Alano, taunting me over how he's special and I'm not. But there's something more haunting than any sex they've had.

"How did you feel about him?" I nervously ask.

"I was in love with him," Alano confesses.

I hate Rio even more because Alano loved him.

"That's that, then," I say, breaking down in tears.

"What is?"

"Us. I got enough ghosts in my life, I'm not gonna try and win a war against Rio as if he isn't everything you wanted."

"That's not fair, Paz. Everyone has pasts. Things we're not proud of."

"Are you swinging at me for killing my dad?"

"No, never! I'm trying to open up about my regrets—"

"Yeah, you regret Rio so much that you're moving in with him. I'm not gonna be your long-distance boyfriend when your boy who got away is down the hall."

Alano reaches for my hands, but I back away. "I want to explore a future with you, Paz. I promise Rio is in the past."

I wanna believe this promise so bad. "How long in the past?"

"I told you. Three years ago."

"No, I mean . . . nothing has happened between you since then?"

Alano is quiet as he looks around, trying to hide his tears. "This shouldn't matter. Everything Rio and I have done was before I met you."

"How long before? Six months? A year?"

Alano closes his eyes. "Two weeks."

Hot tears blind me as my stomach twists in knots. "You are so stuck in the past."

He starts sobbing. "Please don't say that, Paz, you have no idea how much that hurts—"

"You know what hurts, Alano? Staying alive for you!"

Alano wants to pull me in for a hug so bad, but he knows I'm never letting him touch me again. "You aren't supposed to stay alive for me. I've only ever wanted you to live for yourself."

"If you wanted me to live for myself, you should've shown me I was worth loving." I get in Alano's face, one last time, close enough for the kiss I'll now die without. "You're dead to me."

The tears fill Alano's green eye and brown eye so fast, ready to suck me back in, but I turn to leave. Alano grabs my hand, tugging at me, hard.

My blood boils as my fingernails dig into my palms.

I spin around, my fist held high, and—

I stop myself from punching Alano, but he flinches anyway. I made Alano flinch.

Dane comes to Alano's rescue, shielding him—shielding him from me.

I spin in a full circle to find people around the park filming me.

I stare at my fist. Did I almost just punch Alano in the face? That's not me, I don't go around getting mad and hitting people.

But I almost did.

Then I'm hit with an even more devastating blow: I'm becoming my dad.

Everyone was right about me. I'm a threat to society.

Nothing hurts more than the fear in Alano's eyes as he finally sees me for the monster I am.

I run away.

The Begin Days are dead, but I don't know how I'm gonna survive my Not-End Days without the boy I like—the boy I love.

PART FOUR

How to Survive an End Day, Whether You Like It or Not

I am not alive, and I will not fall

into the trappings of life.

—Death

(Golden Heart *by Orion Pagan)*

July 27, 2020

PAZ

7:57 a.m.

Death-Cast didn't call, even though they should've since I almost attacked the heir. Maybe Alano told them how badly I wanna die, so Death-Cast's retaliation is to make me live. Or maybe they're waiting for the media storm to blow over before they send an assassin to quietly deal with me. That's a stupid-ass conspiracy, but according to the news, I showed my true colors yesterday as a Death Guarder, which is another stupid-ass conspiracy, but no one believed my truth before, and they definitely won't now, since I can't hide behind only being violent to save Mom's life.

It took less than an hour for a video of me threatening to punch Alano to go viral. It took a little bit longer before I was identified as the latest Death Guarder out for blood, but the damage has been done. My name has made headlines and is being dragged all over social media. What's really disgusting is watching Carson Dunst's supporters praise my anger against Alano. You know you've done something wrong when that crowd is backing you up.

Mom has asked me to stay off social media until this blows over. I refuse.

People think self-harming is only physical. Reading hateful comments cuts deeper.

I open Twitter and type in my name to see what people are saying:

@theOriginalOP123: I KNEW Paz Dario was a Death Guarder!!! We all know he loves people dying without warning RIP Daddy Dario

@IDoTheLeastAlwaysss: PAZ DARIO FOR PRESIDENT

@manthony12: my best friend Rufus had anger issues too. doesn't mean he was bad. #PazDario

@The1nOn1yPeck: wow Paz Dario threw hands lol he should've finished the job #DeathGuard

@WereWolfie57: bro I watched GRIMMED MISSED CALLS and Paz Dario's dad was a piece of shit who needed to die but Piction+ needs to do a part 2 because Paz is a piece of shit too

@SaveFacePublicity: Paz Dario needs a PR team. Hire me $$$

@ByrdSong27: whoever paid Paz Dario to take a hit out on Alano Rosa should've been clearer #maybenexttime

@ScorpiusIsMyDemonKing: RT if "how to get away with murder" should do 1 more season and cast Paz Dario since hes got EXPERIENCE

@aRealSeerNYC: like father like son. #PazDario

@TheBadNewsHerald: why was Alano Rosa hanging out w/ Paz Dario???

I stop and stare at that last tweet. Would anyone believe that Alano and I were hanging out because he liked me? If so, they're as stupid as I am.

Mom knocks on the door I agreed to keep open and unlocked since she was so concerned about me, especially because I didn't wanna talk about what went down with Alano.

"Here you go." Mom hands me two Prozac and water. I swallow both pills, but she doesn't leave. "We need to talk."

"I don't wanna talk," I say, scrolling away and letting strangers define me.

Mom snatches my phone and holds it away. "What are you going to do? Hit me?"

Apart from threatening to kill herself, this is the worst thing Mom has ever said to me. I can hate random-ass people for saying "like father, like son," but Mom is the only one in the world who I never want thinking that. Hitting Alano isn't me, but I'm sure Dad told Mom the same thing over and over and over. That didn't stop him, not even when she was pregnant with me. I wanna act like I'm different and safe, but I don't get that right.

"That's what I thought," Mom says. She hasn't been this stern since she was laying down the rules of my suicide watch. "I can only assume Alano isn't pressing charges since the police haven't arrived yet, but I'm still terrified they are going to knock on this door any minute now and take you away from me, as would be their right, for threatening violence against Alano."

Between all of last night's crying and secretly self-harming myself like never before, I've barely slept, but what's really kept me awake is waiting for the cops to arrest me. That's how traumatic my first arrest was.

The night I killed Dad, two police officers rolled up. The bad cop found me cowering in the corner of my bedroom. I immediately held my empty hands in the air because that's what I always saw police tell people to do on TV shows. I wanted them to see me as a good kid after what I'd done, but the bad cop still handcuffed me anyway, saying it was procedure and for their own safety, which didn't make sense because they were adults with guns and I was nine without one . . . anymore. Mom begged the officers to be gentle with me, and the good cop took me away from the bad cop's grip, but in all that commotion I missed Mom's warning to not look at Dad's body on the way out.

Of all the moments surrounding Dad's death—from grabbing the gun from the closet to shooting him twice—it really sank in that I had killed Dad when I saw his corpse lying in the blood that was spreading across the same floor where I took my first steps toward him.

I thought I was a hero for saving Mom's life, but I felt like a villain when I was sitting in the back of the cop car, escorted into the police station when everyone looked at me like my crime was written on my face, when I posed for that mug shot, when I got my fingerprints stamped, and when I was interrogated for killing Dad. Mom thought we didn't have anything to hide, so she let me speak to the detective before we had any legal backup, but as I answered every question truthfully, I was still scared that I was gonna make a mistake and be written off as a liar and be charged with premeditated murder and locked up for the rest of my life.

Maybe that's where I belonged all along.

"And?" I ask. I can't stop the police from arresting me.

"Why did you almost hit Alano?" Mom asks.

The viral video shows me and Alano arguing, but you can't really make out what we're saying, same deal with the other videos people posted. What's clear as day is Alano grabbing my wrist when I try walking away and me swinging back, ready to punch him. I would rather go to jail than watch that horrific video again.

"It doesn't matter."

"I called Ms. Cielo—"

"What? Why?" I interrupt. Ms. Cielo was the public defender in my trial.

"In case we need to fight this in court."

"There's no fight. I didn't even do anything."

"That doesn't mean your intent can't be used against you. Instead of having you spend time in prison, we can work with your therapist and psychiatrist to get you into an anger-management program and help prevent future outbursts with cognitive behavioral therapy." Mom loves me so much that she can't even be mad enough to send me to jail before I can become a true terror like Dad. "I can only help if I know what possessed you to hurt Alano."

I've been possessed by a mental disorder because of Dad abusing Mom. I've gone from being terrified to becoming the terror.

"I wanted to punch Alano because he obliterated my heart," I cry out. No one goes to jail for heartbreak, but that should be a crime too. I want Alano tried in court and forced to explain to a judge and jury how he thought it was okay to prey on my dying soul.

That's all I'm able to say, but it's enough for Mom. "I'm sorry, Pazito."

I let Mom hold me as I cry, remembering how badly I missed her when I was sent to a juvenile detention center in the Bronx the night I killed Dad. My throat got so raw as I screamed for Mom, scared I would never see her again. I cried in my cell so hard that I threw up and I cried until I fell asleep and I cried when I woke up and I cried when I was released back into Mom's arms the next afternoon. That one night without Mom—and even Dad—felt like forever.

And now nothing feels lonelier than life without Alano. I'm ready to give up.

"I'm sorry to disturb you," Rolando says at the door, "but there are vans outside."

The police are here, but vans? Like, more than one? Did they send a SWAT team or the military to arrest a nineteen-year-old boy whose only weapon is a knife he uses to hurt himself? I'm gonna have to make a run for it. Then I remember that I self-harmed like never before last night and don't stand a chance of outrunning anyone when I can barely walk. I break out of Mom's hold, hiding my limp as I go to the window and pull back the curtains.

I'm blinded by lights.

It's not the police coming to arrest me. It's the media here to destroy me.

If I'd known surviving would lead me here, I would've pulled the trigger.

ALANO
10:30 a.m.

Death-Cast can't call me, but instead of a company that alerts people before they die, aren't we better off having a service that predicts how long our romantic relationships will last? Love-Cast, if you will. This will give everyone the necessary foresight to prepare for their heartbreak. To get closure. To lean in for that last kiss, or even the first kiss before the chance is lost forever. At the end of the day, I don't need Love-Cast to know that my relationship with Paz was always doomed. I just never envisioned my past with Rio being the downfall of a future that felt destined.

I've locked myself in my bedroom with only Bucky because I got overwhelmed with my parents watching the media coverage and my father's urging to press charges against Paz. What I'm doing instead is trying to better understand Paz's eruption by watching videos and reading articles on my laptop about how romantic relationships affect someone with borderline personality disorder.

For starters, someone with BPD might fall in love fast, recognizing their partner as the soulmate who will save them from their turmoil. There's also a phenomenon known as splitting because while someone with BPD will fall in love fast, they will switch to hate just as quickly if they've been betrayed or rejected. I don't know if Paz loved me, but I'm certain he hates me now.

You're dead to me, Paz said. That's been haunting many of my waking moments.

I'm dead to Paz because I failed at effective communication, which is a must in any relationship, especially if your partner has BPD, since their depressive thought spirals will negatively fill in the blanks for anything unsaid. If only I could've handed Paz an Alano Rosa Encyclopedia so he could know everything about my story, even the pages I wish I could burn. Instead, Paz had to find out about my past with Rio during a heated moment. Of course Paz will only see Rio as a threat.

How can you be so brilliant, Alano, and so clueless? Paz said.

I was clueless because this is new territory for me. I'm moving on from unrequited love with Rio to mutual attraction with Paz as well as being mindful of Paz's borderline personality disorder along with protecting myself from a psychotic break. It will take years of experience before I even hope to be brilliant at navigating relationships of that nature, but I care enough to keep learning now.

My research has brought me to my biggest question: Can I repair this broken relationship? There are a lot of good answers to further reflect on for both the person with BPD and the partner, but what immediately resonates most with me is making sure I'm not put on a pedestal. Paz won't treat me like a flawless soulmate once I come clean about my imperfections.

That's assuming Paz gives me a second chance.

You know what hurts, Alano? Staying alive for you! Paz said.

My desperation to atone for past failures was a driving force behind getting Paz down from the Hollywood Sign safely and that gun out of his possession so I wouldn't have more blood on my hands, but there's no denying the Begin Days were a genuine effort to help Paz live for himself. I didn't anticipate falling for Paz along the way or pushing him over the edge.

I don't regret saving Paz.

I only regret making his life worse than when I found him.

PAZ
11:05 a.m.

All these cameras outside my house make me feel like I'm on a movie set.

What role should I play to make these reporters go away? I'll look like a psychopath if I go out there with all smiles as Happy Paz, but I can put on a show as Sad Paz by getting down on my knees and begging for forgiveness. I can stare into the camera and apologize directly to Alano. Once I'm done apologizing, I'll stand there and wait for the reporters to apologize to me. They're out there acting like I'm the same as Dad, a man who abused Mom over and over for years, when I didn't even lay a finger on Alano. How the fuck is that fair? It's not, but they don't give a shit, just like they don't give a shit about an apology; all they want is more proof that I'm Crazy Paz. I'm gonna go outside and give them what they want—

No, no, no, I'm not gonna be defined by this one moment. That's not me—

Actually, they're right, it's not this one moment, I now have multiple offenses—

I made a mistake threatening to punch Alano, one I would apologize for—

No, Alano should apologize because he did more damage by messing with my head—

I have no right to hit another person unless it's self-defense—

Not even then, according to a shit ton of people—

I wish I never raised my fist at Alano—

I wish I never met Alano.

My phone buzzes in my pocket, rescuing me from the spiral. My heart races, hoping it's the boy I wish I never met, but it's just an email from the Make-A-Moment manager following up about my job application. I'm not surprised Ross is rejecting me for the position, but I'm surprised by how pissed off I am. This job was supposed to be Alano's proof that I could still have a future, and now I'll never know if I'm not being hired because I almost punched Alano or because I killed Dad.

I get up from the couch, limping toward my bedroom.

"Where are you going?" Mom asks, trapped at home with me.

"I'm gonna call Raquel."

Nothing like the closed-door privacy of a fake call with my therapist to self-harm in peace.

ALANO

"You have a guest."

I'm still waking up from my depression nap when Agent Dane repeats himself. It doesn't make sense for Paz to be the visitor, but I hold out hope anyway when I ask who it is.

"Mr. Rio," Agent Dane says.

Of course it is. He's been calling and texting since last night. I haven't responded.

My phone has been on Do Not Disturb mode since this morning because I was overwhelmed with messages from associates checking in on my well-being after another hate crime. This wasn't so much a hate crime as it was an I-hate-you crime. That's why it would probably surprise many to learn that Paz is the only contact I've marked as an exception in Do Not Disturb mode in case he needs me during this time of distress. This wishful thinking that he would ever want my help again is sinking me deeper into my depression.

I get out of bed to go deal with Rio. Bucky shadows me as I make my way through the mansion, and he does a big stretch by the front door with his tail wagging as if we're about to go for a walk. Agent Dane steps out onto the porch first, and Bucky runs outside, losing his mind when he spots Rio as if he didn't see him two days ago. There was a time when I had this same energy for Rio.

"Hey, Buck-Boy," Rio says, leaning over to pet Bucky, his balance shifting because of his oversize travel backpack. Then he looks up at me. "Are you okay?"

"No," I say. My arms are crossed.

Rio takes off his backpack and sits at the patio table, expecting me to join him. "You're being cold, as if I'm the monster that threatened you."

"Paz isn't a monster."

"He's no angel."

"You provoked him."

"You needed to see he's still dangerous. You were so blinded—"

"I saw him in ways you didn't."

"What I saw matters too, Alano. I saw him threaten to kick my ass. I saw videos of him ready to punch you. What I didn't see was your bodyguard tackling the shit out of him . . . ," Rio says, turning to Agent Dane, who is choosing to ignore him. "Even though Paz was clearly a threat."

In that moment it was Agent Dane's responsibility to shield my body as if it were his own, especially since we were surrounded by a crowd of strangers who could've mobbed me. In no world did I believe Paz would kill me. Then again, I never imagined Paz would come that close to assaulting me either. I blame this on his unmanaged borderline personality disorder, which needs to be addressed, but just as I won't share Paz's diagnosis with my parents, this isn't Rio's business either.

"You shouldn't have dismissed the pain behind Paz's suicide attempt," I say.

"He was trying to make himself sound noble when he's just suicidal," Rio says.

"You're doing it again."

"And you're still defending him as if he's completely innocent."

If only he knew about how I should be called Death for the way I've made people grieve.

"My relationship with Paz isn't your business, but now I've lost him because of you."

Rio gets up from the table and steps toward me. "You can't hate me for being your best friend who wants to keep you alive, Alano."

I try responding, but he's not done.

"You have so many life experiences, but even though your family profits off death, you don't know what it's like to actually lose someone." His dark eyes fill with tears. "There are no words for how painful life is without Lucio or how guilty I feel every time I have fun or how often I wish I was dead instead of Lucio so Antonio would have a better big brother." He squeezes his eyes shut, and the tears slide down his face. "It's so hard to remember Lucio alive without also remembering his corpse with no eyes or limbs . . ." He shakes his head like that will make the memory fall out. He takes a deep breath before looking at me again. "Do you want to know the real reason I didn't want to be with you?"

This is not where I thought this conversation was headed. I've always believed Rio didn't have feelings for me. I wish I could live in ignorance, but I have to know the truth. "Why?"

"You have always acted so invincible. I don't know if it was because of Death-Cast or you thinking you know everything about everyone. All I saw was someone who was going to get himself violently killed, and I couldn't go through that again." His dark eyes become angry and sad and hopeful all at once. "I almost lost you, Alano, and I'm so happy I didn't."

"It's nice to have a friend who cares."

He scratches his head and sighs. "I'm not doing this right."

"Doing what right?"

Rio takes my hand. "I'm not some poet, but I want to be with you."

This declaration might not be poetry, but I instantly recall the poet Alfred Tennyson's elegy about his best friend, Arthur Henry Hallam, who died suddenly: "*'Tis better to have loved and lost than never to have loved at all.*" For all of Rio's pro-naturalism and returning to the old ways, his solution isn't to sign up for Death-Cast again so he won't lose me suddenly. It's to live pro-naturally together, even if that means grieving me after an unpredictable death.

After Rio broke my heart, I would revisit memory lane daily, wondering how I mistook our relationship as romantic. It was hard to disprove this because all the signs were there that he liked me, at least according to my parents, his parents, Ariana, Agent Dane, and anyone else who spent more than five minutes observing us. We would go for the longest walks around the city, and whenever we had to go back to our own homes, we would video chat to keep talking until it was time to fall asleep. We took interest in each other's hobbies, like playing his favorite video games or him doing deep dives into my daily fun facts. We opened up about our struggles in ways we never had with anyone else. Great friendships are built on these elements too, but I never felt like I was only getting to know a friend. I was sure that I was discovering my soulmate.

During a moment of vulnerability on Sunday, June 25, 2017, Rio kissed me.

That kiss was as transformative and inevitable as getting older.

"I waited so long to hear you say this," I say.

My heart is racing as our bodies get closer, an electricity buzzing between us that I've grown so used to signaling a shift from two boys hanging out as friends to two boys seeking intimacy as lovers. Rio smiles as he leans in, his lips an inch from mine before I pull back.

"I'm sorry, but I stopped waiting."

Completely moving on is impossible. I will always hold love for Rio whether I want to or not, but I have already survived all the sleepless nights wishing he were there to hold me. Now I'm losing sleep over someone else.

Rio's hand releases mine. "This is embarrassing."

"Don't be embarrassed. This doesn't change anything."

"Is that how you felt when I rejected you?"

Every day was harder and harder. "No, but we got through that together."

Rio grabs his backpack as if he's about to walk away, but he stares at me. "I flew here for you. I was scared of losing you and that's happening anyway."

This doesn't have to be some self-fulfilling prophecy.

"You're not losing me. I'm alive, Rio. I really needed a friend. I still do."

It would be so nice to sit down and open up about how hard this week has been, like other times I've struggled, but Rio lit the match that blew up my future with Paz. Turning to him now would be like if I asked my father to stop me from jumping off that roof when he's the reason I tried killing myself in the first place. Not that my father or anyone else knows this.

"It's too hard to be your friend right now," Rio says, turning to walk away.

It's as if Rio is my Muay Thai opponent. My rejection was a back fist, but before I can block, he knocks the air out of me with a knee strike. We're both still standing but hurt. I want to put an end to this match.

"You're the one who got so moved over the fear of losing me and now you're walking away?" I ask, following Rio as he walks past the fountain and down toward the gate. "Is this how you feel? If you can't have all of me then you want none of me?"

Rio stops in his tracks and whips around to face me. "Do you really expect me to stand around and watch you fall in love with another boy?"

That's the knockout blow that takes me out for so long that I don't notice Rio is gone until the gate door slams shut.

First Ariana, now Rio. I no longer have best friends. Or Paz.

This is the most alone I've been in years.

The poet Alfred Tennyson wrote about how it was better to have loved and lost than to never have loved at all, but I could really use a poem about losing everything because of love.

PAZ

After physically self-harming, I mentally self-harm by reading more hit-pieces.

Twitter has only gotten worse. Instead of just calling me a dangerous Death Guarder, the attacks have gotten personal. I'm an ugly blond. I'm the worst part of the entire Scorpius Hawthorne franchise. I'm exploiting Alano for fame. And my favorite is that I should go kill myself, which I heart from my fake account. There's also a parody account called @PazDariosFist that's challenging Death-Cast employees to fights. Some idiots are speculating that's me, but even if I ran outside and told all those reporters the truth, it wouldn't matter. Everyone's already made their minds up on me, the ugly, exploitative, dangerous Death Guarder who sucked in the last Scorpius Hawthorne movie and should go die by suicide.

I'm about to move on when I see some un-fucking-believable news that has nothing and everything to do with me: the role of Death has been cast in *Golden Heart*, and it's none other than that bastard Bodie, who I met before the chemistry read. He couldn't even bother to read the book and now he's gonna get famous off this story.

I open my nightstand and grab my bloodstained knife. This isn't enough. Self-harm isn't helping. What I really wanna do is hurt someone else, and that thought is so fucking scary.

I wanna punch Bodie; I wanna punch the producers; I wanna punch Orion.

Sometimes a thought is just a thought, but sometimes I don't think, I just act, and if my actions are about hurting other people, then I gotta put an end to this before I truly become Dad.

My life has always been hard, but I believe more than ever that I was supposed to die before Alano interfered because everything has only gotten worse. It's like time travelers are trying to right that wrong, so they've organized a shitstorm to wash out any hope for living, including getting dragged on social media, news vans violating my privacy, Make-A-Moment rejecting me, and my dream of being Death in Orion's movie officially killed.

Message received.

I gotta return to the Hollywood Sign to finish what I started.

ALANO
5:16 p.m.

I'm so alone that I seek out my parents. I find them in their bedroom, where Pa is getting ready for this evening's *60 Minutes* interview at the Death-Cast offices in Hollywood to reflect on the ten-year anniversary and promote his upcoming memoir. Ma is pushing for Pa to wear this navy-blue Dior suit, but I go into his closet and pull a lilac Chanel suit he's yet to wear. Styling my father is a good distraction from all my feelings.

I take a seat on their daybed with Bucky, recounting my difficult discussion with Rio. I can see my parents calculating how friendless I am.

"I am so sorry," Ma says.

"It will all work out, mi hijo," Pa says.

"That's what you said about Ariana," I say. *Word for word*, I should add.

"Life's pains do not heal overnight," Pa says, stealing glances at my bandaged arm. "But they will all heal."

The stitches will close my wounds, but what will repair my heart and my soul? Time and time alone will take too long. I'm not sure I have it in me to wait, especially as my life continues to unravel, taking others down with me along the way.

"When do I need to be at the office again?" Pa asks, selecting his watch.

Normally I would know his itinerary off the top of my head, but I haven't really been as active since my assassination attempt. I log in to my company account and search through the many new emails that Aster Gomez has copied me on for Death-Cast duties. The most recent email is about Orion Pagan's film adaptation. She's shared a press release from today about the casting of Death. Even though I know it's not possible, I hope anyway to find Paz's name. An actor named Bodie LaBoy has been cast and Aster is wondering if we should extend gala invites to him and the other lead, Zen Abarca, since Orion's story is so heavily influenced by the first End Day.

"The time?" Pa asks again.

"Oh." I quickly find the itinerary. "Six thirty."

"Thank you."

I return to the casting announcement, wishing I could've pulled some strings to get Paz into this movie.

"What's this look on your face?" Ma asks.

At first I think she's talking about Pa until she calls my name. "I'm concerned about Paz," I say, stopping my father in his tracks as I explain everything about Paz's attachment to that role in *Golden Heart*. "He got so close with the audition but wasn't selected because of the controversy around his name."

"That movie dodged a bullet," Pa says.

That terrible phrasing thrusts me back into that night where I stopped Paz from shooting himself and then the night before, when Harry Hope shot himself. "Paz almost killed himself over this movie before," I say, glaring at Pa. "His conditions are only worse now."

"Conditions he created," Pa says.

"Do you hold him responsible for shooting his father?" I ask.

"Of course not, but I will not give a nineteen-year-old the same courtesy I would a nine-year-old, especially when my son was the target this time around."

He's so defensive of me that he's not recognizing Paz as someone else's son.

"We should alert his parents of the threat," Ma says. At least she remembers.

"They don't know that he self-harms or tried killing himself recently," I say.

Ma sits beside me on the daybed. "Do you believe he'll harm himself over this?"

"He promised a couple nights ago that he wasn't going to self-harm anymore, but . . ."

"But heartbreak turns people inside out."

I imagine Paz literally inside out with his broken heart trapped between his rib cage with deep cuts across the body; it's an image I immediately wish I could forget.

After Agent Dane and I left the amusement park yesterday, accompanied by three other Shield-Cast agents, I shared my concerns about Paz self-harming, which shouldn't have been that surprising to me since I knew he'd attempted suicide, but I was still caught off guard.

"There are always physical and psychosocial signs," Agent Dane had said before sharing some common examples. Impulsive behaviors, self-isolating, overeating or undereating, and even overexercising. He'd noticed Paz's mood swings, but nothing physical like missing patches of hair or wearing long sleeves during summer to hide unexplained bruises, cuts, or burns. Where Paz self-harms is as big a mystery to eagle-eyed Agent Dane as it is to me. "If parents as loving and attentive as Gloria and Rolando aren't picking up on the signs, then Paz must be acting his ass off."

"He's an actor," I reminded Dane.

"Did he share his method? No sharp objects turned up during the bedroom inspection."

Agent Dane still doesn't know his eagle eye missed the knife hidden in Paz's decoy journal.

"He's cutting, but I don't know where on his body." I've never seen any scarring on his arms, and I can rule out his legs after seeing Paz in basketball shorts yesterday. Still, there is so much of Paz's body I never got to explore.

Even after Paz almost punched me, I was still tempted to go check on him, but I was concerned that my appearance might upset him further.

"Do you want to call him?" Ma asks.

"Naya, why would you say such a thing?" Pa asks.

"Alano is concerned about his friend," Ma says firmly and lovingly.

"His enemy," Pa says, firmer and loveless. It's as if Paz has been put in the same camp as Mac Maag, who actually tried killing me. "If you are so concerned about him, mi hijo, then turn on the news. The reporters who have been outside his house all day will certainly be tracking whether he has left."

My concern for Paz skyrockets knowing there's been a beaming spotlight on his house all day. I pull out my phone and go online to various newsfeeds and find clips of Paz's house. What if Paz snaps like Caspian Townsend and gets killed? I've never been more tempted to break employee code by reaching out to a Death-Cast office to confirm if someone is a Decker.

Would Paz tell me if today is his End Day?

I reflect on this while staring out the window, up at the sky that's too bright, considering how dark this day has been. "I'm going to call Paz," I say, ignoring my parents' protests as I rush out of the bedroom.

My mother chases after me. "Alano."

I keep walking.

"You're not calling him," she says. "You're going to him, aren't you?"

I stop in my tracks. "Please don't try to talk me out of it," I say without turning around.

"A mother is allowed to worry," Ma says, catching up and facing me. "Tell me why you must do this."

"You told me to guard my heart in case I can't save Paz forever, but making sure he's alive is guarding my heart." Even if I'm dead to him.

I regret not being more careful with Paz's heart the first time around.

My mother brings my hands up to her mouth and kisses my knuckles. There's pride and fear in her teary eyes. "I love you, my miracle, and as much as it scares me to watch you try to play miracle worker, I love your heart for guiding you toward compassion. This world is so hard, and I endured so much to bring you into it that I questioned if all those miscarriages were the world's way of trying to show me mercy. Those concerns only sharpened when Joaquin first told me about the secret that would become Death-Cast. It made this world scarier to bring a child into, but I was finally pregnant with you, and I didn't want that to change." She looks at me like I'm a newborn all over again. "But your father's vision for Death-Cast was worth bringing to life too. We had to take these leaps of faith and now here we are. Death-Cast has made life easier for millions around the world and you have made life brighter for me and your father." She wipes her tears and smiles. "And I believe you made Paz's life brighter too. If you must go make sure that his soul has not darkened, I will not stop you, but"—Ma squeezes my hand, just like I did with Paz's when we were on the Hollywood Sign—"please come back to me."

I wait for Ma to threaten that she won't live in this world without me like Ms. Gloria did to Paz, but I'm relieved that it never comes. No matter how hard life would be if I died, I want my mother to keep going. Paz feels the same way about his mother.

"I'm coming back to you, Ma."

"I believe your intention, but I don't know your fate. If you go to Paz, do you trust him with your life?"

After hearing my mother's story about the Death-Cast secret, it's only made me feel more confident in taking this leap of faith to be there for a boy who I fully trust isn't a Death Guarder.

"I trust Paz with my life," I say.

"Then go get peace of mind that he isn't harming himself and wishes no harm on you."

PAZ
6:25 p.m.

It's time to go die before I hurt anyone else.

It has to be now before I can fully transform into Dad, a piece of shit who definitely ran his mouth about how he didn't mean to hit Mom and how his anger brought out the worst in him. Then sometimes he would act like that violence never happened, even though Mom had the bruises. I don't wanna become a man who hits anyone and doesn't feel anything.

I gotta stop myself.

Most news vans have left, but a couple are still lurking, waiting me out. They're about to be rewarded for their patience with videos of me flipping them off as I begin my final journey.

Mom and Rolando are in their room listening to spa music to try to relax during this fucked-up day. I gotta go now so they don't get suspicious later. I'm tempted to say goodbye to Mom and tell her I love her, but the suicide note I've left under my pillow will have to do that for me.

As much as I hate to admit it—and I really fucking hate it— Alano was right that if I have to die, the last thing I leave Mom shouldn't be a suicide note. I never got to pay for those gifts at Present-Time, but maybe the shopkeeper will still send them along to Mom and Rolando when she's back in business. On my way to the Hollywood Sign I'm gonna call the shop to leave a message to make this happen. I can't call as myself since I'm supposed to be dead and impersonations aren't my strong suit, but I can probably pull off an Alano impression. All I have to do is be really polite and share a fun fact about the origins of clocks or some shit like that.

Thinking about Alano's all-knowing brain makes me happy for a millisecond before I remember how his lying mouth broke my heart and twisted my hand into a fist.

Everything happens for a reason, even being saved by Alano so he can wreck me. Maybe if I had gone through my original suicide plan I would've somehow survived and been worse off. I won't have the gun this time, but maybe that's why it would've all gone wrong, because nothing good comes out of guns.

My new plan is simple: jump to my death. That was enough for the Hollywood Sign Girl and it'll be enough to turn me into the Hollywood Sign Boy.

I didn't know a damn thing about Peg Entwistle or her suicide before meeting Alano, but telling me her story has really boosted my confidence in this plan. It's almost like Alano came into my life to be some powerful herald who not only tells me I'm about to die but also how.

I hate that I can't stop thinking about Alano. What sucks the most is that it's mostly the good stuff. How Alano never treated me like some cold-blooded killer. How Alano made me feel seen and heard. And how Alano became a reason to jump out of bed and celebrate not getting a Death-Cast call. But it feels wrong thinking about the good stuff, just like when Alano asked about a childhood memory that makes me smile and I told him about Dad caring for me. I need to remember the bad. How Dad abused Mom and tried to kill her, so I killed him first. How Alano made me so angry I almost punched him. How I might grow up and try to kill the person I love.

For as long as I live—hopefully just another six hours—I'll never forget all the heartbreaks I've been through; my body won't let me, especially during the long, painful journey ahead to the Hollywood Sign.

I fight back tears as I limp to the front door, opening it fast to rush out, but I freeze.

I've gotta be hallucinating because I'm seeing the guy I was never supposed to see again. His green eye and brown eye are staring at me in shock too. He's wearing a gray hoodie and baggy blue jeans with a brown leather satchel hanging from his shoulder. One hand is balled into a fist like he's about to get his revenge hit—or like he was about to knock on the door. Every rapid thought about the guy coming for revenge flies out of my head when I see something in his other hand that's as unbelievable as him being here.

Alano holds up the star rug from the market. "I figured you needed this now more than ever," he says sympathetically—no, lovingly.

I unfreeze, but instead of taking the star rug, I break down crying, and even though I don't deserve to ever touch him again, I ask, no, I beg, "Can I hug you?"

"Yes," Alano says.

I step into his arms, ignoring all the pain that is supposed to be warning me away from guys like him, and I sob as he pulls me even closer against his body, like we're one person.

I will lie and lie and lie to anyone, but I can't lie to myself about how much holding Alano feels like hanging on for dear life so I don't fall off the Hollywood Sign.

"Paz?"

I hold on tighter because I'm scared he's about to leave again. "Yeah?"

"Mind if I come in? We're being filmed."

I look over Alano's shoulders. There are reporters and camerapeople on the street. Agent Dane is also waiting by the curb, locked in on us like the cameras. We step back, and Alano closes the door behind us.

"How are you doing?" Alano asks.

A minute ago I was defeated and on my way to jump to my death, and now I wanna fly, but I know how life works—I'm only gonna crash down again.

I just shake my head.

"I'm here for you, Paz. Agent Dane is going to knock on this door any moment now to conduct a search if you want me to stay. Is there anything you need to hide?"

It kills me that Alano knows me well enough to suspect self-harming. I'm ashamed to nod.

There's a knock on the door. "Go put it away," Alano says.

I rush without thinking to my bedroom, pain shooting up my right leg, so bad that I almost collapse. I grab the knife out of my journal, and Dane knocks harder as I'm rinsing the knife in the kitchen sink before tossing it into the dishwasher. As Alano opens the door for Dane, Mom and Rolando come out of their bedroom, the spa music humming down the hallway.

Once Mom sees who's here, her hand flies to her heart. "Please do not send my son to jail," she says, tears flowing. She's about to cave in until Rolando helps hold her up.

"I only came to check on Paz, Ms. Gloria," Alano says.

"Pazito?" Mom asks, trying to catch her breath.

I hate that I was almost guilty of a crime and she's still fighting for me as if I'm completely innocent.

"He surprised me, Mom," I say. I still can't believe he's here after what I almost did.

Dane is tense when asking permission to do his inspection, but I don't fight it, obviously. I'm just grateful that Alano gave me the heads-up because I'm sure Dane's search will be a lot more thorough this time. Even though I became a monster who almost attacked Alano, Alano still trusts me enough with his life. And he still cares about mine.

Mom embraces Alano. "Are you doing okay?"

Alano nods. "I'm sorry I startled you, Ms. Gloria."

"I've been thinking about you. If you need to talk, I'm here for you too."

"I appreciate that," he says.

I hate that Mom and Alano have been bonded over this. I'm losing the will to live again, knowing I'll never be able to shake off this shame.

"Can we get you anything?" Rolando asks.

"Is it possible to have some time alone with Paz?" Alano asks.

"We're down the hall if you need us," Mom says.

I'm not sure if she's talking to me or Alano.

After standing around awkwardly as Dane finishes his inspection, Alano and I go into my room. He closes the door behind him, another sign he trusts me. I sit on the bed, my heart racing as he approaches, but he only sets down the star rug before moving on to my desk chair. He might trust me, but he's still keeping his distance.

We're both quiet, stealing looks at each other, and at the same time we say, "I'm sorry."

I shake my head. "Why are you sorry?"

"I wasn't careful with your brain or heart," Alano says, his linked hands pinned between his knees, like he's the one who almost attacked me. "I've done more research on borderline personality disorder, and I understand now how my lack of transparency about my past with Rio triggered your reaction."

I sit up fast, and Alano flinches, like I'm about to actually hit him. I remember when Mom would get scared around Dad, and how even when she mistook movement as an incoming attack, she would still hug me so tight I felt her heart pounding. "I hate myself for almost hitting you," I tell Alano, hating myself even more for how I've made his heart race out of fear.

I feel like I'm on trial again, except Alano is the judge, jury, and executioner. "I'm so scared I'm becoming my dad, like this is just in my DNA to hurt the people I . . ."

I can't bring myself to tell Alano I love him after almost hurting him. "To hurt the people close to me."

Alano's head hangs low. "You've grown up with unprocessed anger and you almost lost control."

"I've totally lost control before," I admit.

"What do you mean?"

"Back when I was nine," I say, telling the story.

My attorney, Ms. Cielo, did her best to keep us from going to trial, but she always suspected it was inevitable because this was the first court case where Death-Cast's involvement was gonna factor in the ruling. She advised Mom to stay in the city and do her best to help me settle into my new life while we waited for the trial to begin.

Easier said than done.

A few weeks after killing Dad, I started fourth grade, and people were acting like I walked into that classroom with blood dripping from my hands and a gun holstered at my hip. Kids told on me for looking at them funny when I was only looking at *them* funny because they were looking at *me* funny. The friends who were brave enough to talk to me kept asking stupid shit, like if it was fun to shoot a gun, or wanting to hear more about the killing like it was a cool story I brought back from the Scorpius set. Parents freaked out, filing complaints to the principal that their families were losing sleep every night while waiting for Death-Cast alerts as if I was gonna shoot up the school. Mom even agreed to have me patted down by security every morning, just to give everyone peace of mind, but there were still fears that

I would grab scissors or staplers to hurt the kids who were still seen as kids, unlike me, a kid who had hurt once and would likely hurt again.

I transferred to a Catholic school after the holiday break because Rolando thought I would find more compassion there, which was true for the teachers, but the parents were even crazier. They believed the devil was following me everywhere I went as punishment for choosing the unnaturalness of Death-Cast over their God, who was the only entity that should know when we are fated to die. Some kids ganged up on me at recess, always getting away with verbal warnings and detention, but when I fought back and gave one boy a bloody nose and punched in another's loose tooth, I was expelled before the final bell.

"Those kids and parents and administrators treated you unfairly," Alano says.

"But see, I've always been violent."

"That was self-defense, Paz."

"Punching you wouldn't have been."

"Are you ever going to try that again?"

"N-no, no, no. Never," I say, like I'm begging a jury of twelve Alanos to believe me.

"What safeguards can you take to make sure it never happens?"

Last night I almost cut up my hand as punishment, knowing that I wouldn't be able to hide those scars, which would then get me thrown in a suicide-prevention facility so I would be forced to learn how to never hurt anyone, even myself, ever again. Then I got scared over how powerless I would be in a facility.

A harsh truth about being suicidal is that you can wanna die and still fear for your life.

Since there's no way in hell Alano will back a plan that involves me cutting up my hand, I know what has to be done if I'm ever gonna learn to live with this brain.

"I'm gonna tell my therapist I wanna—that I *need* to start dialectical behavior therapy."

"I think that's the right choice. Do you want to do it now?" Alano asks.

I can't tell if he's being some accountability buddy or doesn't trust me. He's right to have his doubts. I've already lied once today about hitting up my therapist.

I grab my phone and write to Raquel, asking when's the soonest I can start DBT. I stare at the words. This is like signing the Begin Day contract all over again. Something has to change. I'm gonna either be moving forward no matter how long it takes to get the help I need or end everything now. I hit *Send* before I can change my mind.

"Done," I say, tossing my phone onto my pillow.

"How do you feel?" Alano asks, sounding more like a therapist checking on my well-being than people in court deciding my fate.

"Like I'm scared it won't be enough. Like I can't stop my evolution into Dad."

"Did your father ever go to therapy?"

"No."

"Did your father ever change his ways?"

"No."

"Did your father ever apologize?"

"No."

"Did your father ever regret his actions?"

"No."

"You can't speak for the dead, but your father's actions spoke for him," Alano says, coming closer, sitting beside me on the bed. "If it was written in stone somewhere that you were destined to become your father, you've just smashed that stone with your remorse and fear and actions. DBT will only help you unlock your best self."

My best self won't ever wanna hit Alano—or anyone—ever again.

I try staring into his eyes to thank him for this compassion he's showing me, but I'm still so ashamed. I have to fight off this urge to punch myself over and over and over until I'm bruised and bloodied.

"I'm sorry, I'm so fucking sorry," I say, choking on my apology. "I promise I'll never hurt you."

"I trust that you won't. I'm more concerned about you breaking your promise to yourself."

I hate being reminded that I already broke my promise to stop self-harming. My word means nothing. "I'm fine," I lie, not deserving Alano's support. I should lie and lie and lie until Alano gets out of here and stays far the fuck away from me before I can break my promise to him.

Alano calls me out for lying. "I already know you had a knife in this room. What happened? Were you self-harming or did you try taking your life?"

"No, I was gonna try again tonight, right when . . ."

Alano doesn't finish my sentence. He just sits with the weight of what would've gone down if he was five minutes late. Alano's timing has always been amazing. Actually, not always. He was nowhere in sight last night when I could've used him to stop me from making a big mistake.

"I wish you would've called me," Alano says.

"I didn't think you would be there for me," I say, sobbing, and feeling pretty damn stupid considering how he's here for me now without being asked.

"You self-harmed because of me," Alano says, his voice cracking. It's not a question, but I can tell he wishes it was and that the answer was no. We both know better. "I promise all I want is to take care of you, but I was not careful yesterday, and for that I'm sorry." He holds my hand in his like I'm glass. "I'm here now, and I'd like to help any way I can."

I desperately want Alano to help, but it's hard, it's like asking Dad's ghost to help undo everything that went wrong with my life because I killed him.

"Do you mind telling me what you did to yourself?" Alano asks after my long silence.

I flinch at the memory. "I don't wanna scar you."

"You might not be able to see them, but I have my own deep scars. I promise I can handle learning about yours. That knowledge will help me protect you from yourself."

I've never told anyone about how exactly I self-harm and it feels like a second coming-out.

"I started self-harming after that first trailer dropped for *Grim Missed Calls*," I say, trapping both my hands between Alano's as if I'm at risk of hurting myself by reliving everything. "I was eating Thanksgiving leftovers in my room when my Instagram comments got crazy out of nowhere. People were saying that the truth was gonna be out, that they never forgot about what I did, that I'm screwed now. I found the trailer online and told myself not to watch, but I didn't listen. I literally choked on air when my old headshot flashed in the trailer for the longest second ever." I'm crying so hard that I have to catch my breath, all so I can spit out, "I didn't even think about it, I took my fork and started scratching my thigh over and over."

Alano leans his forehead against mine and continues pressing his hands into mine. "I'm so sorry," he whispers, failing to hide another voice crack.

"That was just the start," I say, my eyes rolling over as I go through everything.

I kept self-harming throughout the holiday season, even after I deactivated my Instagram account so I wouldn't be flooded with daily hate comments from people who are out for blood even though they'll never know the full story, especially if they're only working off that docuseries. But I didn't need strangers calling me a psycho or murderer or dad-killer to set me off so bad that I turned to self-harming. Rejected from taking an acting class? I self-harmed. Rejected by agents and managers?

I self-harmed. Rejected for a commercial? I self-harmed. And I started exploring other ways to hurt myself. I switched from a plastic fork to steel. I burned myself with hot water. I started smoking. I wrote hateful things on my skin. And after my first failed suicide attempt and those three torturous days in the psych ward, I upgraded from a fork to a serrated knife to get through my Not-End Days.

"I always cut high up on my thigh so no one would ever know, but last night I wanted to hurt myself somewhere new." I squeeze my eyes shut, just like I had to last night while suffering through that unbearable pain. It's so horrific that I don't wanna tell him where. Turns out I don't need to.

"Your foot," Alano says. I open my eyes in shock and look down to see if I'm still bleeding. "You've been favoring your left foot."

I shake my head, not because it's not true but because I'm so ashamed. "I figured if I could make walking painful, I would never forget how bad heartbreak is," I tell the boy who broke my heart. I have so many regrets, and cutting myself isn't even the biggest one. "I shouldn't have told you this, I'm sorry, I shouldn't have told you, I shouldn't have told you, I shouldn't have told you." This has been nothing like coming out as gay, I felt good about that, but right now I feel guilty for not only putting this on Alano but also blaming him. "I'm sorry, I'll shut up."

"Don't apologize. No matter how hard this is to hear, I want to hear it."

I rip my hands out of Alano's grip. "Okay, but now you know. You should go, I'm okay, I got it out of my system, thanks." I'd like to meet the casting director stupid enough to buy that unconvincing line delivery.

Alano gets up and watching him walk away is more painful than that knife slicing my foot. He stops at the door and kicks off his sneakers. "I'm not going anywhere until I know you're okay."

"That could take years."

"Then we better get comfortable."

I go out into the kitchen and grab some iced waters, pretzels, and fig Newtons as Rolando is cooking a real dinner. By the time I'm back, Alano has laid out my weighted blanket on the floor for our indoor picnic. I've been starving myself since yesterday, but Alano says that if I won't take care of my body for myself to please do it for him, which is enough to get me to start filling my stomach. My headache from all that crying is gone by the time I'm done running my mouth about how the news vans and Make-A-Moment rejection and *Golden Heart* announcement all happening today felt like a sign from the universe to kill myself on top of all my shame.

"It's hard to believe in Begin Days when your past twenty-four hours look like that," Alano says.

"Yeah."

"That's not all that happened, though. If you're interested and feel as if you're in a good enough headspace to talk about my history with Rio, I'll be fully transparent so you have all the information you need. I don't want to keep you in the dark, but it can wait until you're sure it won't trigger a spiral. I just wanted to offer you the opportunity before I leave for New York on Wednesday."

I'm on edge, scared of learning more, but if there's a world where I can have a future with Alano, even just as a friend, I can't be haunted by his past with Rio. And if I'm ever gonna confront this, it's now, when Alano is still in LA to ground me.

"Let's talk," I say nervously.

"Before we do, I think it might be helpful if I shared some self-regulating tips I've been learning from this guidebook by Marsha M. Linehan, the psychologist who invented dialectical behavior therapy," Alano says.

He rattles off the four modules and seven skills I'll be learning in my DBT program. The first module is *mindfulness*, which includes observing my environment without judgment so I can improve my mental clarity and describe what I'm feeling so I can figure out how best to manage the emotions. The second module is *distress tolerance*, which involves a temporary solution called TIPP (temperature, intense exercise, paced breathing, progressive muscle relaxation) that I can use to de-stress quickly; Alano tells me to take note of that one especially, like it's not the hardest one to remember so far. The other half of distress tolerance is radical acceptance, which means accepting reality so you don't get lost in spirals of denial, like I have. I really doubt that radically accepting my life fucking sucks is gonna make me feel better, but we'll see. The third module is *emotional regulation*, which begins with the opposite action from whatever my negative emotions are telling me to do, something like, if I don't wanna eat, I go eat anyway, or if I wanna be alone to self-harm, I go hang out with someone. The other part is checking the facts, which I'm gonna be able to do with Alano as he tells me what actually went down with Rio instead of making shit up in my head. And the last module is *interpersonal effectiveness*, which is supposed to help communicate what I want and need without, let's say, yelling at the boy I love in an amusement park.

"I'm not gonna remember all that," I say. "I don't have your brain."

"Be grateful you don't. My brain is a blessing and a curse," Alano says, as if there's something bad about being a quick study. "You don't need to memorize everything I said now. You'll study this soon enough, but until then, I'll be your talking textbook. Do you remember the TIPP skill?"

"I thought you were remembering everything for me, I'm not ready for a pop quiz."

"Try."

"Um, *T* is for 'temperature,' *I* is for 'I-don't-remember . . .'"

Alano laughs, which is the brightest light in this darkest day. "*I* is for 'intense exercise.' *P* is for 'paced breathing,' and the other *P* is for 'progressive muscle relaxation.' These are the skills that will really help manage any panic attacks or negative impulses. For instance, instead of self-harming, you can hold on to ice for a minute. It lowers your heart rate to calm you down, and it gets so painfully uncomfortable that it can also scratch that itch to hurt yourself without inflicting actual harm on yourself. Or if you have anger to expel, you can throw ice around your room. Harmless destruction."

Unlike the almost-punch seen around the world.

"Why are you teaching me all of this?"

"If my past with Rio triggers you, I want you to self-regulate. Throw the ice, do some crunches, meditate. Deal?"

I'm now terrified that this is gonna be worse than I thought, like Alano and Rio got secretly married by one of those End Day officiants. No, this is where I got to take a step back and check the fucking facts as Alano tells the story.

"Deal," I say.

First Alano apologizes again because even though he suspected I had feelings for him, he didn't set me up for success when he didn't clue me in to his complicated past (and present) with Rio. That's when he dives deeper into the origins of their friendship.

"I first met Rio at his brother's memorial," Alano says, his voice quiet like it will ease the sting of hearing Rio's name. "There was an open invitation to the public, and I wasn't sure why the Moraleses didn't want more privacy, but I felt compelled to go. Then everything made sense during Rio's wrathful eulogy. He was using the memorial as a rally. The only thing that mattered was gathering supporters to hunt down the Last Friend serial killer. Rio spent more time talking about avenging Lucio than about his life. At the end, I offered Rio my condolences. He proceeded to grill me on Death-Cast not using its power more efficiently. I didn't fight him. I just let him be angry at a time when no one else was validating his trauma or grief. I gave Rio my number, but it was almost a year later when he finally reached out on the evening of May twenty-fifth, hours after the serial killer had been caught. The arrest didn't close any of Rio's wounds. He was so angry and sad . . . and empty. Everything changed when we started hanging out."

I unfortunately know all about agonizing sadness, burning anger, and depressive black holes that swallow up everything happy so you're left feeling like a shell of yourself. I also know firsthand how Alano is so powerful that he can fish out smiles and laughter and hope from someone who is feeling everything bad or nothing at all. I would be devastated to lose his company, and as Alano tells me more about his evolving friendship with Rio, I begin understanding why Rio felt so possessive of Alano and threatened by me.

That summer, Alano and Rio became inseparable, hanging out so much that Ariana got annoyed with Alano for not admitting that they were dating, but he was telling the truth. They were just friends and nothing more at the start. Alano was always getting Rio out of the house, and they got to know each other on long walks across Central Park, Althea Park, the Brooklyn Bridge, and the High Line, and they would also get lost in random neighborhoods, challenging themselves to get back home without outside help.

"Things took a turn on June twenty-fifth, when we were supposed to be attending the Pride March."

I'm so jealous of Alano and Rio's closeness that I'm already itching for my knife, and as much as I'd like to do some jumping jacks right now, my foot can't handle that shit, so I grab an ice cube, holding on to it until it burns so bad that I drop it back in the glass. Alano is right, my heart rate is going down, and it's hard to focus on anything else except how much holding ice hurts.

"I can skip ahead if you want," Alano says.

"You're good, go on."

I have to get through the good memories before seeing how it ended.

Alano seems cautious, like when I first tried climbing the Hollywood Sign on my birthday and then fell down the ladder, but unlike me, he pushes on. "That morning the police uncovered the remains of the serial killer's last victim. Rio wasn't exactly in the Pride mood anymore, but his mother wouldn't stop watching the coverage, so my driver took us up to Riverdale, and we walked all the way from the Bronx to Brooklyn. Over those nine hours, Rio and I talked about our callings in life and how hard it is to find happiness after tragedies, especially one as brutal as his brother's murder. He swore he was going to be broken forever. I told Rio that I was sad that I would never meet Lucio or know who Rio was before losing him, but that I liked the person in front of me. His passion, his grief, his curiosity, his anger. Every last piece." Alano stares off toward my window, like he's lost in this memory. "That's when we kissed like it was our End Day."

As Alano goes down memory lane, he sounds as if he's falling in love with Rio all over again, or like he's never stopped loving him.

I should've gone on my own painful long walk across the city instead of listening to this.

"That's really special" is the best I've got for him.

"It was until it wasn't. In my head we were boyfriends, especially after we started having sex, but I got a rude awakening that September when I confessed my love for him. Rio was stunned. He didn't even think we were dating," Alano says, no longer sounding lovesick, just heartbroken. "We agreed to be best friends and nothing more."

I cross my arms, remembering how they hooked up two weeks ago. "How long did that last?"

"About two months," he admits sheepishly. "Rio was vulnerable on Halloween. It was another birthday without his brother. He needed to get lost and be loved."

"But he didn't love you, right?"

"No, but it allowed me to get lost too and pretend he loved me back."

I don't wanna know how many times they've gotten lost together, but I bet it's a lot. I can't even imagine what it's like to be wanted by someone so much, and I'm scared I'll never get to find out with Alano. "I got to be real, you both hooking up for three years looks a lot like you're in love. Moving in together doesn't help. Listen, I appreciate you checking in on me, but I'm not stupid, I can see this for what it is—"

"You're not stupid, but you're wrong," Alano interrupts. "My position at Death-Cast has made it hard to trust people's intentions, but I do trust Rio as a safe person who I can be with when I'm lonely. It helps that we love each other, but we're not in love." He stares straight into my eyes when he declares this, like he's begging me to believe him. "At least, I'm not in love with him."

Anger flashes through me. "You said he doesn't have feelings for you."

"I didn't know he did until this afternoon. Rio stopped by. My near-death scared him into confronting his feelings, but I don't feel the same anymore."

My heart rate is coming down. I got the facts from Alano. I fucking hate the facts, but I got them. It's hard to believe that Alano won't fall back in love with him. "Are you still moving in together?"

"No. Even if Rio didn't have feelings for me, I see now how our past not staying in the past can risk my chances of having a future with someone else."

Yesterday I swore I would never see Alano again for the rest of my life, and if I did, I definitely wouldn't trust him. I even punished myself as if that would break the Begin Days contract so I could go back to living my Not-End Days in peace—well, not peace, but without the special hell of heartbreak. Tonight I'm regretting cutting my foot more than any other time I've self-harmed because it was all for nothing. Alano has a past, but I was wrong, he's not trying to live there. He wants to move on, and I wish I was walking into that future without a mutilated foot, but that's gonna heal, just like my heart.

I grab Alano's hand, massaging his palm. "You've given me a lot of advice on living Begin Days, and I got something for you."

"I'm listening."

"Only be with someone who wants to be with you," I say, tearing up over two other regrets. If that's the only advice I ever give him, it'll save him a lot of pain.

"That's all I want," Alano says, his head leaning against my bed. "Is that what you want?"

"I've only ever wanted to feel wanted, but . . . ," I say.

"But what?"

I don't wanna just grab an ice cube, I wanna dunk myself in a frozen pond while thinking about these betrayals I never like talking about. "I lost my virginity to my second Last Friend."

Carter was this beautiful guy who had childhood dreams of being in the NBA. He wanted to spend his End Day playing basketball, so we bounced between courts and gyms around the city to find him some challengers. He dunked on this one guy so hard he broke the backboard. I legit thought the raining glass was gonna somehow kill him, which he thought would've been an epic way to die. Carter challenged me to a game and I sucked, but he had a lot of fun teasing me. I honestly swore I was about to have one of those magical and painful End Days worthy of an indie movie where the Living Last Friend falls for the Decker, especially when Carter dragged a wrestling mat into the empty locker room for us to have sex.

"He finished, showered, and left without saying goodbye."

"He's an asshole," Alano says. "Was."

To this day I have no idea how Carter died. I only remember going home that night glad that he did so he couldn't hurt me or anyone else ever again.

I had promised myself I would never have sex with another Last Friend. It was hard to imagine having sex with anyone after being ghosted by the Decker who took my virginity.

Unfortunately, I'm a human who was lonely and wanted to feel something—someone.

Enter my sixth Last Friend. Over the app, Kit invited me to his dorm room since he was agoraphobic. Helping a Decker get out into the world would've been the most rewarding feeling as a Living Last Friend, but when I got there, Kit wasn't trying to leave. He called me hot and kissed me and brought me to his bed, and I would've preferred talking more, but time was obviously running out for him. Or so I thought.

"He wasn't a Decker."

There's a fire burning down the forest in Alano's eyes. "He lied to you?"

"He saw me on the app and thought it would be hot to have sex with someone famous, but he wasn't trying to play the long game of getting to know me, so he posed as an agoraphobic Decker."

Now Alano's eyes are being flooded. "I'm sorry you experienced that."

"You know what's the worst part about all that?"

"Worse than these monsters using Last Friend like Necro? Worse than ghosting you? Worse than lying about dying?"

"They both saw my scars and never asked if I was okay." I'm rocking back and forth and crying over how dehumanizing that was. "Imagine taking the time to call someone a D-list actor who got upgraded to a B-list celebrity because of the docuseries that made them self-harm but never ask if they're okay."

Alano pulls me in, letting me cry against his chest. "You deserved better, Paz."

I wish my first time had been with someone like Alano. No—I wish it was Alano, period.

I don't know how long Alano holds me, but when my cries finally quiet down, he doesn't let me go. His chin rests on top of my head. I snuggle my face deeper into his chest, being moved like a wave as he breathes in and out. I can't believe I'm so close to his heart that I can hear it racing, to feel it pulsing against my cheek. I never thought I would be able to touch him again, and now I'm the closest I've ever been and it still doesn't feel like enough. I need more—I grab the back of his neck, clutch on to his forearm, and I swing my legs over his. I want every inch of my body touching his. And judging by his heartbeat, he feels the same way. Or I think he does until he winces. I freak out, embarrassed, and let go, giving him space.

"Sorry," I say.

"No, I'm okay. That was nice, but . . ." Alano rolls up his sleeve, revealing his bandaged arm. "You squeezed too hard."

I forgot about his own wound that's scarring. "Do you need

help rebandaging again?" I ask since it has to be done every forty-eight hours.

"My mother helped this morning, but what about you?"

"What about me?"

"Have you treated your foot today?"

Washing that wound in the shower was its own circle of hell, but it might be time for another cleaning. I unroll my sock, and we both immediately see the blood staining the bandage.

"I got to re-up."

"I can help if you'd like," Alano says.

"You don't have to do that."

"I'd like to repay the favor. I want to."

It's been scary enough to open up about the self-harm, but letting Alano witness the damage I've done to myself is straight-up terrifying. What if he's disgusted by me? What if he doesn't care like my Last Friends? Nope, nope, nope, I'm not letting my mind tell me more lies about Alano when he showed up here uninvited to make sure I wouldn't do the very thing I did. There's a lot to figure out with Alano still, but one thing is true: he cares about me and wants to take care of me.

I direct Alano to the old camera bag in my closet where I hide my first aid supplies. I'm running low on gauze and petroleum jelly after the brutal Not-End Days I've lived through lately, but there's enough to get us through.

Alano undoes my bandage, and we both brace ourselves, as if we know our future hinges on how he reacts in this moment. His gaze falls on my bare bloody foot, and while his eyes tear up, they don't gloss over my wound. He cleans the blood, gently applies the petroleum jelly, gives me new gauze, and rebandages my foot.

"You won't need stitches," Alano says, holding my hand. "You'll heal with time."

Friday marks ten years since I killed Dad, and I'm starting to believe that there isn't enough time in the world to heal those scars. Maybe it's time to accept that I'll always be scarred.

"Are you serious about staying until I'm okay?" I ask.

"Do you think you're in danger to yourself if I leave?"

"There's something I wanna try."

"What's that?"

"Finally watching *Grim Missed Calls*."

"Do you think that'll help you?"

"It's why I started self-harming. Maybe watching will help me end it."

Alano stares off, like he's scared this is gonna trigger the shit out of me. "If you believe this will be healing, then I'm here for you."

I'm done trying to win back love from the rest of the world.

I only wanna be loved by someone who sees me for who I am, scars and all, and never looks away.

I only wanna be loved by Alano Rosa.

ALANO

9:17 p.m.

My father is furious.

It was bad enough in his eyes that I left the house without his permission; my parents have been arguing over this in my absence. But my father is especially frustrated because he discovered I was at Paz's house in the middle of his *60 Minutes* interview.

"When the world sees that I do not know that my son is at the home of a known killer who publicly threatened him, it invites criticism against Death-Cast during these already challenging times," my father says over the phone. "How incredibly selfish do you have to be to not care about the company or your own father being alarmed by this infuriating choice?"

"Selfish?" I shout in Paz's backyard, then lower my voice because I don't want to disturb his family or his neighbors. "How am I selfish for making sure my friend doesn't self-harm?"

"Did you do it for the Dario boy or to ease your own guilty conscience?"

"If protecting Paz makes me selfish, then I'm selfish. You got me, Pa."

My mother interrupts him before he can fire back. "When are you coming home?"

"I was thinking about spending the night. Paz needs company."

"Alano, sweetheart, that's a security concern for everyone," she says.

"Dane is here. If you want me protected, you'll send extra protection."

"Tone," Ma says.

I apologize—to her.

"I'll send along additional security detail to surveil the house, but are Paz's parents aware of the risk?"

"*His* parents? What about us?" my father interjects. "*I* am not okay with this."

"I didn't call for permission, Pa. I'm only keeping you posted." This energy is why I need my own place. "Ms. Gloria and Mr. Rolando have been gracious hosts who have cooperated with every inspection. They're delighted I'm staying. We all agree Paz can benefit from my company."

My father must grab the phone back because his voice booms over their speaker. "You do not know these people! How can you trust the Dario boy after he threatened you?"

"He doesn't withhold secrets from me."

"Meaning?"

"You have never told me about Death-Cast."

"It's for your own benefit that you have not been granted the secret," my father says, fury building. "Frankly, you have proven that you are nowhere near ready to be trusted with that delicate information! You distance yourself not only from the company's proven power and your status as heir, but now from your family, mi hijo, when we only want what is best for you."

Those words are meaningless after all I've said and done to prove how unhappy I am in the life I've been living. "For a man who values family, you're only interested in protecting yours. When do I get to start my own?"

"You're nineteen."

"You were eighteen when you knew you wanted to be with Ma. I'm older with far more wisdom and life experiences. I don't know what the future holds between me and Paz, but my time with him is limited before we return to New York, so I'm going to find out."

I hang up on my father.

PAZ

Alano and I get into bed together.

My room is dark except for the glow of my TV, and it's hard enough trying to watch this documentary already without a beautiful boy in my bed. All I can think about is how Alano and I are freshly showered and now wearing each other's clothes: me in his hoodie, him in my everything else. The air conditioner is blasting cold air because Alano loves the cold, which kills my dreams of him ever moving to LA since he loves winter in New York, but it's a good excuse for us to be pressed against each other for warmth, even with the weighted blanket sitting heavy on our legs.

This might be my only night to be this close to Alano, to share a bed, to be alone with him, but attacking my traumas can make me healthier so we can try building a legit future together.

I grab my remote and scroll through Piction+ and find the finale for *Grim Missed Calls*. The thumbnail is my old headshot in black and white, dotted with drops of blood. This episode is off to a bad start before I can even start it. Maybe I shouldn't. This is supposed to be therapeutic, not traumatic.

Alano reads my mind. "We don't have to watch if it's too much."

Then he grabs my hand, and it gives me strength.

Mom never wanted this show made because it would reopen closed wounds, but those wounds never closed. Maybe now they can.

I press *Play*.

"The Last Missed Call" has a run time of one hour and nineteen minutes. The episode opens with pictures from the crime scene: the gun, the blood, the corpse. I'm already nauseous and shaking so hard that Alano wraps his arm around my shoulders, holding me close.

The trial began in late June. It's so weird seeing this courtroom footage, knowing that this was my real history that became news and entertainment for millions, only for them to watch something else when it was done as if my life was just something on their to-watch queue.

The courtroom was packed all five days of my trial with so many reporters and cameras that I was nervous even though I had truth on my side. In the prosecutor's opening statement, he argued that I would be a threat to society if I wasn't sent to a detention center to receive the necessary rehabilitation for the violent impulses that led to me killing Dad and attacking classmates. Ms. Cielo countered that both incidents were defensive acts and that my school records and character witnesses would support that I was a good kid who found myself in a devastating position on the evening of July 31, 2010.

I spent my tenth birthday in court, being questioned by the prosecutor.

Sullivan Murphy was old even back then, and my routine

Google check-ins show me that he's still alive and kicking, and unsurprisingly, he represents a lot of pro-naturalists. In retrospect, it makes so much sense why he was showing no mercy toward a young birthday boy because this case was gonna determine Death-Cast's legitimacy.

As they begin replaying the questioning, Alano holds me closer, better than any weighted blanket.

"Is it correct that you shot your father to save your mother's life?" Sullivan Murphy asks.

"Yes, sir," Kid Paz says. Manners won't get him anywhere.

"But you knew Death-Cast hadn't called your mother, yes?"

"Yes, but Death-Cast made mistakes that day."

"Were you aware of those mistakes when you shot your father?"

I was prepped for that question, but I still remember feeling hot. "I didn't know Death-Cast made mistakes when I did, but it was the very first day. Anything felt p-p-possible," Kid Paz stutters.

"We know Death-Cast neglected to warn Mr. Dario of his death. Did you warn your father at all before firing the gun?"

Even though I personally know the court will rule in my favor, I still tear up as I watch my ten-year-old self squirming in the witness stand. That tight brown suit I had long outgrown felt like it was shrinking more and more with every second, as I am now against Alano's body.

"No," Kid Paz manages to squeak out. "I didn't warn him."

The prosecutor paces back and forth with his hands in his

pockets, like this whole trial is a walk in the park. "You shot Mr. Dario twice. Walk us through those shootings. Where did you shoot him? How much time between the first and the second shots?"

The camera zooms in on Kid Paz as tears slide down his sweaty face. They show Kid Paz staring into the crowd, but never pan around to Mom, who was crying too, like I was about to lose. I guess that would've humanized the father-killer who was clearly close to his mom.

"I shot Dad in his side," Kid Paz says.

"Is that where you were aiming?" Sullivan Murphy asks.

"Not really. I was just shooting him so he would stop beating up Mom."

"So that first bullet struck Mr. Dario in his side—his left kidney, to be exact—and then what?"

I was so hot on that stand, but I began shivering as I relived that fatal moment; I'm still carrying that trauma in my body a decade later.

"Then I stood over Dad, and I shot him again."

"Where did you shoot him the second time?"

"His chest."

"Is that where you were aiming?"

"Yes," Kid Paz says.

I remember thinking that answering the question honestly was gonna be like landing on the Go to Jail spot in Monopoly and how scared I was because I didn't have any Get Out of Jail Free cards, and this wasn't a game. And I was so scared of

537

getting locked up that I shouted, "I was scared that Dad would hurt me too if he got back up!"

Sullivan Murphy was quick. "Had your father ever harmed you before?"

"N-no, but—"

"No further questions, Your Honor," the prosecutor says, silencing me.

That was my worst birthday for years before last month when I failed to kill myself.

Here's where the documentary gets extra tricky. It's one thing to leave out details about relocating homes and getting bullied, but another to omit a lot of Ms. Cielo making her case for the defense. There's nothing about my dad taking his rage out on my mom for as long as I could remember or how that night was the first time my mom cried out for help, so I helped, or how I wasn't thinking about whether or not my dad was gonna die and only if Mom was gonna live or even how after all the ways my dad terrorized my mom I still somehow missed him—miss him. It's great that the jury got to hear all that, but it doesn't help me exist in a world where millions and millions of viewers don't know my side of the story.

Where no one knows the truth.

What they do show is Mom getting called to the stand. She explains how this wasn't premeditated and how her decision to leave Dad was simply inspired by the first End Day, which had the entire world asking themselves who they wanted to be and what lives they will have wanted to live before they die.

For Mom, that was a life of love and safety for us, but Sullivan Murphy questions her integrity because she registered Dad for Death-Cast's services behind his back, suggesting that she wanted proof that he was gonna die before coordinating an attack on him. Ms. Cielo objects because that was speculative—and a total lie—but that doesn't stop Sullivan from accusing Rolando of having insider information from his shift at Death-Cast that very same day I killed Dad, opening the doors for Rolando to finally be with the love of his life.

"I can't believe we won this case with all this lying," I tell Alano.

"You won because you told the truth," Alano says, his arms wrapped around me.

Instead of showing the character testimonies, the documentary cuts to their recent interview with Sullivan Murphy, whose dark hair has grayed and wrinkles have deepened: "They brought in all those celebrities," he says with disdain. "The author of those children's books, the Hollywood stars. The jury ate all that up. The character witness that still frustrates me to this day is Orion Pagan."

They cut to a clip where Orion Pagan is on the stand, being questioned about my dad. Orion holds his hand to his heart and says, "That monster killed Valentino."

It cuts back to Sullivan Murphy, who is shaking his head. "It was the Decker who tried killing Frankie Dario, but apparently self-defense only matters when it's against someone who doesn't believe in Death-Cast. Not to mention, we will never know if Valentino Prince would've naturally recovered from his brain injury if Orion Pagan hadn't undergone that heart surgery for his own physical benefit. Financial benefit, I should add, since he's exploited that sham of a love story into a bestseller."

This disrespect against Valentino only makes me more infuriated that Orion let this damaging, nonsense narrative block my future.

The documentary shows the final people who were called to testify: executives from Death-Cast, including Alano's parents, who spoke about the Death's Dozen. I'm not sure how much Joaquin Rosa gave a shit about what happened to me as he was protecting his company's reputation, given how much time he speaks about Death-Cast's perfect record ever since the first End Day. They cut to Naya Rosa with her arm wrapped around Kid Alano.

"There you go," I say.

"There I go," Alano says.

Even before we really knew each other, Alano was on my side. Now he's holding me as I relive this nightmare. The episode is almost over, but I hope I get to stay in Alano's arms longer.

Once the closing statements are done, there's an intense, escalating score that gets my heart racing, especially when the cameras cut to Mom and Kid Paz hugging so hard; I remember fearing it might be the last time I ever got to hug her. Then the music fades and there's a heart-in-your-throat silence before we hear the magic words: "Not guilty."

Just like Kid Paz, I full-on sob, relieved that the docuseries didn't rewrite history here, but knowing that my life played out in a way as if it had.

I was naive—no, I was fucking stupid—to think people would let a ten-year-old move on with his life after the jury recognized the incident as a justifiable homicide. All that happened was things got so bad that I've never been able to move on, that I've never been able to close this wound, especially because of this goddamn docuseries that caused so much harm that I started hurting myself.

The worst part is how my almost punching Alano only makes *Grim Missed Calls'* character assassination look legitimate.

I stare at my nightstand, wishing my knife was inside.

"It's not fair; it's not fair," I cry over and over, like I'm Kid Paz. "I'm never gonna be able to live my life." I try wrestling out of Alano's arms, no longer wanting to be held, I just wanna go into the kitchen and grab my knife and cut, cut, cut, just cut out anything that makes me feel.

Alano strengthens his hold. "I'm sorry for this nightmare you've had to live through because of Death-Cast," Alano says through sobs. "You deserved a better life without that trial or having to kill your father. He put you in that devastating position. Not your mother, not Rolando, no one but your father, no matter what this sad excuse of a show says. You were right to save your mother's life, and I'm sorry it cost you yours. You deserve peace, Paz."

I'm never gonna have peace, not with this borderline brain. Not in this life. The Death-Cast calls are beginning soon, maybe

I'll get one, ahead of the tenth anniversary of killing Dad, so I can be spared further pain as the waves of harassment and hate will only keep growing.

I cry about wanting to die, about wanting to be reincarnated as my mom's new baby, and about wanting the fresh start that winning my trial promised.

I wanna self-harm so bad, I don't even care how. Cutting. Burning. Smashing Orion's big-ass book into my head over and over. Anything can be a weapon, which is frightening. "I'm so scared of myself," I cry out, hating my brain for making me my own greatest enemy.

"You don't have to be," Alano says, locking his arms around me.

I'm a sword, and he's my shield, protecting me from myself.

GLORIA MEDINA
11:49 p.m.

Death-Cast did not call Gloria Medina because she is not dying today, but the sound of her son crying has always made her die inside.

Down the hall, she hears Pazito crying, so she gets out of bed, ready to knock on the door when she hears Alano Rosa comforting her son. Gloria wants to barge inside and hold Pazito, but she must let him grow up, to be held by the boy who cares for him.

Still, Gloria wishes Pazito had watched that terrible documentary with her. After all, it's their traumatic history that was documented, not Alano's. But Gloria is one to talk. She secretly watched *Grim Missed Calls*. She only ever lies to protect the people she loves. She didn't think it was wise for Pazito to watch the documentary so soon, especially after its very twisted existence led to his suicide attempt, but she knew the day would come when he would need to see it for himself.

Gloria planned on being ready for that day. She did not plan on how painful it would be to watch this documentary herself.

It was devastating to relive that tragic day. To see Frankie's violence justified. To have her true love for Rolando treated as a ruse in a murder plot. Most heartbreakingly, to watch Paz treated like a cold-blooded killer. She had called their attorney for the trial, Martina Cielo, and asked if she should be pressing charges for the lies and misinformation in this documentary. There was a case to be built on defamation alone for Pazito's career, but Martina Cielo was concerned with winning, simply because Hollywood is a very subjective business that turns down millions of young talents every year, and the fact that Pazito hadn't booked work after winning his trial would be used against them.

"I would still be willing to take this to court," Martina Cielo had told Gloria, giving her hope, until she asked: "But are you willing to put Paz through another trial?"

After rewatching her precious son in court at ten years old, Gloria had her answer.

Hours after her call, Gloria maintained a brave face during dinner, a survival skill she gained in her years of raising Pazito with Frankie, but deep inside she was still so heartbroken and angry over the documentary. She'd wished she hadn't watched it alone after all. She was *this* close to inviting Rolando to keep her company, but he carried his own guilt from that tragic day. If Rolando hadn't confessed his love on that first End Day, Gloria wouldn't have been inspired to leave Frankie. The fight would've never broken out. Gloria would've never screamed for her life, and Pazito would've never come to her rescue.

If only Gloria had left Frankie sooner . . .

If only Gloria had taken Pazito and run away . . .

If only Gloria had thrown out that gun . . .

If only, if only, if only.

The reality is that Gloria stayed, just as her regrets and shame stay with her now, like scars.

Unfortunately, scars don't just appear out of nowhere. They are all wounds first. Some painful, others not. The loud cries of her son let Gloria know that Pazito's wound has been ripped open again before it can heal; she's grateful that his wound is metaphorical, not physical, but pain is pain.

A body needs a survivor's spirit to keep it alive. Only then will it heal, only then will it close all wounds, only then will it scar, and only with time can a scar fade.

One day, Gloria and Pazito will be survivors with faded scars, but today is not that day.

JOAQUIN ROSA
11:50 p.m.

Death-Cast did not call Joaquin Rosa because he is not dying today.

He is, however, alone in his office, away from his wife and close to his alcohol.

Joaquin's sobriety is being tested by the continued attacks against Alano as well as Alano's rebellion against security measures that's making it harder and harder to keep him alive in this new unpredictable life of his. Yes, Joaquin has suffered blackouts from drinking in the past, but losing sleep over Alano's survival isn't exactly keeping him sharp either.

He walks over to the bar cart and grabs a shot glass.

No, this is not the way.

Joaquin sets down the shot glass and grabs the whole bottle instead.

July 28, 2020

ALANO

3:00 a.m.

Death-Cast still cannot call me, and thankfully they did not call Paz tonight.

I've been holding Paz for over four hours as he's been recovering from that documentary. He's cried, grieving the life he should've had. He's fought me to go hurt himself, but I never let go. And he's fallen into deep silences to the point where I thought he fell asleep, but he's awake. He's just haunted by his past. I know that feeling well. Would Paz have it in his heart to comfort me if I share the secret I plan on taking to the grave? What's even more upsetting to wonder is if Paz will take himself to the grave first.

"My End Day is coming up," Paz whispers.

"No one knows their End Day in advance," I say. I never have, and I definitely don't now.

"This Friday. July thirty-first. The day I killed Dad is when I'm destined to kill myself."

"You're not destined to take your own life, Paz."

"I am. That's why Death-Cast hasn't called. It wasn't my time yet."

"Now isn't your time either. We're living to one hundred, remember?"

"I'm not strong enough to keep surviving, Alano."

"We're building your strength. You'll be starting DBT and—"

"No, I . . ." Paz sobs, his body caving in. "I feel like a liar when I talk about the future."

Somehow, I'm even more scared of Paz taking his life than I was when we were on the Hollywood Sign. He has it in his head that he's supposed to die on the anniversary of his father's death. This feeling of doom is certainly a reaction caused by his borderline personality disorder. He's committed to dialectical behavior therapy, but that isn't an overnight solution. That's a six-month program and many patients require multiple cycles before they trust themselves. I'm nervous to remind Paz of this, knowing that the lack of an instant cure is one of the reasons he was giving up that night we met. Even if Paz cries for the rest of the night and wakes up tomorrow in a better mood and something goes wrong, he'll take it as a sign that he's supposed to die on Friday, when I won't be here to stop him. To save him.

I refuse to let the only future Paz believes in be one where he kills himself.

"I'm not going back to New York," I say.

Paz freezes. "Don't say something like that, you've got your gala—"

"That's my father's gala. He has to be there for Death-Cast, and I have to be here to prove that you have a future beyond Friday."

"You don't have to do that, it's better if you move on now—"

"There is no moving on if you die, Paz, and I won't lose you to a self-fulfilling prophecy."

Paz rolls around in my arms to face me with his teary eyes. "I'm sorry I said you were dead to me."

I hold his face to my chest and let him cry. "You're forgiven as long as you never become dead to me."

My staying is the only way to ensure Paz's survival. And my own.

PAZ

Death-Cast didn't call last night, but if I had to die, I'd love for it to be in Alano's arms.

It took forever to fall asleep, but Alano soldiered through the night with me. And now he's staying in LA. I roll over in bed, wanting to wrap my arms around him, but he's gone. My chest tightens. Did he break his promise and abandon me? I check my phone, and there's no missed call, no text explaining himself. I gotta ground myself. Alano wouldn't ghost. Ghosts don't hold you all night and beg for you to live.

I get out of bed to investigate, bracing myself for my first painful step of the day, only for my wounded foot to land on the star rug that Alano has laid out. Hope swallows doubt off this one gesture, this one reminder that Alano gives a shit about me. I limp out of the bedroom, straightening up as I get to the living room, where Alano is sitting on the couch, watching the news; it's like I've time-traveled into a future where we're boyfriends living together before I remember that we've been a nationwide story.

Alano mutes the TV. "Morning."

My heart races as I start getting sucked into a spiral. "They're talking shit about me, right?" Maybe the world is wondering if I'm holding Alano hostage or if I've killed him. Then before Alano can say anything, I check myself. "Okay, I don't have the facts, that's . . ." I snap my fingers, trying to remember the DBT term. "That's in the emotional regulation module?"

He smiles. "Correct. You're a quick study too."

"Are they saying anything about us?" I ask, trying to get that fact so I know what's what.

"Only that we hugged."

"So nothing about me holding you hostage or killing you for the Death Guard?"

"Nothing like that. Shield-Cast even urged the news vans to leave to give us privacy."

"What about online?" I ask, nervous.

"Let's not pay attention to strangers critiquing our lives," Alano says.

I read between the lines: people *are* talking shit online. Instead of self-harming by reading those comments, I'm staying offline. "Good call."

"I'm only even watching the news this morning because Carson Dunst is hosting a rally in New York. I'm curious if he'll finally condemn the Death Guard's assassination attempt."

"I doubt it."

"Me too, but I will wait for the facts," Alano says with a wink. "How are you feeling after last night?"

"Okay. I'm sorry about all that crying."

"You have nothing to apologize for."

"Fine, then thanks for keeping me company." I sit next to him. "Did you get any sleep?"

"Some sleep. I woke up early to call my parents about skipping the gala. My father is not thrilled with my choice, if you can believe that. Agent Dane, however, is excited to get more time in Los Angeles. He's outside discussing logistics with Shield-Cast."

So Alano is really, actually, definitely staying, but I'm scared to treat it like it's really, actually, definitely happening. "It's all good if it doesn't work out."

"Do you not want me to stay?"

"Oh, I definitely want you to stay."

Alano smiles. "Fantastic. As long as I'm a support and not a hindrance to your mental well-being, I'm not going anywhere. Speaking of." He grabs a pill container from the kitchen counter. "Since Gloria is at work and Rolando stepped out for a job interview, I've been tasked with distributing your antidepressants. How many have you been taking?"

This past week I've been all over the place with taking one, doubling up, and skipping my meds all together, but I gotta get back on this, especially if I wanna be in the right headspace so I don't hurt myself or Alano or anyone. "Two, please." I swallow both pills.

"You have therapy on Fridays, right?"

"Yeah, Dr. Alano."

"Would you like me to accompany you that day?"

"Are you scared I'm gonna run back to the Hollywood Sign?"

"I'm scared of you doing anything that endangers your life," Alano says seriously.

If I'm gonna have any chance of surviving past Friday, I'll need to finally embrace all the people working to keep me alive: my mom and stepdad, who need me around to be a big brother to their baby; my therapist, who can guide me through my borderline brain; my psychiatrist, who can up meds or prescribe something better; and now the boy who has become my life coach and the shield to my sword.

ALANO
11:30 a.m.

Right on time, Carson Dunst takes the stage at his rally in New York.

I met Carson Dunst in DC on Sunday, March 31, 2013, at President Reynolds's memorial service at the White House, five days after the assassination that started the political war against Death-Cast. While all in attendance were grieving and distressed, Dunst pulled my father to the side, blaming him for the assassination and many other crimes against the country. Dunst condemned Death-Cast for its encroachment on people's freedoms, and my father countered that Death-Cast provides peace of mind to citizens worldwide to live more freely than ever before. Dunst said the company emboldens people to pursue violent crimes knowing they will survive, and my father made it clear that the success of those crimes is not predicted. And of course Dunst called Death-Cast unnatural with such venom I thought he was going to spit in my father's face.

"Any world that does not allow you your lifelong privileges will always be treated as unnatural, but that does not make it so," my father had said. He offered Dunst condolences before pushing me along back to my mother and other genuine mourners.

I unmute the TV as Dunst finishes waving at all his rabid supporters and steps to the mic. He rolls up his sleeves, masquerading as a pro-natural middle-class American to appease his base of bigots even though he was raised by parents who made hundreds of millions in the oil industry.

Dunst wastes no time talking about Death-Cast being a failed experiment; I wonder if Rio is somewhere in that crowd, cheering for the fall of Death-Cast. He then veers into his usual lie that millions of users are abandoning our services. "I applaud everyone who has seen the light and returned to the pro-natural way, but there's someone who deserves a special round of applause for fighting his way out of the darkness," Dunst says. His crowd is silent, anticipating who is the latest in a line of public figures like politicians, musicians, and actors to opt out of the service. "None other than the Death-Cast heir himself, Alano Rosa!"

Hearing my name is as shocking as Harry Hope shooting himself over the phone, as shocking as Rio's confession that he wants to spend his life with me, and as shocking as Paz almost punching me, but this goes beyond me. This affects the world.

How does Carson Dunst know I deactivated Death-Cast? No one knows . . .

That's not true. There are many people who know. My parents. Shield-Cast. My friends.

The question isn't simply who leaked this information and more about who hates me enough to ruin my life.

All signs point to the pro-natural boy whose heart I broke.

"What the fuck is going on?" Paz asks.

Once the roaring crowd settles down, Carson Dunst continues boasting. "I celebrate Alano Rosa's victory in overcoming a decade of brainwashing and renouncing his claim to Death-Cast so that he may return to his pro-natural life, and I welcome Alano's vote on Election Day so I may accomplish the crucial work of dissolving Death-Cast once and for all. After all, why would anyone invest in a future with Death-Cast when even the heir himself wants nothing to do with the company?"

More cheers.

I never renounced my claim to Death-Cast. That's a lie, but who told my truth?

"I would never trust a man to manage my death when he cannot satisfy his own son's life," Dunst says as if my father is his political opponent in the presidential race. "If it wasn't enough hearing from Deckers who never died and from people who lost loved ones that never received their alerts, then I hope Alano Rosa joining our pro-natural movement is enough for the American people to wake up to the dangers of Death-Cast and how it threatens the natural order!"

I'm hyperventilating so much that Paz runs into his room and grabs my inhaler, but this isn't an asthma attack. I'm panicking over these lies for political gain and their ramifications.

Paz takes my hand.

Dunst continues. "Death-Cast has not only failed the heir and the public who trusted the company's unnatural power, but Death-Cast has failed their employees too. The heralds especially work under grueling conditions without the necessary psycho-logical support for the demands of that dark profession. They are expected to sweep their many errors under the rug to protect the company's false record. Lying to keep their jobs doesn't spare them from the verbal abuse of their leader. Don't take my word for it. A brave woman has come forward to use her voice despite Death-Cast trying to silence her."

"Oh no," I say.

"What?" Paz asks.

I sit at the edge of the couch. "Oh no."

"What? What?"

Carson Dunst leans forward on the podium, like he's letting America in on a little secret. But he's not. He's leaving that to his lying whistleblower.

"Let's give a warm welcome to a former head herald, Andrea Donahue!"

NEW YORK

ANDREA DONAHUE
2:40 p.m. (Eastern Daylight Time)

Death-Cast cannot call Andrea Donahue, thank you very much.

Ten years, ten forsaken years Andrea devoted her life to Death-Cast, only for Joaquin Rosa to demean and terminate her in front of colleagues, all because she exploited her power as head herald.

Allegedly.

Andrea is not delusional. She knows she is guilty of many crimes, more than Joaquin is aware of himself, and his investigation will discover some, ensuring her incarceration, and the remaining crimes Andrea shall take to her grave. She doesn't fear death, but she does fear for her daughter's future.

This is why Andrea Donahue is at a campaign rally, ready to tell the world her truth (even if her truth is built on many lies) so she can not only exact revenge against Joaquin Rosa, but use her voice to help elect Carson Dunst as the next president, all so he can pardon her if she is to be convicted.

Has there ever been anyone in this world more efficient than Andrea Donahue, a woman who has broken records at

Death-Cast for most calls in a night and for leveraging her position by alerting not only Deckers of their fates but also the well-paying press? She thinks not.

Behind the podium, Andrea braces herself, her injured leg wobbling more than usual, triggered by a stage fright that is foreign to her Broadway-bound daughter. Andrea is used to sitting behind a monitor and speaking with the dying over the phone, one at a time, but she's currently staring out into a lively sea of pro-naturalists, some of whom would've been extreme enough to hurt her just last week when she was still employed as Death-Cast's dutiful messenger.

"I was hired at Death-Cast before the first End Day," Andrea Donahue says, reading her prepared remarks from the glass teleprompters flanking her. She speaks about serving the company loyally for ten years before her wrongful termination. "Joaquin Rosa threatened to have me imprisoned if I didn't keep quiet, but our country deserves the truth about what happens behind closed doors at Death-Cast."

She does not possess the charisma of a politician, but she earns cheers anyhow because this crowd is not exclusively made up of pro-naturalists who simply wish to live as all did before the age of Death-Cast, but also Death Guarders who are out for blood. Andrea only makes these extremists thirstier by speaking of Joaquin's outburst when firing her. "He toyed with every herald, demanding that we forget Alano's name and existence, all because someone raised the valid concern that the heir he was grooming to take over couldn't even function in the call center as we have, night after night, year after year. Joaquin made me the scapegoat to intimidate the other heralds. If he was willing to terminate a veteran like me, then no one was safe." She shakes her head, as if disappointed, when truly she wants to smile over how much this crowd is eating up her speech.

"If Joaquin wants to use his 'inexhaustible power' to imprison an innocent woman, then I will make sure I'm guilty of the crime, because I will not be bullied into protecting company failures when innocent lives and deaths are at stake!" Andrea couldn't care less about Deckers, but that line prepared by Carson Dunst's speechwriter elicits more applause, as if Andrea is yet another champion of the pro-natural movement when in fact she only cares about these idiots because they're voting to give Carson Dunst pardoning power. "A brave informant shared this intel about Alano because they refuse to be silenced by Joaquin's intimidation tactics. If he wanted our loyalty, he should have respected our humanity."

Andrea is reaching the end of her speech and now has to bring it home by speaking about the truest thing about herself. "Over the past decade I've been asked why I worked at a company as unnatural as Death-Cast. The answer is simple: I live and breathe for my daughter, Ariana, and I will do whatever it takes to grant her the best life possible."

Not that anyone asked, but Andrea Donahue's dream End Day is to sit in the front row for a Broadway show that her daughter is headlining. How special would it be to see Ariana's name lit up on a marquee? There are no words. And after Ariana is done performing and taking her final bow of the night, then Andrea could die in peace.

But Andrea doesn't need to play the game of Death-Cast like the thousands of Deckers she's called over the years to live her best life. That will come with Death-Cast's downfall.

Andrea points at the center camera, as prepped by Dunst's political advisers earlier today. "As for you, Joaquin, you may be a protector of your son's secrets, but you better make sure your own skeletons are buried deep because we all have shovels and are working hard to dig up everything you've been hiding from the world, especially Death-Cast's dark powers."

As the audience cheers for Andrea, she heads toward the stage's exit, snaking around Carson Dunst. "Pardon me," she says, trading winks with the next president of the United States.

Then she basks in the chants for the death of Death-Cast, knowing she has played her role in destroying their reputation, but the true destruction is still to come.

For a decade, Andrea Donahue encouraged Deckers to log on to death-cast.com to fill out an inscription for their headstones, and now she is envisioning what that would look like for Death-Cast itself:

DEATH-CAST

JULY 31, 2010–JULY 31, 2020

GOOD RIDDANCE

LOS ANGELES

ALANO
11:54 a.m. (Pacific Daylight Time)

This isn't the end.

Those were Andrea Donahue's final words before being escorted out of Death-Cast—her final threat. I shouldn't have underestimated a woman who has nothing left to lose and everything to gain by aligning with Carson Dunst and the Death Guard.

Paz mutes the TV. "What bullshit."

Andrea's diabolical speech blended facts with fiction, but there were indeed facts, which has me wondering if there's any truth behind this Death-Cast informant. Could my father have truly upset another herald so much that they're now feeding information to Andrea to destroy Death-Cast from within? But who? Roah Wetherholt, another senior employee who started at the company alongside Andrea? What about a new and young herald like eighteen-year-old Fausto Flores? Could he have been swayed or bribed or even inspired to betray Death-Cast after the threats my father made to protect me?

For the first time, I truly feel guilty that I'm not returning to New York because I can't help but feel like everything here is my fault.

I didn't plan on spending my day dealing with Death-Cast affairs, but it's the least I can do considering this is also my mess to clean up.

I call my father, but it goes straight to voice mail. I try my mother and can't reach her either. I try my father's office line, text him, and call his cell again. Nothing. I send a text to Agent Andrade, and he confirms my parents are alive and well, just occupied. I'm sure my mother will return my call the moment she's available. My father, on the other hand, might never speak to me again.

JOAQUIN ROSA
12:23 p.m.

Death-Cast did not call Joaquin Rosa because he is not dying today, but he has murder on the brain.

Joaquin sits at his desk, alone with his thoughts about whether he would survive prison. Should Joaquin get his hands dirty, there is plenty he is willing to sacrifice: his spacious homes for a cramped cell; delicacies such as Nova Scotia's bluefish tuna and his wife's bacalaítos for chow-hall fish patties; the ethereal sunrises of Svalbard and the golden sunsets of the Riviera Maya for harsh ceiling lights and mandated lights off; trips to El Yunque for trips to the courtyard; his dignity, his sanity, and even his security as he's surrounded by convicts who foolishly used their lack of Death-Cast alerts to act on criminal plans as if dying is the only way to stall life. Joaquin would even be willing to bunk with his target's ghost until his own End Day, but as long as Naya and Alano are alive, Joaquin will never sacrifice a long life spent with them, no matter how much he wants to kill Carson Dunst.

No one has ever made Joaquin Rosa as bloodthirsty as Carson Dunst. Of course in the heat of a moment people have infuriated Joaquin so much that intrusive thoughts of wishing them dead surfaced, even some where he imagined killing them himself, but that heat always cools down, that moment always passes. Carson Dunst is different. That son of a bitch created a movement that seeks to undo Joaquin's greatest creations. It is one thing for Dunst to build his campaign by lying about Death-Cast, even to dissolve the company nationally if elected president, but should anything happen to Alano then Dunst will become the match Joaquin uses to set this world on fire.

The nerve of Dunst to not only weaponize Andrea Donahue against him but also issue a statement about welcoming Alano's vote on Election Day when he never even condemned his young zealot's attempt to assassinate Alano. Joaquin is so furious that he will be asking Aster Gomez to compile anything and everything he needs to do to run for president as an independent candidate—and he does intend to run to take down Dunst and even President Page, who is not nearly as outspoken against the Death Guard as he should be. Some might say that there is not enough time for Joaquin Rosa to make the most out of this election cycle, to which he would say that if Deckers can live fulfilling lives in a day, then he can change his own life between now and November to secure the presidency—and Dunst is out of his mind if he thinks Alano will still be casting a vote for him once his father enters the race.

At least, Joaquin hopes Alano will vote for him.

There are more urgent matters at play now, such as Joaquin fielding calls from his board members, executives, lawyers, politicians, security force, the media, and his son, who created this mess. He's reminded of the first End Day, when he believed his company was about to collapse before it could soar. Death-Cast survived that, and Joaquin believes—hopes—they will get through this too.

Perhaps these journalists should stop hounding him and investigate the true source of this leak. He would very much like the answer himself.

For most of his life, Joaquin has been called overly cautious. Paranoid, even. How could he not be? He has been holding close the greatest secret of the world. No, the universe. Apart from his wife, the only souls trusted with the knowledge of Death-Cast's apparatus were key members of Central Intelligence and President Reynolds, all of whom have since died: an extraordinary coincidence that keeps the secret close to the Rosas. That responsibility makes a man second-guess those around him. It makes a man reject the Secret Service and instead create his own security force. It makes a man limit how many heralds work the call center because having more employees risks more betrayals—more Andrea Donahues. And it makes a man question who has it out for his company and his son.

Anyone and everyone told about Alano opting out of Death-Cast is now a suspect.

Joaquin can safely rule himself out, as well as Naya, because only the worst mother in the world would endanger her child's safety and future like this. Then again, she did send Alano out to make amends with the Dario boy. He wants to rip his hair out for questioning his wife's integrity. Naya did not persist through heartbreaking miscarriages to ruin their amazing son's life. He firmly rules her out.

This is where things get tricky. Everyone must be questioned, including the heralds back in New York, but Joaquin suspects this is a more intimate inside job. He wonders if the only Shield-Cast agents who were in the know before this rally are responsible: Agent Andrade, Agent Chen, and, of course, Agent Madden. Joaquin is especially suspicious of Agent Madden retaliating after his eleven-hour termination, but he not only got Alano home safely, his report of everything that occurred at the theme park lined up perfectly with Alano's account. No one is fully ruled out, but having to suspect any of the bodyguards sworn to protect him and his family has Joaquin eyeing the bar cart once again, even though his hangover is the worst in recent memory.

There are four suspects Joaquin believes have motives for destroying Death-Cast.

Ariana Donahue, the daughter of a woman fired for leaking private information about Death-Cast and Alano. Joaquin fears the apple has not fallen far from the tree. He is not sure how she would have possessed this knowledge, seeing as she has not checked in on Alano once since the assassination attempt, but that makes her suspicious in his eyes.

Rio Morales, a new pro-naturalist who believes Death-Cast should be ended and had his heart broken by Alano yesterday. That is a vote Carson Dunst can actually count on this fall.

Paz Dario, a boy whose life was ruined on the first End Day.

Sound familiar? Mac Maag failed to get his revenge for Death-Cast's error, and the Dario boy might be trying to finish the job. What if exposing Alano's secret—which he's known longer than anyone else!—is Paz's way of keeping his hands clean but allowing the Death Guard to do his dirty work? For his son's sake, he truly hopes this is not the case, but he's not sure.

And the fourth and final suspect is none other than Alano himself. He has made many questionable choices lately, but he is still brilliant, so brilliant that he may be strategizing for Death-Cast's collapse to experience a true freedom he will not be able to enjoy since there is no other calling on this planet that will ever need him as much as Death-Cast.

Joaquin wants his son to live his life, but not at this cost.

Not at this cost.

Joaquin's phones keep ringing.

For the first time in forever, for the briefest moment, an intrusive thought like those he had for wanting to kill others, Joaquin Rosa wishes Death-Cast was calling to spare him of this misery.

ALANO

3:00 p.m.

My past is coming back to haunt me.

PAZ

Alano is staying in LA to look after me, but I've actually been taking care of him all day.

For the past seven hours, I've been occupying Alano as best as I can to get his mind off Death-Cast's integrity being dragged, something I know a thing or two about. That's meant keeping him far away from the news by playing video games, dusting off the coloring books Mom bought during the COVID-19 lockdown, eating leftovers while watching the second Nightlight Saga movie (*Old Sun*, my favorite), and planting flowers, fruit trees, and vegetables in the garden. I even drew Alano a nice hot bath with Epsom salt to help relax his body after the gardening, but the water went cold because he was making a list of suspects at Death-Cast for Dane and Shield-Cast to investigate.

I suck at taking care of other people just like I suck at taking care of myself.

Mom was able to break through to Alano like only a mom can. She got home from work and sat Alano down, asking if he was okay, and he couldn't shrug her off. He admitted that he was concerned about his parents, especially his dad, who treats Death-Cast like it's another son.

"I'm scared he's never going to talk to me again," Alano had said, something he hadn't even confessed to me.

"I don't know Joaquin, but I'm sure he is just hurt," Mom said. "The best parents strive to put their children's feelings first, but that doesn't mean we don't have our own."

I wish Mom acted on her feelings more, but I'm glad she shed that light for Alano. It helped him see what I've been trying to break through to him all day, but it's gotta matter more coming from someone who actually has a kid.

Then Mom embarrassed the hell out of me by mom-ing us so hard. First she sent us to go take showers since we were both dirty from gardening and then had us help her and Rolando with dinner prep. It was a rough start, since it was the four of us trying to cook in our tiny kitchen, but it got fun when Mom put on a Bad Bunny playlist because every time we knocked into someone, they became your dancing partner for a hot second, even if something was getting overcooked. Mom taught us how to make spicy black bean patties, mango avocado salsa, a vegan nacho platter with our own freshly baked tortilla chips, and even smoothies from our leftover mangoes.

Alano and I are setting the table, the cutlery all mixed and matched from different sets since we're not fancy like that.

"I'm sorry I haven't been very present today," Alano says to me.

"You're here. That's pretty damn present to me."

"Well, I hope my mind catches up with my body. I'd like to create more fun memories with you in the city."

"I looked into some fun stuff going down this week when you were on your Detective Alano flow. The Griffith Observatory has a new exhibit about space sounds. The Hollywood Bowl is doing a live concert of the sixth Scorpius Hawthorne movie. The Last Bookstore is hosting a dystopian romance author tomorrow. And this weekend we can catch a movie at the Hollywood Forever Cemetery."

"A movie at a cemetery?"

"Yeah, this organization Cinespia decks out the cemetery with a big-ass screen for people to watch movies every summer. It seems cool, but I've been too scared to go."

"Because of all the dead people?"

"The living ones."

He chuckles. "That sounds very LA. I'm in. I hope it's okay that Agent Dane and other Shield-Cast agents will have to tag along now that I'm a bigger target."

"No shit that's okay, anything that keeps you alive."

There's a knock at the front door. Rolando looks around, counting everyone, including the baby. "We're all here."

"That's Dane with Bucky," Alano says. His dog is spending the night here.

Mom tries fitting a fifth plate for Dane at our already cramped table and goes back to slicing carrots for Bucky even though he had dinner at home.

I'm so excited to meet Bucky that I open the front door, but he's not there, it's just Dane with two Shield-Cast bodyguards I've never seen before. I tense up, like they're about to attack me even though I didn't do a damn thing, or like they're about to take Alano away, in which case I might do a damn thing.

"Alano," Dane calls from the door like I'm not here. "Your presence has been requested."

Alano approaches. "By who?"

The bodyguards all step aside, revealing Death-Cast royalty.

"By us," Joaquin Rosa says, joined with Naya Rosa in one hand and holding Bucky's leash with the other.

The creator of Death-Cast glares at me like I'm some secret Death Guarder.

I glare back because Joaquin Rosa ruined my life.

ALANO
7:59 p.m.

My dog runs into my arms as my parents stand outside Paz's house uninvited.

"I'm not going back to New York," I say.

They were already struggling with my decision to stay in Los Angeles before Andrea Donahue's speech, and they'll want me back more than ever to help resolve this. I honestly wish I could help out, but there's more time between now and Election Day to save Death-Cast than there is between now and Friday to save Paz. I have to stand my ground.

"Hello to you too, mi hijo," my father says.

My mother pulls me into a hug. "We're not here to fight you on New York. We only came to bring Bucky and say bye before our red-eye."

That's the reason? It's almost as surprising as their visit.

I notice Paz has rejoined his parents in the kitchen. They're all watching us intently. It's been intrusive enough to have Agent Dane going through their belongings, but they didn't sign up for my parents and their security detail. "I'll be back in a minute," I tell the family, closing the door behind me as I step out onto the front yard with Bucky running around my legs for more attention.

"I've been trying to reach you both all day," I tell my parents as Shield-Cast gives us space.

"It is a rather distressing feeling, is it not?" Pa says, cocking an eyebrow. "We did not mean to leave you in the dark, mi hijo, but we were addressing the endless concerns of our board members and the frantic users who do not know if our heralds are to be trusted to deliver their alerts. We haven't seen this volume of fear since the first End Day," he says, looking at the house, well aware the family inside was victim to those errors. "Time will tell if the statements we've issued the media will halt the damage Andrea Donahue and Carson Dunst are causing."

"You should've gotten back to me sooner. I could've helped with the media."

Pa crosses his arms. "How was I to know this when your devotion to Death-Cast has been victim to many changes of heart as of late?"

I mock his arm-crossing. "By answering the phone."

Ma intervenes with time-out hands. "How were you wanting to help, Alano?"

"I'll tell the world that I haven't renounced my claim and I'll condemn Dunst for his lies."

Pa smiles for the first time this evening. "That's a welcomed surprise."

Ma isn't as happy. "Are we really going to pit our son against that cult leader?"

"Even children get their hands dirty in wartime," he says.

How quickly I change in my father's eyes from undevoted to Death-Cast into a soldier in his war against the Death Guard.

"And we fail as adults every time a child must fight for us," she says, haunted. "Speaking of, how is Paz doing today?"

"Why don't we ask him ourselves?"

Paz is standing on the porch. I don't know how long he's been there, but he looks like he has stage fright. "Hi. Um, my mom said you're welcome to stay for dinner if you want."

"We don't want to impose, sweetheart," Ma says. "But it's nice to finally meet—"

"Dinner sounds great!" Pa shouts. "We will be right in."

"Oh—okay." Paz returns inside.

I eye my father suspiciously. "Are you really joining us?"

"Family dinner is inevitable, is it not?" he asks, still clearly hurt that I've chosen Paz's family over my own.

"Ma?" I'm hoping she sees reason.

"Honestly, I would sleep easier at night knowing his parents better," Ma says.

"Especially since you are still without Death-Cast," Pa adds.

"It'll be lovely getting to know Paz too," she adds, almost pleading.

"Fine. Please be normal."

"Of course we will be normal," my father says before communicating to our bodyguards that we'll need Agent Andrade stationed outside the house, Agent Dane manning the back, and Agent Chen surveilling the block.

As I walk my parents to the door I share a critical reminder. "Do not mention anything about my meeting Paz on the Hollywood Sign. His parents don't know he was planning on killing himself that night. They would send him to a suicide-prevention facility if they did."

"Maybe that's better than you taking this on," Ma says. "You're not a psychiatrist, and you've done so much already while possibly going through your own psychotic—"

"If it ever got that bad, I would call the professionals myself," I interrupt, not wanting this turned on me. "Please respect Paz's wishes in the meantime."

She nods, knocking on the door as she steps inside.

My father grabs my shoulder and leans in. "Do not worry, mi hijo, his secret is safe with me," he whispers before entering Paz's house.

Meanwhile I'm frozen outside, still breathing in the alcohol on my father's breath.

PAZ
8:12 p.m.

How long can hallucinations last?

Like, is it possible that I really did imagine Alano on the Hollywood Sign and that hallucination has now stretched out so long that I'm seeing his parents inside my house? About to have dinner? I also used to think hallucinations only tricked your eyes and ears, but when I was researching them as side effects of BPD, I discovered they can be tactile too.

How do I know if something is real if I can see it, hear it, feel it?

Is Alano's mom real? Naya definitely has this elegant beauty that's hard to believe in person, with her warm eyes, long lashes like Alano's, tanned skin, and a streak of silver in her wavy pitch-black hair. I can see her.

"It's wonderful to finally meet you, Paz."

I can hear her. She clasps my hand between both of hers. I can feel her. None of this makes her real.

I watch as Naya embraces Mom like they go way back or something.

"Thank you for inviting us into your home, Ms. Medina," she says.

"Oh, it's my pleasure, but I will kick you out if you don't call me Gloria."

Naya laughs. "Noted, Gloria. I hope our son hasn't been any trouble."

"He's been an absolute doll. Very bright, very well-mannered. You raised him well."

"As have you. Alano speaks so highly of Paz."

I can't possibly be imagining all of this, can I? It's gotta be real, but is Naya actually telling Mom that she raised me right when I killed my dad and almost punched her son? That doesn't make sense.

Then Alano's familiar hand finds my shoulder, turning me toward him—and toward his dad. "Paz, this is my father, Joaquin," he says as if the man who launched Death-Cast and ruined my life in a single day needs an introduction.

Joaquin Rosa looks like if fifty-year-old Alano time-traveled back from the future. Dark brown hair that's peppered with grays, thick brows and beard, bow-shaped lips, a few inches of height on me, and a strong build in his burgundy suit, but Joaquin doesn't have a full forest in his eyes like Alano, only the dark brown of trees. As he shakes my hand, I'm pretty damn certain that Joaquin isn't some time-traveling Alano because I hate his touch.

"Great to finally meet you, Mr. Dario," Joaquin says.

"Just call me Paz," I say, sharper than expected.

His smile is nothing like Alano's. It's wrong, it's so wrong. "I will do just that, Paz," he says before pardoning himself.

"Are you okay?" Alano asks.

579

I don't answer. I just follow the Death-Cast creator as he crosses my living room to the kitchen as if he might be a threat to my family.

"Hey, look who's here," Rolando says, extending his hand out to Joaquin. "I didn't know Death-Cast was making house calls now."

Joaquin shakes his hand. "No, no, no. We all know it was hard enough for you to hang up as a herald, Rolando. A house call would have only gotten you roped into dinner and a movie with your Decker." There's this tense silence before they both bust out laughing, and I don't know Joaquin like that, but that's definitely Rolando's fake laugh. "Thank you for hosting us. I am looking forward to catching up now that fate has reunited us." He turns to Mom. "And to finally meet you, Ms. Dario."

"Medina," Mom and I say together, but I come in hot again. She gestures for me to let her speak for herself; I just hate when she gets tagged with Dad's name. "I prefer Gloria than all these formalities anyhow."

"My sincerest apologies, Gloria," he says, and it legit sounds sincere.

Mom waves him off as she takes a pizza out of the freezer. "*My* sincerest apologies for not having more food prepared or a bigger dining table. It's usually just the three of us, but we'll get comfortable in the living room. Boys, go grab the chairs from outside."

This is the first time I've seen Mom embarrassed about our living situation, and who wouldn't be when you gotta put frozen pizzas in the oven for supermillionaire guests or bring in lawn chairs for more seating?

"Slow down," Alano says outside, blocking me from bringing the chair in. "Are you okay?"

"Yeah—no. I'm just thrown off."

"I am too. I can discreetly ask them to leave."

"No, it's fine."

The truth is that if I'm ever gonna be Alano's boyfriend, I gotta get used to his dad.

Alano and I return inside to find Naya apologizing for any stress she's causing Mom, which Mom denies, of course, because not only is she a people-pleaser, she's a planner, and there's no way in hell she planned a dinner for the whole Death-Cast family.

"Do your guards need to inspect the house? Or the food?" Mom asks.

"If Agent Madden's sweep is good enough for Alano, it's good enough for us," Naya says.

Rolando starts preparing the plates. "Alano also helped cook dinner, so blame him too if you get food poisoning, or lethal poisoning."

Mom pats his back. "Maybe we save the poison jokes until they know us better."

Alano and I carry the dining table and chairs into the living room, inviting his parents to make themselves at home before bringing them our home-cooked dinner on mixed plates since we don't have a matching dining set. This meal is really exciting for my family, but I bet Alano's parents are dreaming about the five-course meal their chef must've been preparing back in their mansion. Mom and Rolando settle onto the couch as Alano and I sit on the lawn chairs with our food in our laps.

If Alano and I were boyfriends, this would be one hell of a triple date.

Maybe one day, if we survive this unexpected dinner.

GLORIA MEDINA

8:22 p.m.

Death-Cast did not call Gloria Medina because she is not dying today.

Gloria is a planner, her affairs are certainly in order should the grim reaper knock on her door, but she hadn't planned on opening her home to Joaquin and Naya Rosa tonight. They are absolutely welcome here, especially as Gloria is hosting their wonderful son, but she does worry if they will all get along considering the ramifications of the first End Day and recent events between Pazito and Alano. She will plan on a good night and hope for civility.

"Cheers to new friends," Gloria says, and everyone clinks their mango smoothies. "Now dig in."

The servings feel too shallow to dig in; that pizza better heat up fast.

"Do you have any wine?" Joaquin asks.

"Pa," Alano says.

"One glass among new friends," he says.

"This is an alcohol-free home," Rolando says.

Ever since Pazito took Rolando's bourbon and tried killing himself.

Gloria shivers at the memory while also wondering why Alano is scolding Joaquin. Is it because they know of Pazito's history and Joaquin has forgotten? Or because Joaquin has his own relationship with alcohol that needs minding? She suspects the latter after Joaquin says not to worry about the lack of alcohol, since Alano seems worried. She studies Naya, fearing that maybe Joaquin's spirit goes dark the more he drinks, just as Frankie's would, but Naya does not seem scared of her husband. That is not to say abuse does not happen in their home, only that Gloria will be keeping an eye on her guests tonight.

"You helped make this salsa?" Naya asks Alano as she scoops some with her tortilla chip, which feels more like a distraction from Joaquin's drinking. "Gloria, Rolando, I hope you're honest about enjoying Alano's company because I need you to teach him everything you know."

"Happily. He's a fast learner," Gloria says. She means it.

"You're a patient teacher," Alano says.

"How about you, Paz? Do you like cooking?" Naya asks.

Pazito shrugs. "Not really, but we had fun today."

"It was good to get our mind off current events," Alano says pointedly.

Joaquin snickers. "Eating the dinner you prepared is good for that too."

"Speaking of work . . ." Naya glares at the men of her family before relaxing her gaze as she turns to Gloria. "You're an intake coordinator at a women's shelter?"

Gloria smiles proudly. "I am. Did Alano tell you?"

Naya blushes. "Honestly, Shield-Cast informed us. I should be fully transparent that we had security do background checks on everyone after our boys started hanging out. I apologize for the invasiveness."

"Not any more invasive than Dane going through my underwear drawer," Rolando says.

"We understand wholeheartedly," Gloria says. If she had the means, she would do the same to protect Pazito. Bodyguards, background checks, inspections, the whole nine yards. All she can offer her son is guidance, hope, prayers, and a subscription to Death-Cast. "I'll give you my number after dinner so you can check in whenever you like."

"It's already saved in my phone for emergencies," Naya says, which they laugh about. "The background check, however, doesn't know what brought you to the Persida Women's Center."

Gloria feels Frankie's shadow looming, like those times where he would follow her around the apartment to scream in her face or worse. This fear continues to live in her body, and as much as she wants to be a good host who keeps things light for her guests, she refuses to sit in silence ever again.

"I know what it's like to be a woman who needs help," Gloria says, owning her past. "My ex-husband was abusive, but I always thought he was going to change, especially when I was pregnant with Pazito. He never did, but he never laid a hand on our son, so I got it in my head that being the best mother meant keeping the family together. I couldn't give Pazito everything he wanted, but I made sacrifices so that he would at least have his father around." Her heart is beating so hard she wonders if anyone can hear it in this silence. "I will never regret that relationship completely because it gave me my Pazito, but being the best mother would've been leaving Frankie forever after he lost money gambling in Atlantic City and took it out on me when I was five months pregnant. I lived in fear of my ex-husband until the day he died."

Until the day Pazito killed Frankie and set Gloria free while imprisoning his own destiny.

"I'm so sorry," Naya says. "You didn't deserve that violence."

"No woman deserves that violence, and I wanted to serve the women who believe they do. As an intake coordinator, I get the privilege of being the first woman to support a woman's choice to start over. I'm able to empathize with my own regrets about not leaving sooner without ever judging them for staying as long as they did." Gloria puts a hand to her chest. "I loved being a stay-at-home mom with my whole heart, but I love supporting my community in my own small way."

"There is nothing small about what you're doing," Naya says.

This recognition means the world to Gloria as she knows her job is not one that pays for a house with its own dining room and dining table and matching dining ware, but it allows her to help women find new homes, humble as they may be. "The shelter is no Death-Cast, but I am very proud of the work I do," she says on the verge of tears.

Naya comes and kneels before Gloria, taking her hand. "We are all serving the community, Gloria, but the work you are doing is what keeps our heralds from speaking to the women at your shelter before they can live the lives they deserve."

That is the moment Gloria breaks, hugging Naya as she cries. "Thank you for saying that. I always wish I could do more."

"All great heroes do."

Like all great heroes, Gloria Medina is a veteran in life's wars. A survivor.

PAZ
8:31 p.m.

I'm so damn lucky to be Mom's son.

I wanna comfort Mom right now as she cries, but I hang back as Naya shows her some love; Naya's kindness definitely passed down to Alano.

"You have done excellent work," Joaquin says to Mom.

Then I notice he's glaring at me.

Joaquin is no doubt judging the work Mom does at the shelter since she raised a son who almost hit his. I'm the one who raised my fist, not Mom.

"You're the best, Mom," I say while glaring back at Joaquin.

If Joaquin has some shit he wants to say about me almost punching Alano, he can say it.

I'm ready to swing back over Death-Cast ruining my life—and this time I'll hit hard.

NAYA ROSA
8:36 p.m.

Death-Cast did not call Naya Rosa because she is not dying today.

If only there was truth to the rumors that Death-Cast employs psychics because Naya would like to have known what this day would hold when she woke up. It is a blessing to know that she will not die, but that does not warn her of life's troubles.

Naya thought the hardest part about her day was going to be when Alano called in the morning, informing her and Joaquin that he will not be returning to New York for the gala as he feels an obligation to help protect Paz Dario from himself. She admires her son's character. There is no celebrating ten years of Death-Cast when Alano knows this company's historic failure upended Paz's entire life. As upsetting as that news was, that was nothing compared to Alano's Death-Cast status being exposed by Carson Dunst and Andrea Donahue.

Now that the world knows how vulnerable Alano is, Naya is desperate for him to return home with her and Joaquin, or to return to the mansion, where there's a panic room should the Death Guard coordinate another attack on his life. But she

589

cannot scare Alano into this decision or he will rebel against her as he continues to do with Joaquin. It would be one devastation for Alano to die and another for Alano to cut Naya out of his life.

There is a small comfort in meeting Gloria Medina, a woman so extraordinary and heroic that Naya knows that Alano will be loved under her supervision (and safe thanks to Shield-Cast's).

Naya rejects Gloria's apology for starting dinner on a heavy note.

Gloria dabs her eyes with her napkin. "Well, I haven't had my people do a background check on you all yet, and I'd love to learn more about you."

"All you need to know can be found in my memoir," Joaquin says.

"We'll go pick up a copy," Gloria says, reaching for her phone as if to order one now.

"He's joking," Naya says.

Gloria blushes. "Oh!"

"What would you like to know?" Naya asks.

"How did you two meet?"

It's been over thirty years since Naya and Joaquin met, and while the basics of their story are agreed upon—such as Joaquin falling in love with Naya's laugh while they were two eighteen-year-olds hanging out at Sip-N-Serenity, a charming coffee shop in Queens that did not survive the Great Recession—many other details have become cause for many he-said, she-said debates:

Naya says she was laughing at a friend's joke, and Joaquin says she was reading a funny passage in a book.

Naya says she welcomed Joaquin's presence, and he says Naya wasn't trying to give him the time of day (which, let's say Naya *was* reading a book—and she was not!—then of course she would want to get back to reading).

And Naya says Joaquin offered to buy her coffee, but he says he offered a scone.

What Naya does not say to her hosts is how whenever she and Joaquin tell this story, playfully fighting over the details, she wishes they knew the truth. If only they were more like their remarkable son, who captures the world as if holding a video camera, then they would know not only if it was a joke or book that Naya was laughing over, but which joke or book, as well as the coffee order or the type of scone. Those memories are all lost, but it is indisputable that after thirty years together, Naya has given Joaquin the time of day.

She says, "I confessed my love first."

He says, "Those words made her laugh my second favorite sound."

They both agree on this so deeply that Joaquin wrote about it in his memoir, *Life and Death-Cast*, as well as other details from their relationship, all of which they now tell their hosts, including how they shared a shoebox apartment, saved up for weekend trips, created traditions, and supported each other's dreams. Dreams as wild as Death-Cast that allowed them so many luxuries like houses and traveling.

"I never got to travel as much as I'd like," Gloria says.

"We are looking forward to our honeymoon in Puerto Rico," Rolando says as he pulls the pizza out of the oven.

"Well, we'll see. Our funds might be going elsewhere now."

Joaquin shakes his head. "You have this one life, and you have spent most of it caring for others. You must treat yourself. In fact, let us treat you to an all-expenses-paid stay at our resort."

"That's too kind," Gloria says.

"It's our absolute pleasure," Naya says.

"I am not sure if I'll be able to go . . ." Gloria places her hands on her belly. "We're expecting."

Naya is overcome as her body—her *heart*—remembers the many times she was struggling to conceive as loved ones not only started their families but also continued to grow and grow their families while she still awaited one child. Then her brain catches up and she remembers she has her remarkable son and she celebrates Gloria's news with another toast.

She overhears a conversation between the boys.

"You didn't tell them?" Paz asks.

"I wanted to respect your mother's privacy," Alano says.

She raised her son well.

As Joaquin excuses himself to the restroom, Naya checks in on how Gloria is feeling.

"Very nervous. Very, very, very nervous," Gloria says. "It's high-risk, obviously, so I'm constantly living in fear of miscarrying."

"I didn't know that," Paz says.

Gloria puts on a brave face for her child. "I'm fine, Pazito. It's normal to be worried."

"Were you that stressed with me?" Paz asks.

"Yes, but I wasn't forty-nine."

"Maybe you should do a nine-month stay at that resort," Paz says—jokes?—no, says.

"If that is what you need, we can make that happen," Naya says. Peace during pregnancy is invaluable. "I'm always available if you need to talk over your fears. I had twelve miscarriages before getting pregnant with Alano."

Gloria is shocked. "Twelve?"

Naya will never forget the first time her cramps led to the discovery of light spotting. "Twelve."

Gloria offers her condolences.

Naya tears up. "Not a single day has passed where I haven't stopped to imagine life with each and every baby I lost. I wanted to be their mother so bad. My pregnancy with Alano was terrifying. I didn't want to get my hopes up, not even as he was surviving longer than the other babies. Then Alano was miraculously born, but my fear of carrying him to full-term now shifted to keeping him alive."

"That fear will never leave us," Gloria says.

"No, it won't."

Naya and Gloria smile at their attentive children, but Naya feels a twinge of guilt because Gloria does not know Alano saved Paz from killing himself.

Does Naya not have a responsibility to tell Gloria that her son was literally on the edge of death, not as an employee of Death-Cast but as a mother? Naya would want to know the same if her son—the son she risked her life to birth—ever found himself high above the world, wanting to fall.

ALANO
9:04 p.m.

After watching my mother cry over the children she lost, I'm even more certain that no matter how much I'm able to confide in her, I must take the secret of my attempted suicide to the grave.

That's what my heart is telling me to do, at least.

My brain knows that doesn't make any sense.

Logic hardly matters as my alarming thoughts get louder and louder.

PAZ

9:05 p.m.

The creator of Death-Cast returns and learns of the news.

"Are you excited to be a big brother?" Joaquin asks.

"Yeah, but I just hope my mom is gonna be okay," I say.

If this pregnancy kills Mom, I won't survive her death.

ROLANDO RUBIO
9:06 p.m.

Death-Cast did not call Rolando Rubio because he is not dying today.

The job of a herald is not for the faint of heart, Rolando remembers well—unwell, he should say. He served his Deckers by alerting them of their fates, but it was a difficult undertaking. He still remembers speaking with a teenage girl around Paz's age now, he believes, who was excited about her first date until Rolando called with the bad news that she was dying. He does not know if that girl went on her date or not. What about the husband whose wife was finally returning home from deployment weeks after his End Day? Was he able to reach her? Is she well today and moving on as Gloria was able to do with Rolando after Frankie died?

Of the many Deckers who Rolando called on the first End Day, he was only ever able to get some closure from his very first, Clint Suarez, a wealthy man from Argentina whom he met at a café in New York early in the morning, hours after Rolando quit Death-Cast. Over coffee, Rolando listened to Clint's life story, and years later, he attended the opening of the dance club he'd heavily invested in before his death, so heavily, in fact, that it was changed to a dance club for Deckers and named Clint's Graveyard. They don't serve alcohol at the club, but Rolando ordered a mocktail martini called the Eternal Espresso and toasted to Clint, the Decker whose wisdom transformed his life.

If Clint hadn't encouraged Rolando to not only redeclare his lasting love for Gloria but also warn her of the dangers of remaining in a marriage with Frankie, who knows what would have happened?

Maybe Frankie would still be alive and married to Gloria.

Maybe Frankie would be serving life in prison while Gloria was six feet deep.

Thanks to the first Decker he ever called, Rolando is living his dream life.

Well, maybe not dream life.

In the decade since he worked at Death-Cast, Rolando has only ever regretted quitting during times of financial struggles. Times like now, where the job market is hard. At the end of every day since being laid off, Rolando has gone to bed worried about not having any money, but he knows his soul is intact. This is what allows him to get out of bed the next morning and apply for jobs and smile in interviews and to keep climbing and climbing until he emerges from this financial hole, especially now as he needs to support his firstborn.

He prays there will be a firstborn to support.

Rolando goes from staring at Gloria's belly to Joaquin and Naya. "Given your personal history, is there really nothing that can be done about Death-Cast predicting miscarriages?"

"If we could, we would," Joaquin says.

"You are already doing something we couldn't before. Why not the extra push?"

"If we could, we would," Joaquin repeats more sternly. "We do not want anyone to go through the terribly unique grief of losing a child they hope to bring into this world, but that is simply not insight we can provide."

Rolando leans forward on the couch, almost like he's about to drop to his knees and beg. "I am trying to keep my family together. I am finally with the love of my life, and we are expecting our first child together—my firstborn—so if there is any assistance from Death-Cast that can enlighten us on the viability of this pregnancy—"

"There is not," Joaquin interrupts. "This has not changed since your time with the company."

"Then why are you not advancing?"

Joaquin takes a large gulp of his drink and then rubs his forehead, as if the smoothie has given him a brain freeze when Rolando actually believes that he is just annoyed. "We are advancing, and even if we were not, we have advanced society plenty."

"That is a shame," Rolando says. He is terrified of losing the baby, of course, but of losing Gloria most of all. "What about someone's End Day? Any way you can know that, even if it is years away?"

"Would you like to go through the training program again to refresh our capabilities?"

"You said you were advancing," Rolando says tensely. He recalls Clint's advice back on the first End Day to speak up while he could to protect the woman he loves.

Joaquin folds his arms. "Tell me, Rolando. How are you contributing to society?"

"Pa," Alano says.

"I am catching up with Rolando," Joaquin says.

"I'm sure your background check told you everything," Rolando says.

"Our team at Shield-Cast unfortunately misses things sometimes, as I am sure they have done while looking into your current place of employment."

"I was working as a career adviser at Claudi University—"

"Was?" Joaquin interrupts.

Rolando blushes. "I was laid off because of funding."

Joaquin scratches his beard as if bored. "Where are you employed now?"

"Currently unemployed."

Naya cuts in. "What would you like to be doing, Rolando?"

"I want to help people," Rolando says.

"Unemployed for almost two months now?" Joaquin says. It appears his Shield-Cast investigators must have found Rolando's records within the past few seconds. "It is very revealing when a career adviser does not have a career himself. Are you sure you were laid off because of funds and not incompetence? History supports that theory."

Both Naya and Alano tell Joaquin to cool it, and Rolando

senses that Gloria and Paz are coming to his rescue too, but as humiliated as he may be, he will not yell, because Rolando never wants Gloria to mistake him for Frankie, or to set a bad example to Paz. But that does not mean Rolando will not speak up for himself. "This disrespect that you show your employees—"

"You do not work for me, nor will you ever again—"

"—is exactly why you found your son's name on the news today," Rolando says.

That shuts up Joaquin instantly.

There is no attacking a man on his success when his company has granted him enough cash to build a tower into outer space, but before Joaquin was the creator of Death-Cast, he was a father, and Rolando calling out those failures is how he drags this man back to earth.

JOAQUIN ROSA
9:12 p.m.

Death-Cast did not call Joaquin Rosa because he is not dying today.

Many, many calls today believed otherwise for Death-Cast, but Joaquin kept his empire in check, ensuring all that Death-Cast will live on despite the threats. He did not take kindly to the board members who were overly concerned about Alano. Joaquin firmly reminded them that not only does Alano know the ins and outs of this business at nineteen years old better than they do, but that he recently survived an assassination attempt. Had any of them survived an assassination attempt? No. That is bound to mess with anyone's brain, even a brain as brilliant as Alano's.

"What about Alano deactivating Death-Cast?" was asked by many.

It was such a popular question that Joaquin worked with his team to prepare a press release that would explain how the assassination attempt by the Death Guard led to Alano's carefully worded "nervous breakdown." Joaquin urged that they avoid identifying Alano's psychotic break until a psychiatrist diagnosed it as such because he does not want the board members concerned about Alano's ability to lead; after all, they would challenge Joaquin's sanity too if they knew that he speaks with ghosts. The press release is designed to redirect blame on the Death Guard and rebuild confidence in Death-Cast, the Page–Paquin ticket, and Alano himself.

This press release needs to be approved, signed, and shared by Alano, whose reputation would strongly benefit after what has admittedly not been his best PR week. Between the story of Alano's freakout in the call center on his first night as a herald, the assassination attempt, the incident with the Dario boy, and now his pro-natural status exposed, the name Alano Rosa has been cycling through the news far more than Joaquin likes, making Alano look more and more vulnerable every time he's mentioned.

Joaquin will always defend his son, always clean up his son's messes, like a good father.

No one—and he means no one—will ever use his son against him.

How dare Rolando Rubio challenge Joaquin's parenting. "Are you suggesting that I put my son's life at risk?" Joaquin asks.

"I am not suggesting anything," Rolando says coolly. "I am telling you that even a family on top of the world like yours is not untouchable."

"I am very aware of my family not being untouchable because not only did an assassin attempt to kill him, he was threatened by your stepson."

The silence in the room is tense, much tenser than when Joaquin's blood was boiling over Rolando blaming Andrea Donahue's betrayals on him. Paz glares at Joaquin, as he has many times, but now he senses a danger, like daggers in his eyes—bullets in his eyes. He is not alone. Alano himself has murder in his teary eyes: Is this what a son looks like when he wants to kill his father?

"We said we would not do this," Naya says.

Yes, they did agree to shelve the matter of the Dario boy almost punching their son, but tensions are high and alcohol has been drunk from his flask in trips to the restroom and poured into his glass of this delicious mango smoothie. Joaquin has not blacked out this agreement, but he is ignoring it.

"Pazito was wrong to raise his hand at Alano," Gloria says firmly. "There is no excuse, and I have made that clear to my son. If I didn't believe in Pazito's restraint, we would not be hosting Alano and endangering his well-being."

"You understand why I am concerned for Alano given Paz's father," Joaquin says.

"Pazito is not Frankie and you will not villainize him in his own home," Gloria says.

As Paz tears up, Alano holds the hand that almost hit him.

Why is his son always taking the side of this boy over himself?

"D-do, do you know everything about your son?" Joaquin asks Gloria, slurring as he imagines what could have happened if Paz had shot Alano while trying to kill himself on the

Hollywood Sign. Maybe it's time she knows how their sons really met.

"You don't know everything about *your* son," Alano quickly says.

Joaquin tilts his head. "Is that what you think?"

Once again, Joaquin will always clean up his son's messes, like a good father.

Does Alano truly believe that he got away with murder on luck alone and not because Joaquin cleaned the blood on his hands?

ALANO
9:16 p.m.

Past alarming thoughts are getting stronger and stronger, like a Death-Cast alert ringing through my head. I'm the only one who knows my full story no matter what my father believes.

I consider keeping my family's personal business within the family, but seeing how my father has treated Paz's family, I can't help myself. "It's impossible for you to know everything about me when you can't even remember everything because of your blackouts."

My father's smugness vanishes in an instant. "What of my past blackouts?"

The alcohol on his breath. The slurring of his speech. The rudeness. It's all a bad look for my father, but no one knows how bad this can get when he's deep into a bottle or two. I've unfortunately witnessed his dark transformation.

"You promised you were done drinking," I say.

"It has been a calamitous week," my father says.

"You broke your promise."

"You have not been a model of honor either, mi hijo."

"I'm nineteen. I'm not supposed to be the role model. You are."

"I am your father when you mean to shame me but not when I aim to protect you?"

He can't even remember that he's not always protected me.

My mother knows nothing about my father's forgotten episode either. Only that this argument is uncomfortable and she moves for the door, asking us to take it outside and apologizing to Paz's family.

"This concerns Paz too," my father says, staying put.

"Leave him out of this," I say as Paz squeezes my hand like it's a stress ball.

My father ignores me, like usual. "The rumor spreading around the world is that Alano Rosa and Paz Dario are joined by a common cause to destroy Death-Cast," he says, studying us as if there's any truth to this rumor. "It is in both of your best interests to put an end to these claims about you being secret Death Guarders."

It's absurd how the media is pushing the narrative that living pro-naturally means I hate Death-Cast so much that I would serve the Death Guard in their mission to upend the company. As for Paz, I might know the truth of who he is, but I understand how even well-meaning people can write him off as an enemy of Death-Cast based on the public's perception.

"How would you want us to put an end to these claims?" I ask my father.

"I've had our team prepare a press release that you can issue, but a statement is far more powerful. You can use your voice so no one can mistake either of you as the bad guys in this political war," my father says, glancing at Paz, as if he hadn't villainized him minutes ago. "You have the power to repair Death-Cast's reputation too."

I scoff. "Is this why you came here? To save your company?"

"To protect your inheritance, mi hijo. Death-Cast will be all yours one day."

I'm not sure that's the right decision. "Maybe the Death Guard is right. Maybe Death-Cast should die."

My father's silence is chilling.

"You don't mean that, Alano," my mother softly says.

I don't believe in the Death Guard's radicalism, but I might be seeing reason in their core belief that the good Death-Cast has been presenting is no longer outweighing the bad.

"I'm not sure a Decker's right to closure on their End Day is a good enough reason to keep Death-Cast alive if it means war breaking out," I say, trying to be realistic. "Our heralds are traumatized. Our power has been abused by serial killers. Our very existence is creating violent division around the world." I flash my bandaged arm. "The Death Guard targeted me, the heir, to kill Death-Cast's future. Think about how many lives we can save by shutting down Death-Cast now. Mine included. I don't want to spend my life hiding from the next assassination attempt just like you don't want my ghost for company," I tell my father, knowing that he fears my ghost haunting him more than any other soul. "Death-Cast created countless miracles, but it has destroyed lives too." I watch tears obscure Paz's beautiful light brown eyes. "Maybe instead of serving Deckers, we make the ultimate sacrifice to protect the survivors whose lives we left in ruin."

I am among those survivors.

My father slowly shakes his head. "You would watch the whole world fall back into an age of mystery over a fraction of lives being disturbed by my creation?" he asks disapprovingly.

"It may be a fraction of the millions you've served, but it was whole lives for individuals."

That's when Paz rises. "I'm not getting my life back, and it's all your fault."

PAZ

9:21 p.m.

I never thought I would ever get the chance to tell the Death-Cast creator he ruined my life.

Joaquin wants to run his mouth about us using our voices to clear the air, but guess-fucking-what, the truth has never gotten me anywhere with the world before, but it's about damn time that the man responsible for everything horrible finally hears my side of the story.

"Sit down, Pazito," Mom says.

I'm standing over Joaquin like I'm about to get aggressive. "Don't worry, I'm not gonna kick his ass," I tell Mom.

"Good. There is no need for bodyguards," Joaquin says as he relaxes back in the dining chair. "I am glad to see you showing restraint."

I'm telling the truth when I say I won't hit Joaquin because any punch I throw is another step toward becoming Dad, but wow, his attitude is trying to make a violent liar out of me. "Don't get me wrong, Joaquin, you definitely deserve an ass-kicking after your life-ruining fuckup, but I already gotta go to my grave with shame for almost punching Alano. You're not worth the extra guilt."

It's pretty clear that no one stopping me as I tell off this grown-ass man is proof that I get to feel all these feelings.

"I had a bright future before the first End Day," I say, my voice cracking. "I've only ever had one dream and that was to be an actor, and I busted my ass trying to make that happen. And just like that"—I clap my hands so hard my palms sting and everyone gets startled—"it was gone. I lost my dad and my dream in one moment. Yeah, I killed my dad, and I would do it again in a motherfucking heartbeat to save my mom, but *you* killed my dream and *you* destroyed my life." I rub my fists into my eyes, clearing the tears. "And instead of ever getting an apology, you roll up in here treating me like I'm some criminal even though my shitty life is all your fault."

Joaquin holds up a finger. "We did reach out to apologize on . . ."

"August 15, 2010," Alano says.

"On August 15, 2010, but your mother said no."

Mom wipes her tears. "Your apology was not going to give him back his childhood."

"Well, for the record, I am sorry—"

I interrupt Joaquin. "I get that you don't give a shit about me, but imagine Alano being the only nine-year-old getting patted down for weapons when he went to school."

"That is horrible," Joaquin says. "I am sorry—"

"I got bullied by students and their parents. Switching schools didn't help. Rolando had to homeschool me. College was never in the picture."

"You should not have been treated that way. I am sorry—"

"Then *Grim Missed Calls* blew up my life all over again."

"We tried stopping production but failed. I am sorry—"

"My life got so bad that I tried killing myself!" I shout, red in the face. I gotta calm down, I gotta calm down, I gotta calm down. I can't lose control. I should go hold ice until it burns or do jumping jacks even though it'll hurt the foot I cut open. I bite down on my lip before I can tell Joaquin all the horrible ways I've self-harmed because I don't want Mom and Rolando knowing.

Joaquin rises and looks me in the eye. "I am sorry, Paz."

"I don't need an apology anymore! The damage is done. I need to know why."

"Why? Why what?"

Alano taught me to get the facts. I'm gonna do that.

"What happened on the first End Day that my dad never received his alert?"

My family is quiet while Naya is breathing heavily and Alano is crying, and I hope I'm not triggering him as I go off on his dad, but there's no way that Alano and I would be in each other's lives for years to come without me and Joaquin having this showdown.

"That is private information," Joaquin says.

"Is that code for you getting drunk and blacking out?" I ask.

Joaquin has been sobering up, but I still smell the alcohol on his breath as he says, "The blackouts began years later, if you must know."

"Yeah, I must fucking know because that night ruined my life. What really happened?"

"A system error," Joaquin says.

"People died and lives got ruined because of a system error?"

"Unfortunately yes, but I put in protections to make sure it never happens again."

"That doesn't do shit for me," I say, turning away from Joaquin before my rage takes over.

My heart is pounding fast.

I gotta calm down, I gotta calm down, I gotta calm down.

My life got ruined over some bullshit system error? This is not like when my camera's memory card failed to store my self-tape or when my audition sides got jammed in the printer, this is Death-Cast we're talking about. Lives and deaths are actually on the line here.

But, hey, it's never gonna happen again!

I'm dizzy, and my chest is tight. I gotta sit; I gotta get it together.

"Take a deep breath," Alano says. He blinks, and a tear slides out of the corner of his green eye. He holds my hands between his as if he knows I'm trying so hard to not attack his dad, which I really, really, really am because that's not me. Alano takes the deep breath with me and ends by saying, "You're okay."

I am okay.

My heart is slowing down.

I let out one last big breath.

"I'm not a Death Guarder, but I've hated Death-Cast for a

long time," I say, staring up at Joaquin as Alano keeps holding my hands. "And I have every right to hate Death-Cast, and I have every right to hate you, but I don't have it out for Alano like that asshole assassin whose life you also ruined. Everything sucks, but Alano has been coaching me to keep trying anyway. My life won't get better if I quit and Alano has shown me I got a lot to live for."

Rain falls in the forest of Alano's eyes. "*So* much to live for," he says softly.

I'm up against a world that doesn't know me but hates me anyway, but I'm gonna keep fighting until my life looks like my dream obituary. But if I fail at getting cast in a mega-hit franchise or winning an Oscar or receiving a star on the Hollywood Walk of Fame, this life is still worth living because of Alano Rosa.

And one day—one day really fucking soon—I can't wait to tell Alano how much I love him.

ALANO
9:34 p.m.

My past alarming thoughts have continued ringing through my head like a Death-Cast alert, but it's as if Paz answered the call and told the herald "Not today!" before hanging up.

At a time where best friends are turning me into a stranger and assassins are trying to kill me, I feel safest when I'm with the boy known for his destructive spirit because underneath this hardened shell and facades and scars is the biggest heart with so much love to give and receive.

I need to overcome the many unknowns and obstacles ahead. Only then will Paz and I be invincible.

JOAQUIN ROSA
9:35 p.m.

If Joaquin thought he was losing power over Alano before, he now knows he is completely powerless as Alano and Paz stare into each other's eyes like Deckers who have fallen in love on their End Day.

He can only hope these boys will not be the cause of each other's deaths.

ALANO

"You boys have given me much to reflect on," my father says.

I'm not hopeful about seeing any real change because of my father's ego, but it brings an end to what has been a tense evening. Everyone picks up after themselves, bringing their dishes to the sink for Mr. Rolando to clean. My mother swaps my father's flask for a glass of water. Paz and I bring the lawn chairs and Bucky outside. I'm grateful for this fresh air.

I turn to Paz. "How are you feeling?"

"I don't know. It's weird. I won't lie, I wanted to Hulk out on your dad a few times, but we're using words and not fists and that feels great now, but it sucked how shoulder shrug–y he was about the first End Day error. Like it was nothing."

I almost tell Paz about my father seeing ghosts, but that's not my secret to tell. I'm preparing to share my own soon. Maybe this Friday on the anniversary of Frankie Dario's death so Paz won't feel alone in his trauma. For now Paz needs to know that my father has many flaws, but detachment isn't one. "My father has been haunted by that error for three thousand six hundred and fifty days."

Paz looks at me and then up at the night sky like the stars will show the equation. "That's bad math."

"Math isn't bad."

He rolls his eyes. "Your math is off. It hasn't been ten years yet."

My math teachers always said to show my work, even if the answers come quickly to me. That's what I do now. "A year is usually three hundred and sixty-five days, so multiply that by ten and you end up with three thousand six hundred and fifty days, but then you have to add the three Leap Days from 2012, 2016, and 2020, which is almost unnecessary since you have to subtract them again because we're three days away from the ten-year anniversary. Leaving you with . . . ?"

"Three thousand six hundred and fifty days," Paz says.

"Three thousand six hundred and fifty days of my father being haunted by your past."

Paz sits with all of this. "Okay, your math is good, but it really doesn't feel like your dad cares about what happened to me."

"I imagine he's struggling to treat you as a victim when he sees you as a threat."

"I'm never gonna live that down," Paz says, his eyes going blank.

I grab his hand, bringing him back to me. "You will with the only person who matters," I say. There's no forgetting that Paz almost hit me, but once he honors his word by undergoing his treatment, I can forgive him. Especially since I know what truly birthed that anger. "I'm really proud of you for addressing the first End Day with my father. His apology didn't give you any closure?"

"Saying sorry doesn't change how bad my life got screwed up," Paz says.

"I'm sorry to hear that." I shake my head. "Poor choice of words."

"It's fine, it's whatever."

"Paz . . ."

He sighs. "Look, getting an apology from your dad just really throws me in my feelings because I'm never gonna get one from mine."

If Frankie Dario had received his End Day alert, maybe Paz would have gotten an apology. Gloria too. We'll never know. "Have you ever tried getting closure?"

"Like what, doing a séance?"

"If that's what you want." It may not have been what I meant, but I would respect Paz engaging in that practice just as I do others around the world who commune with their ancestors. "Anything that helps you move on, especially as we approach the anniversary."

Paz shrugs. "I wrote a letter to my dad on my birthday. It was also Father's Day."

I never pieced that together. "What did you say?"

"What I wish I had said before killing him," Paz says.

I'm curious if he'll open up more about that, but before I can ask, my mother pops her head out of the door and asks if we can come back inside. "Something's happened," she says.

Dread fills my chest. I call Bucky, and we all return to the living room. "What happened?"

My father glances at Paz's parents. "We should speak privately."

"Why? Does this concern Paz? Are they talking about us on the news?"

"It does not concern Paz, but . . ." He closes his eyes in frustration.

My mother hands him another glass of water. "They will all find out soon anyway."

My father nods. "There's been a death—or there will be."

Everyone is quiet. I'm dizzy thinking about the possibilities. Who could be dying that has my parents worked up? One of our heralds back in the city? Roah Wetherholt? An executive like Aster Gomez? Or is this less about my parents getting worked up and more about them sharing sensitive info that will break my heart? I might faint as the fear overwhelms me.

"Please don't say Ariana or Rio," I say on the verge of tears before remembering that there's no way of knowing if Rio is about to die or not. If he's even alive this very moment. Maybe this isn't about a Death-Cast alert but a death threat made to Rio like I received. Is someone threatening him because he knows me? Because we're friends? Used to be friends?

"Sweetheart, no," my mother says immediately. "It's not Ariana or Rio."

I could still cry from relief. "Then who?"

"Marcel Bennett," she says.

"Who's that?" Paz asks.

"A new hire," I say. Marcel was originally in the running for Death-Cast's secret Project Meucci promotion before we decided on a different actor who lost out because he refused to sign the NDA. That's when I persuaded my father to hire Ariana because we could trust her even without the NDA. Then he had to fire her once her trust was called into question. "When did this happen?"

"Minutes ago," my father says. "Marcel Bennett graciously reached out to Aster after receiving his alert, thanking us for the opportunity."

Death is the ultimate callout for not coming to work.

"I'm sorry he will be lost," I say.

"That's so tragic," Ms. Gloria says.

"This promotion is starting to feel cursed," my father says, as if the ghosts he sees are conspiring against him. "But we will persist."

The gears are turning in my head as I remember some of the incredible self-tapes that were submitted to us. Tons of new local talent from colleges and the theater scene, even some television stars with many credits to their names. But I turn to the boy who needs more than an apology to turn his life around. "What if Paz filmed the promotion?"

My father and Paz look at each other before staring at me.

"A young man just discovered it's his End Day," my father says. "I am not sure now is the best time to be discussing this."

I'm not falling for my father believing that I'm being insensitive. He has often said that life goes on even when a Decker's is coming to a close. No, my father's resistance is that he doesn't want Paz.

"You need an actor by Thursday morning. Paz is an actor," I say.

"Absolutely, but we are filming at headquarters."

"We'll go to New York together," I say. I turn to Paz. "Would that work for you?"

Paz looks between his parents and mine. "Um . . ."

"The job pays," I say. I'm sure Paz would do it for free, but we all know that's not the problem.

My father says, "While I would delight in your return to New York, mi hijo, you understand that this promotion is delicate."

I can read my father's mind. He's concerned about the optics of unveiling his next phase of Death-Cast with a figure as controversial as Paz. I have to reason with him politically. "Casting Paz in this project will show the world that he and I can't be secret Death Guarders if he's the face of the new Death-Cast campaign," I say, knowing that I'm appealing to my father already. I drive it home with guilt. "Death-Cast ruined Paz's life and now Death-Cast can give it back."

The best apology isn't words. The best apology is action taken to make things right.

My father glances at Naya before staring at me. "I would like to rebuild everyone's hope in Death-Cast. We are not perfect. No person or company is, but we have done good for millions worldwide." He turns to Paz. "I am sorry that Death-Cast failed you, but I will grant you this opportunity along with an invitation to the gala so you may witness the heartfelt speeches by those who have benefited from our services. Of course, Alano will need to be in attendance too."

"I'll be there," I say before asking Paz, "Will you?"

Paz runs his hands through his curly blond hair before turning to Ms. Gloria. "Mom?"

"When is this gala?" she asks.

"Thursday evening," I say.

Ms. Gloria grabs Paz's hand. "I want this for you if you want this, but Friday is . . . well, you know. We should be together on that day, Pazito."

"You're invited to New York too," my mother says to Ms. Gloria and Mr. Rolando.

"I've missed a lot of work already."

"Then we can arrange for Paz to return on Friday morning or put him on a red-eye after the gala. First-class, of course, as we do for all our stars," my mother says, winking at Paz. I'm thrilled that she's on board with this plan.

Ms. Gloria nods slowly and inhales a deep breath. "This is your call, Pazito."

Paz is quiet. I should have discussed this with him privately. I definitely don't want to pressure him into doing promotions for a company that upended his life, I only want his wounds to heal. Everyone around the world will see this campaign. Maybe that's a bad thing. The last thing I want is to invite more chaos into Paz's life.

Now I'm scared I'm doing just that.

Paz walks up to my father. For a moment I'm nervous he's

going to hit him, but he shakes his hand instead. "Thank you," he says before hugging Ms. Gloria as Mr. Rolando cheers.

My father comes over and shakes my hand too. "Excellent negotiating, mi hijo," he says. "I have taken your words to heart, and I hope you see that I can be receptive to your needs. I cannot help but be overprotective as your father, but I will work harder to find a balance that allows you more freedoms. It would mean the world if you will reconsider giving Death-Cast your full commitment, both in its service and in one day serving."

If I'm granted the life I want, I can see myself leading in the future. "Maybe," I say.

"I will do what I can to regain your confidence," my father says.

That is a long road, but it's as if we've walked miles of it tonight.

As my parents speak with Ms. Gloria and Mr. Rolando about the arrangements of me going home to pack and what time Paz will need to be ready for tonight's takeoff, I pull Paz into the kitchen.

"I'm sorry for putting you on the spot," I say.

"I've had worse spotlights on me," Paz says. Then he throws his arms around me and gives me the tightest hug. "Thanks for making me an actor again, Alano."

Honoring the Begin Days contract is far more fulfilling than my original promise to help kill Paz when he was desperate for his End Day.

I'm so happy that this has worked out so I can still be there for Paz on the anniversary. "How are you feeling about returning to New York?" I ask.

Paz steps back. "The timing is wild, obviously, but what better time to face my ghost."

"Maybe this is what was fated all along," I say before lowering my voice. "It was never about you dying. It was always about moving on."

"I hope so."

This will be the most healing trip if I can restart Paz's acting career and give him closure on his father's death. "What about bringing the letter you wrote Frankie?"

"For what?"

"To say goodbye, Paz. In reading about different programs for confronting trauma I saw that CBT—cognitive behavioral therapy—has a practice where they encourage people to write letters to move on from unhealthy relationships or negative thoughts. Some people even burn their letters for closure on unfinished business. Or we can bury the letter somewhere Frankie took you. How about near that movie theater where he carried you home when you were crying? You said that was a happy memory."

"My old building," Paz says softly. "I wanna end this where it all started."

I really hope this will help Paz get rid of his ghost.

If only burning letters would stop my ghosts from haunting me.

GLORIA MEDINA
10:22 p.m.

The best of planners are prepared as if they have already seen the future, but no one, not even Gloria, could have foreseen that such an intense family dinner would have led to an opportunity for Pazito to act again—for Death-Cast no less!

It is tragic, of course, that the closing of one door has led to the opening of another for Pazito. Gloria feels for Marcel and his family on this young man's End Day. She knows that Pazito has often felt as if his life and dreams ended on the first End Day because what is a life without dreams, even when you're still breathing? But today a family will mourn their own son as he takes his last breath, if he has not already. It's ripping Gloria apart, and since she cannot go to New York, she wants to hold Pazito close here, but between Alano's amazing influence, the protection of the Shield-Cast agents, and the loving care of Naya, and yes, even overprotective Joaquin, Gloria knows that Pazito will be in good hands. That he needs this trip to get his life back on track.

The road to this moment has been long and winding, but you can only overcome roadblocks with persistence. Gloria could not be happier that Pazito is being rewarded for staying the course.

As Pazito showers and Rolando continues his job search in

the bedroom, Gloria is tidying the kitchen and enjoying fla-menco guitar songs on the radio. She is getting so lost in the music that she almost misses the knock at the door.

Who could it be at this hour? Did the Rosas forget something? She hopes this isn't some bold reporter disturbing their peace.

Gloria opens the door to find a woman around her age. "Hello?"

"Good evening. Are you Gloria Medina?"

"I am, but I am not speaking with reporters. Have a good night," Gloria says, closing the door until the woman asks her to wait.

"My name is Margie Hunt. I'm the shopkeeper at Present-Time in Hollywood." She pulls out a light green gift box with a beige bow. "My store was attacked a few nights ago, and the cleanup has been a mess, but I wanted to deliver this personally along with my apology and condolences."

Gloria is confused as she inspects the gift box. It's not as if Gloria has many friends out here, but someone regarded her enough to take time out of their End Day to send her a present. Her heart breaks over the possibility that it was a woman from the shelter, but she can't find a tag.

"Who sent this?" Gloria asks.

The Present-Time shopkeeper is confused. "Your son . . . ?"

"My son is not dead," Gloria says. What a horrible thing to say.

Then Gloria's heart breaks because Pazito may not be dead, but he tried to die again.

PAZ

10:38 p.m.

I can't believe I'm going back to New York so I can act!

This Death-Cast promo isn't a movie or TV show obviously, but it's a commercial that's gonna be seen by everyone around the world. That'll kill all the rumors that I'm some secret Death Guarder and also show everyone—directors, producers, studios—what a great actor I am.

Once I get out of the shower (without using any burning hot water or hurting my wounded foot), I spend some time cleansing and moisturizing my face to get camera ready. I'm definitely gonna need some concealer to treat the bags under my eyes, but that's an easy fix, unlike my hair that's been getting yellower since I haven't been using the recommended purple shampoo because I didn't really give a flying fuck about how yellow my corpse's hair would be.

I gotta care about my life again, and that means staying on top of basic needs: brushing my teeth, washing my face, eating right, staying hydrated, and getting back into working out. These are all the ways I can show love to the body I never wanna harm again.

I get dressed and limp down the hall. I gotta check for

any last-minute things to pack before Alano returns at eleven thirty.

I go into my room and it's been trashed—clothes thrown around, doors and drawers opened, my mattress knocked off the slats. It's like I've been robbed, but why would Mom and Rolando, the only other people in my room, rob me? And why is Mom on the floor crying?

"You tried killing yourself again," Mom sobs.

My nightstand and closet door and copy of *Golden Heart* are all open, and Mom is surrounded by everything I've been hiding from her:

The 365-day journal's secret compartment.

The dream obituary written on the back of the Hollywood DIEner waiver for Deckers.

The bloody sheets I forgot to wash.

The gauze, petroleum jelly, and bandages for my wounds.

Thankfully the gun and knife are gone, but nothing is more incriminating than the suicide note in Mom's hands.

This is bad. This is *really* bad.

Why the hell did they start going through my stuff? Did Joaquin call Mom and tell her that I tried killing myself once he got Alano back home? Was that all some game? Is this job in New York even real? I should've known better than to get hyped about my life turning around for the good, I cut my foot open so I would never be this stupid again. What's it gonna take before I never forget that life is nothing but pain? Cutting the other foot? My hand? My face?

No, no, no, no. I gotta get the facts. I gotta know why Mom and Rolando went through my shit.

"What are you doing in here?" I ask.

"A package arrived," Rolando answers since Mom is incoherent. "From Present-Time."

Son of a bitch. My will to live has shifted so much since Present-Time that I kept going back and forth on whether or not I was scared it would bite me in the ass or give Mom closure. Those gifts are biting me in the ass.

Am I supposed to say some shit like "This isn't what it looks like!" even though it's exactly what it looks like? No, facts go both ways. I gotta own up.

"I wanted to die so bad," I say.

"Why didn't you come to us when you were struggling?" Rolando asks.

"Because I'm struggling every day."

His eyes water. "I love you like you are my own son, Paz-Man. If you are struggling every day, then we will be there for you every day."

"That's the last thing I want. I hated being on suicide watch. You guys were all over me, I couldn't even sleep alone—"

Rolando grabs the bloody sheets and shouts, "This is why!" He's never yelled at me before. He seems just as surprised as he takes a breath. "How long have you been hurting yourself?"

I should lie, I should just lie. "Since November," I confess. I explain that the self-harming started after the *Grim Missed Calls* trailer dropped and how I could already see the writing on the wall that my life was gonna become totally unlivable. "I wasn't wrong."

Mom cries as she rocks back and forth on the floor. I bet she thought this started after my first suicide attempt in March, not months before.

"Are you still doing this?" Rolando asks.

"I've been trying to stop."

"When did you hurt yourself last?"

I really should just lie because every time I tell the truth it's like I'm cutting Mom. "Yesterday," I say because I'm trying to show them how honest I am and not even as a Happy Paz trick. "I was heartbroken and hating myself for almost hitting Alano."

Rolando stares at the blood on the sheet. "Where are you hurting yourself?"

That feels too far. "That's private."

"Privacy is for journaling and masturbating. Not self-mutilation!"

"His foot," Mom says. She's talking about me like I'm not in the room. Like I'm dead.

Rolando nods. "You did not stub your toe on the bed. You cut yourself."

"Yeah."

"You have not been limping like this since November. Where else?"

"This isn't helping, it's just torturing Mom!"

"You not letting us help you is what tortures your mother! You can be mad at us all you want for not giving you your privacy after you attempted suicide, but protecting you is our responsibility. We want to watch you have a full life—"

"That's all I wanted too, but it wasn't fucking happening!" I shout, breaking down in tears as I remember everything that brought me up to the Hollywood Sign. "Nothing was changing in my life and everything was changing in yours. You got together. You got engaged. You got a house. Now you got a baby on the way. You got a happy life, and I got nothing!"

"You have us," Rolando says.

That's not enough, even he's not enough for Mom if I kill myself.

"I need to have my own people, my own friends, but no one invited me to any parties or out on any dates because I was the school freak who killed his dad. For fuck's sake, I was so lonely that I started hanging out with Deckers from the Last Friend app. This life sucks."

Mom cries even more, like she's failed me, but she hasn't, I said that in my note.

"Things will get better," Rolando says, which I hope is true, but it's honestly really fucking annoying to hear that when I need things to be better now. "You are still very young."

"But I feel so old," I say.

Time moves differently when you want every day to be your last.

Mom slowly gets up from the floor, crying so hard that she's struggling. She pushes Rolando away when he tries helping. She's red in the face as she waves the suicide note. "This is how you were going to say goodbye, Pazito?"

I never expected to live long enough to learn that my suicide note sucks. I did try personalizing that Present-Time pendant for Mom before the Death Guarder destroyed the shop, but I doubt that would've been good enough either. "There was no saying goodbye to your face, Mom. I'm sorry."

"How am I supposed to trust your apology or anything you say when you have been lying to me? I had to find out about your borderline diagnosis from your suicide note? Your self-harming from your blood? What else do I not know?"

"I wasn't myself, and I'm still trying to figure out who the hell I am, especially after that diagnosis, but everything has been different since Alano saved me. It's like I can finally see a future now—"

"Alano saved you?" Mom asks.

I fucked up.

"He saved you from suicide? Where?"

I'm scared to keep telling the truth, knowing how much it's gonna hurt Mom. This is why I have spent this year lying as much as I have, but we're in too deep now.

"On top of the Hollywood Sign," I say, and Mom looks like she's about to faint. "I know that sounds scary, but Alano's timing was amazing. If it wasn't for that assassination attempt, he wasn't even gonna be in the city. That night, Alano said our meeting was written in the stars and I didn't agree then, but I do now. He's been this amazing life coach, and I'm finally getting hyped about my future again."

Mom drops the suicide note and holds out her hands for me to take. I do. She squeezes.

"I love you, my Pazito, but you can't go running off to New York when we all need to be working together to heal as a family. To get you the care you need."

"Like what, some suicide-prevention facility?" I ask, pulling my hands out of Mom's like I'm about to have to run for it.

"Whatever it takes for you to get better."

"I will fucking kill myself before I go there," I say, which is, no shit, the worst thing I can say but I'm losing control. "Look, I'm sorry, I didn't mean that. I already hit up my therapist to start DBT. That's gonna be an intense program, but Alano is helping me get ready for that."

"Alano is very bright, but he is not a psychiatrist. You need professional help."

"Yeah, I'll start my DBT program when I'm back from New York."

"You're not going to New York, Pazito."

I'm nineteen, I don't need permission.

I walk past Mom and grab the bag I packed, and I'm about to head out early. The only way that I can prove I'm not going to New York to kill myself is to come back alive with new opportunities.

Mom blocks my door. "You're staying."

This is even more childish than Joaquin's dick-measuring contest.

"Mom, please move."

"No."

I turn to Rolando. "Can you talk some sense into her?"

"I agree with Gloria," Rolando says. "It is best that you stay with us."

Why did I bother with him? "Mom. I'm leaving."

"No, you're not."

"Yes, I am."

"No, you're not."

"Yes, I am."

"No, you're not! No, you're not! No, you're not!"

"Come on, Mom, move!"

Mom glares with teary eyes. "Or what, Pazito? Go ahead and hit me like your father!"

I've never started crying faster in my life. It's not just that she's compared me to Dad, it's that she's looking at me like I might actually hit her.

"I killed Dad to save you, Mom," I say, choking on my words. "That ruined my life, but I did it because I love you. Because you screamed for help. Because you needed a hero, but now you're treating me like the bad guy."

"Oh, Pazito. I'm sorry—"

"How would you like it if I blamed you for not leaving Dad sooner?"

"I wish I had," Mom says, clutching her chest. "Every day, I wish I had."

"But you didn't, and now my brain is broken."

In some other universe, Mom ditched Dad sooner and they got divorced and I maybe saw him on weekends for a few months before that fizzled away and Mom and Rolando got together while Dad rotted in that apartment and my life got to be good. But I live in this hell where I get punished over and over and over.

Mom looks haunted and ashamed. "I thought I was doing what was best for you."

"No, Mom, I'm not actually blaming you! Dad's the asshole who tortured you."

"No matter your feelings, I will always regret not leaving before my nine-year-old had to come to my rescue. Now I'm begging you to let me do my job as your mother to support you in your time of need. I love you too much to live without you, Pazito."

I feel like I'm waking up in the hospital after my suicide attempt, handcuffed to the bed. "That's why I gotta lie to you! You can't handle seeing me in pain."

"No mother can!"

"But you're not only a mother! You deserve your own life, Mom. You spent years stuck in a marriage for me, but you're finally free of Dad's bullshit, you gotta let me go too. But I know you won't, so even in my lowest lows, I forced myself to keep living, but then I got so happy that there's a new kid on the way because it means you can't make good on your threat."

Mom's hand goes to her mouth. She knows what I'm talking about.

Rolando doesn't. "What threat?" he asks.

"To kill herself if I kill myself," I say.

Now Rolando knows that the woman he's marrying, the

woman whose life he's so concerned about, will not live for him if I take my own life. "Glo?"

"I love you, but that's my son," Mom says, almost like she's ashamed to admit this.

"What about our child? Will you survive for our child?" Rolando asks.

Mom puts her hands on her belly and closes her eyes, crying against the doorframe. I'm scared that the new kid won't be enough. That Mom will give birth and leave the baby with Rolando. That my death will ruin everyone's lives, even the new kid's.

I should've taken this secret to the grave.

Instead of hugging Mom or saying sorry for blowing up her relationship, I sneak past her while she's crying and limp as fast as I can out of the house.

"Pazito! Pazito, come back!" Mom shouts, following me outside. "Pazito! PAZITO!"

I run so fast that my wounded foot is screaming in pain, but I gotta go get my life back, even if that means leaving Mom behind before she can make living unlivable.

NEW YORK

July 29, 2020

PAZ

3:35 p.m. (Eastern Daylight Time)

Death-Cast didn't call because I'm not dying today, but Mom's son, Pazito Dario, died.

I never thought Mom would feel like a stranger.

After leaving home last night, I ran a few blocks and crashed outside the tar pits. By the time Alano rolled up in his car and found me, I was a wreck: foot hurt, head hurt, heart hurt. He held me as I cried for who knows how long before we had to meet up with his family and Shield-Cast.

We got to the hangar where the Rosa family's private jet was parked, but we weren't cleared to depart until after 3:00 a.m., when we were sure that no one received their Death-Cast alert (Alano excluded, obviously). It was easy to keep busy as Alano gave me a tour of the jet's interior, which his mother designed.

"Welcome to *The Safe Heaven*," Alano had said. That's what his parents named the jet since Alano was still scared of heights at the time.

I expected the jet to be on the smaller side with maybe fifteen seats, twenty tops, but the spacious main cabin alone can sit sixty people in faux-leather chairs with Death-Cast hourglasses stitched on all headrests. There are twelve bedrooms on board and the smallest one is bigger than mine at home. All the private bathrooms have showers, makeup stations, and the softest bathrobes and slippers. Then we went upstairs—upstairs!—where there are two kitchens with private chefs, two dining rooms, a wine cellar, a conference suite, a small home theater, and a video game room that's been updated over the years as Alano got older.

Something else I never thought I'd see on a plane was a painting—or many paintings. Alano's parents wanted to pay tribute to some of their favorite innovators: Antonio Meucci and Alexander Graham Bell for their advancements in telecommunications that Death-Cast lives off of today; Ada Lovelace for writing the first algorithm to be processed by a machine; Max Planck, a physicist known as the father of quantum theory; Albert Einstein for every damn thing he did; and the psychologist Herman Feifel, who started the modern death movement that had everyone rethinking their mortality, only for Death-Cast to take that convo to greater heights.

A couple hours into our flight, we stopped playing *Mario Kart* and *Super Smash Bros.* to get some rest, but I didn't wanna go to sleep. Alano may have flown on this jet one hundred and thirty-four times (he's been counting) since he was thirteen, but that was probably my only chance of living high like that. Sleeping would've been a waste when I could've spent the entire flight just playing video games or watching movies on a big screen or taking hot showers over forty thousand feet high, but when Alano invited me to sleep with him and Bucky even though I could've had my own room, I jumped into that bed with him.

"I don't ever wanna leave," I said to Alano.

"Me either," Alano said. "The real world is down there."

It really did feel like that as long as we were in this palace-in-the-sky private jet that we were living outside of time and space, especially when we woke up and I looked out the window to watch the sun rise. That view made me second-guess if heaven is real.

During breakfast with the Rosas, Naya was gently encouraging me to make things right with Mom because some problems are so huge that they shouldn't be left to an End Day. She was also super transparent that she would be checking in with Mom during my visit whether we were talking or not because as a mother herself she hates being left in the dark about her son. I couldn't fight her and was even secretly glad that Mom would know I was okay.

Then, before landing, Alano and I hopped into a shower—our own showers, obviously and unfortunately—because we wanted to hit the ground running while it was still light out, since his parents want him home before it gets too late, even with Dane protecting him.

We helped rebandage each other's wounds and buckled up, and I stared at New York during the entire descent. I remember putting the city behind me as we moved to LA, thinking my life was gonna change for the better. It only got worse, but I'm finally seeing some promising progress, like an actor struggling to sink into their character before everything clicks into place.

This glimpse into Alano's life has been wild. Private jets, private security, private chefs, private drivers, but still not as much privacy as Alano would like. I get why someone who used to be so scared of heights likes staying in the sky, especially when we're returning to the city where he was almost killed.

Where I killed Dad.

At LaGuardia, one car took Joaquin and Naya to the Death-Cast headquarters, another brought Bucky home with everyone's luggage, and a third dropped off me, Alano, and Dane in Manhattan for Alano's fitting.

While Alano is in the dressing room with his stylists, I wander around Saint Laurent, playing a guessing game on how much the clothes cost. I lose every time, missing the real price by hundreds, sometimes thousands of dollars. I don't know how much this Death-Cast campaign is gonna pay, but I'm not dropping six hundred dollars on socks unless they give me super speed or something. I'm picking up a pair of three-thousand-dollar sweatpants when I notice the security guard staring. Does he think I'm trying to steal? Or does he recognize me as my dad's killer?

Before I can fully spiral, Alano comes out of the dressing room.

"What do you think?" Alano asks. He's still wearing his blue jeans and green T-shirt that brings out the forest in his eyes.

"Um. It's super casual for a gala, but do you?"

Alano flexes his arm, and it takes a second before I realize he's showing me black silk wrapped over his bandage and not his fist-size muscle.

"I love it," I say. I'm not talking about the silk.

"This wrap feels classier," Alano says, unwrapping it and handing it back to the stylist. "Though not ideal for life-renewing contracts."

"Where's the full look?"

"You'll see tomorrow," he says with a wink.

I obviously don't have gala-worthy clothes back home, since it's not like I was ever on anyone's invite list for anything fancy, but Alano is gonna play stylist with his wardrobe when we get back to his place.

Once we get into the car, I ask where we're off to next.

"The park," Alano says. "There are some things I need to get off my chest."

"Did I do something wrong?"

"No, it's about me. I've been building the Paz Dario Encyclopedia," Alano says, reaching across the back seat and grabbing my hand. "It's only fair you get the missing pages from my book."

ALANO
4:04 p.m.

Death-Cast still can't call me, but that might change soon.

There's an uneasiness being back in New York, one that can be mostly quelled if I'm certain that I'm not about to die. It doesn't mean that someone won't try to kill me again, but I'm growing interested in knowing about my survival now that the future has some promise once again. My brain is overactive enough without also adding unnecessary paranoia into my every waking moment. Even back at Saint Laurent I was questioning if the stylists in my dressing room harbored enough ill will toward Death-Cast to pull out a knife while I was busy admiring my suit in the mirror. Everyone was lovely, of course, but once word gets out that I've returned to the city, who knows if there will be another assassination attempt. I'd like to know if there's any hope to survive, which only Death-Cast can offer.

I'm nervous about dodging not only enemies, but my best friends too.

As Paz and I enter Althea Park, I'm remembering the times I came here with Ariana and Rio. This is where Ariana told me she got into Juilliard and where Rio first shared his dreams of being a detective. I hope they're both able to pursue their futures, as sad as it makes me that I would be unwelcome in any theater where Ariana is performing or that I'm more likely to see Rio if he's investigating Death-Cast. I have to focus on my future too, it's just harder in a city where I have so much history with two people who won't talk to me anymore.

I can only hope that Paz will still want me in his life after I share the secrets I've been hiding.

PAZ
4:09 p.m.

I haven't been to Althea Park since the first End Day.

Strolling—limping, really—through this park feels like a walk down a literal memory lane. I'm not even mad at how my foot is slowing me down, it's giving me a chance to take in how much has changed in the past decade—trees with plaques, interactive kiosks, bigger playground—and I tell Alano about the last time I was here.

I had finished my audition for some educational toy commercial when Rolando hit up Mom after quitting his job at Death-Cast, inspired to take bold leaps like everyone else that day. He joined us for lunch at Desiderata's Restaurant, which I later learned was where Rolando had first professed his love to Mom when they were college students. Then we kept the fun going here at Althea, and while I was playing around on the jungle gym, like this little girl is now with who I'm guessing is her mother and grandfather, Mom and Rolando were having a deep talk.

"They were here on one of these benches," I tell Alano, wondering if the blue bench we're now sitting on could be one and the same. "Rolando was urging Mom to divorce Dad for her safety. She got inspired, and the rest is history."

"That's incredible," Alano says. "He helped save your mother's life."

I should text Mom a photo of us here at the park so she knows I'm okay, but I can't get myself to do it. It's like my brain isn't sending the signal to my body to grab my phone. I think I'm still too hurt by everything that went down.

"I missed coming here," I say.

It sucked moving from our apartment in Manhattan to Rolando's in Queens, but it wasn't like I could go to my usual spots anyway without being treated differently. The pizza maker next door used to throw in free garlic rolls with our pies because he liked Dad, but sometime after I killed him, Mom finished packing up our old apartment and went to the pizzeria for dinner, only to be thrown out before she could order. A couple months after the incident, we went back to my acting studio to continue my training, but when we noticed that my headshot had been taken down from their Wall of Fame, we took the hint that the coach no longer wanted to be associated with a kid who she helped book a role in one of the highest grossing movies of all time. And as much as I loved Althea Park, I couldn't play here anymore because I couldn't handle the harassment from parents and kids who saw me as a threat. That's when I saw the move to Queens as a fresh start, where I could go to a new park and swing on monkey bars and go down the slide and be a kid without anyone knowing my face.

"Smart move," Alano says. "I got bullied here."

"Why?"

"It was Fourth of July, three days after President Reynolds announced Death-Cast. There was no Pro-Natural Order or Death Guard yet, but people were scared of how life was going to change once we started predicting deaths. I became a target. Kids were shoving me around. One punched me. They were all telling me to die."

I hate anyone who hurts Alano. "I wish I was there, I would've kicked their asses for you," I say. That was obviously a big summer of playing hero.

"Thanks. It was really sad. I walked away crying and . . ." Alano stops and stares at the hopscotch board on the ground, but I don't think he's actually paying anything any mind. He's deep in thought. "And I think you were there, Paz."

"Um . . . what?"

"On our first date at Make-A-Moment you mentioned that your gay awakening happened over the summer when you were nine."

"Yeah . . ."

"You thought that it took place on Fourth of July at a park."

"Okay."

"Were you at Althea Park on Fourth of July in 2010?"

It takes me a minute to remember because sometimes my family would barbecue in Central Park or up in Riverdale, but that year was definitely Althea Park. "I was here. Dad was manning the grill and giving Rolando shit for applying for the Death-Cast job. Mom told me to go play to get away from the bad language."

"That means . . ."

"That we were both at Althea Park at the same time," I say. The only crazier coincidence is Alano finding me on the Hollywood Sign. "Wait, wait, wait. You don't think I'm the kid who punched you at the park, right? I had never been in a fight before then."

Alano shakes his head. "No, I know who that boy was. It also couldn't have been you because I don't actually think we were here at the same time. You may have been arriving to the park as we were leaving."

"How do you figure?"

"Your gay awakening happened when you saw a boy wiping his tears on the street. You don't remember his face, but you said he gave you that butterfly feeling that told you something was different in yourself." Alano works through this equation. "What if that crying boy was me?"

I obviously know what Alano looked like when he was a kid, but I didn't know him back then. I guess that light-skinned, dark-haired boy could've been Alano? I can kinda see him now, but it's hazy. I don't know if I'm now forcing Alano into this memory or not, and I can't exactly trust my brain.

"I guess it's possible," I say.

Alano smiles. "If I'm right, this means that we were each other's gay awakening," he says.

Kid Alano saw Kid Paz in the Scorpius Hawthorne movie and Kid Paz saw Kid Alano outside Althea Park.

Alano and I have always grown up knowing about each

other, but what if we could've actually known each other before the Death-Cast stuff really kicked off? Does this mean we could've met if Death-Cast never happened? What if his family didn't go to the park that day? What if they did and Alano wasn't bullied because there was nothing to bully him for, so he was still at the park when I got there? And what if Alano and I met at Althea Park and had been in each other's lives since then?

"I don't know if this is true," I say, smiling back at Alano. "But I like this theory."

"I love this theory," Alano says, looking between my hand and my eyes.

My heart is racing. "I wish you had stuck around. Life could've been so different."

"Me too. Though leaving Althea Park explains why I don't remember seeing you that day."

"Why would you remember me?" Who knows how many kids were out and about then.

"This is what I actually want to talk to you about," Alano says. He takes a deep breath as he taps his foot. "I have a secret I've been keeping from almost everyone, but I . . ."

Alano stops speaking as that woman, the little girl, and the older man slowly approach. Dane is quick to block us, and I shift closer to Alano too, ready to shield him in case this innocent-looking family tries some shit.

"I'm sorry to bother you," the young woman says, holding close the little girl who looks like her clone. They both have light brown skin, straight dark hair, and the same brown eyes. "My daughter wanted to say hi."

"You're not bothering us," Alano says. He tells Dane not to sweat it and he backs off. He turns to the little girl. "Hi. What's your name?"

"Penny," she says. She squints at Alano then looks up at the woman. "I don't think that's him, Mommy."

"Your mother is right. I'm Alano. It's nice to meet you, Penny."

"My mom said your name is Paz."

Alano blushes. "Oops," he says, turning to me.

My heart is racing as I look up at the woman.

"You're Paz Dario, right?" she asks.

I brace myself now. "Yeah . . ."

"I thought I recognized you from the news."

"If you're some Death Guard weirdo—"

The woman sucks her teeth and laughs. "Oh no, we have brains in this family. I'm Lidia. Last week I started watching the Scorpius Hawthorne movies with Penny in honor of her god-father's birthday. We were only supposed to watch the first, but she got really sick and wanted more so we had a big marathon. She's scarily become a big Larkin Cano fan."

I'm speechless. It's been a minute since someone said hi because they liked me.

Penny lights up. "I like when you cast that curse at Professor Indigo and that fire snake ate his insides."

Alano laughs. "You didn't find that scary?"

"I don't get scared," Penny says.

"Oh yeah?" the older man says. "Remember your nightmares?"

"Nightmares happen when I'm sleeping, Tío Teo. I can't be brave when I'm sleeping!"

The man laughs. "That's very smart, Penny."

Penny sits on the bench next to me. "Was it fun casting magic?"

I don't know if I'm supposed to keep up the illusion that the magic was real; it's like trying to figure out if I gotta lie about Santa. "It was a lot of fun," I say. The magic didn't have to be real for the fun to be true.

"My Tío Mateo really loved those movies," Penny says.

"He loved the books more," Lidia says. "No offense."

"My mom says I'm too young to read the books," Penny says, swinging her legs.

"That's okay, you can read them when you're older," I say. "Maybe with your Tío Mateo?"

"I can't. Tío Mateo died," Penny says.

I'm quiet because I don't know what to say.

"Mateo was her godfather," Lidia says. "And Teo's son."

"I'm so sorry," I say. "How—I mean, when—did he pass?"

The last person in this circle I expect to answer is Alano, but he says, "September 5, 2017."

Teo and Lidia stare at him. "How do you know that?" he asks.

"How the *hell* do you know that?" Lidia asks.

651

"Ooh, bad word, Mommy," Penny says.

"I recognized your names from the *Time* magazine article about Living Last Friends," Alano says. "You have an impressive record, Teo. I think it's so extraordinary how you and Lidia and those Plutos commemorate your losses by making sure Deckers aren't alone on their End Days."

We're all still surprised at how Alano pulled that out of nowhere.

Lidia and Teo exchange glances. "It's what Mateo would've done for us and what Rufus would've done for his friends," Lidia says.

"I was in a coma when my son passed," Teo says, tearing up. "Without Death-Cast, Mateo would have died alone. Instead Mateo and Rufus lived a beautiful End Day. I thank your family for making that possible."

Alano nods. "Of course. You know, I've never been a Last Friend before, but Paz has a few times."

"That so?" Teo asks.

"Not as many times as you," I say, which is obvious because he wouldn't be the record holder if I had as many Last Friends as he did. "Sounds like you're the good ones on Last Friend. Some people on that app suck."

"You mean like that serial killer?" Lidia asks. "Mateo was so creeped out by those stories. He was obsessing over every news report."

"No, I mean, yeah, that guy too, but there are other ways people abuse that app," I say, thinking about my two shitty experiences with one real Decker and one fake Decker. "It's just good to see someone doing good on it."

Teo nods. "I've met many people who were treated unfairly in life. It hurts my heart, but I can rest knowing that I helped make their final hours easier. I will do this for as long as I can, in honor of my son."

If I had died, there's no way in hell my dad would've spent the rest of his life honoring me. Honestly, it's more likely he would've spent the rest of his life behind bars for being the reason I was dead. Whoever this Mateo was, he had a great dad.

Surviving the death of a loved one isn't easy. Penny lost her godfather. Lidia lost her best friend. Teo lost his son. I wonder if there've been times when Teo and Lidia didn't know if they would keep breathing. Or if they no longer wanted to. If Lidia didn't have Penny, would she want to take her own life, like Mom was planning? Was Teo put on suicide watch after he woke up and found out his son was dead? I don't know, but even if they wanted to die, they're still here, breathing anyway.

"Do you mind taking a picture with Penny?" Lidia asks.

For a moment I think she's talking to Alano before I remember Penny is my fan. Somehow.

"I'd love to," I say.

Penny grabs a stick for the picture and holds it up like a wand. "Cheese!"

It's honestly the sweetest thing and a glimpse into the life I could've had if I only became famous as that child actor from a Scorpius Hawthorne movie and not from you-know-what. It gives me hope for what might happen after I film the Death-Cast promotion.

Lidia tears up. "This would've made Mateo so happy."

"This is making Mateo so happy," Teo says, gazing at the sky.

They thank us for being so sweet to Penny and return to the playground where Penny uses her stick to cast curses at her mom.

"You've come a long way from getting harassed at this park, superstar," Alano says.

I should call Mom to let her know there are people in this world who think I'm cool, but there's bigger business to get to.

"I'm kind of dying here, I gotta know this secret," I say.

"Absolutely. I don't want to keep you in the dark. It's about my brain."

"And how you know everything?"

"I don't know everything."

"You almost do. What's your deal? Do you have a high IQ? Are you actually an alien?"

"I'm not actually an alien. Not that I'm aware of, at least."

"So you're just supersmart."

Alano blushes. "I'm technically a genius."

"That's not a secret. It doesn't take a genius to know you're a genius."

"It's more than that. My parents and teachers sensed I was gifted and had my IQ tested when I was six. The WISC—Wechsler Intelligence Scale for Children—examined my verbal comprehension, visual spatiality, problem-solving, working memory, and processing. The average score is anywhere between ninety and one hundred and nine. I scored one thirty, marking me gifted with two percent of the population. The psychologist suspected I had eidetic memory, better known as photographic memory, but when I tested again four years later with another psychologist, he identified my ability as something rarer."

Okay, so we've ruled out that Alano is an alien, but maybe he's a real-life demonic wizard. Honestly, if Death-Cast has some secret ability, maybe all the Rosas do too.

"Do you have some magical power or something?" I ask.

The longer Alano takes, the more I start suspecting that's true. Like I'm about to find out that Alano Rosa is the Clark Kent to some Superman who's been flying around unnoticed.

Alano takes deep breaths, squeezing his eyes shut. "I'm sorry. This is scarier than coming out because I've only ever told this secret to one person outside my parents."

My chest squeezes. "Rio?"

"No. Ariana."

I hope Ariana doesn't run her mouth like her mom and keeps Alano's secret, but I know I will. I reach out and hold his hand. "You can trust me, Alano, but you don't gotta tell me."

"I have to if anything is going to happen between us," Alano says, gazing at me with his brown eye and green eye. Then he takes a deep breath and squints like the sun is in his eyes as he sheepishly says, "I have the power to remember everything."

Did Alano just say he has the power to remember everything? Is that a thing?

This makes perfect sense but also no sense.

"What do you mean?" I ask.

"I have hyperthymesia, also known as highly superior autobiographical memory. There's approximately a hundred documented cases of this ability; I'm not one of them, as my parents don't want anyone knowing. I understand why. If I was harassed for being the Death-Cast heir, what would happen if anyone knew I had this power? My parents feared someone might try and dissect me as if I'm all-knowing like Death-Cast. That's not true, though. Death-Cast is not all-knowing about death, and I'm not all-knowing about life. Not all life, at least. Unlike eidetic memory, which has a short-lived recall, my power allows me to remember my entire life."

"Hold up, hold up. You can remember your entire life? Like even when you were one?"

"My entire life," Alano says.

"No fucking way."

"Test me."

"How do I test you?"

"Ask me anything about my life. You can get specific."

I look around, not even knowing where to start. I guess here at Althea. "Okay, who was the boy that punched you?"

"Patrick Gavin, later known as Peck once initiated into a gang. He was arrested on Tuesday, September 5, 2017, for trying to kill Rufus Emeterio at Clint's Graveyard and Rufus was saved by"—Alano points at Teo—"that man's son, Mateo, which I only know because she"—he now points at

Lidia—"was an eyewitness who is quoted in the police report that I read on Saturday, September 9, 2017, at exactly 11:12 a.m. Not that I could've said any of that just now without coming across as even more of a stalker than I already did by knowing about their Last Friend experiences from the article *Time* magazine published on Monday, July 20, at 10:00 a.m., later read by me during my lunch break at 12:46 p.m., when I was eating leftover rigatoni in my father's office."

Alano stares at me with this smile like he might say, "Gotcha!" But he doesn't. He's serious.

I'm tempted to go find this police report or look up that *Time* magazine article to see if the timestamp matches what Alano said, but I don't need to. "So if I asked you what was the first thing I ever said to you, you would know?" I'm not even sure I do.

Alano nods. "You lowered your gun after I asked you not to shoot me. Your voice trembled as you said, 'Get out of here.' I didn't, so you shouted, 'What are you doing? Alano, go!' I was terrified, but I got closer. That's when I recognized you. I said to you, 'Your blond hair threw me off. But I never forget a face.' The whole truth is that I never forget anything."

Alano Rosa knows everything. This is why I always thought of him as a walking encyclopedia. My own memories start playing back, not with times and dates and other super-specific details, but enough that helps me look at Alano in a new light: he knows so much about Peg Entwistle, the Hollywood Sign Girl, like he's her personal biographer; he knows about those

Hollywood stars who made comebacks despite their troubled pasts; he knows so many languages, I don't even remember how many because I don't have this power; he knows about those women who had late-in-life pregnancies; he knows when exactly Present-Time opened; he knows the exact day that Joaquin was supposed to meet Mom; and he knows way more than me about borderline personality disorder even though he wasn't familiar with it until I gave him my diagnosis. Anyone can know all these things too, but if asked, how many of them can answer as quickly as if being asked their name?

"This is fucking amazing," I say.

"Like all superpowers, there's a cursed side to being gifted," Alano says, shifting around again. "Remembering everything means never forgetting anything. When I'm reliving a moment, it's as if I'm time-traveling back to that day and experiencing those feelings all over again. Good and bad."

"So when I asked you about that boy punching you . . . ?"

"It's as if I was reliving that moment," Alano says.

Instead of bringing that up again, I should've just punched Alano myself—oh shit, I actually almost did. I already hate myself for almost hitting Alano, but I couldn't survive knowing that he would forever relive that punch. Still, knowing that I almost did is gonna haunt him anyway.

"I'm sorry I almost hit you, I'm sorry, I'm sorry," I say as if my apology will be all that he remembers.

Alano squeezes my hand, like he knows I'm about to get sucked into a violent tornado of a spiral. "I accepted your apology because that's the only way I can move forward to create better memories instead of getting stuck in the bad ones."

I think about some of the bad memories that could've been, like Alano watching me blow my brains out on the Hollywood Sign, or even shooting me himself, and yeah, no one would forget those violent memories, but only Alano would relive it like it's happening right then and there. It's not just violence that traumatizes people. It's words too.

"I'm seriously so sorry I said you were dead to me," I say.

"That was honestly the second worst thing you said that day."

My blood was boiling in that argument, who knows what I said in the heat of the moment. I'm struggling to think about what's worse than telling the boy you love that he's dead to you. Was it how I regretted staying alive for him?

No. Oh fuck, no.

I remember the moment Alano started sobbing. "I told you that you were stuck in the past."

"And I said, 'Please don't say that, Paz, you have no idea how much that hurts.' Now you know why, but I'm not telling you about my power to guilt you. Between my hyperthymesia and your borderline personality disorder, we both can't escape our pasts, but we have to know about each other's conditions if we're going to build a future together," Alano says. He scoots closer on the bench, so close that our shoulders are touching. "I really want a future with you, but I have to protect you as much as I need to protect myself from a total psychotic break. It's so hard to stay afloat when I'm trying to remain grounded in the present only for my mind to get whisked away to another time, or how I can't even find peace in sleep because my vivid memories trigger horrible nightmares. I think I finally snapped after last Thursday at 12:03 a.m., when I heard Harry Hope shoot himself and then less than twenty-four hours later I was almost killed by Mac Maag." He's shaking and twisting, like a gun has been fired and that knife is still inside him. "I'm in this time loop where someone is trying to kill me over and over and over—"

"Remember our first date?" I interrupt, rescuing Alano from those horrible memories and the pain they bring. "And when we were laughing on the Ferris wheel? And cooking with Mom and Rolando and dancing to Bad Bunny? And how happy you got when I gave you the vanitas vase?"

Alano relaxes as he travels back through time. His brown eye and green eye water. "Thank you," he says.

"I'll always save you, and you'll always save me," I say, locking my fingers through his, like a promise that can't be broken. "Remember that."

Alano's unforgettable smile comes out. "I'll remember that."

I wanna lean in and kiss him so bad, it's like my chest is on fire, but I gotta cool it. "And I'm down to take it slow to make sure our heads are good."

"I really appreciate that. I was scared to bring that up to you because I didn't want you to get the wrong idea. I'm really trying to be careful, and I regret when I wasn't. It's easy for me to memorize an entire textbook, but emotional intelligence is only learned with experience. We'll have our bumps in the road, but we'll get over them together."

There's gonna come a time when I get sucked into some stupid-ass spiral over something Alano says and I'm gonna bust out of it by reminding myself that Alano wants a future with me, even though he knows that's gonna come with highs and lows.

"Thanks for opening up about all that. I'm gonna keep it a secret, obviously," I say, almost mentioning how I won't even tell Mom when I remember that I'm not saying anything to her right now. "Was that all you had to tell me?"

"Actually, there is something else," Alano says, then pauses. I can't tell if he's lost in the past or just his thoughts. "I don't know if you . . ."

I sense one of those stupid-ass spirals circulating. "You don't know if I what?"

"I don't know if you're going to think I overstepped here, but I know time is of the essence for you to face your father's ghost. You're filming the promotion tomorrow before the gala and then you're returning to Los Angeles to spend the anniversary with your mother."

I mean, I'm not sure that's still happening, but that's gotta wait. "I don't get where you overstepped," I say, getting nervous.

"One of the reasons I chose Althea Park is because it's ten blocks from your old building," Alano says.

"I never gave you my address," I say. If I did, I definitely forgot.

"No, but I remembered it from when my father was supposed to meet you and your mother."

That's wild and gonna take some getting used to.

"Anyway, I went online and saw there were some apartments listed for rent. One of them is 6G," he says, and gently adds, "I made an appointment for us to check it out."

My old apartment is vacant. "I'm not moving back there," I say.

"Of course not. If you want to return to that space to confront your father's ghost, I'll be there with you. If you don't, no harm, no foul. I can cancel the appointment and we'll stick to your original plan."

"What time is the appointment?" I ask.

Alano checks his watch. "Twenty minutes from now."

That's so soon, it's too soon, I don't know if I can do this, or if I should.

Alano reminds me that I don't have to. "I've only known you for five days, but you've shown me so much strength in that time. You got down from that Hollywood Sign. You applied for a new acting job under your real name. You committed to dialectical behavior therapy. You watched *Grim Missed Calls*. You stood up to my father. You survived over and over, even when you reached new lows. The only thing holding you back is your father's ghost. You will never forget him, but you can leave your guilt in the past so he can't haunt you anymore." He offers a gentle smile. "If it's too overwhelming, I'll be right there. Don't forget: I'll always save you, and you'll always save me."

It's now or never if I want closure before the anniversary.

I get up, taking the first of many painful steps through the park, all so I can finally close my most painful wound.

ALANO

5:00 p.m.

I discovered I have hyperthymesia on Friday, March 18, 2011, at 5:37 p.m.

For the past nine years, four months, and eleven days, only four people have known about my condition, which I've been calling my power ever since Friday, March 18, 2011, at 5:44 p.m., and the first person on my list, Dr. Angelica Knapp, told me that some individuals with hyperthymesia don't view this ability as a superpower. Those individuals weren't ten years old like I was. I'm not ten anymore, but calling this condition my power has stuck. Dr. Knapp was very kind, trustworthy, and took this secret to the grave when she died on January 4, 2013.

The next two people on the list are my parents, obviously. Given how difficult it was to conceive me, they were blown away to have a child so naturally gifted.

That night at dinner (mashed potatoes with white gravy, peas, mushrooms, and roasted radishes) my parents sat me down for our first talk about keeping my hyperthymesia discreet. They were concerned about the misconceptions of my power coming from the same source as Death-Cast's, but now that we understood that my IQ score was born out of this ability, we

664

wanted to be respectful to the other students by not accepting any honors determined by grades. It didn't seem fair back then. I may have had advantages in history, science, and literature, but over the years, I was having to fact-check everything on the off chance my original sources were wrong. I also had unique challenges with abstract subjects like math since maintaining focus on the equation was difficult when my brain would get carried away with random details such as what the teacher was wearing on the day she taught those particular lessons.

As I got older and started working at Death-Cast, I began utilizing this power very effectively. I would take minutes for all meetings, but I only ever wrote down the notes to keep people off my scent; I started using the dry-erase boards and tablets because I hated how much paper was getting wasted for this charade.

When I was promoted to executive assistant on Wednesday, July 1, at 9:43 a.m., my father told me, "Your job is to know everything possible." He then patted my shoulder. "Until it's time for you to know the once impossible." This meant I was regularly on secure lines and in private meetings with global leaders, acting as my father's personal recording device of what was said and by whom.

It also meant that for how confidential those communications were, there is still something holding my father back from telling me the Death-Cast secret. He claims he's waiting until I'm older and wants to keep me safe, but this power has made me grow up faster and my life has been regularly threatened.

There must be some other reason he isn't telling me the family secret.

The last person on my list of trusted contacts is Ariana Donahue. I told her the secret on December 25, 2018, after making snow angels in Central Park around 4:30 p.m. (I only don't know the exact minute because I wasn't looking at the time, but I can tell you the sun was setting behind the bare trees.) Ariana envied my hyperthymesia because she would love the ability to read play after play and instantly memorize all the lines, but otherwise she had fun testing my memory and was very honored that I trusted her with this secret. I hope this holds true even though we aren't friends anymore. If she told anyone, I imagine it would've found its way to the press by now.

For nine years, four months, and eleven days, only my father, mother, Dr. Knapp, and Ariana have known this secret. Today Paz is added to this small list.

Trust is so fragile, which is why after telling Paz about my hyperthymesia, I couldn't bring myself to share my other secret when he asked if I had anything else to tell him.

People have limits for how much they will forgive.

PAZ
5:28 p.m.

My old building is like a haunted house. I'm scared to go in, like I'm gonna walk into spiderwebs and trip over skeletons and have ghosts pop out, but the only jump scare is the leasing agent stepping out onto the curb to invite us in. She instantly recognizes the Death-Cast heir but not me. I'm not mad at that, but it does mean she's chatting up Alano and Dane about Death-Cast while leaving me alone with my thoughts as I take the first step inside; I wish Alano were holding my hand, or even Mom.

The building hasn't undergone any real renovations, just some paint jobs; the ugly yellow walls are now white, and the brown trim is black. I hate to say it, but this place had more character when Dad was the super. I'm sure the residents will happily trade color for the functioning elevator, something Dad kept claiming he would get around to; who knows if he would've ever made good on that. The elevator is a tight squeeze, so I let Alano, Dane, and the leasing agent ride up. I'm super anxious anyway and one of those DBT modules said that exercise is a good way to blow off some steam. I hobble up the stairs, trying to remember which ones would creak, something Alano would easily know if he lived here, or even visited once. By the time I reach the second floor, I can hear Alano and the others exiting the elevator. Their voices travel down as I keep going up.

I stop at the fifth-floor landing.

"Out of breath?" Alano asks one flight up. I don't respond. He rushes down the stairs. "Are you okay? Do you want to turn around and leave?"

I'm shaking, but not because I'm scared to go up. It's because I'm remembering what—who—went down here. "This is where Valentino . . . ," I say.

I can't bring myself to say it, but Alano takes everything in himself. My dad knocked Valentino down those stairs, and Valentino landed right where we're standing. He may have technically died at the hospital, but his life ended here. It's been ten years, but it's weird that there isn't anything here that memorializes Valentino Prince, the first Decker, the boy who heard me cry out for help and fought off my dad long enough for me to get the gun and—

"You're okay," Alano says, pulling me into his chest.

I bite down on my lip, not wanting to cry.

"Is everything all right?" the leasing agent asks.

"Give them a moment," Dane says. Even he knows what's up.

I gotta get it together.

There's no plaque here for Valentino, but that doesn't mean he's forgotten, and he never will be, thanks to Orion's 912-page book as well as that movie I won't be in.

"Okay, let's go."

This last flight of stairs feels like I'm climbing a mountain, but I get to the top.

The leasing agent opens my door—I mean, my old door—and welcomes me inside what used to be my home for nine years, but I don't go in. She must be so confused why a wannabe renter is taking so damn long to check out the apartment. She stands in the doorway, telling me about the appliances as if I'm gonna run in because of the new washer and dryer.

"Can I just take a look around?" I ask even though I'm not actually sure I can get myself to step forward.

"Sure," the leasing agent says, staying at the door.

Alano crosses the threshold and holds out his hand. I take it and go in.

This is it.

My old home. The scene of the crime.

The apartment is smaller than I remember, but I don't know if that's because I live in a house now or because I just got bigger. Everything else is basically the same except for new kitchen counters, new window frames, and what has to be new floorboards because there's no way in hell they got the blood out of that wood. I step around the spot where Dad died as if his corpse is still lying there, and I show Alano the closet where Dad hid his gun, Mom and Dad's bedroom, and mine. It's not much, but I got to play with my trains and magic wands in here. It's also where I hid when things got bad.

"How's it looking?" the leasing agent asks.

Alano walks over and says, "Still giving it some thought. We're going to speak privately if you don't mind."

"Of course."

Alano closes the door and quietly says, "Take your time."

I don't wanna take my time, I wanna get out of here.

I pull the letter out of my pocket, smoothing it out. If the Begin Days contract was my promise to keep surviving, this letter was my promise to die at any cost on the anniversary.

My hands start shaking as if Dad is in here right now. I can picture him drinking beer and watching TV, his feet kicked up on the hamper like it's an ottoman. I used to talk to him about what I learned at school and acting class, and he wasn't really listening then, and I don't know if he's listening now, but it's all about me getting this off my chest.

I start reading the letter: "'Hey Dad, today is my nineteenth birthday. It's also Father's Day. I've never tried talking to you before, not because I don't know if you can even hear me, but because I figured you wouldn't wanna. Why would you? I killed you. Don't fucking worry, I'm gonna die soon too.'" I stop to catch my breath as everything I felt writing this letter crawls back to the top. I was so sad but so confident. "'I went for a hike after Mom and Rolando gave me my presents, but all I could think about was how the only thing I wanted was to die. Then I saw the Hollywood Sign and thought I could give myself that gift. There was no way I would survive jumping off the sign, but I couldn't even get up there before falling down. And I got scared to die wrong and decided to make a plan to die right. That's gonna be a gift for both of us when I kill your killer on the anniversary of your death.'" I stare at the last two words, not wanting to read it, like it's gonna undo everything, but I can't stop myself and say, "'I promise.'"

Teardrops fall onto the letter.

"Are you okay?" Alano asks.

This was supposed to give me closure, but this wound hasn't closed. It's like all I did was rip into my wound, using my fingernails as knives. And now I'm digging up all the words that I never thought to put down in writing, to say, or even think. "I hate you."

"What?" Alano says.

I stare down at the letter like Dad is there. "I hate you for making me violent. I would've never picked up a gun or raised a hand at anyone if you weren't in my life." If only I was raised by Mom, someone who's always shown her strength without putting her hands on another person. "Dads are supposed to be role models, but you're the role model of who I don't wanna be." I cry as I rip up the letter, this letter that puts all this guilt on me as if I was wrong to save my mom's life, as if I was supposed to watch her die, as if I had some other power at nine years old to stop my dad from killing her. I wish there had been some other way. I wish he had made better choices. I wish he had just been my dad. "I somehow still love and miss you even though you ruined my life. But I'm also happy you're not alive to screw me up anymore because I'm gonna keep living whether you like it or not!"

I collapse onto the floor, hard, crying as I slam my fist on the pieces of paper, screaming.

The door opens, and Dane rushes in, surprised that Alano is safe.

Alano helps me up, wrapping my arm around his shoulder. "Do you need anything?"

"I wanna go," I cry.

"What's going on?" the leasing agent asks.

"We're going to keep looking," Alano says. "I'm sorry to waste your time."

Every step down the stairs is another step away from the scene of the crime, from the promise I made to myself and Dad to go die. And when we get into the car and start driving away, I'm leaving behind that haunted house and Dad's ghost and my guilt.

I killed Dad to save Mom's life, but saying goodbye is helping save mine.

ALANO
6:27 p.m.

By the time we drive straight from Paz's childhood home to mine, there are six Shield-Cast agents waiting outside my building. Civilians are being told to cross the street, and once there's no one on this block except for those paid to keep me alive, that's when Agent Dane opens the car door and lets us out. He's still trying to rush me inside as if there's a sniper, but I freeze.

The bloodstain—my bloodstain—outside the building is faint, almost like this one part of the sidewalk has been discolored. I thought for sure I wouldn't have come home to this. It's difficult to remove blood from concrete, but we have the resources to get this handled. Why weren't power washers and enzymatic cleaners used to remove my bloodstain? Or a painter to redo the entire block? How about a construction crew to jackhammer this slab of sidewalk so I don't have to see this eyesore? I don't need this reminder to remember that this is where I almost bled to death.

I'm transported back into the night of the assassination attempt. It's so upsetting how Mac Maag got around my hyperthymesia because he used a different name and matured since I last saw pictures of him five years ago when he was fifteen years old. If only I had recognized his voice when he threatened my life over the phone, I wouldn't be staring down my blood right now.

Paz also wouldn't be grabbing my hand as he is now. He doesn't even say anything. He knows what it's like to stare down blood, both his father's and his own. There's something about staring at my bloodstain that enrages Paz so much that he squeezes my hand.

"I could've lost you before I knew you," Paz says.

If I had been assassinated, then Paz would have killed himself back in Los Angeles.

We would have both died without ever meeting.

That's a dark thought, but that's all it is. Some horrible alternate reality. "You didn't lose me," I say. "And I didn't lose you."

We're both here, surrounded by Shield-Cast agents tasked with keeping me alive, but it's almost as if Paz and I are becoming each other's personal bodyguards.

The stakes are higher, though.

If one of us dies, the other will have to fight like hell to survive.

PAZ
6:31 p.m.

I can't believe I'm about to finally go inside Alano's home, but then I can fully believe it when Shield-Cast agents are searching me as if I've picked up secret cameras or guns during our supervised day out. Even Alano thinks this is ridiculous, but honestly, I get it, they gotta treat me like a criminal to keep him and his family safe. I relax once I'm cleared, knowing they got no reason to suspect me of trying to harm anyone.

Waiting for us at the front door is Bucky, the best boy ever. Both Bucky and Alano are hyped to see each other, like they weren't together hours ago. Bucky's even happy to see me after our cuddles on the jet, but he quickly runs back to Alano, who grabs Bucky's paws and stands him up like they're dancing. I still don't know why Alano tried killing himself, but I can see how hard it is to be so suicidal when you got a dog that loves you this much. I should look into adopting a dog.

"Come on in," Alano says.

Any penthouse this close to Central Park was gonna be crazy, especially if owned by a family that flies in the kinda jet they do, but I'm still blown away.

The floor-to-ceiling windows are so damn high and the living space is so damn wide. There are two couches, a chaise, a big-ass TV, so many plants and flowers, a grand piano that belonged to Alano's grandma, Naya's rosewood guitar, a fireplace. And while there are many framed pictures on the walls, mantels, entertainment center, and coffee table, the oil-painted family portrait of the Rosas steals the show. They're only in suits, but they don't need crowns to look royal.

"My father's idea after I turned eighteen," Alano says. "He wanted to celebrate our legacy."

He seems embarrassed, so he takes me through the gourmet kitchen, where I meet Chef Lily while marveling at the marble islands, the empty wine fridge, brick pizza oven, and all the other standard equipment except not standard in the slightest because my toaster doesn't have a touchscreen display so I know how toasted I want my toast and my fridge sure as shit doesn't have a camera inside to see what's stocked remotely. The pantry is hooked up with enough organic food and sweets if the Rosas ever had to wait out an apocalypse.

I shouldn't have stepped foot inside this dining room, it's just got me feeling bad that last night I had these mega millionaires sitting on mismatched chairs that we bought at a flea market while they're used to this long-ass dining table with a dozen matching chairs, a crystal chandelier, and a six-foot hourglass that Naya had custom-made for family dinners because she felt like she wasn't getting enough time with Joaquin and Alano as everyone got older and busier. Family dinner with Dad used to mean sitting on the couch with him while we ate our food and watched TV.

Alano continues the tour through all the other rooms on the lower level: the gym where he works out and practices Muay Thai with Dane; the gift-wrapping room that's also stocked with quality gifts for last-minute presents; the game room with old-school pinball machines, a pool table, and every gaming console; the library where Alano likes to read and study languages, complete with a ladder that I play on because I'm still secretly nine years old; and the wellness center for spa treatments, meditation, massages, cold plunges, and yoga.

As Bucky leads the way upstairs where all the bedrooms are, Alano explains that there used to be a wing for employees, but because Joaquin wanted more privacy, he instead bought apartments within the building for his most trusted staff, including Shield-Cast agents, house managers, housekeepers, cooks, chauffeurs, and his and Naya's personal trainers. This way everyone is on call if the Rosas need something, but the staff can also live their own private lives with their families.

This wing is just for guests now, which these days has only really meant Alano's friends. My chest tightens over how unlikely it was that Rio was staying in any of these rooms when he and Alano were hooking up as much as they were. But there's no point letting Rio get to me when he's not in the picture anymore and I am.

All the guest rooms are themed after nature, but before I can choose between the tropical room, the mountain room, the winter room, or somewhere else, Alano takes me straight to the rainforest room, where I've already been set up because he knows I miss the rain. The room is wallpapered like a forest, and the diffuser sticks on the nightstands make it smell like spring rain. There's a white-noise machine that ranges from gentle rain to heavy thunderstorms to bring it all to life. The bedframe is wooden and the comforter is a sage green with plush brown pillows. Some house fairy has already hung my backpack in the closet alongside my three shirts, jeans, and basketball shorts, and put my underwear and socks in a drawer. The private bathroom is decked out in bamboo—bamboo trays if I wanna read in the bath, bamboo plates for jewelry, bamboo soap dispenser, and bamboo mirror frame.

"What do you think?" Alano asks as I step out of the bathroom.

"It's so relaxing."

"Does it make you want to add more color to your bedroom?"

"Oh, definitely." The black-and-white vibe is too sterile now.

"Sounds like we'll have to return to the Melrose Market," he says with a smile.

I'm so happy we're confronting our pasts and fighting for our future.

"You owe me a tour of your room," I say.

"I do. I hope I can live up to your five-star tour of your room."

"I mean, I'm sure your Siri or Alexa can take over for you if you suck."

"We actually don't have AI assistants in the house since those devices are always eavesdropping."

"Then I guess you gotta crush this tour on your own."

Alano leads me down the hall, and once he opens his door, I'm expecting to find something futuristic and tech-heavy with all the best consoles and tablets and TVs that money can buy, but there isn't a single screen in here. It's actually super minimalistic.

"Welcome to my sanctuary," Alano says.

That's the perfect way to describe this peaceful room. The walls are all a solid light cream except for one that has a geometric sunrise painted onto it. Natural light filters in through the linen curtains that are burnt orange, just like the bedsheets. A door leads out to the terrace. It smells like sweet earth thanks to the sage diffuser sticks. There are stones, rocks, and crystals of all shapes and sizes and colors scattered across the room. A desk with notebooks. A small fountain shaped like a boy drinking water. Bonsai plants and peace lilies on the floor and wood stools. Himalayan salt lamps. Plush meditation cushions. A dove statue wearing Alano's necklaces while his rings, bracelets, and earrings live in the nest. Polaroids strung across one corner like a smile. The steel clock with a rose gold face stands out when everything else is so natural, but I'm honestly more thrown off by the platform bamboo bed in the very center of Alano's room.

"Why there?" I ask.

"I've been told to watch my back ever since I was nine," Alano says, sitting on the bed with Bucky. "I took that very seriously during the early years of Death-Cast. In school I always kept close to walls and corners so no one could sneak up and hurt me. Then I started bringing that behavior home around the staff. I hated feeling so paranoid, especially in my own home. I needed a psychological reset, so I created this sanctuary where no enemies could ever harm me. I centered the bed so it felt like my own personal island where I felt so free that I wasn't concerned about watching my back. Instead I surrounded myself with my plants and flowers and rocks and woods. I feel safe in this dangerous world."

I would happily get stranded on an island with Alano and no one else. Actually, we'll take Bucky, since he would never try to ruin our lives and happiness, unlike strangers on the street and the internet. "Is the island vibe also why you don't have any electronics?"

"My brain is overactive enough." Alano gets up from the bed and puts his phone inside a small box on his desk and picks up a notebook. "Instead of absorbing more heavy news before bed, I try journaling to offload my thoughts."

I really should've journaled instead of self-harming. "Does it help?"

"Sometimes. It's easy to obsess over the negative moments, so I do my best to focus on the good memories. It's almost like building a dam in my mind. But at the end of the day, there are some words that never leave you, no matter how many times you write them down," Alano says, freezing as if he's reliving some harsh words now. I wonder if it's from the night Ariana rejected him, or the day he rejected Rio.

Or how I scarred Alano by telling him he's stuck in the past.

"It's gotta be hard living like this," I say.

"That's why I have this sanctuary to help me find some peace."

"You killed it in here. You got that cozy bed, your fountain, your pictures—wait, why do you even have pictures? Your brain is kinda your own personal camera, right?"

"Just because I can remember everything doesn't mean I don't benefit from reminders of favorite memories. Besides, it might not always be this way."

"What do you mean? You're gonna take the pics down?"

"No, I might forget these moments one day," Alano says, which is a dizzying flip from a few hours ago when he told me he remembers everything. "My grandfather, Jacinto, had early-onset Alzheimer's. It started developing four months after I was born when he was only fifty. He kept calling me Joaquin while not recognizing my father. His brain gradually deteriorated over the next three years before he died, sooner than the doctors had anticipated." It's wild to think about the Death-Cast family being caught off guard about someone dying. "Every couple years my father and I go to top clinics for comprehensive genetic testing. Between my father turning fifty and his blackouts, he was especially concerned during our screenings in February, but we're not showing any signs of the disease as of yet."

"But you think it might be a good thing if you get Alzheimer's one day?"

Alano shakes his head. "I would never say good. I don't wish Alzheimer's on anyone, myself included. I do accept that it might be inevitable given my family history. I'm simply taking solace in knowing I might be able to forget one day, since I don't know what that's like. Hyperthymesia can be so unbearable, especially during states of distress. It's as if the dam I painstakingly built can come undone in a moment and flood me with terrible memories and the feelings they bring. Do I really want to die remembering an entire lifetime of memories? It seems more merciful to forget life's most heartbreaking moments."

For all our talks about living to one hundred, I never knew that Alano carries more life with him than anyone else at any given moment. He reminds me of the Immortal in *Golden Heart*. Vale sometimes regretted getting so attached to the dying, knowing that he would be shackled to that grief forever. I totally get why Alano doesn't wanna be on his deathbed reliving his assassination attempt as he's actually dying, just like I don't wanna think about shooting Dad or all the harm I've ever caused with a gun and knife and fist and words. But our lives are not just the bad moments.

"I would hate for you to lose your good memories," I say while dreaming up memories of events that haven't even happened yet, like our first kiss and becoming boyfriends and getting married and starting a family and dying old together.

"I'm not going to have any control over which memories I forget, but after observing how my father was with my grandfather, I decided to prepare my family with the necessary tools to help me find my way back onto memory lane," Alano says, as if it's not totally wild that he learned lessons on how to get ready for a life with Alzheimer's from things he witnessed at three years old. "Jacinto wasn't a particularly sentimental person. He didn't keep infant clothes or locks of hair or even a baby book for old photographs. My father gathered household objects from Jacinto's apartment to try and jog his memory. He found this rock in the closet that had a date written on it in my grandmother's handwriting: August 18, 1969. Their wedding day. They got married young because Pilar was pregnant, and every time Jacinto held that rock, he kept remembering the happiest day of his life. My father buried him with the rock."

That legit gives me chills. I'm sure Joaquin must've been so damn happy to get his dad talking about how his family got started instead of being treated like a stranger.

"So are all these rocks special?" I ask, looking around.

"I personally collected all these rocks, stones, and crystals from around the world, but they're not so special that I think I'll be buried with any of them," Alano says. He points at his Polaroids. "If I ever start forgetting, those are the memories I'd love to remember."

I go over to this smiling string of Polaroids, and without moving from the bed, Alano tells me about them: the first is Alano in a cap and gown because even though he was homeschooled through high school, his parents still celebrated him with his very own graduation here at home; Alano with binoculars as he embarked on a wildlife safari in the Serengeti; Alano on what looks like a beach but is actually the Skeleton Coast, which is apparently a real place in Namibia even though it sounds like a setting in the Scorpius Hawthorne books; Alano shirtless in the Blue Lagoon without a single scar on his body; and then I freeze up when I see a picture of Alano, Ariana, and Rio dressed up as Spider-Man, Black Cat, and Venom.

"Halloween 2017," Alano says.

I pull an Alano, doing some life math in my head because I'm pretty sure Alano said that the first time he hooked up with Rio after getting his heart broken was that Halloween. My chest tightens as I look at their smiles and wonder if Alano getting to have sex with his first love again is why he always wants to relive this memory. I gotta walk away because I don't wanna make a scene in Alano's special sanctuary, I've already done enough mental and physical harm. But walking away is only gonna make a scene too. So what do I do, stay here and get mad because Alano has a past with someone I don't like? If I'm gonna keep Alano in my life, I can't pull a Paz. I gotta keep growing; I gotta keep facing my ghosts.

"Do you miss them?" I ask. He pauses like he knows his answer could set me off. "You can be honest."

"I miss them," Alano says.

It twists my insides even though I knew the truth.

I've never had best friends before. I don't know if Alano counts me as one of his, but he's definitely mine. If our friendship was able to survive some shit, I'm betting he's gonna make things right with Ariana and Rio at some point, and if Alano and I become boyfriends, I'm not trying to be at war with his best friends.

"Maybe you should hit them up," I say, hoping that I'm not digging my own grave.

Alano gets up from the bed and looks at the Halloween

picture, as if it's not stored away in his perfect memory. "How many times do I have to reach out to Ariana, who didn't call when I almost got killed? Or Rio, who was perfectly okay keeping me around when he knew I was in love with him but now that the tables are reversed he wants nothing to do with me?"

Judging by the tears building in Alano's eyes, I know he wants his best friends back in his life. "If today were your End Day, would you hit up Ariana and Rio?"

No one knows Alano's End Day. He could die right now from an asthma attack or crack open his skull on his fountain or—ugh, I don't wanna think up more deaths for him. The point is that it's on Alano to live like he might die at any moment.

"I would call them," Alano says, keeping the picture on the smiling string. "We've had more good times than bad, but I'm scared that even if we rectify everything our friendship won't ever be the same."

"Maybe it'll be stronger. Like I think we are after everything?"

Alano nods. "We're definitely stronger. In fact, I have to add your picture to this wall. I haven't really been inspired to add new pictures. Things have been so hard, especially these past few months, but you're someone I always want to remember."

My heart races, and I kinda wanna happy-cry too. I never thought someone who wasn't my mom or stepdad could be this nice to me. Could show me this much love.

Alano gasps and breaks out in a smile. "I know the perfect thing for you to take a picture with," he says, skipping over a wood stool and rushing to his closet. He comes out with the brown ceramic skull vase I got him at the Melrose Market along with the 3D flower bouquet he bought. "My vanitas vase!"

I wish I had Alano's power to replay the memory of giving him this gift in high-def, but I'll settle for being in this moment where he's happy planting his paper flowers inside the vase.

I pose in front of the sunset wall, hugging the vanitas vase to my chest.

Alano aims his Polaroid camera. "Say 'Remember you must die!'" And as I'm staring in confusion over why he's bringing up memento mori instead of just asking me to smile, he snaps the picture. He busts out laughing. "The look . . . on your . . . face."

"I'm gonna burn that photo."

Alano taps his head. "Go ahead. I still have it stored here."

"Then I'll burn your brain too."

"Please don't. I promise the picture is not bad. It's just funny."

Alano shows me the developed Polaroid and okay, I look stupid, but watching Alano laugh all over again makes me not give a shit. This picture could one day have the power to unlock Alano's memory if he ever starts forgetting and I wanna be remembered for making him happy instead of holding a gun to my head or showing self-harm wounds or almost punching him.

He pins the Polaroid to the wall. "There. You've added peace to my sanctuary."

"Gotta live up to my name."

I hope to only bring peace to Alano's life and keep finding it in mine.

11:39 p.m.

The rest of the night flies by.

First, Alano made me feel like an A-list actor the way he was styling me for the gala with all the super fancy clothes he has in his big walk-in closet. He pulled some outfits and made me promise to speak up if I wasn't feeling something. So I did. The classic tuxedo didn't feel special enough. The glittering gold suit was maybe too special. The red cloak that was supposed to be a nod to my Scorpius Hawthorne days had more of a Little Red Riding Hood vibe. After several more pulls and combos, I fell in love with this black velvet shirt with shimmering sequin stripes and its scarf that drops down like a tie, paired with some fitted black pants and penny loafers with extra comfortable insoles to protect my wound.

Then Chef Lily served us ginger sesame noodles with tofu, which we ate alone outside Alano's bedroom in the rooftop garden, since his parents are still busy at Death-Cast. Over dinner, Alano shared more about his hyperthymesia—the story of his diagnosis, how he navigated school, more highs and lows—and he got self-conscious from talking too much, but I honestly loved every second because not only was the spotlight off me, I was getting to learn more about him.

After dinner, Alano drew me a warm bath because he wanted

me to experience what it's like to really luxuriate in a tub big enough to fit me and my long-ass legs. He lit one of the reusable candles he bought at the Melrose Market and hooked me up with a body scrub and chamomile oil to show my body some love.

I could get used to this life. It's not even about the fancy clothes or fancy meals or fancy baths. I just love spending all day with Alano.

Now, we're back in Alano's bedroom, lit up only by his Himalayan salt lamps, and we're not just in his bedroom but on his bed, fighting back yawns and losing every time.

"Sorry," I say after another yawn breaks free, interrupting Alano as he's telling me about the day his parents surprised him with Bucky, who's already fast asleep at our feet. "I swear I'm not bored."

"I trust you're not. Today was draining."

I honestly don't know what time my body thinks it is. I rub my eyes open, trying to stay awake. "Okay, so some kids were being dickheads and your parents got you a dog to cheer you up."

Alano laughs. "You can go to sleep, Paz."

I really should sleep because I gotta film the promotion in the morning, but I wanna keep learning about Alano. "So, some kids were being dickheads and . . ."

"My extremely difficult life got easier once I had Bucky. Not easy, of course, but easier," Alano says, smiling at Bucky, who's running in his sleep as he dreams. "I didn't know how hard making friends would be as society adjusted to Death-Cast, but my parents did. I'm starting to suspect that I can read a hundred books about parenting and I still won't know any better than my parents who never got to read up on how to raise a son in the age of Death-Cast."

I'm only just now realizing that yeah, parenting must be hard, but for the past ten years, Mom, Rolando, Naya, and Joaquin definitely had challenges that other parents won't ever know. How do you raise a son who killed his dad? How do you raise a son whose dad rewrote the rules of death? How do you raise sons who've tried taking their lives because life got too hard? Not that Naya and Joaquin even know that shit got that dark for Alano. I don't even know what went down that got Alano to that place, but however you're supposed to raise a suicidal kid, I doubt a parent should ever threaten their own life as a way to trap their kid into theirs.

"Are you asleep?" Alano asks.

I didn't even realize my eyes were closed. "Sorry, I'm awake. Just thinking about how hard it must've been raising me and how I'm still putting Mom through it."

"You're not the reason raising you was hard. That was society's fault."

"And Death-Cast's, no offense."

"And Death-Cast's fault," he whispers. Now Alano is so quiet that I think he's fallen asleep, but he's staring up at the ceiling. "If today was your End Day, would you call your mother?"

I threw this question at Alano hours ago about his friends, and now he's throwing it back my way.

If Death-Cast called right now, there's this voice in my head telling me to get revenge on Mom by not telling her I'm about to die, but no matter how angry I am, I love Mom too much to ever do something so cruel. "She would be my first call," I say. That's the truth, but it also doesn't mean I have to talk to her right now, or that she even wants to talk to me.

Life is hard when your biggest crime is loving someone too much.

"What about you?" I ask Alano. "If today was your End Day, would you call your dad?"

ALANO

11:47 p.m.

If today were my End Day, would I call my father?

Thursday, October 24, 2019. The day I attempted suicide. I could see that the sky was clear from here in my bedroom. I hadn't received an alert, but I was still determined. I didn't let myself think about my mother or Bucky. Only my father, who made me want to die. There was no need for a suicide note because he would've known what pushed me over the edge.

"There was a time when I wouldn't have called my father," I say. I anchor myself to the present because I don't want my brain flooded with every awful memory that led to my suicide attempt. I scroll through my memories and confirm that I never told Paz about this. "I bought this time capsule at Present-Time."

Paz sucks his teeth. "That place." If Margaret Hunt hadn't delivered Paz's gifts straight into Ms. Gloria's hands, he wouldn't be at war with his mother right now.

I'm transported back into Present-Time, hiding behind the grandfather clock as the Death Guarder destroyed the shop. That fear of being killed stays with me, thrusting me through a sequence of memories: my assassination attempt, which led to my deactivating Death-Cast, which led to my sneaking away to the Wisdom Tree, which led to climbing the Hollywood Sign to save Paz, which brings me back into the present with him, only to throw myself back into the cold past when I say, "I bought this time capsule on December first."

"When does it unlock?"

That question anchors me since it's about an unknown future. "Depends on when I die."

"It unlocks when you die?"

"It's technically supposed to, but since it's connected to my Death-Cast profile, the link has been severed. I would have to resync the capsule with my identification number."

He squints at the clock with his tired eyes. "It's not super big. What do you even fit in there? A note?"

"A voice recorder, like the tech used in the objects you selected."

"Is it too personal to ask what you said?"

"Parting words for my parents. Caretaking instructions for Bucky. And . . ." I stare at my blurry reflection in the clock's rose gold face, but in my head I see the memory I've locked away. "A confession."

Paz wakes up at this. "A confession? Anything you wanna talk about?"

"I should, but I've ruined my life enough for one lifetime."

My heart is racing as gunshots ring through my head.

Paz reaches over and squeezes my hand. "Just because I'm trying harder to live doesn't mean you can't trust me anymore to take your secrets to the grave."

Trust isn't the problem. "I appreciate that."

"No pressure, obviously, but in the meantime, you might wanna consider leaving your secrets somewhere safe since this won't unlock anymore."

"That won't be an issue."

"Why not?"

I gaze into Paz's light brown eyes. "I've been doing some soul-searching as I finally see the potential for the future I want. I need to know that I'll be around to live it. I'm going to reactivate Death-Cast for peace of mind."

Paz fully sits up now. "Are you serious? But what about your dad?"

"Last night my father asked for the opportunity to prove that he can give me the space to live my life. I believe in him," I say, which feels so powerful and relaxing. I don't want to be at war with my father. All that does is make everything a thousand times harder and pushes us to that place where I'm willing to die without him knowing as payback. Besides, everything my father has done was to keep my blood off these streets. I'm lucky to have a father who is so overprotective instead of destructive like Paz's father.

"I like knowing that you're gonna survive the day," Paz says.

"I like you liking that," I say. I read the time on my clock. "Ten minutes to midnight."

"Your last ten minutes of living pro-naturally."

"Only if I reactivate in time," I say, getting up to grab my phone out of its lockbox and then returning to my bed. I open the Death-Cast app and begin filling out my profile.

My father is going to be so happy to hear the news of my reactivation.

This pro-natural experiment was heartbreaking for my father, and as liberating as it was for me, it's not worth the trouble it's causing between us or the rest of the world. President Page and the company's board members have been hounding my father over the severity of my choice, a choice that has my parents stuck at Death-Cast tonight. Undecided voters are reportedly leaning toward Carson Dunst since my deactivation has spoken volumes about the harmfulness of Death-Cast. Agent Andrade has had to station more guards inside and outside this building now that the world knows I'm vulnerable. One quick peek on social media shows strangers welcoming me back into the pro-natural fold, which makes me long for the days when they were threatening my life. I don't want my life to cause any more pain. Tomorrow morning I'll release the statement with the news of my reactivation to quell all concerns about where I stand with Death-Cast.

I submit my profile information and receive an error notice telling me that I'm already registered. Have I not been pro-natural all this time? No, I received my confirmation on Friday, July 24, at 8:45 p.m. PDT. This must be some glitch. I review the account history and see that my alerts were reactivated on Tuesday, July 28, at 1:49 a.m. PDT. Unless I'm beginning to lose my memory, I didn't do this. But who . . .

I can't breathe, and I'm not sure if I need air or my inhaler.

My father isn't going to be happy to hear the news of my

reactivation because he already reactivated my profile behind my back.

This is an absolute violation of not only company policy but also our relationship.

I get up and throw my phone against my sunset wall, shattering it. It surprises and scares Paz and Bucky and even myself. I've never thrown anything in anger in my entire life.

"What's going on?" Paz asks, following me around the bedroom.

My breath feels stuck inside my chest, like my father is squeezing my lungs. "He's never going to let me live my life," I say, repeating it until hot tears burn my eyes.

"Who?" Paz asks, trying to steady me, but I keep shrugging him off.

"My father!"

No matter how empowered I feel, my father will always use his power over me.

I storm out into the rooftop garden and fall to my knees, gasping for air. This isn't asthma. This is suffocating anxiety. Paz follows, keeping Bucky inside.

"Talk to me," Paz says.

"He signed me up for Death-Cast against my will," I say.

This isn't like when my father sat me down to tell me about Death-Cast on Monday, June 28, 2010, before the company's intentions were officially announced on Thursday, July 1. Even then my father had the decency to ask me if I'd like to be signed up with the rest of the family, a choice he didn't have to respect when I was underage. This isn't even like when my father abused his power to make sure I wasn't going to die in the hospital after Mac Maag's assassination attempt. This decision is so violating, and it's one I can't wrap my head around. I can almost pardon this violation if he'd done this after Andrea Donahue and Carson Dunst teamed up to expose my pro-natural status. But according to the timestamp, my father did this when I was in bed with Paz, protecting him from hurting himself. My father must've been fearing that Paz was a danger to me, but he's the real threat to my life.

"That's fucked up," Paz says. "But I need you to breathe. I've never seen you like this."

I haven't felt like this since October 24.

This is a signal that life was never supposed to work out.

I stare up at the stars, wondering if Paz was right when he said we aren't meant to be together. I've kept hoping that our meeting was part of some grand plan to save us, but it's not. We're doomed and we have been since the start.

Time blurs between now and then, this moment and memories. It's like I'm time-traveling at warp speed. It's dizzying, and my usual trick to anchor myself to the present by focusing on the future is compromised because all I see is darkness right now. There is no future for someone responsible for more deaths than he could ever know. No dream life.

This is how you survive an End Day. You don't even know that you were safe all along.

I will prove my father wrong. He has already controlled my life, but he will not control my death too.

Memento mori. Memento mori. Memento mori.

Remember you must die. Remember you must die. Remember you must die.

I remember I must die.

I remember. I remember. I remember.

That is my future, and when I'm back in the present, I find myself on the edge of my rooftop. One step forward and I will drop thirty stories and die where I was almost assassinated.

My father forced Death-Cast's warnings on me. I will die without one.

July 30, 2020

PAZ

12:00 a.m.

Death-Cast hasn't called yet, but the heir is gonna kill himself.

This is the psychotic break Alano has been fearful of all along, the snap.

"Alano, that's not safe, get down," I say, trying to play it off like there's a chance Alano has forgotten he's at the very top of his roof.

Alano doesn't respond. He keeps staring out into the city.

Is this how Mom felt when she found me drunk and drugged and near death?

How do I save Alano from this? Should I remind him that he used to be scared of heights? Will his hyperthymesia trick him into making that fear feel real again? Or what if I do that and he freaks out and falls forward? Fuck, fuck, fuck. How about getting help? By the time I run inside and find Dane in that big-ass apartment, Alano might already be on the ground. I need some intervention, like the helicopter that appeared when I was on the Hollywood Sign. No, the helicopter didn't save me. Alano did. He climbed up that Hollywood Sign when I was a stranger and saved my life. Now I gotta be the X factor that saves Alano's life.

I gotta be careful. I'm so scared of accidentally doing something that makes him fall before he can change his mind, before he got me to change my mind. What did he do to get me to change my mind? I don't have his memory, and those few minutes on top of the Hollywood Sign were so intense. He told me not to jump. He recognized me—no, he saw me, like, really saw me. He told me that he had tried killing himself before too. That he had found himself up here before.

I'm not trained for this, and Alano wasn't either, but he was a natural. I gotta speak from the heart.

"Alano, I know what you're going through," I say. Fuck, I fucking suck at this. It's the truth, but even I'm not buying this delivery. I sound like an actor playing a crisis negotiator on some shitty network show and not someone who actually knows this pain. "I know what it's like to wanna die. To feel powerless. To feel like the world will make all my choices for me and never hook me up with any wins. But you've shown me that I have more power than I ever would've thought."

"My father is more powerful," Alano says.

"You can't let him have power over you."

"There's no stopping him. He said it himself: he has inexhaustible power. He will always abuse it and claim that it's for my greater good."

"You don't need him!"

Alano begins muttering something about the night Andrea Donahue was fired. Or repeating something about everyone forgetting Alano's name. He closes his eyes and shakes his head, and I don't forget Alano's name, I call it over and over until he opens his eyes because I'm scared he's about to forget where he is and fall over. He opens his eyes. He's back with me.

"Alano, if I can begin again, so can you."

"My father won't ever let me begin. The only life he wants me to have is the one he has planned for me."

"He wants you alive, Alano, that's all. He would be devastated to know that you were up here right now, thinking about dying."

"I've only ever been up here because of him," Alano says.

"What do you mean?"

"October 24, 2019. A Thursday. Beautiful weather. Clear skies. A Thursday," Alano says, like he's not aware that he's repeating himself. "I was taking a long weekend from classes because I was overwhelmed by everyone's stories. Everyone tells me their pain and it never leaves my head, it never leaves. I can't quiet all their stories."

I wish I had never said anything to Alano, I wish I had killed myself minutes before, or waited until Dad's anniversary, anything that would've stopped us from meeting, knowing how much my pain has tortured Alano, who doesn't deserve that.

"My father was drunk during the day," Alano says. "I could smell the tequila on him as he opened my door and started yelling at me in my sanctuary. I wasn't living up to his expectations. I wasn't taking on more than I can handle. I wasn't ready to lead this company if something happened to him that night. My memory bank was an asset to him when he needed it, but he could never empathize with what I actually feel. I fought back. He wanted me to train as a herald, even though I had told him I didn't want to do it because it would be too traumatizing. He told me to be stronger like he had to be when he was founding this company. Then I finally worked that shift and I heard a man kill himself and now that gunshot can never leave my head!"

Alano flinches like a bullet has just passed by him. He twists so sharply I'm sure he's about to fall back, but he finds his balance.

"He endangered me! This is what I was avoiding. But he sees death as a part of life and wanted to throw me into the fire. I didn't want to get burned. My father got so furious that he said if I can't see the value in making those calls myself, that maybe I don't deserve to know when he dies. That I disappointed him so much that he wanted to die without me knowing." Alano is sobbing. "That's when I decided that I would kill myself and he wouldn't know either. But if I had gone through with it, my death would have been a complete mystery to my father because he blacked out that whole conversation. I'm the only one who knows—who remembers."

All this time I've been so mad at Mom for threatening to kill herself if I died first, but Alano has been secretly battling these feelings of Joaquin bullying him so bad and saying that Alano was such a disappointment that he wanted to kill himself. That only led to Alano surviving his attempt. And Joaquin has only fucked with his life even more since then.

I don't know if Alano will survive this time.

I'm not enough to live for.

Connecting with him didn't work, what else did he do to save me?

The stars catch my eye. Alano said fate brought us together. I might think I'm not enough to live for, but Alano definitely did. I remember him shouting at me on the Hollywood Sign that he believed fate brought us together. I gotta remind him.

"Fate didn't bring us together so I can watch you die," I say, doing my best to echo him.

Alano turns, his back to the city. "Maybe it did."

"It didn't, you have changed my life—"

"You should kill me, Paz! Mac Maag was right to target me. You should get your revenge—"

"I don't give a shit about Death-Cast ruining my life, I only care about saving yours!"

Alano shakes his head and closes his eyes, saying something that doesn't make sense at first, until I realize he's quoting me from earlier when I was talking to Dad's ghost. "'I hate you for making me violent. I would've never picked up a gun or raised a hand at anyone if you weren't in my life . . . I somehow still love and miss you even though you ruined my life. But I'm also happy you're not alive to screw me up anymore because I'm gonna keep living whether you like it or not!' You should live, Paz, you should live. You should kill me, and you should live."

Would guilt-tripping Alano help? There's no way I'm gonna live if he mysteriously falls from the rooftop garden on the very same night he brings me home for the first time, especially since I'm the only one who knows he attempted suicide before. No one's gonna take my word. But I don't think guilt is how to get through to him right now, I don't fucking know.

What else did Alano do with me?

The deal!

"Alano, you gotta give me three hours," I say. And as much as I hate saying it, I hope I won't have to act on it. "You gotta give me until two fifty a.m. like I gave you. If that's not enough, I'll push you off this roof myself."

"No," Alano says.

"Please. We can go wherever you want, do whatever you want."

"The only place I want to go is down," Alano says, eyeing the street. His legs are shaking.

I'm losing, I'm gonna lose him. "This isn't your End Day, Alano."

"It is, Paz. I'm so sorry. Please take care of Bucky and yourself."

I don't even think about it, I just rush and hop up to the edge, a few feet away from Alano. The guardrail comes up to my knee, which isn't enough to guard anyone from falling over, not that anyone should be standing up here in the first place. This is higher than the Hollywood Sign. I feel so much closer to the stars and moon. And I know that there is no surviving this drop.

I wonder if I'll hear our phones ringing with Death-Cast alerts any minute now.

"What are you doing?" Alano asks.

I take a couple steps toward him. "I'll always save you, and you'll always save me. Remember?"

Alano remembers our deal, but this time he isn't smiling. "You shouldn't save me. You shouldn't want me alive."

"I'm not one of these assholes who wants you dead."

"You should be."

"Alano, I hated being a survivor until I met you," I say, getting closer. "Now you got me going to bed hoping Death-Cast won't call and excited to wake up to start my day." I reach out, hoping he'll take my hand. "I'm proud to be a survivor because of you."

Alano ignores my hand. "You should forget about me, Paz. Go live your life."

My heart races as I close the space between us. "You are unforgettable, Alano," I cry, hating this pain in his beautiful eyes. I grab his hand, locking my fingers around his. "And I'm not gonna live without you."

"You have to," Alano says.

I've been trying to follow in Alano's footsteps since he was able to save me, but none of his tricks are working on him. I gotta tap into someone else's playbook.

"If you kill yourself, Alano, I'm gonna kill myself too."

This is why Mom did what she did. It wasn't to guilt me. She was telling the truth. I know in the pit of my stomach that I can't watch Alano dive off this ledge without wanting to jump after him.

He shakes his head. "Don't do this to me. I told you that I only wanted you to live for yourself."

"And I want the same for you, but I know how hard life can be. If you don't have it in you to live it, then I'm not gonna stop you, but I won't live without you, so we're better off doing this together." I squeeze his hand as my legs shake.

"Trust me. You don't want a life with me. It won't end well."

"Then we should end it now. Today was a powerful End Day, but before we do . . ." Sudden movements are dangerous, but that doesn't stop me from finally pressing my lips against

Alano's. If we were to fall to our deaths right now, I hope our lips would stay locked. Alano comes alive and kisses me back. I slowly pull away and give him a sad smile while staring into his beautiful eyes. "If we're about to die, I had to know what it's like to kiss the guy I love."

Alano stares like he's about to call me out for lying. "You love me?"

"Don't play dumb, you know-it-all."

His bottom lip quivers. "I love you too, Paz."

I smile because I'm now Happy Paz, but it's not an act. I thought I would die before hearing a boy say he loves me. This feeling . . . it's like flying. And in a blink, that's what it really feels like when our feet leave the roof's edge. There's nothing to do but accept that I've lost this fight to save Alano's life and my own. I wasn't enough to live for, but I was enough to love, even if it was just for a few days. Except we don't lose because we don't fall forward toward the street but slam backward onto the rooftop.

Alano pants after saving us and stares up at the stars, and I roll onto him, wrapping my arms around him to hug him, to restrain him, to hold on and never let go.

This isn't our End Day.

There are some Deckers who manage to live perfect End Days, but not everyone's got a life where you can get a happy End Day. Some of us got wounds and brains and hearts that need more than twenty-four hours to heal. Days, weeks, months, even years. That time can be suffocating, and planning those futures can feel like telling lies, but love saved us tonight, and as long as we stay together, love will keep us alive.

ALANO

12:07 a.m.

Death-Cast hasn't called to tell me if I'm going to die today, but I want to live.

My world went dark as I was being buried alive by so many memories that I wanted to die until Paz saved me. His courage, his defiance, his kiss, his declaration, these are all the memories that make me want to stay alive.

There are also the memories that make me feel so guilty to live.

If I had died, my time capsule would have unlocked and the secret I've been taking to the grave would have been unearthed for all.

The thing is, I can remember my entire life. This includes before I was technically born. This might not seem significant to anyone that I can remember being in the womb except for the fact that while it's true that my father has never told me the secret to Death-Cast, he did tell my mother while she was pregnant. I've known the secret since before I was born, before I could absorb the words, before I could make sense of what was said. My parents stopped talking about the secret around me when I was four because they were scared of me learning it, which only made me keep my own secret from them.

HOW TO SURVIVE AN END DAY, WHETHER YOU LIKE IT OR NOT

On the first End Day, I went into the Vast Vault at Death-Cast to see the secret for myself.

I shouldn't have gone in. If I hadn't, the Death's Dozen might be alive today. I don't know.

All I know is that love will not survive once Paz discovers I ruined his life.

PAZ AND ALANO
WILL RETURN IN

NO
ONE
KNOWS
WHO
DIES
AT
THE
END

RESOURCES

988 Suicide & Crisis Lifeline: If you need immediate help, you can always call 988. You can also visit them online at 988lifeline.org for additional information and other resources.

Borderline Personality Disorder Resource Center: This organization promotes education about borderline personality disorders and connects people to resources for treatment and support. Contact them at 1-888-694-2273 or at nyp.org /bpdresourcecenter.

Crisis Text Line: Text HOME to 741741 for free and confidential support.

National Alliance on Mental Illness: For support, please call 1-800-950-6264 or text HELPLINE to 62640. For other resources, visit them online at nami.org.

National Domestic Violence Hotline: To reach an advocate, please call 1-800-799-7233 or text START to 88788. Additional resources and a live chat are available at thehotline.org.

Safe Housing Partnerships: Visit safehousingpartnerships.org /for-survivors for resources and additional helplines for survivors of domestic violence.

Self-injury Outreach & Support: sioutreach.org provides

resources to people coping with the urge to self-harm as well as guides for loved ones looking to help.

The Trevor Project: This organization, which specifically works with the LGBTQ+ community, is available online and via phone. The resources listed below are available 24/7, year-round:

- Website: thetrevorproject.org
- TrevorLifeline: 1-866-488-7386
- TrevorText: text START to 678678
- TrevorChat: instant messaging service available through thetrevorproject.org

To Write Love on Her Arms: The website twloha.com/mental-health-toolkit/ is a helpful tool kit that features exercises related to mental health, information, affirmations, and playlists.

ACKNOWLEDGMENTS

After one of the most heartbreaking—if not the most heartbreaking—year of my life, I'm genuinely surprised I survived to not only finish writing this book, but to pay tribute to the extraordinary people who supported me along the way.

First of all, to my best friend, Luis "LTR3" Rivera, who has always been the MMVP (Most Macho Valuable Player). He saved my life with an out-of-the-blue phone call when I was twenty-one, unaware he'd done so until years later when I finally started opening up about the struggles I'd been facing since I was a teenager. Luis, thank you for getting me to step down and thank you for stepping up in countless other ways since then. And thank you for letting me bounce a million ideas off you for this book, and for all the Ping-Pong breaks. LYTM, Kidd!

My mom, Persi Rosa, who called me when I was feeling like a liar as I talked about the future. Thank you for flying across the country at a moment's notice to be at my side when things were bad. We've survived a lot, Mom. I love you a lot lot lot lot lot lot lot lot lot lot.

My agent, Jodi Reamer, who knows how I'm doing in the first few seconds of any phone call. It's not lost on me how lucky I am to have an agent who guides me to prioritize my mental health over my book, especially a book so personal that it kept taking and taking and taking before giving anything back. Thank you for always reminding me of my value in the times I felt worthless. Jodi deserves every ice cube this world has to offer.

My editor, Alexandra Cooper, who showed me so much grace during my chaotic process and while I dealt with a hurt heart. I still can't believe this never-ending story came to an end. (Sort of!) Thank you for reading so many incarnations of this once never-ending story at so many different stages. Remember when Paz and Zen met on the Last Friend app and when Paz met Orion at the book launch and when Paz was the only narrator for Part One? Fun times for our eyes only! I have an entire novel's worth of dead scenes, but thanks to Alex's sensitive touch and thoughtfulness, we've honed in on the best version of Paz and Alano's story.

My publisher, Rosemary Brosnan, who tagged in to help get this novel across the finish line. I often think back to our conversation at ALA Midwinter in 2016 when she showed me that she not only cares deeply about the work, but the people behind the work. I'm so lucky to be published by someone as bighearted as Rosemary.

My assistant, Kaitlin López, for everything she's done on my last five novels and everything in between. So many things would fall through the cracks in my books and my life without her.

My Writers House family: Cecilia de la Campa, Alessandra Birch, and Sofia Bolido for all you do so I can make the world cry in over thirty languages. And Anqi Xu for your attention to detail in the real world and in the fictional world I built.

My HarperCollins family: Allison Weintraub for the extra backup on all things editorial and administrative; David Curtis for partnering with artist Simon Prades to give me another phenomenal cover; Michael D'Angelo and Audrey Diestelkamp for always making marketing these sad books fun; Samantha Brown and Jennifer Corcoran for getting the word out about Death-Cast; Patty Rosati and the School and Library Marketing team for all you do, now more than ever; Kerry Moynagh and the Sales team for making walking into a bookstore and finding my stories on shelves a dream come true; Shona McCarthy,

ACKNOWLEDGMENTS

Erin DeSalvatore, and Allison Brown for spending decades of your lives on the production of this behemoth of a book so I can look smarter than I am; Rich Thomas for being a wizard behind the curtains, but, like, a real wizard who casts real magic on my books; and Liate Stehlik our new leader who immediately felt like a longtime partner.

My Epic Reads family: Sam Fox, Sonia Sells, Emily Zhu, Maureen Germain, and Rain McNeil for coming up with fun things to film when I visit the office, and Blake Hudson, Luke Porter, and Blake Buesnel for getting it all on camera.

My film agent, Jason Richman at UTA, for believing in me since the very beginning.

My therapist, Rachel, for the diagnosis that helped me understand my brain and for all the work she does on my heart. I look back on who I was before therapy with empathy, but I don't miss being that person at all. Here's to many more years of growth and surviving.

My dog, Tazzito No-Middle-Name Silvera. His company got me through the pandemic and his cuddles made me safe from myself. I love my Papacito Man.

My friends: Anita Lashey, Arvin Ahmadi, Jeff Kasanoff, Tyler Alvarez, and Robbie Couch for all the cheering on and for always letting me vent, cry, and even vanish when I needed to; Jordin Rivera for all the grace and Georgia and Miles for the much needed hugs and cuddles while writing this book; Alex Aster for always riding this unicycle with me; David Arnold for letting me send him insane monthly unboxing videos; Jasmine Warga for knowing this work well; Nicola and Dave Yoon for continuing to show me the love I want; Sabaa Tahir, Victoria Aveyard, Marie Lu, Tahereh Mafi, and Ransom Riggs for always, always, always caring; Dhonielle Clayton,

ACKNOWLEDGMENTS

Patrice Caldwell, and Mark Oshiro for a group chat full of laughs and gut checks; Angie Thomas for letting me know when I fall on her heart; Ryan "Good Morning, Charlie!" La Sala for staying on the phone for an hour while I talked to myself about how to rewrite this book; Jeff Zentner for the (fictional) legal advice; Amanda Diaz, Michael Diaz, and Cecilia Renn for being there since the beginning; Sandra Gonzalez and Mike Martinez for loving me so much that I sometimes avoid their company because I don't always feel worthy of their love; Victoria Mele and Ben Miseikis for keeping my body strong during brutal deadlines, which kept my mind strong too; Scarlett and Cooper Hefner for the socially distanced hangout at a low moment that proved to me you were keepers; and Elliot Knight for serving as the Alano to my Paz many times over the years.

And as for my friends who aren't in my life anymore, but once helped save mine, you know who you are: thank you.

A special thanks to Lauren Oliver, who first got me to call a suicide hotline a decade ago. Both calls saved my life.

And another special thanks to Lisa the Psychic. Everything she foresaw about my future husband and my future children and my future life got me so excited to stick around when I was deeply suicidal. Lisa the Psychic, your visions didn't come true when you said they would, but you saved my life anyway. That was $60 well spent.

For all the booksellers and librarians who've supported me this past decade, I'm so grateful that you've kept this dream of mine alive and well.

And lastly, for all my readers, but especially the ones who have struggled with life. You know who you are. I know who you are. There are so many more pages in our stories, so please don't close the book. Keep turning and turning and turning.

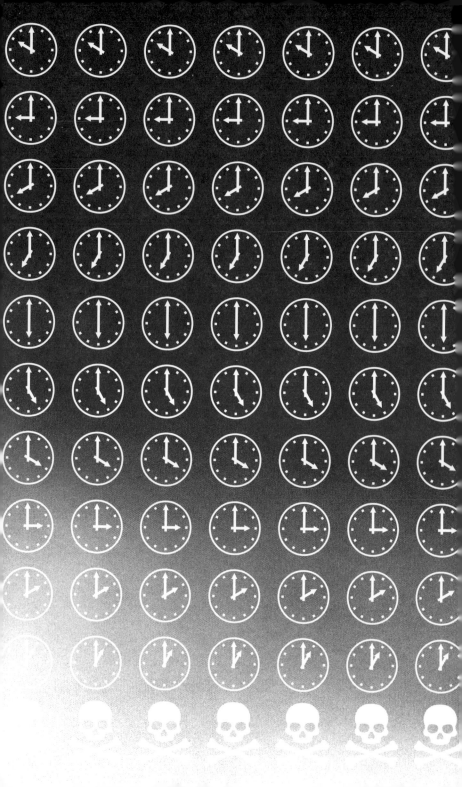